CW01658844

What he was was a wa[illegible]

Where had he co[illegible]

The place out of which all who wasted emerged: scraped from the caves of Thanatop[illegible] a universal saprophagus as it fed upon cosmic dead atoms, or spat from the morphon-heretical parasites which sucked at dark matter.

Where had he visited?

The usual places. The slums and cesspools of Calcutta, Mogadishu, Buenos Aires, Ankara. The open-after-sunset slave markets of Marrakesh and Matamoros. The all-you-can-eat weanling raggamuffin buffets of Manila and Bangkok. He'd smiled through the throngs of deceivers and desecraters. Perverts, pariahs, and Poo Bahs. Reapers, rapers, raveners.

Wasters.

He listened to the poems of lamentation that those who were doomed to die painfully whispered in their sleep. To the evensongs of debauchery peculiar to the undersides of third world nights. He always sought nouveau methods of employing the wasting, turning it into art, trying to be different, original, inspired. So that he never had to view it afterward and feel he'd done less than his best.

After all, just because it was his station—his dharma—to be this, didn't mean he shouldn't take pride in it.

SOMA

CHARLEE JACOB

Macabre Ink

Copyright © 2003 by Jim Jacob
ISBN 978-1-63789-109-4
Macabre Ink is an imprint of Crossroad Press Publishing
All rights reserved. No part of this book may be used or reproduced in any manner
whatsoever without written permission except in the case of
brief quotations embodied in critical articles and reviews
For information address Crossroad Press at 141 Brayden Dr., Hertford, NC 27944
www.crossroadpress.com

First Edition - 2024

For Jim, Who Taught Me The Night
Doesn't Have To Go On Forever.

Foreword

Well, I have never done one of these before and I ran screaming when Shane Ryan Staley asked me to do this one for the special Delirium Books hardcover edition of *Soma*. I insist that I write this foreword under extreme duress and following many Spanish Inquisition-style torments by an array of editors and their associates in skimpy black leather costumes and each with tight buns. This reverse sexist assinity aside … welcome to my nightmare. Oh, been done? Yet, it applies here. So I will steal it.

I am a rather ordinary woman, all in all. Just over fifty years old as I write this, a bit frumpy, kind of quiet most of the time. Occasionally catty. The only thing which is genuinely worth mentioning about me are my nightmares. I can fall asleep in the middle of the day on the sofa for only three quarters of a minute and still have a dream. I have dozens of them every night. Some of these are your basic, silly, loaded with day-crap pap. But many fall under the heading of sticky-boned, fear-sweat-in-the-crack-of-the-ass get me out of heres. The sort that after I manage to claw myself to consciousness and stumble to the bathroom to switch on a light (so I won't wake up Jim, my husband … providing I didn't wake him up shrieking bloody murder), I recall the horrors and tell myself, "Damn, I need to write that down!" The ones that come in regular, Rapid Eye Movement sleep make the most full-fledged scenarios, of course.

But I've been known to suffer night terrors and hypnogogues, too, which only leave me with fleeting yet visceral images (from the first) or a few lines of quirky poetry (from the second). I once read an interesting book titled *Nightmare* by Ernest Hartmann (Basic Books, Inc. 1984), being *The Psychology and Biology of Terrifying Dreams*. The text says that it is rare for anyone to suffer all three types of nightmare.

Ain't I rare? Ain't I lucky?

I didn't used to think so as I woke up to discover myself on the opposite side of the bedroom door, having slammed it after I ran out into the hall, fleeing a very three-dimensional vision I'd glimpsed when I thought I had just awakened in my bed. Or as Jim had just shaken me awake, hoping the neighbors weren't telephoning the police because it sounded as if we'd been home-invaded by slavering demons who never chewed through their victims' voice boxes first. Messy eaters, demons, and none too concerned about authority figures.

Now I go to sleep *almost*—not *quite*—hoping to have just such an experience. It makes terrific fodder for those such as I who compose like the mad and the damned. At this writing I have had almost 600 publications for poetry and roughly 230 publications for short stories, as well as the novels *This Symbiotic Fascination* and *Haunter*. Mostly because I either dream badly from too much Texas chili on my stomach—or from this life's personal history of depression, suppression, and impressionability—or from too many evil previous incarnations and their subsequent guilts and curses—*or* I go through highly creative but teeth-chattering bouts of insomnia. It all deals with the dark, with being able or not being able to shut the eyes and let go. With vulnerability and the shadow of death every fucking way we turn.

This novel was written going deeply into troubled psyches plucked from dream characters, wrung from the 3:00 A.M. heart and crotch grip of mortality, all the worst nightmare bits of what we may be capable of. Of what we inhibit through conscious morality but which the dark may be capable of. It's about the god parts of ourselves and the devil parts … sometimes frighteningly the same parts! It's about the shapeshift we undergo when we go under, visible in the figment's warped mirrors which stretch or compress us to discover outrages and blasphemies in 31 groin-delicious or gut-nasty flavors. And even at the risk of sounding pretentious (probably too late, huh?), I feel a crime or two in this book may strike a chord in you—if only because . . . if there is one thing we all share, it's dreams. Whether or not some folks remember theirs. The nightmare is as universal as fear.

So read on. Share with me.

Charlee Jacob
September 30, 2003

" … Life and Death are but words …"
Bhavagad Gita

PART ONE

Dancing The Beginning And End

No-Logue

What he was was a waster.

Where had he come from?

The place out of which all who wasted emerged: scraped from the caves of Thanatopsis, or squeezed out the ass of a universal saprophagus as it fed upon cosmic dead atoms, or spat from the morphon-heretical parasites which sucked at dark matter.

Where had he visited?

The usual places. The slums and cesspools of Calcutta, Mogadishu, Buenos Aires, Ankara. The open-after-sunset slave markets of Marrakesh and Matamoros. The all-you-can-eat weanling raggamuffin buffets of Manila and Bangkok. He'd smiled through the throngs of deceivers and desecraters. Perverts, pariahs, and Poo Bahs. Reapers, rapers, raveners.

Wasters.

He listened to the poems of lamentation that those who were doomed to die painfully whispered in their sleep. To the evensongs of debauchery peculiar to the undersides of third world nights. He always sought nouveau methods of employing the wasting, turning it into art, trying to be different, original, inspired. So that he never had to view it afterward and feel he'd done less than his best.

After all, just because it was his station—his dharma—to be this, didn't mean he shouldn't take pride in it.

Chapter 1

"The great gods together piss
out the lovely Soma."
—The Upanishads

At the entranceway to the east gate of Nagas Wat was a neatly-stacked pile of artificial limbs, glass eyes, and hook appliances.

Since the people of Phnom Yohp wanted to present themselves before their god as they really were, every article of medical detritus designed to supplement catastrophic physicality had been placed here. Except for those attached to the four women who'd remained home to tend the twenty-five children, all the other female villagers sweated in the jungle humidity, saltwater running off them in rivulets thick as blood loosened from opened veins. The women didn't mind this industry a bit, some squatting on the grassy swathe of the main garden on legless hips or working with feet in lieu of missing hands.

This was for their deity. And for themselves, too, ultimately. Only the men, the chosen, sat aside, not needing to toil. Their part would come later. Now they waited, sitting lotus, thumbtips touching fingertips, under the watchful eyes of serpent-faced priests.

The mushrooms had been brought up from the lower catacombs of the temple, the only place it was cool enough to grow them. It was impossible to have subterranean passages in most of the jungle because of the amount of groundwater, but natural caves burrowed through the mountain that the temple had been built upon a millennium ago. In some places the enormous roots of silk cotton trees had grown through the rock, relentless as the claws of some giant rakshasa sprung through a fruit pulp face. Liquid seeped in silver chains to gloss where the mushrooms bedded among sacred shadows.

Yellow straw baskets of fungi gleamed like a collection of varying sizes of transparent diamond. Crystal clear, until they might have been comprised of that ground water. Or of tears.

Every one of the villagers was deformed in some way. Mutilated by the Khmer Rouge over twenty years ago—or since, considering the fighting hadn't really stopped there in the northern mountains until recently, with Pol Pot's death. They resembled a menagerie of broken Bodhisattvas and apsaras, brutally maimed by cruel and thoughtless soldiers. There was only one villager older than thirty-five, all of them having been children when the terror visited their part of the forest. Orphans of the most repellent punishment. New offspring for their people had just come again. And that only after God re-united with them. But those young ones were safely back in the village. Twenty-five of them, a real gift! The deity had brought so much since returning a few years ago: fertility to the fields, healing to the nightmares, hope.

The women pressed the mushrooms between heavy stones. Loose wads of flesh and pulpy stumps slapped as whatever limbs they possessed worked tirelessly to draw the juice. Others who hadn't actually been dismembered still struggled to manipulate shriveled and twisted parts around their tasks. They strained the clear fungi blood through a measure of undyed silk, afterward mixing it with oxen milk.

Hisssssssssss. One of the priests gestured to the dark threshold beneath a gray gateway. An intricate raised relief had been sculpted long ago, depicting the great god Shiva, interrupted from his contemplation by Kama, the god of love. Shiva had been so angry by the unwarranted disturbance that he burned Kama horribly with the laser of his third eye.

A figure was emerging in the gateway, just a head at first, as this was where the initial light fell, from torches set about the garden. A beautiful face, carved from topaz and moonstone, regarded the peasants serenely. The voluptuous body glistened under the torchlight, reflecting from twin sets of melon breasts the way four mirrors would. It stepped out into the courtyard, flanked by two of the priests in saffron robes, the hems susurrating around invisible feet. They seemed to have no noses; their heads were too long and flat; lipless mouths almost reached from ear to ear. The skulls swayed on their necks, king cobras ready to strike should any enemy military spring from a stand of bamboo.

Sarun Chhuon, the only man there not to be waiting with the others, was the oldest man there at forty. Just old enough to really remember the last embodiment of the god to dwell in the temple. He held out the libation to a priest who then gave it to the deity. The gorgeous one drank, eyes rolling back to whites. Slowly, this being began to dance in ecstasy.

Belled bracelets around the ankles tinkled as the holy feet glided gracefully across the carpet of humus. The hands gestured at the ends of slender arms which swung as if in one piece down through the shoulders. The fingers pantomimed stars being born in explosion, then wisping out to nothing. The penis bobbed as the divine form leapt, revealing a clitoris behind the testicles, testifying to the androgynous nature of this god. But the full breasts were already an indication, given the omnipresent erection. As was the soft glory of the face, which anyone not of the village would first guess as belonging to a perfect woman.

The dance became convulsive, limbs fluttering like a swiftly spun cable, which moved so fast it no longer displayed each single vibration. One which has reached the state of a wave, carrying its disruptive but hypnotic current through any field of energy, bringing with it a chaos both shattering and creative. The hips twitched as if to seduce, as if beginning to give birth. The quadruplet breasts rotated in separate directions, clockwise and counterclockwise. The belly moved in and out, in an act resembling the terrible peristalsis of a snake, of a cobra—Shiva's symbol animal.

The muscles in the glistening thighs began to flutter spasmodically. The taut buttocks clenched.

I dance creation into existence, Shiva thought, arching his hip until it seemed to dislocate backward into the spine. The vertebrae popped like firecrackers, each emitting a spark as if struck on a flint.

Or I dance the end of the world ...

The dancer threw his head back, black hair in long knotted cords and waterfall ripples fanning behind him. He could see the stars caroming in a circle overhead as he spun in dervish, waiting to be possessed. How like the incarnations they were, points of lighted souls going round and round. A smear of milk like the Soma itself, a filigreed wall of jewel. White. Silver.

Green. Solid as the jungle.

And he lost his mind. It left his body to travel the years. For wasn't Shiva Lord of Time, as well as Lord of The Dance?

PFC Harrold Tyler shook his head, wondering if he was flashing on some drug he'd taken in Phonm Penh while last on leave. A little herbal or chem R & R was fine as long as it didn't mess you up on patrol too much. A man's life depended on being sharp to every movement in the bush. A whole company's existence often depended on it. Death came in fragmentary blinks. And crippling-for-life came faster than the pico second it took for the eyelids to shutter halfway down. One didn't drowse out here. Or daydream. Or hallucinate.

Probably something that little whore, what had been her name?—Uma—had fed him, on the houseboat on the Tonle Sap River. There were a lot of these floating brothels, outfitted with anything from twenty dollar squeaky eight-year-olds to sloppy eighteen-year-olds as cheap as 50 cents. Hell, sometimes just a bottle of cold Bayon Beer could cost that much.

But she'd had something Harry hadn't seen before, not even at Mere Shum's opium den in the heart of the city. The girl was fully double-jointed, a former dancer in the Cambodian ballet before she'd been knocked up.

The career was subject to a patina of medieval notions of either virginity or at least a marginal respectability. Only girls danced in the national ballet. Once a female gave birth, her dancing days in this country were at an end.

Yet Uma still had a broad range of gymnastic talents at her disposal in this new career. She could spin on Harry's dick like a tight, greased hula hoop, and wrap her arms and legs around him even as he bored into her from behind. He was surprised that, with a talent like this, little Uma didn't work at one of the bordello's run on property owned by the Queen Mother.

But now the squad was patrolling out in the middle of nowhere, some place of slimy pastorality called Choeung Ek. The streams were full of leeches. Stopping to pluck them off once they'd bloated on your blood was nasty, like trying to sling some other grunt's jizzum off your fingers. The banks of the water could be black with clouds of mosquitoes until it made a guy think demons were rising from the earth.

In swarthy shapes, with abysses churning in their cunts and assholes, inviting him to come fuck them. To enter those orifices that telescoped out into some Oriental hell. Not all these Cambodians were Buddhists. Some still believed in the old Hindu gods, adopted from Indian traders a couple thousand years ago. And there were members of that pantheon as horny as they were scary, able to suck and fuck you till all your bodily appendages vortexed in a bloody cyclone up your own rectum. Nearly sounded worth it, such a horrific end—if it was the denouement of the total cosmic blowjob and chasm-rut.

Harry groaned and slapped the side of his head. Wake up, you dickwad!

He felt the weight of the M-16 cradled in his arms. The rice paddy stank of jade moisture and malarial larvae. The sounds of insects was such a loud buzz, he felt his skull thrum. Like it had during a Stones concert in Paris a couple years ago, before he began his first tour in the butt crack of the world. The amps had ground out droning wavelengths of pain that night, turning the outermost layers of his bones to silt.

"Hey, Tyler," called somebody up ahead. "There's a sexy bit of meat up here, if you've got your usual boner."

There were chuckles and a few serious gasps for breath from other soldiers. Harry came alongside and saw a dead female water buffalo, half-in, half-out of the water. Its splayed legs revealed gaping genitals peppered with flies. The udders were swollen with either gas or ruined milk.

"Fifty says he'll fuck her," said Rosh, a grunt from New Jersey. He began digging in his pockets for the cash.

"Not even Tyler's that sick." Jansen turned away, suppressing the need to puke from the stench of sour gut-fruit.

"I got fifty more says he is," added Corporal Crowell.

"I saw this guy do a tango on a napalm-burned pinhead in Saigon a few weeks ago. Could hear her skin crackling like cellophane on hard candy. With blisters the size of your ass popping against his skin as he rode her," related Graham, a blond surfer from California.

"Damn! I've heard the capitol whorehouses got some of the strangest snatch. What dya suppose he had to pay for that?" Katzeff—a newby just arrived from Oklahoma—asked.

"Nothing," Harry said with a straight face. "*She* paid me."

The kid guffawed.

"No, really," Graham told him, shrugging. "He's got some kind of condition they call Per … Par … Pree …"

"Priapism," Harry finished, eyeing the buffalo. Observing as flies crawled into the ruddy vulva and around the mouth where a tongue the length of a gangrenous forearm lolled.

"What the hell is that?" Katzeff asked, stepping back from the big Texan as if it might be some kind of venereal disease.

Graham sniggered. "It means he's always got a boner."

Katzeff snorted dismissively. "That's crazy …"

He thought about it, recalling that the front of Tyler's pants always seemed to be tented. But he'd just figured the guy was wearing a jock-cup or had a pig-sticker down there.

"Well, whatever. I'll bet that much easy that nobody'd stick it in a rotting ol' cow," Katzeff argued.

"Put your money where your mouth is, boy," Crowell advised.

"And be glad you aren't expected to put your mouth anywhere near anyplace this intrepid perv would go."

Harry'd only served with this bunch for about a month. He'd been with another squad till then. But he was something of a legend in the whole company.

Harry unfastened his fatigue trousers and knelt, insinuating himself between the stiff upthrust back legs of the buffalo. It didn't mean anything to him to screw an animal. Hell, they were all animals, especially on the maternal side of his family. Nor did death bother him. Everyone died eventually. The aging state of the body was one of slowly creeping death from birth onwards. And he'd seen so much … It was just one more crusty hole. Warm or chill, the difference was only in a few degrees of temperature.

"At least there aren't any maggots yet," he murmured and slid in. Depending on how many hours something had been dead, it might be lubed up sufficiently to prevent any claustrophobic dry hump.

Harry's vision swam. Suddenly the fields and the water were crowded with corpses. People who'd been smothered, people with pickaxe holes, people who'd been bludgeoned. Some had blindfolds with the fabric rotting into the mesh of their decomposing flesh. Harry had seen folks done a lot of different ways, and he recognized the nature of injuries. Surprisingly none of these bore gunshot wounds. As if the killers had been saving their bullets for 'worthier' causes. There were so many that in some places the ground could no longer be seen at all and the streams were dammed up. Men, women, babies. Thousands of them. They stretched to the horizons, the smell rising in a visible mist the color of spoiled mangos.

And there was a figure moving among them. Harry saw a very well-developed bosom. A woman, not close enough he could see her clearly, but still obviously more beautiful than all the whores he'd seen since the U.S. army brought him to Southeast Asia's shores. Lovelier than any Hollywood movie star or Playboy pin-up and more graceful. She danced across the corpses, putting delicate feet against elasticizing backbones and down on breached, brain-curdled skulls. She swayed to an unheard music, both sculpted metal blossoms and real exotic flowers adorning her shoulders and hips. Her arms snaked out like catwalks extending from a main stage, the hands slinking out like sublime featured players, performing solos as if totally independent of the rest of the body. They curled into dreaming fists, a study in fetal sleep, rings on the fingers flashing the way of dying spirits struggling to send a last message. The fingers then opened, uncurling orchids or spiders, summoning the rest of her body to begin a manic pirouette. When she drifted closer and then turned fully to him, Harry saw that her magnificent bosom was actually four breasts. He also spied the erect penis and shuddered.

A little over a month ago, as the squad had been patrolling farther north, in the mountains about fifty kilometers or so from Angkor Wat, they'd stumbled on another ancient temple crumbling amid the vines and bombox trees. Doing recon, suspecting Vietcong of hiding in such a place, they'd flushed out a creature part man/part woman/part fox/part night terror.

"Hey, Tyler! We know you like some strange knotholes but we bet you a month's pay you won't fuck this moi!"

So Harry'd done it, naturally. He'd fucked the Khmer. Because he always had a hard on and he'd never been able to pass up pussy, no matter what state it was in. That was part of the human experience, wasn't it? Variety? Adventure? Seeking answers in the blackest depths?

Two grunts had held it down so Harry could climb aboard, because it was fighting like some kind of demon. He'd landed a blow on its jaw that broke with a sound similar to a fragile crystal champagne glass. But it still struggled, eyes staring up at him all ebon star sapphires mounted into pupils of hammered red metal. Harry rammed his dick into its cunt and gripped the cones of its tits. It had a yellow cock and balls jiggling between the two of them, rubbing Harry's sweaty belly. It bared betel-black teeth at him and snarled curses in Khmer. Or did the teeth just seem black? The mouth gaped and there was darkness down there, spiraling up from the throat like a flock of nightmares flapping up from the point in space that generated them. It didn't really have too many teeth left. Harry had knocked half of them out when he slugged it in the jaw to shut it up.

He slogged in and out, jerking side to side but couldn't come. He'd banged lepers and cripples, headless trunks and trunkless heads, chancred whores, and even a dead Buddhist nun who'd been boiled alive in her bath when American bombs started a fire in Kampong-Rau. But he was so freaked out by this unearthly mutant that he was actually going limp. And *that* was something he hadn't been in ten years, not since he'd been a kid and his dog-muffed mother had invited him into the bedroom, shedding garments as she glided backward, revealing her shapeshifter state with each step.

But the moi came. Right in Harry's face as he sat up on top of it. The yellow cock squirted like some poisonous jungle mushroom, in gushing streams of rice gruel and goat curds. Harry'd passed out from the stink.

And he'd dreamed of a whole crowd of walking wounded and raised-from-the-pitiful-dead naked bodies. They begged with diseased hands out, or with withered limbs where only a wrist bone protruded from the arm to gesture with. They rolled up rotten egg eyes and thrust their pelvises at him, covered in hair that moved like worm follicles, or bald with running pink sores. They opened their mouths, and black rumbled from their throats in a mantra.

Wia neuv ch'ngaay te?

This was Khmer for "Is it far?"

Over and over. Is it far? Is it far?

Was what far?

The words whirpooled out of them and descended on him, wrapping him in tornadic blackness. He could hear them screaming in it even after their ruined faces and wrecked bodies vanished. Then all he could see was darkness in a long tunnel. At the end of which was a small circle of a pearl.

Harry'd opened his eyes to see the gibbous moon overhead. There was a mango tree nearby, and the gook's skin was hanging from the branches. Some of the guys had skinned it after Harry lost consciousness. The others were asleep. Harry couldn't even move when he saw it start to climb down, animated by the moonlight. It scuttled off, boneless arms and legs dancing.

That is, eventually it rustled away.

The men were dead in the morning. Everyone but Harry. Had VC traipsed in as these guys racked out? Not seeing Harry somehow as they methodically swung machetes through the bodies, like almost silently harvesting wheat? The soldiers were laid open from throat to crotch crabs. Organs steamed in the heavy dew. Jigsaw faces didn't betray if they'd even seen what hit them.

And Harry hadn't seen either. He'd been asleep. Or he'd been flashing on recent drugs in his system, and he hadn't imparted much credence to the resulting hypnogogue of a creature formed from pimply papier-mâché, outside rippled and crinkly because it had no insides. Because he'd been frozen inactive. And it was common knowledge that you could be in a nightmare where you just couldn't even twitch a finger. Such surreal paralysis was one of the things that told you the panorama wasn't genuine, even as its images unrolled before your eyes in a similar fashion to flayed skin unrolling as it's stripped from a trembling body.

Harry was transferred to another squad within the company. If he suffered nightmares, he didn't scream with them. So he still had to be fit for duty.

But now Harry watched the exquisite being dancing on the vision of thousands in killing fields to be. Lord of the dead. Haunter of cremation places, graveyards and battlegrounds. And it turned enough he could see that throbbing erection like a waving golden baton over the vulva the color of sugared cinnamon and scented with patchouli.

It turned enough Harry could see its face looked very much like his.

Time gathered itself forward again, about thirty years. And the god was drunk on Soma. He stopped dancing and began to urinate into a trough provided in the temple garden. The splashing foam was dark as topaz and streaked with blood.

The serpent priests hissed. "Sing a praise-song to Soma brown of hue, of independent might. The Red, who reaches up to heaven …"

It smelled like jasmine and high mountain snowmelt. Part of this emission was given to the men who sat lotus on the ground, beneath the watchful gazes of the cobra priests. They prayed and then consumed it, chanting part of a hymn from the Rig Veda, "We have drunk the Soma; we have become immortal; we have gone to the light; we have found the gods. What can hatred and the malice of a mortal do to us now, O immortal one?"

The men became highly intoxicated, faces taking on the contortions of damned innocents in the grips of a horror they were totally unprepared to handle.

Back in the village, those who remained behind to tend the twenty-five children looked up, hearing screams of terror and pain rip through stands of sugar palms and fig trees. Vines whipped like downed electrical wires. Tigers raised their heads from hunting and roared with empathy.

The women took some of the Soma from the trough. They began smearing it on the statues and bas-relief that decorated Nagas Wat. The ferociously hideous were depicted cavorting with creatures of breathtaking divinity. All sported inhuman body cavities which were being despoiled by every manner of razor-flywheeled nipple, taloned fist, serrated phallus, and corkscrewed tongue. Some of them had erect parts that defied description on any biological level known to man. They ravaged each other or took turns bending to be-garlanded sacrifices bound to altars, mastering poses of cannibalistic delight such as no mundane Kama Sutra had ever imagined.

These weren't the delightful erotic athletics of Tantrism, those so offending puritanical Christians who visited Devi Jagadambi at Khajuraho that they defaced the sublime architecture. There was nothing life-affirming here.

No, creation destroys as much as it gives. MORE than it gives.

The Soma was rubbed on them, like ghee butter to lubricate dust-dry dicks and clitorises, like snow to revive the sleeping. Slowly the carvings began to move, enacting in torturous rub and milky mouthful all the obscenities their statues portrayed. Anyone who bent close enough to the damaged monuments could hear whispers of rapture coming from the cracked sculpture.

Shiva watched as the men who'd drunk his heavenly rearrangement of the Soma suffered and shrieked. He wanted to touch them, to murmur what a mother/a father would to children in the grips of any violating passage. That it would be all right. Not to be afraid.

He wanted to bless them. But he knew it was unnecessary. He'd already blessed them.

Hours later, near dawn, their screams died down. The looks of abject affliction on their faces smoothed away. To be replaced with the serene smiles of transcendence. The haloes surrounding them brightened as the stars winked out overhead.

Chapter 2

"Go away, death, by another path that is your own,
different from the road of the gods."
—The Rig Veda

Cheanneary Ry was lying on her side near one of the temple pools. She sighed, thinking of the god she'd seen, emerging from beneath the graceful yet crumbling archways, always accompanied by bells and some unseen flute.

She blushed, wondering, is it possible to be in love with a god?

The old stories related tales of mortal women and deities coming together, such as Krishna and his milk maid Radha. And she'd heard that this incarnation of Shiva had once been but a mortal man.

She leaned across the water to cup a lily in her hand, catching rippling sight of her own reflection. All she could see was ugliness there. Oh, to be sure, there were no scars upon the face, nothing terrible upon the shoulders, the breasts, the smooth unblemished arms. Her waistline and hips rivaled any carved in stone in and around the temple. They could never be as flawless as Shiva's, of course, but it wasn't the feminine attributes of the god that drew her anyway, causing Ry to moon about and neglect her duties in the village just in the hope of catching a glimpse of what her heart yearned for. A conception of darkness and light, the power that comes from the exerting of complete discipline and the other resonating kind of power that was derived from unbridled wildness.

But back to ugliness.

Cheanneary Ry had only been a baby really when Sarun Chhuon found her in the woods. She'd still been inside her mother's womb. The woman had just ceased breathing, eyes doubtless staring up at a cruel red sky where moments before there'd been horrible faces grimacing and laughing above her. Swinging their machetes down, slashing at her head, her limbs, the swollen belly on her torso.

Her crime was to have been caught with a letter in her pocket, a note from her lover, Cheanneary Ry's father. It proved to Pol Pot's fiends that she knew people capable of the offense of writing, also suggesting she herself could read.

Sarun Chhuon had come upon this bestiality in process and had hidden in the bushes, knowing he could do nothing to prevent the things done to this poor pregnant woman. He'd shivered and wept silently, forcing himself to view it so that she wouldn't die without such a witness to her suffering. The blackclad soldiers had hacked and then left. He'd hurried out, and through a gash in the dead woman's abdomen had delivered out the child, its own legs severed.

How had he managed to keep it alive? He was little more than a boy himself and scarred with his own injuries? Yet he had, bathing her with mountain water, tying off the tiny wounds—with silk pulled from cocoons so he told her years later—and stealing the milk of everything from oxen to monkeys to hummingbirds to a sleeping, deaf tigress.

Ry vaguely remembered the first time she realized she loved Shiva—more than just the devotion of a worshipper. She was wearing her artificial limbs so she could work. She had her long black hair under the checkered cotton scarf called a *krama*. Perhaps she was bowling sap from the flower stalks of bristly sugar palms. Or she bent, rhythmically yanking up fistfuls of rice seedlings, knocking them against her wooden legs to loosen the mud. The movements were a kind of dance, performed to a music she heard in her head. A very sad song it was, of the deflowering of a once beautiful country by hordes of Khmer Rouge locusts, of a war waged against dancers and poets and children inside wombs.

And then there was the god, standing not twenty feet away, saying inside her mind, "Don't think any more today of the *peal chur chat*. The sour and bitter time is past ... for now."

Shiva then danced for her, hands gesturing in lullaby and eyes brimming with some fully uncontainable joy. From his body came a smell of musk and jasmine, and the sweet cream that one associates with the skin of very young children.

She grew mesmerized, a state which was an interesting combination of comfort and arousal. She'd never seen a being possessed of more beauty. He would turn and reveal to her the animalism that had filled the eyes of the savage man he'd been, and then turn again and show how these crimes could whirl away. And then he turned *again* and was gone, the place where his feet ought to have left tracks adorned instead with some bit of sanskrit verse.

Even though she couldn't read, she knew it had something to do with the commanding of death to depart. It puzzled her, since Shiva was himself both time and death.

Cheanneary Ry sighed, hoping he would stroll near again, or appear even at a hazy distance, the eyes of the ancient stone demons brightening at his approach. She didn't wear her false legs in this place. But how she wished for real ones, so she could kneel before him. Was it possible—could it ever happen—that he would then see her as a lover on bended knee?

Chapter 3

"Freeing himself he flows away, leaving his body's severed limbs, And meets his own Companion here."
—The Rig Veda

Sirikit was polite as she waited for her client to leave. The Cambodian had been much kinder to her than many men were. Most who came seeking the taboo pleasures to be had on this side of Bangkok did so because the place was infamous for regarding the lives of its children so cheaply. It was probably the most carnal place in the world, even though Thai people as a rule were very modest. Or so she'd heard. Except for one time, years ago, she'd never seen anything but the dregs of either her own native city or those who made the pilgrimage to it.

She gazed around at the damp walls of her tiny humid room: the landscape of forfeited childhood. Where she'd met strangers whose cruel affections only seemed to congratulate her on her lack of innocence. She'd been raped, sodomized, fisted, made to swallow every by-product the human body produced, and had endured three painful forced abortions with a sharpened wire during her thirteen years in the world. She'd nearly bled to death more than once and had crawled on the floor during bouts of infection, causing yellow centipedes of pus to wriggle out from between her thighs.

She'd come to believe there was nothing and no one alive incapable of hurting her.

But this man, Sarun Chhuon, had been the second gentlest person she'd ever met. He'd kissed her delicately on the forehead, avoiding her mouth because her lip had been split by a German client's roundhouse punch a few nights ago. And he hadn't parted her fragile dandelion stem legs or straddled her narrow shoulders. He'd requested only that she lay her cheek a moment in his lap, while he stroked her hair as if she'd been his child. He'd put a cool, dry hand on her shoulder, the left one that the Portuguese-speaking woman from South America had used the extremely slender whip on. The network of strap scars there resembled a bundle of snakes.

Sirikit supposed maybe he'd recently lost a daughter to a landmine. Or maybe it was something far more personal, making it impossible to perform any act deemed suitably masculine.

She'd seen many Cambodian men who were crippled, with wooden legs and plastic arms. A lot of them had fled the Khmer Rouge years ago, coming to refugee camps like Khao I Dang set up across the Dangrek Mountains border. She would glimpse them through her window, on the street: surreal figures in the heavy pollution that fogged downtown. And by the types of scars they bore she'd know immediately that these walking ghosts were probably Cambodian.

Sarun Chhuon was no different there. He sported a long row of dull red gouges that stretched vertically above his groin, as if he'd been attacked by a hole-punch in an effort to make him fit into a notebook. And his shoulders were strangely bowed, suggesting he'd had both of them dislocated at an early age and not received proper medical attention until after warping had resulted.

For most of the others she'd felt a vague, queasy pity. She was separate from them, even though she herself was crippled, wasn't she? She held the vial in her damaged left hand, transferring it to the right so she wouldn't be likely to drop it. The evils which had maimed them were very different from the evil which marred her. The damage they bore still elicited a certain amount of sickened compassion from her.

But she didn't feel this for Sarun Chhuon. Perhaps because of the tranquil smile his pocked face wore. Or the tender way he put the small vial in her palm after paying her the *baht* he owed for her services.

"What's this?" Sirikit asked, turning it over. She saw a translucent fluid slide within, rolling a bubble back and forth.

"Nirvana," Sarun Chhuon replied in a soft voice. "The only kind that can be reached without dying."

She was understandably a little suspicious. "Is it poison or dope or what? Will it hurt me?"

"It will bring you sublime happiness," he explained, fanning out both palms like sunbursts.

She huffed, unable to help it, even if she was trying to be ever so sweet. He was very nice but she hadn't seen much happiness anywhere. And the savage rictal grimace of orgasm displayed by visitors of both sexes could not truly be termed joy. It was just transformation without revelation. Usually via the anguish of her body.

"I've had heroin, opium, ups, downs, even LSD," she said. "Everything made me feel like shit."

He placed a hand on her shoulder and murmured, "This won't do that."

She gazed up at him, at the peaceful expression on a face that could never have been said not to have suffered.

"Have you taken it?" she asked. Did this explain the smiling calm she saw there, as if the torments his flesh had endured were a part of another—distant—incarnation?

"No. I'm but a bearer. Compared to those in my village who have taken it, this serene composure of mine resembles a nervous cat descending into a sea of wild dogs while clinging to a strip of bacon."

She bowed and accepted the gift. She said in Khmer, "*Aw kohn.*"

"*Lia suhn hao-y.*" He bowed back and left.

It was dawn. Through her little window she could see the sunrise like an explosion of magenta orchids and marigolds. They filtered through the visible line of smog hovering above the city, trickling the way liquid blood might infiltrate airy smoke, creating a whole other element only a sorcerer knew the name for. It was the only time of day that her singular view of Bangkok wasn't hideous. Because Sirikit never left this room. Her pimp, Phya, brought water for her basin in which to wash, carried meals in to her, ushered in men. She hadn't even been as far as out in the hallway in three years.

Sarun Chhuon had been her last client for the evening. She would be allowed to sleep for a few hours before the stream of hunger would begin again.

She stared at the vial and shrugged. It was a tip and that was supposed to be handed over to Phya, same as the money. Any drugs given to her must be cleared by him, arranged beforehand. He didn't want any of his girls to be too incapacitated, so that they couldn't perform for the next customer.

But she didn't think she'd tell him. It was hers. And taking it would be a small act of rebellion, the most power she could exert over her own life. Even if it turned out to be poison, would that be terrible?

She would leave this place then. She'd fly out like a bird caught up in a great gust of wind, smelling rain, washed clean by it. Phya would have to go kidnap some other child to lie down upon the stained mat. Someone skinny as she was, naked, crying.

And some vestige of Sirikit's spirit would gaze down at her from the ceiling, whispering, I'm sorry, sister, that he needed somebody to take my place. But I have nothing to give to protect you.

She took out the rubber stopper and drank, eyelids fluttering down.

Closed.

Sealed.

There was a pulsing ebon light.

Or a strobe of very pale darkness.

How long it lasted, she couldn't be quite certain.

But when she opened her eyes again, she was no longer a prisoner in her little room. She was outside on the street.

Admittedly, it had been three years since she'd been out. Yet she'd looked from her window each and every day, and could plainly see now that this wasn't at all what their tawdry block of Bangkok looked like. The buildings were enormous, not in the manner of a modern downtown with western style concrete apartment towers or even the high sky-scraping roofs of palaces. These reached into the clouds till they blotted heaven out almost completely. The slivers of darkness that shone in-between might have been anything but glimpses of night. But the vision of a squashed melon of the near-full moon as it floated between three spires could be nothing else, could it? If she hadn't seen that, she might have suspected she wasn't outside at all but in some massive complex of temples, all brought together beneath one unimaginable roof. In the underground of a world with no fit sky.

Yet it had been dawn when she took the drug.

Not anymore, so it seemed.

There was no gray-brown smog from the millions of vehicles that throttled the city. The miasmic kind that cost local children several IQ points by the time they reached their eighth birthday.

Sirikit inhaled, smelling green cardomom. Sandalwood. Myrrh. Bhat perfumes, pleasantly de-tected when bowing in reverence to a great golden statue of the Buddha. There *were* many figures erected in stone here and pressed in outline into the walls, but none were the Buddha. Some were merely awesome while many were completely horrible. Creatures the like of which Sirikit had only witnessed in nightmares where there were no faces, only genitals arrayed in arsenals of weapons.

There was nothing she recognized as truly Thai. She'd seen similar affectations before—although not as fierce—in opulence of great detail. Three years ago.

She was a ten-year-old *khai long*, a homeless girlchild begging from foreigners to be able to eat, turning a trick when she had to ... which was all too often. Many *farang* came to the infamous Patpong section of the city just to satisfy a lust for very young sex partners, a penchant that would have had them imprisoned or even castrated in their own nations.

She had no family. She didn't know who her father was, but her mother had been like her before a venereal disease rotted the young woman away. It had been a slow death, dissolving her down until she resembled nothing less than a pot of boiled meat.

On one certain day Sirikit was panhandling down by the Chao Phraya River. She didn't feel well and would rather have spit in people's faces.

Still she composed herself, putting her hands together and bowing quickly, brightly chirping, "*Sawadee kha*" to everyone.

She gleamed, having washed her face, hands and hair in the river water. But her eyes were red from the pollution and from tears she'd shed all night. She was exhausted. She'd spent all the previous evening staring into the dark, terrified.

She'd found her best friend stuffed into the trash behind a restaurant on Suriwong Road. Chumbhot had been four years older and like a big sister. Often, when Sirikit hadn't made enough to feed herself, Chumbhot would share what she had. She'd even sewn the beads from her one cherished necklace into Sirikit's blouse, to cover the holes made when some Russian bastard had repeatedly burned holes in it with his stinking Balkan cigarette. And she'd bathed with oil each of Sirikit's blisters from the same unfortunate incident.

"Is this suffering our karma?" Sirikit had asked her big street sister as she cried, watching as each cigarette burn swelled and popped.

Chumbhot had frowned fiercely and shaken her head. "No! It is theirs."

But last night there were needle tracks on Chumbhot's arms, the freshest ones leaking a sallow rice gruel that smelled sweet. Flies swarmed all over this and swam in the shit that leaked out of her, where bruises had swollen her flat buttocks to twice their usual undernourished size. The coccyx bone at the caudal end of her spine was visible, the tender flesh around it carefully whittled. Through the still-wet blood the asshole resembled a shrieking mouth in an otherwise unraveling face. A nose was indicated there, as were two long-slitted eyes, looking for all the underworld like a dragon which has regretted swallowing a large firecracker.

When Sirikit wept and tried to caress her friend's dead cheek, a cockroach the length of a man's forefinger crawled from Chumbhot's ear and scuttled across her knuckles, leaving a tiny wet gray trail. She'd then heard footsteps, heavy with solid boots, heels clomping, running toward her.

Don't scream, *she cautioned herself.* Hold it in. He'll know right where you are if he hears you. If he doesn't already know.

Sirikit had fled down the narrow trashy *soi.* The faces of jaded old beasts and nightlife's children didn't even turn from their sordid business to witness her streaking past. It never even occurred to her to stop and ask somebody to help her. They would think it was only a ploy to seduce them, to offer her body like it was a pussy snack at a street peddler's stall. Or they would melt away from her right into the walls of the strip bars, vanishing into ghosts whose bodies were the same as the poison clouds in the air.

She'd spent till dawn huddled beneath broad sheltering palm leaves in Lumphino Park. *Don't scream ... stop shivering!*

Chumbhot was her only confidante; what would she do now? Whores had few real friends (having little time to spare from the hustle). Child whores had even fewer.

The tree leaves vibrated around her but she never heard the boots again. So heavy and black sounding, as if the heels had been made from basalt. When the sun rose, she'd crawled out and made her way to the river—not going by way of Suriwong Road.

She'd stolen a hibiscus flower from a vendor and placed it in the water.

"I won't mourn you," she whispered to Chumbhot. "You're free."

But she wished she were more sure of that.

Begging along the Chao Praya didn't net her more than a few *baht*, barely even enough to buy a cup of tea. Her shrunken stomach grumbled. She lowered her eyes in embarrassment.

"It sounds as if Indra is singing inside you."

Sirikit looked up at a tall turbaned man who stood in front of her. His skin was almost black it was so dark, yet his eyes were blue as lapis disks. He wore a ruby ring the size of a kitten's head on one pinky finger.

Sirikit blinked. "Indra?"

He smiled. "The god of the wind. Among other things."

"Oh, yes." She blushed before the shining assault of his perfect white teeth. Hindu gods were worshipped by many in the city. At the Erawan shrine for example, though she'd never been there.

He sighed and looked sad. "What a pretty young girl you are. Too young to be out doing this business."

She gazed up at him slyly. "Are you wanting to be my father for a while? Have a daughter to pull your kite string or swallow your dragon?"

He extended his hand. "My name is Ram, little one. You come with me and I'll see to it you are given a good supper."

Sirikit was sure what that was the euphemism for, having been 'fed' by many men whose meals had nearly choked her both in size and sour curds. There'd been mornings when she couldn't speak at all, their deep thrusts down her throat bruising her palate.

Ram helped her to board a speedboat waiting for him and together they were carried north on the river. There was a beautiful house where many windows studded the facade like ornamental mirrors. A servant hurried up as they went through the front door.

"Fetch this starving child a big bowl of Aviyal, a stack of bread, and some fruit," he ordered with a wave of the ruby-weighted hand. "And find something for her dessert also."

The servant quickly ran off to obey. Ram led Sirikit into a grand dining room and bade her sit down at a long polished mahogany table. Murals of sun-diademed gods and sword-wielding heroes in chariots adorned the walls. Life-sized statues of voluptuous apsaras appointed every corner.

"Enjoy," he said and then left.

Every time she turned, she thought she could see from the corner of her eye that the apsaras were dancing, having transformed into smooth flesh with bracelets jangling. Their heavy breasts bobbed firmly. Muscled thighs and buttocks perspired slightly, the sweat tinged sweet so that they smelled more as if they were engaged in a sex act than in a simple dance. But when she swung quickly about she only found them still, frozen in stone. The smiles on their faces were secretive but dry.

"I saw you," she whispered accusingly.

She thought their faces seemed very young, even if their bodies had full breasts and generous hips. It frightened her for a moment, sure that they had been little girls lured to this very house to be fucked by the master, then transformed into graceful rocks.

The servant brought in a tray piled high with food. Sirikit ate greedily, almost becoming sick when she ate too fast. She worried that if she didn't hurry, the Indian man would return, expecting the services he wanted from her, and that she'd have to stop before she was three times full. If she was going to end up a statue, she might as well be a sated one. Maybe she'd first vomit it up on him to show her contempt.

It had been two years since she'd even seen this much food. The vegetable curry was spicy but no moreso than the dishes most Thais preferred. The steam from the stew opened her sinuses, long clogged by the pollution of the streets. She sniffled and rubbed her nose with a madras-printed napkin.

She stood and tiptoed to one of the apsaras, reaching up her hand to place it on the round breasts. They were cold and hard. What, had she actually expected a heartbeat? She stroked and then chuckled. Would she ever have such monumental tits? She touched her own flat chest. Had her mother owned big breasts? No, but then her mother was only about sixteen when she died. And with the plague her little breasts had seemed to bubble and burst, like Sirikit's cigarette burns. There was little other than the horror of this passing that she even remembered about her mother, except for cradle songs crooned in the strange language of gargled semen.

Sirikit jumped when she saw another girl about her own age standing in the doorway. The child was Hindu, like the man, but not as dark. She was draped in a white silk sari, bordered on one edge with a single line of sky blue.

"I'm sorry I startled you," this one said in a lilting birdsong voice.

"Who are you?" asked Sirikit.

"Rajani," replied the Indian girl.

Sirikit snorted. "Did the man bring you for sex games also?"

Well, it wouldn't be the first time Sirikit had been involved in an act with more than one partner. At least this time the third would be another soft-faced girl. Not some *farang* lesbian with a spoiled-fish cunt and a strapped-on dildo. Or some second guy she'd have to suck off while another took her up the ass until she couldn't walk for a week. Couldn't walk *and* couldn't talk. At least the third party wouldn't be an animal. Those were the worst. Some Europeans traveled with their pets, dogs the size of horses, big as the marble Fu lions in front of the restaurants in Chinatown from Charoen Krung to Sampeng Lane.

She knew a girl named Nopphamat who had to wear a tampon up her rectum all the time, because too much ass-reaming by large animals had left her incontinent. The type of client that was attracted by Nopphamat's smell totally freaked Sirikit out.

Rajani shook her head, a modest smile turning up the corners of her small mouth.

"Oh, no, nothing like that," she assured Sirikit. "I am Ram's wife."

Chapter 4

" ... may we be slayers when we war:
Watch, Soma, at our solemn rites."
—The Rig Veda

In flames
Going down
down in flames
Going to die.

He was on fire. Probably the most excruciating on the list of painful conditions to be had. White hot contact with nerve endings, hearing his own mustache and eyebrows sizzle.

Listening to the chopper blades whir and stop, whir and stop. Vietnamese hanging on to the runners were screaming as their hands ignited. So they let go. And fell.

Going down in flames.

1975. Spring. Vietcong marching into Saigon.

The panic everywhere was electrifying. Electro-frying. You could feel it like a lightning-heavy storm, crackling blue static across your skin.

At the base, trying to take off. Vietnamese desperate to board the Huey. American soldiers stomping on yellow fingers grasping for purchase inside. Using the butts of rifles to keep the transport from capsizing under the extra weight before it could even take off.

Elliot was certain that the flesh adhering to the soles of his boots was sticky as bubblegum. He could still see the old woman's face as he crushed her fingers, pleading with him. He could still see the child in another woman's arms as she tried to hoist it into the chopper, before another grunt smashed her in the face with the block end of his M-16.

"Down!" this other soldier shouted at her.

Yes, we are going down …

Elliot hadn't wanted to do this to an old woman, any more than he wanted to see a young mother struck on the bridge of her nose, the bones making a sound like a big walnut breaking. Causing her to slip back, drop the squawling kid. Baby going down, down.

Everybody down …

But he was under orders. The last couple of years, crawling along under the aegis of some buttfuck's commands. Told, hell, it gets easy after the first one, after the first dozen, after the first hundred or so.

And El's stomach in one stupendous knot. His sphincter tight and airlocked. Waiting for the guilt to hit, the self-hatred and disillusionment.

But it never arrived. Because it *had* gotten easy. It was dehumanizing. But, then, Elliot had often doubted if he was totally human to begin with.

Captain Summers cried under the din of rotors starting up, "No one else aboard! No one else!"

No more room. Let go, dammit. We're sorry (*sure* we are) but we've got to go home now.

Blades: slash, rrrrurrrrurrrru, *slashash,* rrrrurrrrurrrru.

Then a grenade launched, or a mortar, or some stray full metal jacket bullet struck a vital spot in volatile mechanics. A sudden gasp of muffled explosion or the sound steel makes when it sighs with resignation. Either this or Elliot's ears had just gone softly deaf. Thunder from all that lightning, surely.

They hadn't been airborne long, a few feet above the tallest trees, and weren't nearly as high yet as they might have been if there hadn't been so many gooks clinging. The chopper went down in the street, annihilating a group of five or six whores who'd chosen a poor moment to flee their brothel. One girl wasn't slaughtered outright but lay like a misused toy, stumps of arms and legs waving, head jerking back and forth, spastic on the last dregs of a battery.

Captain Summers was trying to slide away, burning still. One of the airfoils, dangling like a strip of lethal muscle, swung wild, decapitating him. The dog tags flew from the severed neck. Elliot's own tags had grown so hot he'd yanked them off. Of three other soldiers, two were dead, the last was frying bacon trying to scream. But all that came out of his mouth was smoke, much too red, like blood turned to steam.

El tumbled from the crashed chopper, rolling. Hands—his own?—slapped at him. At his uniform, limbs, gray relic of face.

It was about all he remembered prior to going to sleep, positive he'd never wake up again.

Yet he did. Inevitably. In a snug bamboo cage too short to stand up in and not wide enough in which to fully recline.

Elliot knew there were other Americans imprisoned nearby. He heard their voices drifting from other cages. Some mumbled, little snatches of weird shit reaching his ears in a funky osmosis through the tangible humidity. Some shrieked, things he wasn't sure he really wanted to understand.

Somebody kept singing part of the lyrics from the Jefferson Airplane song 'White Rabbit'. Over and over again, as if that part was all they could remember, "Feed your head, feed your head, feed your head …"

A snatch from a Heinlein science fiction book was whispered, the title, 'Stranger In A Strange Land'. Repeated once every few minutes. No, shit, Sherlock. So were they all.

The mournful lilt of a saxophone drifted through the air. No, man, that wasn't even possible. Did some POW actually have a sax with him? In a bamboo cage? Bullshit. But Elliot heard it, clear as a bell. Or more like a bird. He even knew this number.

Because Harry used to listen to jazz back home in Texas, during fits of being sick of rock and roll. This was Charlie Parker stuff. 'Out Of Nowhere', wasn't it. No wait. It was 'Dark Shadows'. Recorded with Earl Coleman after Parker had been in the state hospital for setting his bed on fire. The mourning alto notes made Elliot shiver.

Someone was mumbling, "The world is a comedy to those who think, a tragedy to those who feel, a feast to those who fuck, and starvation to those who are insane. Look at me: I laugh, I cry, I jerk off, I'm hungry …"

Elliot heard all this, filtering into his ears the way salt slides through a funnel. He didn't really understand any of it. He couldn't call out to them, to ask, "What the fuck do you mean?". He parted his lips but couldn't squeeze out as much as a whisper. The fire had damaged his vocal cords and/or lungs.

He inhaled deeply, sharply. The wind roughened in his throat, slicked with grainy mucous. But his chest didn't seize up. So the lungs were okay.

He felt wasp-stung all over. He examined his arms, his naked chest and stomach, his thighs. Blisters were almost gone, pink weals in sharp contrast to the relatively undamaged patches of tanned skin. How long had he been there? Long enough for deep second degree burns to heal. He searched his face with careful probing. He was bandaged there. Touching the area was agony.

Elliot unwound the gauze. The face ought not to have been burned more than the rest of him. His fingers traced ragged furrows and slippery tendon. These weren't burn damaged.

… happened?

What else …

What else happened to him?

He'd tumbled from the crashed helicopter into the street.

Check.

A miles-per-hour trip across twisted metal onto cratered concrete.

Check.

Then a slow-motion skid in the mode of embrace, up close in a screaming kiss. Hissing across where flames had flinched the hair off his face.

Check.

Half of his face skinned off, lying in shreds that scrawny dogs would find and eat. And then some skinny Vietnamese would find and eat the dogs. Cannibalism—like guilt—by association.

A VC guard walked by, glanced in, noted that Elliot was conscious. The guard squeaked and then ran, screeching in excited birdbabble. He returned with four more VC who stood before the cage, gawking at the injured prisoner.

What are you dinks looking at?

A scene flashed through Elliot's head, of being back in basic training. Boots caught referring to Vietnamese as *Vietnamese* were immediately humiliated by the drill instructor.

Like a fist delivered to the gut or a swat on the head or a tweak on the nose. They were only allowed to call these people who were supposed to be their allies for chrissakes as dinks, slants, slopes, gooks …

Some other prisoner down the way sang out of the side of his mouth, "And it's one-two-three, what're we fightin' for? Don't ask me; I don't give a damn. The next stop is Vietnam!"

Country Joe And The Fish, 'I-Feel-Like-I'm-Fixin'-To-Die-Rag'.

Was this other American trying to send Elliot a message of support? Of sympathy? Of put-your-head-between-your-legs-and-kiss-your-ass-goodbye fatalism?

One of the guards pulled a pistol and prepared to zero in on El. The others first shouted, then quickly hushed their voices to whispers. They restrained the man who wanted to shoot him, emphatically shaking their heads.

Elliot felt bugs crawling across the damaged side of his face. Doubtless energized by the tenderized steak of it. Nothing bit him, to pull off meaty tidbits or suck a mosquito's rusty snootful. They just moved around, as if deciding where to settle down and raise a family. El put his fingers there, gingerly trying to shoo them away. But he touched only himself. The only things he could find twitching were nubs of exposed cartilage and raw cheek slab.

He shuddered violently, shutting his eyes tight, hands flying to clasp and squeeze resilient bamboo bars. He waited to throw up, recalling another face which moved like that. Back home in Texas.

The place he'd joined the military to escape. Hoping to never see it again—to die if necessary before that trait showed itself in him.

He closed his eyes but still got a picture of his mother's skin-walking, flesh-crawling beauty, bending over him when he was a child. Slavering like a she-wolf, saliva dribbling a fringed shawl from her chin. Licking him and his brothers clean as if they were cubs, humid stinky tongue lapping at their little bottoms and winkies. The noises that came from the big bedroom when their father took her to bed. Growling, snuffling as she was rutted, howling when she came.

Dad had split—couldn't fuck an animal forever unless you were one yourself. And then Elliot and brother Harry traipsed off to Southeast Asia, seeking normal horrors, totally unfazed by the stench of the jungle.

"Think Arcan'll be all right?" Elliot had asked Harry, referring to their youngest brother.

"Alone with Mother? Who the fuck can answer that?" Harry'd replied. "Damn, I hope so. He's a tough little guy. But we don't even know if he's got the taint. Only time'll show that. At least we don't have it. I think we'd know by now if we did."

Of course, Harry did fuck animals. He fucked everything and anything. But he didn't change when he did it. His features didn't twist and meld, trying to become something else. So Elliot had just assumed that Harry was sexually perverse but otherwise okay. It was only the change of appearance into something less human that made it wrong.

Elliot didn't do what Harry did. And he didn't really like to hurt things. He'd take orders when told to kill this or that, him or her or them. But he didn't take the initiative. He remembered guys in his squad setting out cages with rodents they'd caught. Rats and stuff, maybe sixty, seventy at a time. They'd array them in front of a bunch of villagers, pretending to do some Buddhist shit. Then they'd pour fuel on the cages and set them on fire, laughing as the animals screamed. Elliot never took part in that crap. And he checked his face every morning and every night in a mirror, or anything that reflected if they were out on patrol. He never saw any indication of change. So he had purely believed it skipped him.

That is, till now. Till he felt his face moving. Must've been latent. Triggered by the trauma of the chopper's crashing. Or maybe it wasn't the shapechanger trait at all. He'd been severely injured, treated with dubious medical efficiency, stuck stark naked into a bamboo cage in a simmering bilge-pot of a jungle. There could be any kind of bugs in there, having burrowed down to the roots of his scraped features. Broken arms and legs itched as they healed. Why couldn't peeled flesh crawl as it improved?

But the VC guards, ogling him, sure saw something. And Elliot wasn't as bothered by the one so freaked out that the guard wanted to kill him as he was by the others, so scared they didn't *dare* kill him.

"Feed your head, feed your head, feed your head," the single-minded idiot kept repeating.

And then El felt the whole scene shift, as if the movement on the side of his face had ruptured exponentially, taking the jungle with it in one infectious ripple.

The floor of his cage plummeted, more like a falling elevator than the trapdoor to a gallows. Dropped about a hundred feet real fast, taking Elliot's gut with it. He saw the tops of trees coming up to skewer him, airfoil blades *slashash* and *rrrrurrrrurrrru* through the branches. Green foliage, red fire, black dream.

Out Of Nowhere. Dark Shadows.

It wasn't a bamboo cage at all. Elliot was on the floor of a cell—or maybe it was a hospital room. One without furniture ... just walls, padded at that. Dirty, filthy, vomited on, shit-stained, pissed in patterns in Rorschachs of blood-tinged urine.

The VC were a gaggle of doctors. Vietnamese ones. The many arguing with a single one who held a hypodermic needle.

"Yes, give the GI another shot to help bring him around."

"No, he's already coming around from the ECT. See, his eyes are open and he sees us."

Elliot could hear other voices, murmuring down the hall, or screaming. But they weren't in English. No Americans singing, reciting homilies, playing alto sax. He'd been in a fetal position.

Did he remember anything after the chopper crashed?

After part of his features went on a journey across the street, without him? On a safari looking for hungry dogs?

After turning slowly toward the whore who was now only a head and torso. And whatever part of her mind was still sane after just having been torn limb from limb—that part looked at Elliot's face, going mad in that glimpse. Her shriek like breaking glass.

Down. Riding that descending chopper again and again. Tops of the trees snapping crocodile jaws, slipping inside them to be chewed up, eaten alive, swallowed into dark stomachs.

Up, toward a light, burning as napalm. Bright as the heart of the blowtorch.

The taste of the rubber toothguard. Two cold steel plates to the temples. Somebody sitting on his legs to keep the bones from snapping when the seizure took hold. Somebody sitting on his chest.

Like the demon squatting on the sleeping woman's breasts in Fuseli's 'Nightmare'. Squatting to take a dump or keep him from folding up like a jackknife. Down. The tops of the trees as the swiftly chopping blades of the helicopter, guillotining, mincemeating, into which he must fall, shredded into ten thousand separate pieces of himself. Conscious in every one and screaming.

Up. Toward a light as beautiful as an aurora. As a woman he'd seen once, on R & R with brother Harry. She'd been doing a fire dance at some disreputable club. One of those exquisite Asians with the long black hair and delicate golden face, eyes dark and perfect as the almonds out of a Hershey bar. Juggling torches till one of them slipped. And her hair and costume caught fire. She writhed on stage, flesh turning every color. Someone doused her, with buckets of water or a hose, Elliot couldn't remember which. And Harry had knelt between her legs, embers still glowing in sparkles along her ruined scalp and on her breasts. Good god, the man was erect, turned on, screwing her, his pubic hair singeing.

(Yet not shifting, not becoming an animal in his face. But she didn't seem human anymore, like one of those rats in the cages being set afire, like a dog that's been barbecued on a spit in some Saigon eatery. Their father's voice crackling out of the coals of her brain: Couldn't fuck an animal forever unless you were one yourself.)

Elliot had been ashamed. Both to be such a callous asshole's sibling and to have to admit that it'd given him a boner, too. Because if you squinted just right, it was as if you were gazing at the sunrise.

Volts snapping, lightning shooting down his throat and up his ass.

He felt his brain catch fire and burn.

Down. Nothing. Dead. The darkness had a shape. Many shapes. Darkness was the definition of every image in hell. And it changed as it willed to be. And everything that had seen this darkness knew the secret of changing, too.

He saw his mother's animal face, the beast's insignia. He saw everyone he'd ever killed in war. He saw a city wasteland where tortured children were forced to abide, little body streets, ass-gutters, face-walls.

Up. Climbing the pillar of some enormous phallus. Slippery as the contact gel they use in the ECT room when they fixed the electrodes, as seepings from sebaceous glands. It just kept going, toward the sky. Always hard ... kind of similar to brother Harry's constant hard-on. Except way up there, where the hole in the head released the semen: bubbles. Not of milky fluid but of light.

Regaining consciousness, curled up until the body must resemble a question mark to anyone sitting on the ceiling, looking down.

Elliot couldn't remember how long he'd been in the mental institution. It must have been nearly forever. He'd suffered many shock treatments. It wasn't the way they gave them in America, with the patient being administered anesthesia or anticholinergic drugs. Here they tied you down and turned on the current. Well, it wasn't really intended as cruelty. They just didn't have the necessary pharmaceuticals.

But why? Elliot wasn't crazy. He'd been injured when the chopper crashed. He'd been burned and ripped. Why had the VC sent him here instead of merely killing him?

Oh, with what the doctors did to him regularly, it could be honestly stated that execution took place. He'd been killed every time he was put under the shock treatments.

And as for why the VC hadn't killed him or simply let him perish of his injuries there on the Saigon street? Well, maybe one of them had a brother-in-law. Every family should have a doctor in it somewhere. Enemy soldiers made great research subjects. Maybe a slope had seen the injured face move and thought, *Somebody pay good money for trick like this*.

El managed to stand up. Harder than it sounded. A monumental effort. His whole body felt emptied out. Really, being killed a couple times a week would enervate anybody.

Something shiny caught his eye. A reflective surface. Window, eyeball, mirror. Whatever. One of the doctors was holding it up, all of silver water and symbols. Elliot stumbled closer to get a look at himself.

The scar tissue on the side of his face slid, swirled like a waterpaint pallet of reds, grays, flesh tones. It flicked, flickered, mimicked features of other people. Elliot saw the face of the old woman whose fingers he stomped so she'd stop trying to get into the chopper.

It's doomed anyway! We can't save you ... Go die somewhere else. This here's our damnation.

The next image woven from wounds and defoliated dermis was his mother, Deborah Tyler. A faded beauty queen. Seductive one moment as she ran the tip of her tongue across her lips, horrific the next as her lips skinned back from her teeth in some night hag's growl. Animals flashed: kitten, tigress, wolf—extensions of her, or she herself as turned totally inward.

And then came the sultry fire-dancer, flames encircling her eyes in the lashes, like fiery hoops some circus performer would leap through. Then the eyes popping like bubbles in boiling caramel. And her mouth opening to scream like an incinerating rat in a cage. The sudden flavor of burnt almonds on his tongue.

The Saigon hooker, graceful arms and legs gone to stunted nubs, who'd seen Elliot and gone insane. (Had she seen herself writhing across his laid-open cheek? Severed into the hopeless freak who wouldn't even live long enough to have to learn to beg?) *Children paving a hell he didn't personally remember.*

Brother Harry, the strangest manifestation of all, crafted from the muscular wreckage, handsome redneck with jaw hard and jagged as shrapnel. Growing softer, beard stubble vanishing, as if adopting a disguise. Turning not into animals but a woman. A sort-of woman. As if dressed in drag. And murmuring, "How far is far? The universe, as it was created, is far in the past. Destruction is always nearer than you think. Put the two together and they make a distance of a single step, good with blood."

Elliot slowly sank back. He lay on his side, knees folding up toward his chest. The scalped side of his face lay against the floor. He felt the scars rolling, churning, some movie with a cast of thousands.

Oh, but this was only replay.

Elliot had been in the institution for about a year. He'd been out now for better than twenty. When he learned to control the moving picture show of his scars. Or perhaps when they'd grown bored with him and left of their own accord.

He remembered often, the burning/crashing helicopter, the shock treatments, the doctors observing as half his face took on personalities. Life was dependent upon memory, and memory was but a series of flashbacks.

Why hadn't he gone home? To Texas and America?

He'd just let his family and everyone else believe he was dead. Captain Summers' body had been burned beyond recognition. His severed head had been absconded with by some VC seeking a grisly yankee trophy, or by some hole-in-the-hooch cafe that had run out of stray pets and rodents for the blue plate special. The rest of Summers' corpse had been linked with Elliot's dog tags and sent home to the Tyler family in Texas. And Summers himself was listed as MIA.

Elliot had broken out of the *dim sum* loony farm with another American. Saab Gestetner and he'd shared a padded wall for about two weeks.

"You the one the staff refer to as *ghostface*?" Saab had asked.

When they'd finally met, Saab had quipped, "Ah, you don't look so bad. I've seen worse. Hell, I've done worse to people."

It was due to Saab that Elliot joined a group of mercs. There was nothing in Texas to go home to. He'd heard that his mother was a suicide and brother Arcan had grown up to become a sexual terrorist, done in by some of his own victims. That Harry had remained in the military for a while and then vanished from the face of the earth. (Which to somebody like Elliot readily meant that Harry just didn't wish to be found. He could personally dig that.)

He'd already been taught how to kill. A man could make some real money off such a skill. Death got easier and easier. Till eventually you didn't have to be told to do it. To Elliot it was just business. And ideologies seldom entered into it. No patriotism was required to cover up when morality came up short. You worked for this guy in some private little war. Next month you might be signed up by his competitor. Elliot had a lot of money stashed.

He took a swallow from his beer, ignored the stares of other patrons in the bar, and let his maimed gaze stray to the entertainment. He'd seen Saab moving up near the stage, then lost him in the crowd.

A girl was demonstrating her unique physical prowess. Many Bangkok saloon girls could shoot rapid-fire balls from their cunts and smoke cigarettes in their pussies. But this one had a box of dumdum grenades. She would pick one up in her twat, actually pull the pin on it with her vaginal muscles without dropping it, and then toss it out into the crowd. As it exploded in confetti and glitter, a few would scrabble for strips of paper that awarded a free drink or even a lap dance.

Saab slid up from behind and tapped him on the shoulder. He gave a jerk of his head to indicate Elliot should follow. They made for a back door.

Suddenly there was an explosion. The walls shook and the ceiling rippled. Glass shattered; people shrieked.

Elliot glanced at Saab who wore not so much as a smirk.

"Oops," Saab muttered. "Guess one of those grenades was live."

"You know her?" the Texan asked.

Saab shrugged, mouthed *no.*

El shook his head. Sometimes Colonel Gestetner could be such an asshole.

Chapter 5

"The Kundalini, in the form of latency,
is coiled like a serpent. One who impels
this Shakti to move will attain liberation."
—HATHAYOGA-PRADIPIKA

(A Stroll Through Harry's Time In Vietnam, After Cambodia)

Fact: Forty-two members of the United States Marine Corps were tried and convicted between the years of 1965 and 1971 of committing murder and other deadly violence on Vietnamese civilians in incidents not having to do with necessity in combat. As for the United States Army, ninety-five soldiers were convicted for crimes of murder and man-slaughter under the same criteria.

Harry hadn't that long ago raped the hermaphrodite in the Cambodian jungle. He'd begun to notice a few changes, sure. Subtle ones. The jungle itself could cause a variety of complaints: funguses springing up which might change a digit's configuration, might seem to spread upon parts of the body to create what looked like miniature worlds glimpsed from space.

Boils could be microcosms which might even seem to speak when the countryside got very dark and the soldier was really fucked up on a sweetly aroma'd Thai Stick, or trying to ride a horse through a needle to the syncopated rhythm of A-K rounds. If he'd had diarrhea for a while and then it stopped, spun a one-eighty and transmogrified into severe constipation, why, he might just have been squatting in the bush trying to pass his last few K-rations and had a turd remain stuck, part in and part out—until, you see, it looked as if he were growing a tail.

Harry had tried to pull it out. Had greased his fingers with spit, peanut butter, and gun oil to work around the anus. Then he finally realized this didn't originate in his rectum. It extended from the base of his spine, the coccyx bone to be precise. In short, yeah, boonie rat, you did indeed have a tail. It grew slowly but every week was a few millimeters longer.

So Harry hid himself in the trees, made sure to the best of his ability that there were no snipers lining up a bead on him and none of his fellow hellraisers peeked between the velvet ferns. He drew out his combat knife and, reaching around and back to take hold without really being able to see behind him, he hacked it off. It took several sawings back and forth, slipping once or twice to slash his buttocks which really pissed him off. Not because he minded having scars on his ass but because it stung. He cut, trying not to damage anything he fully intended to keep as part of the regular inventory. He grit his teeth until he felt a few of the molars start to silt. He chewed his tongue until tastebuds burst like under-ripened olives and blood curled over his lips. Suppressed the righteous scream, shut his eyes as surreal patterns of flashing strobes and incinerated babies in beds of purple roses came and went. His eternal hard-on throbbed in sympathy with that two or three square inches of butt end, then came with a squirt of glowing jizzum that burned like it did whenever he caught a dose from some less-than-fresh whore who probably owned a silent yet controlling interest in a penicillin factory.

Hurry! Cut the mother off!

Finally it severed. He then stared at it in the palm of his hand, the piece coiling like an agonized slug some sadistic kid poured salt on.

He had blood on the seat of his fatigues for a while. The medic just assumed ol' Harry still had the shits to the extent that sanguine dysentery had become unstoppable. Except normally when a guy got that sick, it showed as a tale of woe and turistas in his face. And his gait would become stumbling. And the flies! Fuck! The flies and mosquitos and every kind of bug there was in the fetid, vermin-festooned jungle would zero in for the open bar and free hors d'oeuvre table.

No insects bothered Harry. And he didn't grow pale. And he didn't stagger. Although he did stop from time to time to tug at the fatigue trousers, pinching them away from the crack of his ass. But, hell, what guy (who wasn't presently in the company of his maiden aunts) didn't do that?

He didn't stink like shit and blood. Or of fever which made any soldier rank as vinegar and spoiled plums. Actually Harry had begun to smell ... good. The way some of the better bordellos in Saigon and Singapore did. Not of cheap perfume, but of fresh orchids and gardenias, sandalwood and patchouli.

"You carryin' aftershave in that rucksack?" a new buddy named McCarty asked him, (for all the old buddies had perished near the temple of Nagas Wat).

"Naw," Harry replied, grinning. But it wasn't as if he hadn't noticed. It bothered him, maybe not quite as much as growing a tail did, but what guy wanted to be fragrant as a latrine full of forget-me-nots? "Sign of the pure at heart, don'tcha know?"

"That's our Harry," said Hicks, another new comrade. "The Saint of Eldorado Company."

Then—well—it grew back.

After three tries to slice that bony booger off for good, Harry gave up.

And then he developed a yeast infection. Yikes and cock-suckin' destiny-with-contumacious-space-mites-in-her-brillo! What the damnation was that itchy soreness between his legs? He had a yellowish discharge in his briefs that smelled like an experiment to make your own beer gone horribly wrong. He probed around his bag of gems, tenderly touching the cock and circumnavigating the testicles. Sliding backward, finding his anus, going back more to find his anus.

Two assholes?

Wait a goddam minute ...

It scared him, sitting one night while on patrol, monkeys screaming hysterically in the branches overhead, hurling insults as if he were the target for some great esoteric joke. Bats swooped toward his head with their high chitter which sounded to him suspiciously like "Hey, Har-riette!" Even the wind passing through the tops of the trees sounded like a soughing laughter.

Were these the wages of sin? Or some peculiar prize for having been the meanest sombitch in the valley of the shadow of death?

He had dreams of silk mountains that rose high into the adamantine stars, incense smoke of jasmine and chandan in clouds just below the peaks of these. Of being attended by a retinue of the most outrageously beautiful and hideous who brought him carved teak and ivory boxes filled with the whispers of the dead. And when he opened one of the boxes to hear more, he fell into it, dropping past galaxies of slowly decomposing souls and comets phallic with frozen miracles. Eventually he got his bearings, slowed up, learned to fly.

"Stop," he told the whole swirling menagerie.

And the stars exploded and the heavens folded up into a tiny dark knot which looked to him to be a hermetical anus.

"Start," he told this arcane sphincter.

And gases swirled, brewed, erupted, balling up, heating up, spitting out webs which would make stars and chunks that would be planets: creation upon a word.

He giggled insanely and did it over and over, all the entropic nadas and ever shimmering nebulae his own bag of tricks.

Then he woke up, more tired than when he'd fallen asleep with his rifle across his chest. Blinking his crusted eyes and hearing the tinkle of soft golden bells right next to his ears. And he was confused because there was someone singing. Damn stupid thing to do on patrol! There could be Cong anywhere, listening.

But who was it? It was nothing in English. Nor was it Vietnamese.

An ethereal yet birdlike voice, plaintive or sacred or both, a nightingale or …

Harry discovered it was him singing like that, voice like a canary or a pre-pubescent choirboy or a little girl crooning to a favorite doll. And not a single one of the other men noticed, even the one who had to be awake—on guard duty. As if the sound were above the register of human hearing. He cringed, expecting to hear dogs howl in protest or in answer.

No dogs replied. But far off a tiger roared. Nearby a cobra did him a little dance in the reeds, its neck dilated into the flared hood. When he stopped his peculiar singing, the snake slithered away. The moonlight flashed through branches in stripes of orange upon black as the tiger fell silent.

The sentry looked over at him. "You okay, Tyler?"

Had the grunt heard him after all? Harry mumbled, "Why?"

"'Cause you look as if a boomslang crawled up your pant leg and gave that dong of yours a big black kiss."

"No boomslang. It was your sister. Want her to come out and say hi to all the fellas?"

"You look weird," the sentry told him.

"Yeah, well I think somebody put a li'l synthetic mescaline in my canteen. Wouldn't know anything 'bout that, would ya?"

The guard grinned. "If I had it, I wouldn't be wastin' it on you."

Harry nodded. Then he asked, "You ever had real peyote buttons, Laughton?"

Wondering, because Laughton was the guard's first name—his last was Young Bear.

Laughton made a face. "Back home outside Vegas, during a party that was part mystical Ghost Dance thing and part love-in. Bitter shit. But after we all threw up, we covered each other in Wesson Oil and discovered exactly who had what guardian animal. I fucked an otter, three brown deer, a butterfly, a cougar, and twin rabbits."

"Man, what was it like to fuck a butterfly?"

"Tight. So, you done buttons?"

"I've done everything. On peyote, I did have my dinner come back up, but I kept it in my mouth, chewed it, and swallowed it back down. It tasted completely different the second time."

"Yeuchchch! Like what?"

"You ever done a three-way with a guy and a dead vegetarian girl? I did. After he'd taken her up the ass and right after he came, I moved him away and then sucked his cum out her rectum."

Laughton stared at him, jaw dropped.

"Well, anyway, it tasted like honeysuckle trampled into the earth mixed with the milky juice from loco weed with a little armadillo snot thrown in for spice. Armadillos all have a form of leprosy, did you know that?"

Laughton Young Bear didn't reply. But the moon rolled its rays through the branches again. Orange and black stripes crawled across him until Harry considered the sentry seemed to be inside a tiger.

Then what? The next day they were walking down the road near a village, folks out about their business tending goats or heading to and from cultivated fields or kneeling by the nearest tribulette of the 2,600-mile-long Mekong River to wash their pajamas. A grunt by the name of Strand got pissed off when some old grandpapa-san farmer gave the patrol the finger. Was this an international gesture or had the withered man just learned it from the Americans? Anyhoo, Strand blew his stack, fired off a shot which he swore later up, down and sideways had only been meant to take off the peasant's straw hat but which ended up turning the guy's head into noodle soup. Noggin: noodle. Noggin soup.

People began screaming, hurling curses at the G.I.s. Women grabbed their kids and headed for their huts. A couple boys threw rocks—actually one boy threw rocks and a second kid threw clods of dried water buffalo dung.

"You go home!" a couple of elfin men shouted, pointing where they thought America might lie across the cesspool of dreams. "You barge in say you save us then can't win crapshoot. Get out!" Things had been tense lately anyway. The standard stuff. Some guy claimed he'd been sold a soft drink full of ground glass, another said his stew had been pissed in. Kids on bicycles would ride by and knock some soldier's helmet off. Soldiers had lost their wallets to pickpockets.

Another went coconut-picking and fell in a spike pit, becoming impaled on at least fifty sharpened bamboo stakes. He was still twitching when the others found him. No one could figure how to get him up without making the situation worse. As it turned out, when they finally climbed down and tried to lift him, his body fell apart with him screaming Beelzebub's rendition of the Hellelujah Chorus.

Only three days later yet another soldier encountered a cartridge trap. He'd stepped on an unseen bamboo slat, the cartridge beneath pressed down on a firing pin, and a bullet entered his foot. He didn't die but he was limping.

And then there was the really weird shit. A pimp had led one Corporal Menger to his prize snatch, a really large woman with the biggest breasts in the known world. Just as Menger was kneeling between her thighs and about to submerge, a serpent darted its head from her cunt and bit him on the head of his dick. (Which was why Laughton Young Bear made that boomslang comment to Harry.) She was apparently immune to the venom or else—as it was her pet—it never bit mama-san. His penis swelled up all green and knobby, then burst like a boiled zucchini.

And PFC Lambert who had gotten lost when he dropped acid, was befriended by a shepherd's family who found him when they went out looking for their little son and a prize bull who had also strayed. He helped them search but unfortunately the pair had stepped on a mine. The boy was alive yet would be hideously scarred. The bull was dead, most of its legs and head blown off. It was only the bull's body between the child and the mine that spared the kid most of the shrapnel. Lambert helped them get both child and bull home … the bull because they said they didn't want to waste the meat. They gave Lambert refuge for the night. When he woke up, he panicked to discover they had sewn him inside of the bull's carcass. It was drying in the sun, shrinking in the merciless heat. The patrol happened by, heard his muffled cries, and cut him out.

The patrol was feeling antsy from the get-go. Then Strand had to go start something—or finish it, depending upon your point of view. The soldiers felt compelled to respond. They might have simply kept going. Well, if these people had been VC they ought to have been able to do a lot more mischief than throwing rocks and shit and giving the finger, n'est-ce pas?

Harry sighed as he saw guys just metamorphose into nutso idgits, stress letting go as frustrated G.I.s decided the mission of the moment was search and destroy. They chased down men, women and children, machine-gunning knots of peasants racing helter-skelter. People ran into their huts and it was just naturally assumed they had Kalishnikovs and flamethrowers in there. So grenades were tossed in after them. Hicks knelt in the dirt and zipped a mortar into the middle of the village. Yellow dust filled the air, swirling like a storm of dirty gold.

McCarty stood next to Harry. "What the fuck?"

McCarty was wiping buffalo shit off his flak vest but wasn't lifting his M16.

Harry, much to his own surprise, also wasn't making any move to join the berserking fray. Everything had gone black in his mind. He neither saw nor heard anything (except for what McCarty said). He smelled strong copper, iron, sulphur. He tasted ashes as if he himself had just detonated, an implosion from the profane outside to the secretly mystical inside.

A split second before he'd gone blind he'd seen a group of small children crouched down, gazing up with liquid black sapphire eyes at PFC Alexander. Then the world cracked.

(In that blazing darkness in his skull, Harry saw more small children. Dozens of them, black eyes staring at him, expecting him to save them. Only he could. Only he could …)

But when he was able to see again, these kids were dead. (Not the ones in his mind. They'd been a different bunch, none he'd seen before. Maybe they weren't alive anymore either—or maybe they weren't alive *yet*.)

McCarty had just marched up to Strand and brought the stock of his rifle down against the man's skull. Not shattering it. Not caving it in to reveal gray ridges in pink meat. Enough only to knock him over and make him feel foolish. Strand had been between some young peasant's legs, her mouth bloody from where he'd bashed her to shut her up. She'd convulsed and then went very still, either frozen with terror or dead because she'd strangled on the teeth he'd broken which had gone into her throat. Her squawling infant lay next to her, gummy fingers reaching out to make fists, then release, then make fists again.

Harry just stood there, not feeling even the slightest desire to indulge in outrage. His dick did not yearn. His groin didn't exhort him to vileness. An off day.

"Ah, Jesus," McCarty said under his breath, seeing the bodies everywhere, hearing whimpers and death rattles. He picked up the baby and held it close to his chest. Then he repeated, "Ah, Jesus."

"Fuck me. This is a friggin' flippin' war crime," muttered PFC Lambert, still shaking, his gun empty, shell casings around his boots like perfectly symmetrical pieces broken off a tombstone. He'd developed a twitch since being sewn inside that dead animal. "We'll be hanged fer sure."

"No," Laughton replied softly, who was only the third man not to take part in what had just gone down. "It'll be like My Lai. The brass can claim suspected enemy stronghold. The Hague Convention and 'hostile territory' and all that bullshit. There might be court martials if somebody decides to make a distinction between dink allies and dink VC. This wasn't a military action. It was just murder—or manslaughter since there was no premeditation. I have to be honest. If the chance comes, I'll testify against every one of you motherfuckers."

Guys walking up, dazed, stared at him. Some glared. Harry could see what went through their heads. Yeah, Injun, you keep talkin' like that and you're gonna find yourself sitting on a claymore toilet.

Harry knew that this was not how Laughton would end up though.

"The fuck you will," said their lieutenant, a pussy-bearded fragging-candidate named Womack. "Nobody says anything. This is between us. And if it does get out, well, we were attacked. ARVN's and Cong all look pretty much alike. McCarty, put that kid down. We're moving out."

"Sir ..."

"Down, McCarty. We can't take it with us, now can we?"

"But what'll happen ..."

"Tell you what. One guy stays behind to take care of the baby. I'll give him, say, five minutes to decide on what's the most merciful method."

"Jeeze—fuckin' hell! Haven't we done enough?"

"Can't leave it here to starve or for dogs to find. That would be cruel. So who's it gonna be?"

The men shuffled their feet, stared down at their boots, werewolfism gone to sleep. It was one of those scrawny papa-sans telling them to go home who'd dropped his pants to shake his butt—providing them with the full moon to make their hairy pelts come out. He lay in the dirt now, bottom up, ass blown clean away. No full moon now.

Yeah, and that ass-shaker had farted. And it sounded like gunfire. And it had startled the ever-lovin' out of a bunch of men who'd learned to react with survivalist discipline to anything that sounded like a bang or a pop.

Was this what had started them shooting? A string of farts?

Could any tragedy be that funny?

Harry said, "I'll do it."

Womack's eyes were slits. "Yeah. I'm not surprised."

McCarty reluctantly handed him the baby, his eyes pleading with Harry but he didn't comment. They went on down the road. Harry watched them go, then lifted the infant so he could press his forehead to the child's forehead.

He heard those golden bells again, next to his ears. The kind that were no bigger than the shells to a 22 caliber popgun (the bells, not the ears). He heard fish jump in the river a good three clicks away, too far for reasonable hearing. Rushes swayed, parted by feet in sandals. Long black hair had golden pollen caught in it from flowers that had climbed one tree in a stand of bamboo.

Somebody—a young woman—was coming and would be there in maybe twenty or thirty minutes.

Not a one of those other guys could have sensed this. Harry didn't know why he could.

Harry smiled a little sadly, experiencing some emotion he'd never felt before. He couldn't identify it. He only knew it wasn't this child's time to die nor the time for the girl approaching the village. It surprised him to even contemplate that there might be dates set for demise.

He tenderly set the kid back down on the ground. He reached into his pocket for his wallet and removed every cent he had, folding the bills and placing them under the baby's head like a faded green pillow.

He was definitely changing. No way would he have done that a few months ago.

The next night, Laughton Young Bear went out to take a dump and was eaten by a tiger.

Fact: A grunt with a two-year stint was expected to spend one year of it in the field. The odds were high he'd be knicked, crippled, disfigured, completely basketcased, or downright killed—slow or fast; the gruesome varieties were endless. But if he chose to re-enlist before this time was up, he'd be returned home, re-trained, and then sent back to the Southeast Asian paradise to work a safe job out of the jungles, rice paddies and crazy dark mountains. So there stood the grunt, balancing in one hand a mere two years in the Army where he might get arms, legs, penis, or brainpan blown away ... and in the other hand five years with the assurance of living to go home with a tan from the Vung Tau Beach or maybe the belief he'd been blessed by the large statue of Christ that overlooked the South China Sea.

After particular heinous outtings where firefights and snipers claimed a lot of boys, the patrols would stagger back or be brought in, exhausted and shell-shocked, on board helicopters. The re-enlistment officers would descend like ravenous dogs to take advantage of their freak-outs. A lot of men opted for the second tour to get out of the damned party by the lake of fire, no matter how much they hated Vietnam.

Not that it always worked out that way, especially toward the end of the war. But there wasn't a military anywhere built upon sterling truth. War was the business of death and—like any other business venture—held close its bottom line.

On a pass in Saigon, Harry and McCarty were out looking for some action. It was called a 'search and delight' mission. They'd already been bar-hopping along Tu Do Street. Harry was nauseous on enough '33' beer that, if he barfed, people might think a pink typhoon had roared in. Weird, since he never used to get sick at all, even off the cheapest hooch made from cactus and tarantula venom back home in Texas. (Except for on peyote. But you couldn't really be said to have vomited if you'd re-ingested it.)

That additional asshole he'd sprouted—which he defiantly insisted on thinking of as an asshole and not what he was afraid it was—had begun to ooze some red. He was suffering cramps and feeling bloated. He felt as if there were a snake coiled inside him, trying to rear up for a strike. And it made him think of Corporal Menger and the fat bitch with the snake inside her. Had this been some kind of kundalini, its sacred purpose debauched?

(And then there'd been that cobra on patrol, doing a hoochie coo for him.)

They passed some teenager with a transistor radio, playing the Rolling Stones, 'Let It Bleed'. He gave the pimply kid a five spot to buy the radio, then threw it on the ground and stomped it into crumbled plasticine silence.

McCarty had been drinking Pernod so that his breath smelled of licorice whips. He stood by while Harry killed the radio, his smile faintly lopsided from the hash they'd smoked an hour ago.

At the last bar a hooker with the smoothest skin Harry had ever seen sidled up to him.

"Want to touch me up?" she asked slyly.

He shook his head. "Not tonight, darlin'."

"Want me touch you up?" she offered.

Harry squeezed his legs together, like some prissy li'l thang. Felt stupid as all get out.

And then all the bar babes just pressed too close, eyes all black, nails filed sharp and painted red. One grinned and Harry almost swore he saw stars exploding in every white-hot tooth.

McCarty got close enough to tell him, "Man, these chicks feel like sharks, don't they?"

"Or danavas," Harry corrected him. "Both the siblings to the gods and their eternal enemies."

"Huh?"

Harry frowned. Where had that come from? Yet these ladies leaned so near and something about them reminded him of decaying flesh.

"Tonight big night for you, yes?" another girl said, her legs so long it almost seemed they went up to her chin. So, there she was, a demon with only legs and a head. If he were to stick his cock in her slit, it would enter her mouth: simultaneous hump and blow job.

"We show you things about the night … " she murmured. "You feel different than you ever did before."

"Yeah yeah, love you long time," McCarty said dismissively, joking.

"Forever," every girl there whispered as one, voices a porcelain rumble complete with fine cracks.

A trickle of blood exited Harry's new gender place, slid down his thigh like acid. Something going on here was a turning point.

"You feel weird? I do," McCarty interjected. "Mind if we go somewhere else?"

The girls pouted and hissed as the guys left. Harry noticed one of them held a drink and that the ice cubes were all blue eyeballs. (Had to be marbles.)

Now, Harry knew McCarty was something of a softy. Not a coward, but not a veins-in-the-teeth maniac either. (Like Harry had always been.) If he'd met the guy during his time in Cambodia, he would've had no use for him whatsoever. Why did he tolerate him now?

He supposed maybe he liked him. The guy could take care of himself but seemed so—innocent somehow. Made him think of little brother Arcan at home, too young when Harry went to Vietnam for Deborah to yet have her claws in him. How Harry himself might have turned out if he hadn't had a shapeshifter for a mother.

Anyway, there was this peep show on the next street. Harry thought it would cheer McCarty up. He'd told McCarty about leaving the baby alive, feeling in his gut the kid would be saved by somebody coming. But his pal didn't believe him and was depressed about the brutality that had gone down.

"Aren't we supposed to be the good guys?" McCarty had asked, shrugging his shoulders.

"War's hell—and other crapulent fraudulent platitudes," Harry replied, slapping him on the back. "Hey, you have nothing to feel guilty for. Now me—guilt and I? We go waaaaayyyyyy back."

They saw neon flashing like persistent artillery. At first the bursts of colored light almost had them diving under the nearest parked jeep.

GIRLS! GIRLS! GIRLS! NUDE! NUDE! NUDE! NASTY BUT CLEAN! NO DISEASE! BEHIND GLASS ALL TIME!

"Goddesses dance for you," said a wizened man with wrinkled skin the color of betel nuts. His mouth was a lightless hole, no teeth. The gums resembled the fire-blackened battlements for a ruined fort.

"Goddesses, huh?" Harry said laconically. "Then why does it say 'Girls'?"

"That old sign from last owner. New owner re-vamp. No girls, just goddesses," the man assured them, smiling crookedly like a corner in a pitch-dark labyrinth. "Sex magic give you what you want."

Harry raised an eyebrow and glanced at his friend. McCarty nodded. "Never been in an old-fashioned peep show. Been to regular strip clubs, but not one of these where the girls are like museum exhibits."

They paid to get tokens. Rock and roll was loud, pulsating. Jim Morrison with 'The End', purring out "The killer woke at dawn, he put his boots on …"

Black lights screwed into dragon sconce-lamps didn't do much to brighten the long hallway. It was dark and musty, of sweet-and-sour buttermilk and dead fish. McCarty went one way, Harry another. The coffin-sized cubicle had a wide, tall window. Man, it was steamy in there. Harry inserted a token in the slot, pushed it in. Then he sat down on the greasy chair.

(Prove to myself I'm man enough. Just some ancient VD not even the devil has a name for. It ain't some cunt but just a wound, a chancre that moi up in Cambodia rotted into me.)

A panel rose, as in a cage to release a lion for the tamer's whip. Behind the tall glass was a gyrating woman with her back to him, an apple ass and coils of ergot-black hair. She pirouetted, breasts in mounds she pressed hard against the window. Harry frowned. She had no nipples. Blood seeped in milk there, drizzled like this rain he saw, up above and behind her where there ought to be walls and a ceiling. Some strange effect of light and tinsel, no doubt.

No nipples but there was this wormy scrap too long to be a regular clitoris. It hung like raw bacon, striped as a peppermint but thin as string.

The music changed, wasn't rock, wasn't American or European. It boomed, a rhythmic slogging-through-mud percussion and a thunder that could soften bones given enough time. It squealed like pigs thrown to piranha and skreed like suiciding vultures. It set Harry's teeth on edge and made the blood gouting from his throbbingly tender mystery-orifice boil.

The dancer parted those full lips soft with scarlet, wide enough to take him cock and balls (and whatever else), no tongue to flick, no teeth in the ragged gums still bruised dark.

And then behind her another door slid open and a second woman crawled down the (wall?) to lie supine, legs spread, flesh burned from knees to up high inside. Roasted balls might have been two fried eggs.

And then another door opened behind this and then one behind that. And it telescoped out ridiculously like a battlefield in a hall of mirrors. All these were injured somehow, critically wounded, everything: tits and cocks like frayed ribbons and balls and cunts which were little more than gutted thickets began to dance for him, stroking themselves and each other, stumps where hands were gone caressing fried breasts and pitted hips, undulating with gruesome grace. Skin puckered and fluttered like autumn leaves trying to reach the ground to die. Flesh split and pus foamed like scalding milk. They moved, managing to display their terrible beauty in movements anyone else might have thought agonizing. Suffering—for him.

What could he do? He got up and began to dance, too. He unzipped his trousers and released the boner he always had. It rose straight up, swaying like a snake, the testicles making it resemble a snake with wings.

Coiled Kundalini was female vitality—psychic energy—in a dormant state. It might remain quiescent for a person's entire life. But then it might awaken—a cosmic power which climbed the spine to be joined with Shiva in the head chakra. Shiva who was the Pure Consciousness diffusing the entire universe.

The very symbol of the mantra, the strongest of all the seed-sound syllables—OM—denoted Shiva … and Shiva, in his fourth aspect, was a fertility god associated with bulls, snakes, the moon, and soma.

Pranava was the ultimate sound. It was the serpent uncoiled, merged with Shiva, hissing, hisssssssing Sssssssss-OM-a, the 'a' being the AH of space borning as creation originated.

This good old boy (actually deviant monstrous redneck old boy) had no idea where such knowledge came from, but there it was: thunderbolt and wild. In Harry, Kundalini didn't merely climb his spine vertebrae by vertebrae to bring him to his feet with lightning in his back. It sprung out from his penis as well, perhaps what his priapism had always been/perhaps not. His pubic hair was matted with blood so that his dick looked as if he'd just fucked his way through the vast landscapes of both genesis and omega. He twisted and turned and lasciviously thrust himself out from the hips as the women pressed to the window, calling to him to come break the glass, to let them out, for him to climb into their space which went too far back to be a closet or a room or a massive airport hangar, filled close to that window with pink smoke, it turned a lavender gray farther away, then faded out to a grainy black—the grains of which, upon scrutiny, turned out to be faces of pisachas and nagas, asuras and rakshakas. These last in particular caught his attention, for these were demon shapeshifters.

He saw them sinuous, sensual, torturously tortuous. Gouged cunts behind wormy cocks and flaccid scrappy balls, tits definitely put through a wringer. His brother-sisters, yes. His lovers if he so desired. Go inside! There would be no struggle there, no further pain after he submitted to despoiling, no burden of dharma too heavy for someone who never expected to become a god.

If he went in, would he come out? Or would he be one of them, some aberrant freak who just missed godhood by a devastated inch, the thickness of that glass.

Sweat poured down his face. How hot was it in here?

That snake strained in his back and in his erection. But to force him to flee or to admit he could never be worthy and, thus, give in to the delights he saw behind the window?

This was the pollution he'd always been attracted to. The damage, the scarring one perceived when the veil of reality dropped from the phenomenal world. That veil was known as Maya. Coincidentally, Maya was also the name of a great demon.

Harry lusted for what he saw behind that glass. He almost started to pound his fists on the window. It would be so easy to break, to then rub the shards and spikes across him like diamonds, to embrace those crippled dancers with kisses raw as the lewdest trauma. He wouldn't have passed his test but what did it matter? He'd never thought to rule the universe. Let the demons have it. Let them have it and every human bag-of-crap in it. Oh, this was easy; it was shockingly sweet; it was the negative nugatory he'd secretly always wanted. Warped guys like him had the death wish implicit in every flagrant crime they committed. Right?

What pulled him back? A force within his spine actually drew him backward as if it were a metal, a snake of steel. As if a giant magnet lay behind the curtain into the hall. His erect serpent actually turned, jerking at the scrotum.

Still he couldn't tear his eyes from the vision of those frolicking harlot-freaks. He fought to keep his momentum toward the window. The blood which had scorched down his thighs now turned to ice, hard/red/brittle.

He moaned, gathered up every ounce of power he thought he could summon and managed to cry, "OM!"

It wasn't what Harry had started to yell. He'd been thinking something closer to "Stop!" or "Fuck!" or "Shit!"

But it was "Om!" that came out, both shrill and resonant, a sob and a thunderclap.

The glass in the booth's window exploded. The walls shook and the floor rose up and then dropped. Harry ended up on his ass. For a split second he was blind again, as he'd been in the field when the patrol opened up on that village. He was deaf, hearing only a distant buzzing and hissing as of flies, locusts, fire …

Not blind again. He saw the brilliance out of the corner of his eye. Flames leapt around the room. The curtain that separated this booth from the hallway was a flaming rag. Had he done that with a shout?

He didn't even zip up. He spun, covered his head with his arms, and leaped through the burning entrance to his booth. The corridor was full of smoke.

Behind him, those who'd failed to be Shiva sighed, moaned seeing him leave them. So close.

"Would have loved you … forever," they croaked, ashes spilling from their lips.

"McCarty?" he cried out, stumbling for the booth his friend had entered. "Man, you all right?"

But it was as if he were still blind. There was so much smoke in the corridor, he couldn't see. People pushed past him.

He felt naked skin and then somebody knocked him down. He heard women weeping and men yelling. He tried to crawl but put his hand in the mush that had been some guy's face. He managed to creep close, grabbing for dog tags glinting around the neck.

"McCarty?" Please tell Harry he hadn't caused this.

He could barely see but did read the tag. It said Strand, Thomas. (Motherfucker, Harry added mentally, then realized he had no right to cast stones at anyone.)

Harry crawled on his hands and knees, choking and coughing in the smoke and the rising yellow dust. He got into another cubicle. A lot of fire in this one but he didn't care.

The ceiling had fallen in. The walls were still shaking from the concussion. The window inside that cubicle had been blown out and the dancer, just some little black-haired chick wearing nothing but tattoos in Sanskrit, lay dead, practically flayed from top to bottom in the flying glass. Her hair and blood were burning.

"Goddam rocket!" some American shouted as he ran down the hall.

And, unfortunately, when Harry found his friend, he discovered McCarty had ridden that rocket.

Chapter 6

"Wandering far, with wise designs, the
juice here present is effused,
Made beautiful ..."
—The Rig Veda

"Ram said I was too young to be a whore but he has a wife my age?" Sirikit arched a fine black eyebrow.

"It isn't what you think. We haven't been together as man and wife. He prefers to wait until I'm older. He is a very kind man."

"So what am I doing here?"

Rajani sighed.

"My husband goes back to India frequently on business," she explained. "He believes I should have a companion, someone my own age. You're here only to be my friend."

As the Indian girl showed her the downstairs, Sirikit looked around at the sumptuous furnishings. A bronze elephant the size of a truck, sporting real ivory tusks, trumpeted silently in the garden. There were intricately carved screens, painted silk tapestries, and thick pile mandala carpets in every room.

"I'm to *live* here?"

Rajani nodded.

Sirikit looked again at how Rajani was dressed. The very fine quality of the silk she wore. There were tiny blue and white diamonds sewn into the neckline and at the edges of the short sleeves. Her extraordinary hair was braided with filigreed silver.

"Will I have a nice dress, too?" she asked, acutely aware of her own rags.

Rajani put a hand to her cheek in consternation. "Of course! How slow I am. We'll go and choose something now."

She led the Thai girl up a long staircase, the banister pieces an ascending row of hand-carved *lingas* set into *yoni* bases. A mural on the wall of the stairwell from first to second floor depicted Shiva wearing a garland of skulls and dancing wildly upon a mountain, encouraged in his abandon by demons. But was he dancing up the mountain to embrace the moon or caroming down to unravel the universe? Sirikit couldn't help putting her palm briefly to the wall where blood dripped from the skulls. But it was dry, of course. Just paint. On cool plaster.

Who but a prince—or a rajah—could afford to live like this?

"What kind of business is your husband in?" Sirikit asked, swallowing meekly.

"Oh, he's a broker of precious stones. Here. This is my room," Rajani said as she opened a door on the long upstairs hallway.

She glided in and her guest followed. Sirikit marveled at the paintings on the walls. Rows of beautiful men and women were involved in quirky gymnastic positions not even her most athletic clients had requested. It might have embarrassed her had she not found them so impossible. She couldn't help but giggle.

"I don't believe anyone could bend themself that way."

Rajani nodded. "They are from the Kama Sutra. I study them as I fall asleep at night so that when I finally begin my duties as wife, I'll know how to please Ram."

"But this one's different," Sirikit noted, pointing out the wall with the outside window.

The art depicted a young woman in several poses. In the first, she was throwing cowrie shells to a crowd which avidly collected them. In the second, she bathed in the river and then donned a red sari. And then a third showed her about to leap into the window. The glass was stained in streaks of scarlet and gold, so that the light coming in—facing west with the sun starting to set now, it was so late in the day—was like a burst of flame.

"That's a story of Sati. The woman is a widow. The window is her husband's funeral pyre where she'll immolate herself to be with him in the afterlife," Rajani explained.

Sirikit smirked at the explicitly sexual portraits and the others indicating a fiery suicide. What was this? A room-sized text of what every young Indian bride should learn? It was like walking into an adult cartoon. But she admitted to herself it was lovely. She'd visited many sex markets in Patpong, where the illustrations weren't rendered with as much style or sensitivity. Yet was it or wasn't it the same as pornography? There was nothing gross about it. Her flesh didn't crawl, except where the woman threw herself into the fiery window.

"What about the rocks?" she asked her hostess.

In every corner—as the apsaras had been arrayed in the dining room—were stones that went up to graze the high ceiling. Each were covered with handprints, some still faintly peeling a red ochre paint.

"They're sati memorials. The widows would pass through the gates of the temple where their dead husbands were to be burned. They would dip their hands in vermilion and leave a mark from their palms, there upon a pillar. Later these were chiseled into the stone so their sacrifices would never be forgotten." Rajani beamed as if she thought this very romantic.

Sirikit didn't comment, imagining that anyone stupid enough to jump into a fire got what they deserved. Surely some of those widows were forced into this action. But the others? To suffer like that, so horribly, in free will? She believed that the world was too finite. One had to hold onto whatever they could grasp, for as long as they could keep somebody else from stealing it away. And anybody who believed in romance had never been forced to endure an American inserting a half dozen small ivory figurines of Chinese demons—painted in azure and indigo—to watch her "give birth to the blues".

Rajani opened her closet, revealing dozens of saris in every color. Some of the veils were patterned as intricate golden spiderwebs and ponds full of lotuses. Many had real gold thread woven through them and gemstones stitched into the cloth. Sirikit ran her hand through them. There was no rustle, just a soft whisper.

"Anything you want," Rajani told her.

Sirikit arched that slender eyebrow again. "Anything?"

"Yes, any at all."

How far could she take it? She felt a flash of jealousy—not the first—at this girl who had everything.

"Well, actually … " she paused, "I like the one you have on the most."

Rajani smiled as if flattered and instantly began to take it off. "It's yours," she said.

Sirikit hadn't expected that kind of generosity. It was a lot to be willing to give her a dress from the closet, but the one she was wearing? The Indian girl stripped off the white silk.

"Don't you want to undress so you may put this on?" she asked as she slipped from the skirt, the silk murmuring around her slender thighs.

Sirikit did so but was genuinely shy now. Rajani's skin was flawless, and the same couldn't be said for hers. The two exchanged glances when fully naked and then turned as one to face a large mirror, staring at themselves and at their differences.

Sirikit's flesh bore the Sanskrit scars of intravenous needles and puckered burns round as tiny faces. Of fingernail halfmoon trails and bruises on her nothing-breasts that might have been the scrolls on temple pillars. Of bite gouges on the slopes of her buttocks, like the dead littering a frieze from a Ramayana battle scene.

Downstairs the servant had given her a drink called *lassi,* blended from yogurt, ice, sugar and mangos. Rajani's skin was as smooth as that, as if any moment the liquid of her would lose the precarious shape it held and she would flow across the thick carpet.

Sirikit would give anything to own this sort of skin, perfect, unblemished, new. With such flesh surely the monstrous memories would not be there. Skin like that which had never been terrorized and defiled. Had never been anointed with urine the color of still warm embers.

"How can we ever be companions?" she asked her hostess. "A ten-year-old wife and a ten-year-old whore?"

Rajani plucked a purple gossamer scarf from a drawer and tossed it across the mirror, obscuring their reflections. She kissed the Thai girl's cheek.

"Everything exists behind one veil or another. Kali is both Mother and Destroyer. She's given many names, including those for both *virgin* and *whore.* Neither renders her less holy than she is," Rajani said. Then she added cheerily, "Now let's get this on you."

Sirikit let the other child dress her, wondering how being surrounded by pictures of carnality and death had taught Rajani so much goodness. But she had to admit that she was beginning to feel very lucky. If she hadn't met Ram by the Chao Phraya, what would she be doing that night? Tonguing clean a man who'd just been up her ass? Wondering if the guy who'd paid for the five-minute tumble behind the Robinsons Department Store on East Silom Road carried AIDS, because she'd seen lesions in his scalp? Being murdered by the animal who'd done Chumbhot, his knife carving what sort of filth into her?

Rajani dressed again, this time in a dark pink sari the same color as her lips.

"We'll go show Ram," she said as the two went back downstairs.

He was in the foyer, placing a bowl of milk before a statue of Ganesh, the elephant-headed god of luck. Long stalks of incense wisped to either side. He looked up when he heard them, beaming with those bright white teeth of his.

"What a lovely pair of children," he declared.

There was a commotion outside. A servant cried out and there was the popping sound of a gunshot.

"Rajani! Quick, take Sirikit and escape out the back way," Ram ordered. He pulled a pistol from the drawer of the table Ganesh sat on.

The door was kicked open. Armed men were on the lawn and porch. The boat they'd arrived in bobbed in the Chao Phraya, the engine roaring. The water held a smear of the lingering sunset, half black/half red. Like a sacred river of the dead full of ashes and blood.

The man who'd forced open the door stumbled into the entrance and received a bullet in the face as Ram fired almost pointblank. Another leapt up the front steps, grass flying from his boots, and fired twice, hitting the Indian in the hand and forearm. Ram's gun dropped from the shattered fingers, white bone gleaming backward through the meat of his elbow.

"Here he is, Mr. Tak," this one shouted to a heavy-set Thai strolling up the walk, impeccably dressed like he was just coming to a dinner party.

"Fine. Only don't shoot him again," Mr. Tak said softly. Then he told Ram, "Should have let me buy you out. It was a most generous offer, wasn't it? Now I must make an example of you."

Tak waved his pudgy hand, and another punk stepped up with a flame-thrower. Ram's body jerked in the doorway as the column of fire struck him. The statue of Ganesh exploded into bits of confetti plaster resembling the bone bits of Ram's hand and arm. The statue of Shiva appeared to actually dance.

Rajani screamed and ran forward, trying to push Ram down and roll him, trying to put out the fire with her hands. Her pink silk sari caught like rice paper, turning red as a sati sacrificial dress. Her long shimmering hair crisped as the filigree silver worked into the braids melted. Her flawless skin puckered and charred.

"Damn it, I wanted him dragged out *here* first, you idiot," Tak snapped. Then he sighed with resignation. "Quickly, inside … into the study on the left, across from the dining room. The safe …"

The man gulped, pausing for an instant to gape at the couple incinerating on the foyer floor. Then he jumped through the fiery entrance, slapping himself as flames crackled at his clothes. He rushed into the study.

Sirikit gasped, backpedaling, blinking at the blinding flash of the carpet and curtains catching fire. She could see the fat man waiting on the porch, only slowly making his way back onto the safer lawn. She could see the man hurrying to open the safe, using some high-tech form of mini-explosive in lieu of the lock's combination. The smoke cleared; he grabbed a large leather pouch inside. A long line of flame had flickered across the floor, blackening the borders in the carpet, debauching each mihrab, and then obscenely eating the central mandala. The furniture smoked, then went up. The man, hugging the pouch, threw himself through the nearest window.

Sirikit felt as if she'd become one of the apsaras in the dining room, stiff and solid, frozen in stone. She could see a long bas-relief of multi-armed gods on the wall as fire chewed around it in the plaster, paint running in liquid sores. Their faces seemed to turn toward her, arms reaching out to pull her into some deadly embrace. The edges of her sari began to flutter. This broke her spell of immobility, and Sirikit ran down the hallway toward the back of the house. She was thinking *Stupid stupid! Why did I just stand there? I'll burn up, too ...*

But she could see the open hall door leading to the kitchen. And the door beyond that which the cooks had used to flee the house. Into the garden where the bronze elephant trumpeted amid the jasmine blossoms. She could see their white clothes wisping among the trees like raiments of ghosts, headed for the street. She noticed they weren't screaming. And she thought, *No, because then the men might hear them and chase them down. That's how I have to go out, silently, like before. Noiseless and fast.*

She picked up the white silk skirts, diamonds glittering like lasers, realizing as she ran that Rajani had neglected to give her shoes. The floor was getting hot, blistering her feet. There was nothing but roaring behind her, and the sounds of explosions like some huge firework display. Something whizzed past her face, narrowly missing taking the lobe from her ear. She didn't know if some piece of statuary had just detonated, shooting an arrow of sharp stone, or if one of the assassins had taken a shot at her, seeing the white dress like a swan's feather in the blaze. But then she knew no one could see through all the smoke that was gusting through the house.

The ceiling rumbled and then bowed. One of the temple pillars crashed through from Rajani's bedroom, engraved sati palms glowing red hot. As if coming up to say, Stop! Halt! Come back to us!

Sirikit's throat burned and she was very dizzy, and she wondered if she just should have let herself lie down with Rajani and Ram, committing sati with the only people who'd ever shown her kindness. Let herself lie down and put her arms around the burning corpses, considering she was apparently going to die anyway. Maybe it would have ensured she would be with them, providing there was any kind of afterlife. She still could, probably. She could pass that stone on her way back to them and slap her hand against it. The flesh would stick, leaving a doughy red print.

No, hang onto what you have. Rajani should have run, too. Now what does she have in place of that perfect skin of hers?

Incinerated muck, grease simmering through. Worse than even Sirikit's mother looked when she died.

And then she was outside, through the back door, the door Ram had wanted his wife to take her through. She sucked in the air, feeling it scorch down her throat as harshly as the smoke had. The blisters on her feet burst and she fell down, whimpering with the pain. She forced herself to climb back up, racing down a path strewn with flower petals, which had been jolted from the bushes as the servants ran that way before her. Like the blossomed carpet lain for a bridal march—or a funeral procession.

Sirikit went through the line of longan and bodhi trees. She couldn't see any of the servants anymore when she hit the street. She didn't even see the man who stepped from the shadows and grabbed her, pulling her into a car which then sped off.

It had been Phya who'd abducted her. And even though he was a pimp working for Tak, Tak probably didn't even know about this kidnapping at the sight of his own activity.

Phya was a little disappointed when he saw she wasn't Indian, because he already had plently of little Thai chickens. But she was very pretty AND scarred, a combination that would appeal to quite a few clients. As if every *farong* who'd had her left some bit of intaglio to describe a story of her life. Just as temples had panoramic designs carved in intricate glyphs, like at Bangkok's own Wat Phra Chetuphon or down south in Cambodia's Angkor Wat. But better for the fleshy hedonist because it was interesting to unwrap, and there was no need to be nervous about adding to it.

And people had added to her scars for three years. By comparison to how she'd looked un-dressed with the Hindu girl, her flesh *then* had been flawless. She felt the dermatological detritus ripple across her at every dawn as she stretched out on her pallet to dream for a while, grimacing as they tugged and pulled to wake her up again by noon. She wore razor demons and blazing cigartip moonscapes, knife-point vampires and nail sketched shrieking-mouthed victims. Various clamps and vises had left dimpled deserts. Heated restraints gave her keloid bracelets on her wrists and ankles. Her nipples and clitoris were as etched as ancient rocks beneath a sun-dappled waterfall. She had a picture of a headless corpse tattooed on her belly, accomplished with a heroin needle dipped in ink from a ballpoint pen, then heated in a zippo lighter. The artist had been a Swiss bank exec with a thousand-dollar suit, carrying a briefcase full of high grade white powder and stock market items from around the world.

But the taint which was the favorite of her visitors was her left hand.

She remembered the man who'd done that to her, only a scarce two months after Phya had abducted her. He'd strapped her down and taken out a scalpel. He'd carved the fingers until they resembled tiny totems.

He'd sat naked on her chest as he did this, wearing only his boots and breathing the odor of sour pickled cabbage into her face. He'd stuffed his underwear into her mouth to stifle her shrieks. Even though Phya knew what he was going to do because the guy had paid extra. It was just to keep her from alarming the other *farang* visiting in the building.

"Did you know Chumbhot, sweetheart?" he asked over and over as the scalpel pricked delicately down to nerves, wheedling cartilage.

He had the kind of features that Occidentals referred to as baby-faced. Soft, pretty, almost preternaturally young. Yet there were chips of mica in the blue eyes, the same metallic shade as the blade of the scalpel before it was covered in her blood.

And all she could do was cringe, not even trying to scream amid the wad of boxer shorts. Afraid to make a sound even though he'd found her anyway.

Scar tissue faces and torsos rose from her hand like the rocks of Stonehenge and the heads of Easter Island. One had follicle-feather wings scrimshawed across the first knuckle. Another had a serpentine spine replete with pore-sized scales rippling beneath the second knuckle. A third had seen the bone chipped out in splinters to resemble claws. Done with such precision and skill that they had not fallen out later, nor had to be removed, nor had caused her to develop either blood-poisoning or gangrene.

It had, of course, basically crippled her manually. She couldn't grasp well with it. Hand jobs had to be done strictly with the right, although clients seemed to like it when she inserted one or more of the handicapped fingers up their rectums. Mostly they wanted to watch her touch herself, touch the other inscribed passages on her pictographic skin with it.

Sirikit could taste the drug Sarun Chhuon had given her, lingering on her tongue like a piece of overripe fungus. But it felt like plum wine in her throat. She had abdicated Phya's bondage and now stood on the alien street, realizing she was naked. She looked down at herself and could see the gorgeous devastation of her flesh.

A trick of the moonlight and the drug made her body seem to jerk on the spoke of the neck, wheeling it around so she could view her own back in grotesque detail. Her bones clacked like a prayer wheel as the torso and limbs then rearranged themselves forward again, street seeming to go out from under her feet until she hung like a spastic doll for seconds. The lack of gravity made her gut and colon cinch spastically. The ground returned.

She heard a screech and looked up in alarm, eyes trying to see the misty pointy *chedi* tops of infinite reliquary towers. But the outsides of the leviathans were completely garlanded with rows of brightly painted dancers, performing acts so deformed that the couples engaged in the Kama Sutra drawings she'd seen years before on Rajani's bedroom walls would have been shocked and frightened by the perversity within. Only a shadow zigzagged across a row of these. She heard the high-pitched skree again. She scanned Pagoda-style temples. Their high roofs curved in such a way she could really believe the sky nestled in them. Hindu *Rathas*, or temple chariots, sat before these, roomy enough for rhinoceroses to lie comfortably within, with huge stone wheels which could crush a man as though he were an ant. But there was nothing flitting across them now. No shadow.

She thought she saw something fall, a feather, a sprinkle of dusty dander. Falling across one of the elaborate arches strung between shrines. These were carved as the bends of gigantic human legs, ending in gross genitalia on one base end and in scaled talons on the other. A reflection daubed off a minaret the size of a soccer field, and she tried to follow it. It rippled across a series of *prang* rounded-top domes as large as a mountain range, their tops vanishing beneath a haze of dark cloud.

But then it was gone, no fabulous monster to go with the mirrored spark she'd barely seen in the corner of her eye.

A strident squawk loud as a klaxon went off behind her, making Sirikit shout, nowhere near loud enough to match it. She jumped and saw the grinning slimy mouth uncrease before her face. A tall human female form, surmounted by an ungainly vulture's head, had its arms open wide, all six of them. The breasts, also six of them, wobbled like scoops of thin cheese. Wings the piss-color of a wasp's folded and unfolded behind it, attached to either side of the crooked spine. Crabs the size of U.S. quarters scuttled through the groin hair, pincing their way in and out of the mangy slot between the legs.

Sirikit stumbled backward, repelled. But it snatched at her, winding the half dozen arms around her and lifting the petite Thai girl off her feet to press her against the clotty tits. It then began to carry her between two colonnades leading into a courtyard. Sirikit barely managed to turn her face and see the imprints in the stone of these pillars. Like the paint-flecked hands chiseled into the sati monuments. Except that these were faces, mouths open in shrieks or rictal grimaces, the rest of the features contorted out of all symmetry.

There was a long fissure open in the earth, crooked as a thunderbolt. Black grass growing in tufts around it made it look like the bird-headed female's cunt. Vermin scrabbled in and out of this also. The creature took Sirikit down into it.

She lost consciousness. Or the drug inside her spasmed, making it seem as if a seizure had passed her mindlessly from one level of this nightmare into the next. When she opened her eyes again she was lying flat on her back upon a cold stone.

The subterranean chamber she was in was enormous, sabotaging all symmetry. As if the strange city she'd been above-ground in had turned inside out. The walls and ceiling of it (she couldn't see the floor from where she was stretched out on her back) might have been the interior of some colossal animal. The surfaces were ribbed, musculature teeming with parasites. These tiny creatures would from time to time spin single silk-spittle threads and then scuttle down, grabbing some tidbit from the larger things bent over the countless slabs, onto which other victims were helplessly bound. Then they would rapidly scurry back up, devouring their gory loot while swinging on tightropes of sticky webbing strung from wall to wall. As they descended Sirikit saw they were really about the same size she was. And they had nearly-human faces. But this is where the resemblance to people ended, in size and features. The rest was insectile, chitinous and nasty. Which still placed them above in appeal when compared to the predominating creatures. The ones on the ground, eating their live meals.

Sirikit had seen similar things, carved in stone. But manifesting into animated meat brought them to an almost indescribable hideousness. She tried to close her eyes, willing herself to wake up or sober up, whatever it had to be. Unless the drug Sarun had given her really was poison, in which case she was dead and this was hell. There was no leaving this place. If she'd thought she'd been tortured in life, she'd make some gruesome discoveries now.

Her eyes wouldn't close. Did she no longer have eyelids? Had one of these demons eaten them? Shouldn't she then be shrieking in pain? Others were screaming all around her. Of course. Hell was the nation of pain. Her pupils bulged from the sockets, dry with sand one moment and running with slime the next as muck dripped from the webbed walkways so far overhead.

Sirikit glanced down at her naked body and saw nothing else was missing. She'd not been slashed or gored. Her scars gleamed with sweat. She wished she could close her eyes!

She wanted to stop up her ears. The sound level in the cavern thundered. The demons addressed one another in nuances of confusion. Hungry syllables were tossed out of the fissured throats, ladened with gristle-thick consonants. Slurred drunken vowels echoed canyon-like within the feasting hall. (Yes, because that's what this was … a gigantic dinner party.) It rumbled until Sirikit's skull shook within her head, blood blooming in pore-sized roses everywhere on her face and scalp.

Some of it ran into her eyes.

I want to close my eyes!

A devil turned toward her, the length of its head from top to pointed chin was as long as one of her legs. There were ten to twenty fine eyelashes adhering to one cheek like linear freckles. But they couldn't belong to it for it had no eyelashes, nor eyebrows. Nor hair of any kind. Its bald body was a mass of pulpy sinew. Its firepit eyes were gabled by a chipped red sandstone ridge. Looking into them she saw herself reflected, could see her eyelids were still intact.

It opened its square mouth, revealing knots of rock in place of fangs. Leering at her, its tongue darted out to lick a yellow discharge dribbling from its single nostril.

Close my eyes close my eyes close my eyes close … !

(Don't scream, why? It already knows I'm here.)

But Sirikit couldn't scream. She had so long deprived herself of this release that it wouldn't come now that she needed it most. Her dismembering was going to arrive with her silence, probably the only hushed horror in the vast *jahannan*.

A boy moaned, bound to the basalt to the direct left of hers. The demon swung away from her, smelling the urine the youth had pissed out in terror. It deftly slid glass-sharp talons under the restraints and then lifted him up in a single claw-tipped hand, dangling him above the four raw corners of the mouth. It squeezed his abdomen until the rectum disgorged gruely ropes of pulverized sausage. Some of it was packed with shit, some of it with undigested slop. The intestines jerked as they fell into the demonic maw, as if still in peristaltic throes. Sirikit heard it slurping and tasted acid in her own mouth.

She forced her eyes—still unblinking—to roam about the room. To fix on anything but that. Her pupils seemed unfixed, rolling, dark-centered gyroscopes. She saw thousands of other demons, bodies opulent with knobs and crevices no human could guess the practical functions of. From time to time the knobs brightened or darkened, sharpened, quilled, spun. The crevices squeezed out howling infant-faced fireflies which burned to cinders before they could go far. Or these holes let out loose and languid noodleballs of death-chanting worms. Or the cunty tunnels would spasm and out of them would crawl hauntingly beautiful beetle apsaras, who danced to death some of the victims bound to stones.

Some demons had large bodies but small heads. They buried these between wrenched apart thighs, savoring a confectionary of virgin wombs. Some had no heads at all. They straddled the stones, lowering the mouths that gashed their bellies down to dine on faces marinated in tears. Caressing the mole-like limbs of people who had clearly been raised underground as blind cattle, they plucked out cherrystone eyes that had never seen daylight, popping them like white grapes.

A man was being rubbed up against by a devil bitch with breasts that were paddlewheels of razors. She then licked the splayed carcass clean, only to afterward regurgitate it, puking lumpy pink rivers, orgasmic with bulimia.

Women were disemboweled with phallus fingers. Men were cored like apples with footlong nails, their dying lingas springing up to spew seeds.

Dying? Dying … was anyone dying here?

Sirikit watched corpses fatten up again, plumping with vitality seconds after being discarded. Watched eyes open. *Where am I?*

Heard the screams begin afresh. And she wondered if she'd been taken yet. A night terror memory slid across her mind, dragging chains with it that made her entire body go rigid. She'd died, was being killed right that moment, was about to be chosen again. Bile burned like remorse. Humiliation was a taloned finger up her ass, moving up and down and in and out like relentless degradation. Inescapable with scorching breath on the back of her neck and icy hands clutching her hips to keep her steady with buttocks thrust at the correct angle. And it was like Sirikit was being raped underwater, beneath a stifling current of cadaver swills. The dangerous undertow of nightmare laughed its butt-fuck babble, leaving bloody spit in her hair.

The quality of sanity was inversely proportional to the amount of synapse-sparking agony her injuries relayed to her brain.

Dying. Dead. About to be reincarnated into the same mortality to do the whole thing over. An ever-spinning cycle of the most surreal, unstoppable suffering. No soul, in a new infant with the traditional infinity of possible destinies arrayed before it. The ultimate curse upon the wheel.

Not even a wheel. Just a spirit trapped in a single groove, replayed with variations dependent only upon the depth of the scratch that made it.

Dying. Dead. On the verge of an insanity-inducing catastrophe.

This mantra reverberated from the heart of earthquake. Was she never to be reborn, never to know a flawless flesh? Not to possess a complexion of unwasted innocence? Would she never be restored? Or would she always be a Sanskrit of etched wounds, lining her skin with an indecipherable codex of pain?

Hell was all about helplessness, as was the condition of being human. The things being done to her were exponentially worse than anything the *farong* had ever done.

Sirikit's lips parted. She stretched them so far in an attempt to scream that her jaw sprung. She heard the tendons snap, bone crack. She tasted a flood of bloody saliva. She couldn't close her mouth. She began gagging. A demoness glided up to her, voluptuous everywhere except for a skeletal pube. She leaned over Sirikit's face, her own full black lips dripping a profound cinnamony venom.

Sirikit heard the ropes binding her pop like spines. She was lifted into the multi-armed embrace of her devouress. She was overwhelmed with the sickening tilt of vertigo. As if her stomach were the only part of her this bitch would never get to eat as it floated away.

Sirikit's left arm was free. She brought the hand up, imploringly. She saw the scarred totem fingers wriggling, manically alive with mouths howling, each in a separate blasphemous language. The bone sliver extremities became real tiny limbs. Dragonfly wings rustled, flapping desperately to take off, away from this joining with Sirikit. The palm waved in front of the she-devil's face as Sirikit tried to blot the sight of the demoness out. The monster's face changed.

Into an American soldier, larger than life and with camouflage spurts of green and brown streaking his face, dog tags gleaming white hot metal around his neck. And even though Sirikit was illiterate, she still read the name PFC Harrold Tyler. He opened his mouth wide and inside she saw the bodies of children, birth-defected whores, burned nuns, other beings so mutated they were nothing but a mouth and a cunt … all chewed together, rolled around the bloody gums by the lewd tongue.

Sirikit finally screamed, the sound tearing not from her throat but somewhere deep in her bowels. It splattered out with blood and blue mucous-flecked air. It dislodged several of her teeth with its force and shattered two ribs.

Did it feel good to finally let that noise out? After all the abuse? The torture. The horror?

No!

Yes …

She waved her hand again. The visage changed. It was Shiva's face, the Destroyer, all the visages of hell on earth and beyond frowning down. Dying. Dead. Wrenched around to die again. The eyes held no pity. The third eye opened and she felt herself shrivel inside the exploding universe.

Again Sirikit's palm moved across the demon's face. It softened. Was her mother's. Just a child herself, singing like she had when Sirikit was a baby. There were lines already beginning to track the youthful brow but there were no scars. Her mother's skin had been flawless before she got sick.

The hand spasmed, totem fingers alive. The face was Shiva's again. But not the Destroyer. It was feminine and beautiful, ornamented in gold (with silvery dog tags around the graceful throat). There was compassion in the eyes. A scent not unlike milk. Sirikit was held against firm breasts but she could feel the omni-present erection pressed against her thighs. The god as creator turned his head and gently kissed the maimed fingers as they bayed to some unseen moon. Then he folded her up like a palm leaf and ate her down, breaking her apart utterly against the diamonds of his teeth.

The din of the cavern went out, swallowed to silence. Sirikit saw nothing. She hadn't closed her eyes. Had she any now to shut? The sensation of Dying, Death, and Die again was gone. But she still had a feeling of self as she was washed through Shiva's convoluted exotica of organs. And that self told her it was not going to be the same the next time.

She wended through mercy's greasy sphincter as the god crouched down, his fingers pulling apart the petals of a womb. She unfolded wings as he birthed out a butterfly.

And she was lovely, unmarred. Smooth as gold dust in yellow wine. Sirikit flew up, gazing at herself in wonder. She had the body of a girl but with silken wings flowing from her shoulders like watercolor paints. The scars were gone, the skin smooth and supple. The demons didn't swerve from their dining to watch her go.

Except for Shiva, smiling like a beautiful apsara. Grinning like a skull, face upturned he began to dance.

She passed up through the sticky webs of the parasites without being snared. Up through the cavern's high ceiling of inverted pagodas and minarets. The massive complex heaved, the way the ground buckled during earthquake. It burst open and flopped, becoming the city again, spires and colonnades rearing like ornate serpents' heads.

How Sirikit found herself back in the horrible little room in Phya's brothel, she didn't know. She fluttered just below the ceiling.

But the window was open, the street a couple stories down. What need did she have for a street when she could fly? And she would, fly right on out. She'd just returned to her point of origin, where she'd taken the drug. It didn't mean she had to stay.

She was gorgeous and free. She could go anywhere she liked.

Someone moaned. Sirikit looked down, recognizing the blood- and semen-stained pallet, the piss- and shit-spotted walls and floor.

A girl was on that floor. Younger than Sirikit had been when she'd been brought there … maybe. It was hard to tell this one's age.

Because she'd been flayed.

The skin, in several wilting red-yellow strips, had been draped across the back of a chair.

The little hands and feet twitched. Sirikit wondered how much Phya had made a client pay to let him do this. And what he would charge the next person to fuck the quivering hideless form before the girl died.

"I'm sorry, sister, that he needed somebody to take my place. But I have nothing to give to protect you," Sirikit whispered, so near that window.

She was close enough to smell the girl's tears, see them etching down the raw face like drops of acid.

Yes, I do have something. One thing.

Sirikit didn't even have to land. The only requirement was that she wish it. So, obviously, this was still the drug. This was still a hallucination.

But one she wanted to hold onto! Like the new unmutilated flesh!

Everything worldly ended. Dreams, gifts.

Illusions/Maya.

"I give you my skin," Sirikit murmured, then shuddered as an icy chill wrung her out.

Her newfound flawlessness was gone. She was lying on the floor of her prison. She hadn't been flayed but her scars were returned. Yet she was in no pain. The room was filled with clouds that smelled of milk.

She was smiling, floating in an ecstasy she knew would never end.

Chapter 7

"Make me shine bright like fire ..."
—The Rig Veda

Strolling through the worst of human geography, sordid streets mapped from flesh. Usually pretty girls and boys waiting to be picked up, to be pricked up.

But tonight, oh, tonight! The streetlights, the neon, couldn't outshine them. Sitting lotus on the filthy sidewalks, smiling up at the stars whether heaven was visible or not. Haloes, as if their sleek black hair had been combed through with phosphorous. As if flashlights were somehow positioned inside their skulls to pour such luminosity through their eyes, out their nostrils, ear portals, gusting out from between the lips in brilliant breath. As if they were verging on speaking some diamond mantra capable of pacifying the brutal world.

The customers didn't like it. Neither the locals nor the *farong*. A few had been convinced to try.

"Do anything you like," the pimps said. "They won't argue."

But it was weird, creepy. It felt like something was being desecrated. And, yes, there were the mentalities that went in for that sort of thing.

To a point.

The use and misuse of innocence. The temptation of total helplessness. It was like trying to fuck a soft statue, a limber bodhisattva. Or even Catholic prepubescent Madonnas and Jesuses.

Except that there was an additive to the light they carried. It felt like damnation to those who would abuse it. Touch it properly and be blessed; do it wrong and be cursed forever.

In the brothels where children were held captive. On the streets where their singsong had always energized Patpong's *frisson* with timpani. Now all just simply sitting, lit up like moons on a clear night, like baby Buddhas, like the nativity.

A few tourists snapped photos and took videotaped memories. Of hundreds of glowing kids lined up on Silom Road, reminiscent of the rows of statuary at Angkor Thom known as 'Churning of the Sea of Milk'. Folks began flocking to this infamous section of Bangkok for purposes other than sex, anxious to see this phenomenon. It was far more tangible than lining up to see a vision of the religious figure of their choice, discovered in a billboard advertisement for soup or in the knots of a tree trunk. Someone suggested they'd been poisoned but they sure didn't look sick. Another suggested they were high because of an opiated drug being introduced into the water supply. And somebody else bothered to point out that before these young prostitutes began their strangely sublime meditation, they'd been screaming in wild hallucination, unable to wake up from whatever nightmares held them. The city had rung with their shrieks.

Were they radioactive? A Geiger counter quickly trashed that notion.

They didn't sweat. They didn't piss or shit. Apparently they didn't eat, didn't need to. Was this a surreal type of coma or some form of perfect suspended animation?

A television newscaster quipped that Bangkok's days as the sin capital of the world were ended. Now perhaps it would live up to its name, Bangkok translating out to City of Angels. Actually it was the local name, Krung Thep, which meant that.

And the flesh merchants were understandably upset.

Phya had gone with at least two dozen other procurers to protest the situation to their boss, Mr. Tak. He sent out bloodhounds to find the man suspected of having polluted the ass and pussy pool. Whoever it was had apparently visited many of their whores in a single night, like some Asian version of Santa Claus.

All they knew was that it was some Cambodian named Sarun Chhuon.

Tak himself wasn't happy—and not just because he wasn't getting revenues from the skin trade. His drug business was suffering, too. Figure: a drug became available that—although its start was a bit rocky—its climax guaranteed a bliss that didn't appear to wear off. Hours went by, days, a week. These kids weren't crashing. They weren't coming down and sobering up. They just sat and smiled beatifically. One hit from this stuff and you were hooked. But instead of a monkey on your back, you had myrrh butterflies, jeweled salamanders, nightingales of rapture ... If you were looking to evade reality permanently but were shy of committing out and out suicide, this seemed like the ticket. And nobody taking it had complained yet.

But where to get it? Only from a shadowy figure named Sarun Chhuon, who—if you could find him—didn't charge anything for it. He called it Soma.

Tak had a few of the whores tested. When beaten, they did not phase. When burned, they did not wince. When slashed repeatedly with a razor, knife or machete, they did not blink, although their flowing blood bore the scent of sandalwood and jasmine. When exterminated by any of several means available, the bodies stayed fresh, never developing rigor, never decomposing. The only possible means of disposal was cremation.

Not that Tak gave them time to decompose, past a few days. Well, he was losing his percentage.

Tak's lab managed to get a tiny sample from the residue left in a vial discovered near one of the 'victims'. Analysis showed only that it was some unknown fungi, a mushroom the modern world hadn't seen the likes of before. Meaning it was either some new species or a very old one from a location so remote that its existence had remained a secret.

Clearly, Tak must find the source of this clear and present danger to his organization. He was certain that Sarun Chhuon was only a front man, sent out to test the waters before his network took the product into a broader market. But he could tell Tak who his boss was. He could tell who needed to be taught a lesson. Who needed to be killed.

Finally Sarun Chhuon was dragged in. The little man didn't cringe or cower. Perhaps he didn't understand who he was dealing with here? Hadn't he heard of the very important Mr. Tak?

The fellow just smiled, calm as a monk, serene as a dalai lama.

"Where do you come from? Who is your leader?" Tak asked.

"From the fields of heaven. God," Sarun Chhuon replied. Obviously being vague, being evasive.

Tak had him soundly beaten. The man never uttered a cry, even as his flesh purpled over breaking bones.

"Don't knock out too many teeth. Don't break his jaws. He must be able to speak," Tak instructed. "Everywhere else is fair game."

Afterward the Cambodian still answered the same. Blood spilling from his mouth, from his flattened nose, swimming to obscure the iris in one eye.

Tak had him jolted, wires hooked up to his genitals. The flesh and hair stank as it sizzled, smoking. The man danced a nasty jitter, teeth banging together so hard a few shattered like glass.

Tak then demanded, "Where is this stuff grown? Who is your boss?"

Simply, and without rancor, Sarun Chhuon (after spitting out the shards of broken teeth) answered, "In the fields of heaven. God."

Tak watched impassively as the Cambodian's finger- and toenails were yanked from their rootbeds with plyers heated red hot. Then as the fingers and toes themselves were severed from the hands and feet, one at a time with bolt cutters, producing miniature geysers. Then as the stumps were cauterized (without anesthetic) with the flame from a jeweler's blowtorch.

"Where is the headquarters of your organization? Who is its chief?" Tak insisted, becoming annoyed, tapping the highly polished toe of his left Bruno Magli.

"The fields of heaven. God." Sarun Chhuon repeated, stubbornly refusing to demonstrate that he was either in agony or afraid.

A doctor was sent for. He arrived in scrub whites, wearing sterile latex gloves. As the Cambodian was tied down, this man began making tiny incisions with a scalpel. Into the arms and legs, the buttocks and scrotum, more deeply into the abdomen. Then he withdrew a needle from a bag and injected each of these sites.

"Do you want to know what you are being given?" Tak asked, perspiration shining on his round face.

Sarun Chhuon only smiled. As a Cambodian child who had been tortured and seen others tortured by the Khmer Rouge years before, he'd seen injections with sodium Pentothal, urine, gasoline, chlorine, ammonia and a variety of acids. Been there, done that. And still managed to crawl away with his glowing faith intact. He wasn't sweating. Only bleeding.

Tak shrugged. "Well, you'll know soon enough, my friend. In the jungle, even the holiest of holies rots."

It didn't take long in the hole they kept Sarun Chhuon in—without hardly any air, hotter and steamier than any orchid greenhouse. In a day the fly eggs had begun hatching. The maggots began eating him from the inside out. In two days the Cambodian began weeping.

Tak came to visit again. He didn't stand quite as close, and—from where he did stand to observe—he held a silk handkerchief over his nose. The stench was appalling, of death and living death. Anyone who'd ever been present on a battlefield or where a city had been bombed with carcasses lying about knew that odor.

"Where are you from? Who is your leader?" Tak asked again.

He watched with nervous, giggly horror as the man's penis jerked erect, then spasmed out a crawling white worm jizzum. Then it twitched, stiffened again and juiced out more worm-sperm. The Cambodian's flesh literally crawled as if some obscene book of demons was being writ beneath it.

"Heaven," Sarun Chhuon reiterated. He gasped out, "God."

Tak came back the next day as the prisoner began screaming.

"Where is your organization headquartered? Who is its boss?"

Sarun Chhuon just stared at him with one eye and one socket where the other eye had been consumed. Maggots oozed from his rectum. They came out of his nostrils in wriggling rice puddings of snot. They marched out from the ears mixed with wax, until they took the appearance of hideous figurines from some miniature wax museum of abominations. Swarming from every incision the doctor had made until, at first glance, the Cambodian appeared to be a figure comprised only of worms.

"Why should I tell you? What more could you do to me?"

Tak couldn't help but grin. "Nothing, save for killing you. A quick death instead of this slow torment. A blessing really, considering your circumstances."

Sarun Chhuon began choking. His throat constricted and then disgorged what might have been riceballs but which, of course, weren't.

That's one food I don't think I will ever be able to eat again, *Tak thought to himself.*

Sarun Chhuon continued vomiting out the clusters of maggots, stringy with blood and bile. After a spate of this grisly retching, he whispered, "Phnom Yohp. Go …"

He couldn't finish the last word, God. He'd begun puking again. His whole body contorted in a horrific pantomime of the wriggling of a maggot. Tak could hear the industry going on inside the man as organs finally popped like griddled pears, and synapses in the brain short-circuited before being devoured. The second eye was pushed out, dangling from its optic stem across the cheek, maggots swarming out of the socket, climbing down the stalk to retrieve and finish eating the eye. The man's throat visibly collapsed, like a tunnel unable to sustain itself under the weight of the earth atop it.

That was it, there would be no more words of any kind from Sarun Chhuon.

Tak nodded to the guard who pulled a pistol and shot the Cambodian through the head. Tak quickly looked away as more worms came out with brain matter.

Outside the hole, in the dubious fresh air of the city, Tak turned to one of his men. "Contact Colonel Gestetner. I have a job for his army."

Chapter 8

"And that which hath Real Being
hath never ceased to be—
can never cease to be ..."
—Bhagavad Gita

The well-heeled tourists milled around, chatting each other up, drinking champagne or brandy or the caramel-coffee flavored Thai tea from frosted glasses. They pointed, commented, judged according to criterion of distinguishment, some uncommon trait be it absolute perfection or frisson-inducing flaw.

The gallery's owner, Mr. Ramkhamhaeng, had invited them. No others had been admitted. This was an unusual display and only the most discerning and open-minded collectors could be trusted to behave properly.

(Or so he hoped.)

There were about twenty who had accepted the invitation. There was a British lord and his wife, a U.S. congressperson and her husband, an internationally renowned heart surgeon, and a Greek princess who donated her time helping victims of minefields. There was a couple who'd struck it big in the Powerball lottery. There was a billionaire who'd made his money at the onset of the computer craze. Another fabulously rich-bitch had been born in a trailer but gone on to create a cosmetic dynasty. There was the reclusive rock star who'd made something of a freak out of himself, hellbent on being a connoisseur of nature's most gruesome novelties. He stood by, flanked by bodyguards, shy beneath dark glasses.

The rock star was heard to murmur, "How beautiful they look. Wish I could find me some of that juice."

Glowing smiles, all. And a brightness not unlike from the angels of western tradition.

Statues were lined up. Behind green and blue bead curtains—which were themselves strung behind ornately carved teak screens—musicians played softly on a variety of traditional instruments: wrapped gongs to mute, xylophones, two-stringed fiddles, horns, flutes, drums.

There was a male statue that had no legs, or rather possessed only thigh stumps the color of cinnamon sticks. The ends had been carefully wrapped in very thin bronze foil. Next to this was one as exquisite as a young Siddhartha Gautama, penis erect with its tip like a moist rose blossom. His hair was coiled about his skull in a coif of careful braids. Next to him was a statue with its surface so ruinously etched, it crackled like brittle cellophane.

"I heard about her," the English Lady whispered to the Congressperson. "Poor thing. Only fourteen. A man wanted to marry her and she refused him. He crept into her bedroom one night and doused her with acid. They say it really happens all the time."

And next to this was another boy, his face painted with liquid gold. Not enough to hide the pocks from adolescent pimples. His head was shaved and his scalp also painted gold. He was a bit on the plump side so he might have been made up as an older Buddha to make a set with the younger one.

Beside him was yet another youth, a little older. He reclined on his side, dressed in saffron.

"A reclining Buddha," said Mr. Ramkhamhaeng, "which symbollizes parinirvana, the ultimate state of serenity achieved by the Master upon his death."

"Are they for sale as a trio?" asked the Greek princess.

"Possibly. We do have a temple which had made a bid. We are accepting sealed bids."

And next was a bride in her wedding costume, Hindu in style. Her nose was pierced and delicate golden chains linked this to rings that looped from her ear. Her eyebrows were painted in red ocher. One eye was missing beneath these crimson arches.

"And I know the story behind that," the Congressperson told the Lady. "Some creep purloined that eye while the bride sat in a garden, right where her groom had left her when she was slipped the soma at a party."

The heart surgeon leaned in to argue, "Maybe it was the new husband who took it, needing some memento, angry, not willing to let heaven have all of her."

The women sighed as if this were actually rather romantic.

"See how the socket gleams, damp as if with tears," the gallery owner pointed out. "But this serene face has no room in its expression for sorrow. It has passed beyond ever-changing samsara."

"But don't you have to die to achieve nirvana?" asked the computer genius.

"No, sir. It isn't a place like your concept of heaven," Mr. Ramkhamhaeng explained, folding his hands in front of his chest. "Even a monk who has become 'arahat'—an ascetic with the highest self-control and spiritual empowerment—may attain nirvana during life. A state of neither being nor not being. There is nothing left to desire or accomplish; there are no more struggles and no more wishes. All has been achieved. This is perfect joy."

The computer geek cackled. "Uh huh. Which means you gotta die first."

The lottery winning husband cooed to his wife, "Oh, look sweetheart. The ugly little one, she's emanating!"

The final one. She was scarred as hell: razor demons cavorting on petrified blisters red and brown as rubies and topaz—or white as moonstones. Pictographs enhanced her flesh from a ripper's stylus, decapitated death written on her bare belly. And a hand—oh, that hand with the mutilated fingers, bone and cartilage like a skeleton menagerie for some twisted collector of pain. Somehow this was worse even than the girl whose rejected suitor had acid-burned her face.

They were sure she must be wax over steel wire and wood, for how could this have ever been alive in such a way? None wanted to believe such atrocities on an innocent young girl's body.

Of course, their concept of 'innocence' was simply another one of Maya's many tricks.

The cosmetic queen huffed and shook her head, walked up and down past the exhibit.

"I say this isn't real," fisting up her hands which were covered in gaudy diamond rings, perching the fists on her liposuctioned hips, and jutted out a surgically implanted chin. "They've been made to look like people, but I've been to those wax places where they do Madonna and Jeffrey Dahmer."

The owner blanched and protested, "I assure you …"

"No living person could remain still that long." Then she unclipped an expensive Tiffany brooch from her Versace blouse. She jabbed the pin's point into the bride's empty eye socket. There was no flinch nor twitch nor shriek. And she'd jabbed deep. It *must* have entered the brain. But the bride neither convulsed nor fell over.

There was, however, a stream of gouting blood.

"Seen it in movies a hundred times. Guess it happens a lot, huh?" she challenged. "So you have blood bags put in devious places. It would've moved had it been real. It would've screamed its freakin' lungs out and that's for sure."

Mr. Ramkhamhaeng gestured helplessly with his hands.

"You want us to buy these?" Rich-bitch needled the exhibitor. "You best be able to prove they're the real enchilada."

She shrugged a narrow, tanning-booth browned shoulder, sneering through the thick fuchsia wax on her collagen-fattened lips.

"What would please Madame?" Mr. Ramkham-haeng asked, managing to sound obliging even if he wanted to strip her down to her bones and put her out on Patpong Road to peddle her skinny ass to the same sort of fiends who'd scarred some of these kids. He still smiled and bowed. The perfect host even to the rudest, most barbaric guest. The quintessential businessman.

"Burn one," she told him, licking that ridiculous pouty mouth. "Set it on fire."

He slightly raised his eyebrows. "You mean deliberately destroy a priceless object of art?"

"Oh, come now," Rich-bitch honked. "Hardly priceless. They're sitting on street corners from one end of Bangkok to the other. If it's real life, then it's cheap as all get out."

He bit his lip.

She chuckled. "Here, do this one. It's so ugly nobody with an ounce of class or taste would want it in their house."

She'd indicated the little one with the scarred hand.

"Hey, I'll even pay for it."

And she opened her mesh bag and drew out a bundle of traveler's checks.

A guy in the back of the entourage pushed through. "No, no, no. With all due respect to Madame," and he said the M-word as if it were a crunchy cancerous melanoma on his tongue, "she's already damaged one. What ever happened to 'you break it, you bought it'? No way. Burn *that* one then, not this one."

The boss snapped his fingers and a servant brought over a bottle of brandy from the tray of free apéritifs. Ramkhamhaeng opened it and doused the still life bride with the contents. Then he stepped back, lit a match, and tossed it.

The brandy ignited, at first as fragrant as a chafing dish dessert. The bride's silk costume and the flowers which had weeks before been so fresh and colorful—now dried and frail—flamed, curled, performed a wispy saraband.

Still the bride didn't move, made no attempt to escape, to streak as a comet across the room of notable stars, or to roll herself upon the sumptuous wool carpets in any effort to suffocate the flames.

The stink of burning skin and hair made several people gag, though none left the gallery hall for the bathrooms or for the cars they'd arrived in.

Rich-bitch studied the immolation, tongue in her cheek, trying not to let even a single nuance escape her eye.

"Look!" cried the Powerball wife. "She moved!"

"No," argued her husband. "That's just the contortion of the flames. It creates a mirage, you see."

Sounded so reasonable. As grease and blood foamed. Flesh puckered, crawled, slipped off not dissimilar to wax after all. The smile that transcended a restless destiny shrank back from teeth wrapped around a belch of air expelled from the lungs. The fire resembled greedy fingers. It seemed like tongues in the only consummation of her marriage this virgin would ever know now. It was Maya with veils of smoke, saying, "See? Here are the limitations, the world process of transmigratory existence. Samsara! She is reborn into cinders …"

The smoke activated the sprinkler system in the ceiling. Showers of silver glinted down. The other statues smiled, motionless in time and space. Softly brilliant. At peace which was the only true freedom.

Ramkhamhaeng turned to Rich-bitch. "Well, does this satisfy you as to the authenticity of these objects?"

She nodded. "Yeah. Fair's fair, I guess. I'll take the pretty boy with the dreadlocks and the hard-on."

Chapter 9

"Darkness there was: at first concealed in darkness this All was indiscriminated chaos."
—The Rig Veda

God sat among the lotus blossoms, regal head tilted, eyes half-lidded, regarding the moon. Nearby a rare tiger snarled in a vined tangle below palm trees, its stripes sliding sideways between the wan yellow light and the shadows. Looming far above were the tiered pyramid towers of the primary temple, almost gothic in cathedral aspect. The jungle rot wasn't as obvious now. The place might have been new except for the smell. Except for the heaviness that can only be felt from something psychically ancient.

Faces leered down from the temple bas-relief. If he looked hard enough, he would find the one that resembled the last living embodiment of Shiva. The one that was raped and murdered during the war. The same one he'd replaced when he was Harry Tyler.

Another lifetime. Another incarnation.

Most died before going from an incarnation into the next. But he'd not done that.

(Had he?)

He'd slid into this manifestation of Shiva while he was yet Harry. Like the stripes of that tiger gliding in and out of tender green bamboo, a danger and a beauty—but hard to quite pin down. For one golden stripe might be a bar of moonlight. One slash of black could be a rakshasa, disguised as an arm of night. All four of those things might seek your blood: the tiger and the rakshasa, the moon and the darkness.

Harry Tyler hadn't died to make room for Shiva, had he? He was still there. He carried the memories of himself, tucked into the part of the godmind that remembered the shames of mortality. That held the key to the doors which eventually led to the temple compound of Nagas Wat.

The place known as Angkor Wat was famous. Its name most readily translated out into 'palace-city that has become a Buddhist temple'. Most of the other temples had *wat* as the first part of the name, immediately denoting their function. Nagas Wat had also been something before it was inhabited by Buddhist monks. But whereas Angkor Wat was dedicated to Vishnu, Nagas Wat belonged to Shiva. The sacred serpents (*nagas*) were his favorite king cobras. Those Khmer who had built it had been forced to leave by invading Siamese, just as at Angkor. The Buddhists took up residence soon after, although they had already been at Angkor for many years.

There was a part of the temple complex at Angkor which had been originally dedicated to Shiva, called Ta Keo. The Buddhists had no trouble there. But once the monks transferred to Nagas they began to suffer nightmares.

As Shiva, Lord of Time, he could access the memory of every one of those who'd been his embodiment. At that moment in history, he'd been a Khmer Buddhist named Oum. Closing his eyes fully, he became Oum again. Standing in the grassy courtyard, turning round and round with amazement. His brothers were all afraid, claiming to see the statues and figures carved into the stone moving subtly, gesturing obscenely. He'd seen movement, too, out of the corner of his eye. He could hear the stone beings whispering.

Join the dance, the dance that shakes the loins and spirit!

The trees began to sway, leaves turning to mimic the hands of dancing maidens. The air became perfumed, heavy with orchids, with both male and female musk. Carved phalluses oozed pale seed at their heads. The nipples on stone breasts lactated milk.

Dance with us … open your mouth and legs … open your third eye. We will fill and overfill everything.

"This place is haunted," said one of the monks.

"What manifestation of Shiva was this place built to?" asked another.

The all … the full. The horror that brings us to joy.

Buddhist priests contemplated both ugly and dead in their meditations. They studied mandalas of illusion to better grasp reality. But when the sculpted creatures began to climb out of the walls and colonades, the monks began to run. The mountains rumbled with demons dancing as Oum's brothers fled toward the temple's openings. The earth split and thousands of cobras writhed out of the fissures, snapping at them as they tried to leap over. Every prayer wheel cracked, and candles guttered, flickered, adopted the shapes of tiny dervish monsters. The air popped with a steaming static. Voices so high they rivaled the noise the wind makes as it sings through broken skulls and so low they might have been rocks striking as flint during earthquake, these called to the priests *join the dance, bend and open, join …*

A voluptuous stone goddess snatched at a monk running past. He'd slowed down, curious, seduced by the sinuous movements of this danava. She clutched him to her, squeezed out his seed and soul. He dropped to the ground, splitting at the seams, shedding his humanity in a ream of yellowed rice paper.

Other monks covered their eyes as they ran, barefoot into the jungle. Oum had stopped turning and staring. He stood still, watching with wonder as a few brothers tore off their saffron robes, screaming as serpents slid up their rectums and beautiful devils knelt to suck their hairless cocks. They whirled and jumped, reaching out to every organ they might grasp, rock or flesh, groaning with a frightening pleasure.

The monks changed ... eyes slitting, noses all but disappearing, mouths widening to fill with venom, dicks turning into serpents and fingers turning into dicks, flesh silkening out with dappled scales.

Oum doubled over with a cramp, folded to his knees. Fire seared along his scrotum until he couldn't help slipping a hand beneath his robe to cradle his testicles. And once that palm was there it was only another slight gesture to become an aching, luxurious massage of himself, sliding up and down the erection, as hard as if it also was stone. Then kneading the balls, fingers slipping inside, inside. Inside a womb. Hot, wet, sore with blood.

A young monk, Oum had never even seen a real vagina. Nothing but the artistic renderings in sculpture, usually exaggerated to say the least. But he knew instinctively what this was. Even as he gasped in painful surprise as his own flat chest bloomed into breasts. There was a shocking sharp torment at the base of his spine, burning in his colon the way it would if he suddenly began to pass an acid turd. But this wasn't shit coming out, lengthening in quick inches. It was a Naga's tail growing from his coccyx. He ground his teeth together to keep from crying out but heard twin shrieks anyway. Muffled, stifled by flesh and bone. Opening his fists, he saw the mouths in the palms.

Weeping, laughing, full of the sanity that is universal wisdom and the madness that came with all full knowing, Oum began to dance.

He became the first of the temple's living Shivas. His likeness was up on the bas-relief with the many others.

Harry Tyler had become the most recent one. But his transformation was slower, taking years, decades. And he'd certainly been no monk.

He'd only just begun to change physically while stationed in Okinawa, following the Vietnam experience. Yeah, he'd developed the vagina, hiding in the folds of his scrotum, and a tail, before he left the Southeast Asian war. If he was feeling particularly argumentative, he could grin with a split back to both ears, just to freak you out. But all that erupted in Okinawa was a superfluous set of nipples. Hardly worth bothering the company doctor with, right?

But on the way back from visiting his little brother back in Texas, and before the army was going to ship him off to Saudi Arabia, Harry stopped off in Cambodia. What the hell, he still had most of his two weeks leave remaining. It was after the December 1978 Vietnamese invasion into that country, running Pol Pot's skunks out of Phnom Penh and into the mountains in the north.

He landed first in Bangkok, spent the night in Patpong. Walking the streets, seeing all the whores and whoremongers. Smelling incense, blood and semen worse than the miasma of pollution from the traffic.

Curious that once upon a time he'd been here, sniffing up pussy, low or choice, clean or diseased, hadn't mattered. Seeking out the stray nightmare to ride until dawn. Tasting of death and near-death as if, no matter what he did, his face and body remained a man's, proving he was human. That no matter what, Harry Tyler didn't have a shred of the skinwalker in him.

No animals howled out of his mouth when he fucked tainted light or suppurating darkness.

Curious because now he saw the brothels, the street meat, the mutant bars differently. They weren't avenues to prove who and what he was. No, just the opposite. He walked there, full of changes, strange dreams dancing in his head, and knew he was the path to prove who and what they would become.

The lights along the streets of this quarter were so sickly lush that the darkness never really fell there. It might have been just sunset all night long. The luminescence a body riddled with cancer takes on. Humid as a crotch lined with garish gonorrheal sores.

Harry noticed he was being followed. He could feel the breath almost at the back of his neck. He could smell the kid, the sweat sweet-sour, and need almost overpoweringly metallic on the tongue.

He stopped suddenly in his tracks and turned. The teenaged boy almost plowed right into him. The boy was startled and began to backpedal. His lips skinned back from his teeth in a grimace of surprise.

Harry smiled and held out his hand.

"Don't be afraid," he said.

And since when had Harry cared whether or not his prey was frightened?

It had been such a long time anyway. Had he truly been celibate for a few years? When was the last time he'd had sex?

He remembered and wasn't sure if that could truly be called having sex or not. It had been an act of pure terrorism. (Wasn't love often that?)

He'd been home for his mother's funeral. He'd been trying to get his father to start taking care of brother Arcan, too young to be out on his own. The old man had refused. Claimed his little mistress wouldn't like it. So Harry'd grabbed her by the tits and tossed her out. *And, so now what?*

But the old professor still wouldn't accept those grand parental responsibilities. "He's got his mother's blood in him. I see it crawling in his face."

Harry pushed him face-against-the-wall, told him all about the Cambodian hermaphrodite he'd raped in the jungle. Forced the old guy to feel up the velvety but recessive addition to his manly gonads. And then fucked his father up the ass.

Had to take Arcan to live with an uncle anyway.

Was that the last time he'd had sex?

Yeah. Something had changed inside his mind as well as in his body. It wasn't some Christian notion of lofty self-renunciation. He still had that constant boner. And passing the deformed or the burned or the dead, begging in the streets or laid out in the gutters, still made him more conscious of that ever-present erection.

But things had altered. And until he fully understood—or at least began to get even an inkling of the why's and wherefore's of these new feelings washing over him—he'd wait. He must.

But here was this Thai kid, skinny as beans, obviously sick. The copper-colored rash on his hands and the lesions on his gums instantly told Harry that the boy was probably ill with secondary syphilis. He could feel the waves of fever rolling off the kid.

Don't be afraid.

The Thai took Harry's offered hand. In an alley Harry let him pull down the zipper on his jeans, take out the large erect cock and guide it into that infected mouth. It felt to Harry as if he'd just stuck himself into an atomic swamp. If the boy saw more, saw the gleaming vulva beyond, he said nothing. He just sucked and nibbled, suppressing groans as sores behind the lips broke, leaking trails of highly contagious spirochetes, blending with the seed that burst from Harry after a few timeless minutes.

Harry'd closed his eyes, rocked back on his heels, let the heat bring images to his brain. Of an ancient Calcutta—teaming with ghosts singing songs of love and cannibalism. Of bats swooping out of a rain forest like the fall of night—wings rustling around his face like the caressing black hands of Kali. Of ashes swirling about the Terrace of the Leper King at Angkor, where stands a nude but sexless statue—staring out with an enigmatic smile as somewhere another hapless child steps on a mine.

Then the boy leaned away, spitting out pus, jizzum and blood, wiping his lips. Harry gazed down to see the boy's eyes, the pupils gone all bright. The kid grinned and stood. He stumbled toward the alley's entrance. He paused, one arm outstretched, the other resting on a hip cocked suggestively. He pressed his heels together, sliding the soles across the ground, his gait rolling sensuously, slowly at first, then soaring steadily. The boy began to spin, rotating on one or both feet until he became a blur.

Tourists had stopped to watch, applauding the kid's skill and speed. He whirled, as true a dervish as any in Bombay, pantomiming the circular careening of sun, moon and panoply of stars. A radiant compelling grace, waiting to be possessed by something which, perhaps, had already taken hold.

The kid's entire body was loose as a bundle of silk scarves. He danced as if he was flinging himself into the wind, reaching up to cyclone into the sky. And he spun so fast that pieces of him almost seemed to vanish: the diseased parts, the mortal sections which had always bound him to gravity.

But then he cried out, "Shiva, Lord of the Dance, Lord of All and Nothing, I love you!"

The kid leaped into the street, a standing broad jump of ten or twelve feet. Directly into the pulse of traffic. Horns blared and there was a terrible *thwuummppp!*, followed by a second, softer crackling of bones through flesh. A hiss as a linear splinter from a femur punctured a tire sure as any three-penny nail. The car that hit the kid swerved into another as the tire blew. A woman in that auto screamed as the baby sitting in her lap bulleted into the windshield. Then this car rolled over one of the open tri-wheeled taxis that trolled Bangkok, crushing its wizened driver.

Harry zipped up his pants, slipping out of the alley unnoticed in the commotion from the accident.

A tourist sneezed heartily in the pollution.

"Bless you," Harry whispered.

"Thanks," said the tourist.

But Harry hadn't addressed it to him. He'd murmured it toward the street, and toward the boy who'd just offered up the first prayer to a god's new living shrine.

Taking a train from Bangkok to Aranyaprathet on the border. Not willing to take the major road from there that led directly to Siem Reap and Angkor Wat. Too many of Pol Pot's people slithered there. Crossing into Cambodia by back paths. Into the Dangrek Chain north of the Cardamom Mountains. (Cardamom! Like the spice … heady and almost too sweet for senses to bear without attributing the spice's effect to meat and/or a sex act.) Hearing artillery fire much of the time, coming from east and south. Hiding among trees, camouflaged amid branches like extra pairs of arms and in clouds of insects, watching as bands of Khmer Rouge skulked through the undergrowth.

Here and there a shrine, partially devoured by the jungle, outlines of a face spectral gray, like a cameo of someone he knew in a former life. Everywhere else green as aching jade. Little riverlets which led away from and into the lake of Tonle Sap, lead/silver as eels in the middle of the day, tingeing to gold and finally blood red at day's end.

Harry didn't blink at decapitated heads frowning from sharp bamboo impalements, expressions on faces in slackjawed scream, the eyes already dined on, leaving sockets oddly scritched like the Sanskrit letter for pain. Nor did he gasp at the naked woman tied to a pole, covered in mosquito bites, belly sagging, a gout of blood dried in her pubic hair and down her thighs, bayonet on the ground with a human fetus skewered on it, impromptu abortion. (He shuddered slightly, thinking, *The old Harry would have been unable to just pass by without trying to fuck what was left.*)

And was it the god who shouldered the guilt of that? Or Harry the man, counting his sins? It could scarcely have been the soldier from Texas, stiffened in his pants in an eternal weapon incapable of penance. Nor could it have been Shiva, Lord of Destruction with eyes rolling up to the whites at the ecstasy of the blood scent—even as the Creator/ Creatrix in him reveled only in the hundred jasmine-white butterflies that had just risen from their cocoons.

Maybe that was all this shudder had been: rapture, lust, revelation.

Ah, it was Harry's new womb that quaked, seeing the baby that Cambodian woman had been carrying shishkabobbed out of her and set in the dirt for every ant within a mile's radius to zero in on. Tender as veal. His nipples, both new and old, withered at the sight. Feminine empathy.

He at last made it to Phnom Yohp, the ancient temple nearby but invisible in the heavy forest. But he sensed it there, beckoning, beacon undiminished. Sizzling in the middle of his forehead, the meat of his palms, making his dick throb and his pussy soup-up in anticipation. Knowing all the while it was still only a promise down the road.

Harry had his obligations to the army. A vow. Not that taking such a solemn oath would ever have meant a damn to him, but to Shiva … to any god … vows were holy music. He'd signed up for a twenty year stint, thinking he'd see (and fuck most of) the world. Where else would a man like Harry have found so many diverse holes if not in Singapore, Riyadh, Berlin, Panama. Sticking it in someone whose life wasn't worth two cents American. Humping the diseased, the catatonic, the dead. Feeling vaginal walls or rectal tunnels surrounding him with a hundred and six degrees as whoever or whatever babbled in feverish hallucination. Feeling the drop in temperature in these same orifices as he just penetrated and then waited, secure in the knowledge that his erection wouldn't falter, doing it like an experiment to see what it was like going from body heat to gelid ice in a cooling corpse. And then finding a reflecting surface fast as he could, having it mirror himself back to prove he was human. No animals there. A callous bastard, yes. A brutal, glutted, self-satisfying asshole, sure. Greedy and gorged. But all imperfections of himself as a man, not a beast. If he had no pity it was because he'd never seen it demonstrated.

That was a learned thing, pity was. His father had never shown it as he rutted with Harry's loupgaroux mother, nor when he tired of her and tossed her aside. Nor had Harry's mother shown it as she tormented her children the way any predator does its living food.

There wasn't much left of the village. The Khmer had obviously been through Phnom Yohp, desecrating anything that even vaguely resembled beauty or symmetry. Harry stood in the middle of what had been the village's street and looked around at burned huts, piles of rubbish. Bones.

Had he come back to nothing? Wouldn't that be a joke on him?

Then he saw eyes watching him from the jungle. Several pairs at the perimeter visible between palm fronds and behind gaudy orchids.

"Do you not know me?" he asked.

Then wondered why he'd said that. Harry would hardly have expected Cambodian peasants to know who the hell he was. He hadn't even been hereabouts for years. And since that time the Khmer Rouge had done their worst.

He stood there and asked, "Do you not know me?"

Spreading his hands in gentle supplication, like Bozo the Clown or Jesus.

A small body timidly stood up from the leafy hideaway and began to stumble toward him. Then two more. Then others. Slowly at first. Some remaining slow because they could hardly go faster without legs. They gathered around him as if they did, truly, know him and were therefore unafraid. They all prostrated themselves on the dirt at his feet. He wondered how the ones without arms were ever going to get up again.

All but one were children. Most hadn't even been born when Harry's squad found the hermaphrodite at the temple. Each bore some war-inflicted deformity. Maimed by knife or bayonet or merely sharpened bamboo.

"Johm riab sua," said a young man, the oldest of the group. He might have been about twenty. *"Kh'nyohm ch'muah Sarun Chhuon."*

Harry didn't speak Khmer but somehow he knew the kid had just said Hello. My name is Sarun Chhuon.

Unable to answer back in their language, Harry asked in English, "Are there any adults here? Except for you?"

Sarun Chhuon shook his head, downcasting his eyes. "Khmer Rouge killed them. We are all that's left."

"Do you know me?" Harry asked, not sure what he expected to hear.

(Oh, yes. He knew very well. He knew it in his four nipples, in his balls and in his ovaries.)

Every head nodded.

"God," came the awed, whispered reply from every mouth.

"Have you come to take care of us?" asked a little girl, no more than six or seven years old. She supported herself on the ground with knees and elbows, having nothing beyond these points.

Harry gulped, feeling a knot in his throat that he was unable to swallow away.

"Not yet. But I am coming back. And when I do, it will be to stay with you. And take care of you."

He touched his face and stared in shock at the wetness there.

Tears? He could always blame it on the new hormones.

PART TWO

The Mercs

Nihil-logue

Even wasters must specialize eventually, after the chaos of indiscriminate mangling and mincemeating has left them sated or disappointed by turns. One hopefully, eventually, finds their niche. And the law of station and duty forgives the time it may take you to fully understand the specific twist you are meant to follow.

He'd been pleased enough to discover early that he was best at—and most delighted with—the wasting of the *pneuma minima*. The most altricial of victims: children. He bought or stole, strode up in the dark as the Schrecklichkeit in heavy boots, their karma in his pockets, transfixing with steel and wire the shape their dharma took, rendered in wasted flesh.

He knew the difference. Karma was the acts committed by one in a specific incarnation, accumulated into positive and negative reckoning for the soul. Dharma was the law decreeing you do as you were born to do. Kings ruled, soldiers fought, poets composed, wasters wasted, and certain children were meant to be obscene—not heard.

He was aware that religion generally taught that dharma was meant to keep the world spinning as it should, each drone of samsara in its place, the adherence to fate's law pushing ever out the good frontiers of light. But he perceived a black dharma, separate from the dark and light that were opposite sides of the same coin, exiled from the death and life which were equally cherished manifestations of the same cosmic force. His dharma was the nihilist's canon, apart from death and darkness, and having respect for neither.

Chapter 10

"For all their search
they cannot see
the image in the mirror.
It blazes in the circles
between the eyebrows.
Who knows this
has the Lord."
—poem to Shiva
Allama Prabhu

"Wipe them out," Mr. Tak commanded.

Not the first time an employer gave this order. For that matter, Tak had done it before. It was a couple years back when he hired Gestetner's mercs to go up against a rival drug lord in Laos.

Laos had an effect on Elliot. He'd had never seen a country this completely ruined by modern warfare. Parts were so devastated he thought he was on the fucking moon. He'd seen newsreels of Europe in 1945 that didn't look anywhere near this bad. Bombed-out dioramas of Berlin, Dresden, Stalingrad had nothing on Laos.

Eventually the mercs had reached the location near where the rival's crew was due to show at dawn. To stay well out of sight, they'd ducked into caverns to spend the night, sentries posted outside. The place was not far from Louanphrabang, near Pak Ou, famous for its sacred caves. Elliot trudged in with the rest of the soldiers to bed down, flashlights showing the way in bouncing leaps of illumination, little better than laser scrimshaw. And then it just opened up, and they were dazzled by the sight of lit candles everywhere.

The place was already inhabited. Were the rival's men waiting in here for them? Hell of a place for guns to be going off, below the earth. The ricochet and echo would be like being in a 360-degree shooting gallery. The kind where everybody becomes a duck in a row.

Saab put his hand up so that nobody raised a weapon.

Ruiz had mouthed silently, and Elliot lipread it as "Can you believe this shit?"

Obviously some local temple held services there. Well, after all the years of America dropping bombs on the country—more than two million tons over nine years of undeclared war—they probably thought it was safer underground. Had to be the local equivalent of an old-time revival meeting, judging by how many attended.

But evangelicals back home would be jumpin', swayin' and shoutin' out their hallelujahs and amens till even a deaf god couldn't help noticing. There'd be plates being passed for collections and Jesus opry choirs, drowned born-agains choking out phlegm with accidentally snorted and backed up baptismal water, adenoidal witnessings speaking in tongues, and maybe a few rattlesnakes being fondled just to make sure no one got too comfortable.

Yet, there in the cave, the gathering was very still, mostly sitting in full lotus. Not a fidgetter, secret testicle teaser, or a butt scratcher in the bunch. Only their shadows on the walls moved and jumped. It was eerie. And totally silent—save for the gentle flickering of the candle flames. No wonder the mercs hadn't thought anyone was in there.

And if they look up and see a bunch of camouflage-painted soldiers strolling in, armed to the teeth? Some of us big white people with U.S.A. in big hot blood-pink neon letters shooting out of our crazed eyes? *Elliot prepared for the screams and/or curses to start. This hive must surely begin to buzz.*

Nobody moved. No one made a sound. And, even for Laotians, he realized they were rather small. His eyes adjusted and then he was stunned by the thousands of gold and wooden statues of Buddha, all finely wrought and delicately featured, across the cavern floors, arranged in rocky niches, peering down from stone sconces. It was like walking into an underground inhabited by Oriental Lilliputians.

"Bed down. Try to get some rest," Saab had ordered. "I'm going to find a place to take a dump."

Elliot could feel them watching him all that night. Not judging really. Not shooting psychic questions at him: what are you doing here? why do you bring death to this place? why don't you throw down your weapon and contemplate like Siddhartha, until you grow gaunt and dreamy?

One of the mercs, a Cambodian named Monivong, had leaned over and said to Elliot, "I want to smash them, don't you?"

Elliot had needed to ask himself, "Do I want to do that?"

He found he didn't. He simply wanted to crawl away from them, scar tissue pulled across both eyes like a blanket so he couldn't see them anymore. He didn't really sleep, merely drifted, thinking he was dreaming but not actually far enough gone to.

Then why had he found himself alone, the other mercs gone? He was surrounded by waves of tiny Buddhas, who had crept up to him from their niches, had their hands on his face, pulling the scar tissue aside from his eyes so he had no choice but to see them there. Speaking of Lilliputians, he did then feel like Gulliver. Overrun, pinned down, a ludicrous giant.

Don't hide, they insisted, wheedling.

When he shook himself the Buddhas were gone. The other soldiers were sitting around, smoking, checking their weapons. Some were talking softly, about having just come across the moonscaped country, passing a village where a Laotian funeral was being held for a man killed by a tiger, the body in the process of public cremation.

"They have six categories of death here," Monivong said now, sniffing smugly as if remembering the smoke from the roasting flesh and hair. He proceeded to enumerate them. "Death by illness, by execution, by drowning or dying as this fellow did—by being torn apart by a beast, by falling out of a tree, and by being struck by lightning. These are the violent ways to die and if you go that way here, you get a hasty and not very polite funeral. Your family won't close your eyes and bathe you in perfumed water. You won't get a gold coin in your mouth. Nobody will party over you for a week in joy for your having died from natural causes, which means you were blessed and surely reached nirvana. They just burn you up real fast."

Elliot thought to himself, wonder how many reached nirvana while we were bombing the piss out of them.

"I saw one of those once," Gestetner mused, smoke puffing out from between his lips, twining with the different colored candle smoke. "They were partying over the deceased. They'd put him in a wooden coffin and were going to great pains to protect the crate from wood lice. They still burned 'im up. I think that's what every culture should do. Corpses are filthy things, you know. Spread disease. Nirvana? Crap. Once the worms get you, there's nothing sweet."

"You don't believe there is something beyond death?" the young Frenchman, Vezat, asked. Around his neck a gold crucifix glittered, complete with messianic corpse.

"You mean you do?" Saab retorted, sneering.

Vezat's eyes shifted, away from the men and toward the flickering shadows on the cavern walls. He fingered the cross. "*Je ne sais quoi. Quelque chose.* Something."

"Yeah, well ... by the pricking of my thumb, something wicked this way comes," the colonel recited, from either Shakespeare or Bradbury, Elliot wasn't sure which.

"I think we should take as much of this gold with us as we can," Monivong said.

Gestetner snorted. "Sure, let's be weighted down with that during battle. We can swing back by here after, maybe. Do some souvenir hunting. Till then, mitts off. We're men on a mission from God, remember?" Or so Saab knew Tak liked to think of himself.

When they left the caves just before morning light, the Buddhas watched them go. Blessing them? Cursing them? Ambivalent was more likely. An inscrutable face on each one, perfect for pondering a cadaver's outcome. Whatever that was. Or maybe just being able to see the future on each soldier, viewing ghostly guts trailing from blow-out belly wounds, phantom brains crusting mortar-scooped skulls on those who wouldn't be coming out alive. Elliot took a last look back at them, as gold glittered and wood gleamed sleekly. If he hadn't learned to manage himself, would each Buddha have flickered across his flesh? Would they have made mouths through a hole in his cheek, begging "Take us out of this tomb! Godhood is horrible ..."

The battle itself was a grisly joke. It went on for hours before they finally discovered they were fighting the wrong group. Their opponents weren't part of the drug cartel at all, but only ethnic Hmong opposed to the Vientiane government. More Hmong reinforcements arrived—American trained and Thai financed—and only half of Gestetner's men got out with their lives.

Elliot was reminded how much he detested jungle battles—even if some of that jungle was chemical-defoliated and growing its latest gangrene lush from bomb craters the size of city blocks. The humidity and insects made the worst festering slop imaginable out of rice and shit pooped out the exit wounds in a man's lower back.

Saab was furious at first, shouting about their recon being lame. But deep down, Elliot knew the colonel really just blamed himself. It wasn't like Gestetner to make that kind of mistake. Usually he had the most uncanny instincts about just who and what were where. Or maybe his sources, whoever they were, had fucked up.

Elliot remembered another time when they had the right party, but then wished they hadn't. Some big lumber company in Brazil had hired them to 'remove' some wigged-out Christian militia group taking up valuable rainforest squatter space.

These guys had been better equipped than Koresh's group in Waco.

The mercs rolled up and were nothing short of impressed at the array of rockets with base bleed and flechette warheads, gas-trap and pyrotechnic grenades, breech loading and rifle mortars, and every paramilitary weapon from Auto-Ordnance to Valmet. They used field guns that fired American M483s, a 155-mm shell that struck the ground and fragmented from its bomblet body at a lethal radius of about 20 feet. Able to penetrate a main battle tank, it was hell when it was used on the soft targets of men out in the open. A number of the colonel's mercs were rendered into just so much sifting hashmeat.

The Sons And Daughters Of The Apocalypse obviously had more money than, well—God—to be able to afford such an arsenal. They had a bigger military budget than most small countries. Gestetner got tired of the shooting war and finally resorted to sending a few remote-controlled drones, carrying payloads of sarin nerve gas into the beseiged compound.

Elliot hated that moment, itching, hearing piranha in the water stripping the still-living body of an Ausie named Polk. He'd been the last man to suffer from a blast coming from the compound. The mortar had landed near him, the shock wave knocking him thirty feet ass over shoulders. It hadn't done more than knick him in a few dozen shallow spots but it blew him right into the Amazon.

"Christ!" Elliot had cried out, voice muffled inside his gas mask until it seemed to funnel right back up his nose. He'd jumped forward to go in after the man.

"No, El!" Saab grabbed him by the collar of his flak jacket, yanking him backward off his heels. His own mask made him look like some gigantic praying mantis. "Too late already."

And both of them had then turned back to stare in the compound's direction, knowing the drones must have already released their payloads. They expected to hear shrieks penetrating the reinforced, double walls, because how could that many people be dying without noise? They would surely hear what it must have sounded like when the Nazis turned on the Zyklon B in the showers and people started climbing on top of each other, willing to scratch each other's eyes out just to reach the top of the heap and a few more seconds of life. But all they heard were the thousands of needle teeth as piranha worked their way under Polk's mask or *through it* to get at the man's face, lethal bodies thrashing the stagnant water into a red froth. They tried not to hear Polk attempting to scream through the mask, the holes the piranha had made in it causing the water to rush in, reducing those cries into gurgle-snorts.

There were noises coming from the compound, seeming to float through the jungle, rising and falling wavelengths rippling through the humidity. But it didn't sound human. It was like the distant skreeing shrieks of many parrots and macaws, suddenly finding themselves in jaguar jaws. The tree leaves ruffled with it. But there were no birds around there, not since the battle had begun.

Elliot was thinking, there weren't kids in that compound, too, were there? I was told they were radical celibates, like the Russian Skoptics whose men castrated themselves and women sliced off their own breasts. That wasn't just press bullshit the lumber company put out so we wouldn't think about those eighteen children being burned alive at Waco?

After the bird sounds stopped, Gestetner let a few hours pass. Then he nodded. "Right, let's bomb the shit out of it now. Level the place."

"Then what?" some soldier asked.

The colonel shrugged. "Why don't we salt the earth?"

Now, Elliot imagined this village in Cambodia might be full of stuff the Khmer Rouge had confiscated as they ran amuck through the country. And these peasants were a religiously-inspired group, like the ones in Brazil had been. Fanatics of that stamp were often the most difficult to go up against, especially in jungle areas where nature seemed to always work against intruders, favoring the native sons.

Faith freaks were less likely to turn traitor or just turn tail and run. They were more liable to be willing to die for their ideals, even zealously seeking to die just to prove how deep their beliefs went. To the bone. Through the heart. Down to the last red corpuscle. (The Skoptics again. Anyone who would slice off his own jewels or her own tits *had* to be a wart on the topside of fully dedicated.)

"We're just going in with seven men?" Elliot asked Saab.

"That's all we'll need," Gestetner assured him.

"How do you know that? I thought this guy wouldn't tell Tak much of anything. We barely know where we're going."

Saab punched Elliot's shoulder and grinned.

"You know I can always find out more. Some little local news rag did an article on this village a couple years ago. I remembered it. Said this village near Phnom Kulan was harvesting its best crops since before the war. The info came from a group trying to find American POWs. I happen to be acquainted with a guy in that group. He gave me primo lowdown."

Elliot scanned the weapons they were carrying. Nothing heavy. Hand weapons, both pistols and rifles, plenty of ammunition, ropes of magazine belts crisscrossed across their chests till they resembled Halloween Rambos crunching strawberry flavored veins between their teeth. No howitzers, light mortars, M1 rocket launchers—not even any grenades hooked to their belts. Although the colonel himself was toting a pack on his back bigger than any of the others, and whenever he set it down, he did so mighty lightly.

Guess maybe Saab believed that running into any of the late Pol Pot's missing links in the mountains was a zero proposition. Well, it was reported that the last holdouts of the revolution had surrendered, just a few old gap-toothed rebels coming out of the mountains with their hands on their heads, hoping to retire to Florida. (Much better than their heads in their hands, tucked beneath their armpits, or jammed between their thighs where their generative toys used to be.)

Gestetner was normally a very cautious fellow, not given to slop. He was too fond of winning and got too pissed when he didn't. If he said seven men, carrying light, he must have had his reasons.

El didn't ask more questions although he found it odd. He'd been fighting alongside this man a long time and had seldom had reason to question the colonel's motives for doing things. Still, he must know something more, information he wasn't telling. Like maybe there weren't really any villagers. And no village. Just a small group of armed yet rustic, ignorant farmers in dope fields. Nothing fancy. Hard to reach but little more than a showdown at the OK Corral once you got there.

Weird. Seven guys. Elliot couldn't help thinking they looked more like assassins, a clean-up crew supposed to sneak in quietly, do some moderate dirty work, then slip back out again like *almost* nothing had happened. Leastwise, nothing anybody would ever find out about.

The kind of covert crap that organizations like the CIA were cinematized over.

The precise coordinates for the village were still a mystery element. The guy Saab knew with the POW group had been vague, saying only that it was somewhere near Phnom Kulan, give or take twenty-five or thirty kilometers. They parachuted near the Stung Sreng River, then struck a southeast path into a particularly dense part of the mountainous jungle.

The sun showed in small jagged bursts through spaces between branches. Like silent flashes from gunfire. It reminded Elliot of a large building full of broken windows, a sniper sitting in each one drawing a bead down upon a head, squeezing the trigger, creating a tiny explosion of light. But it was hard to tell whether the flash you saw was from a bullet being fired, or a reflection of the sun upon a glass shard still spiking a windowpane.

Elliot at all times put his attention everywhere. Being in the jungle always did a psychological fuck with his head. Felt like he was tightroping barefoot across razorwire. The stenches made his nostrils flare in indignation, of loose shit, decay, fungal sex. The colors were the garish ones from nightmare or electro-convulsive shock-induced figments. The sounds were—back home. Too much of back home. The cat-in-heat howls, feral growls, noises of hunger-threat. That you in there, Mama?

So why hadn't El gone home, instead of going into a line of work which meant being in jungles often? Why hadn't he become a monk in a desert someplace, where the only sounds he would hear would be blowing sand, scorpions flicking out their dangerous tails, Bedouin women ululating messages from cumin-flavored tongues?

Didn't ghouls originate in just such a wasteland? Cannibal creatures that made you watch as they devoured you, showing you what your testicles looked like after they'd ripped them off at the roots and chewed them for a spell, turning them into a paste which reminded you of deviled ham and snot. The first vampires and were-things originated in the deserts. And there were demons for virtually every dune which might be sifting across an ancient, buried hellhole. They sang to you when the sun went down and the air went cool, to lure you out so they could bathe in your blood. So they could chew open a hole where the knot of your navel was and then fuck you in the warm tangle of your guts.

There were predatory things everywhere. In all places was some semblance of jungle. Being a soldier, Elliot could stride into those areas and kill, demonstrating they had no power over him anymore. Because he wasn't a kid any longer. Because he'd had a generator plugged into his brain until he ought to be able to power a radio off the current still crackling between his ears. He might dream of the animal his mother was. Or of descending too fast in a crashing helicopter with the tops of tropical trees rushing up to impale him. Or of waking up in a small bamboo cage which might or might not eventually reveal itself to be a room in an Asian mental ward. But when he awoke he could face it down, blow holes in its precarious logic, then let the bugs swarm to consume what was left of it as he walked away.

When he was a twelve-year-old kid in Texas he remembered standing in front of the bathroom mirror. The pretense was that he was trying to clean his acne up, squeezing blemishes, scraping red weals practically down to the bone with his nails. But really he was looking for the slightest twitch which didn't belong. Skinning his lips back from his teeth and inspecting for the too-sharp tooth. Almost willing it to START, MOVE, CHANGE, just to get the suspense over with. Was he really relieved when nothing bestial showed? Or, deep down where the wild heart beat, was the boy he'd been disappointed?

And then Harry would stick his thirteen-year-old, remarkably unpimpled face into the room, grinning, biggest boy-dick in town. "Hey, El. When Lon Chaney Jr. is his fuzzy wolfman self on the moors, if he runs into some Doberman in heat, think they do it doggy style?"

START, MOVE, DO SOMETHING. Prove I'm not just another small town-in-East-Texas-nothing, same as every other barely-hung, unsung juvie cock in junior high, smelling of wet dreams in his gym shorts.

Harry seemed to know what Elliot was doing. Didn't fall for that studiously popping the zits crap. He'd unzipped and taken his own out, shotgun barrel flesh-tube filling up his entire fist, big as a grown man's, big as an ungelded range horse's. And said, "This here's the only animal thing you need, brother. If you can get it up and keep it up, the howls'll come for all they're worth."

Then there was that time Harry and he had been on R & R together, staying at a cheap but flashy hotel, decorated like some bargain basement Chinese New Year. Elliot was there in the morning, trying to shave, looking into another goddamn mirror. Harry came up behind him and chuckled. "What? Again, bro?"

"Do you believe people can see into the future? I mean, is this why I do this, looking for a glimpse at what's going to be? For me, anyway. The shift to come in the features, like time showing clips from coming attractions. I mean, like that's what we'd see in Mother's face when she'd do that halfway slither into some crotch-nasty creature. Of her future when she'll be dead and in an after-existence where she's going to be all-animal."

Harry's eyes widened and he laughed heartily. "That's quite a mouthful coming from you, El."

"Seriously …"

Harry grew quiet, as close as he ever really got to being reflective. It must be difficult to think deep thoughts with a constant hard-on, hormones running eternal interference. "No, I don't believe in seeing into the future. I don't believe there is a future."

Elliot closed an eye and stared at him. "Right. I've even seen our baby brother Arcan do this. I've even seen Dad do this and he doesn't carry her blood. Must be afraid he can catch the shift like it was the clap or something. You've never done it? With our heritage? Stared into the glass, looking for—well, for you know what?"

Harry looked past him into the hotel mirror, streaked, greasy with pollution, polka dotted from where his brother had been popping zits again. "Yeah. But all I get's nothing. I don't look for a shift, man. I look into the reflection and then close my eyes. See nothing. Sometimes it's just that void, absolute and empty. Other times I'm falling through it. Or maybe I'm flying through it, like I own it for all it is—which is still nothing."

Elliot smiled. Talk about a mouth full. Then he got a mental image of Harry in the air, like the flying nun only with the slab right and left hemispheres of his scalp peeled from the skull, scraped, and stretched thin on wires to resemble that wingy wimple thing Sally Fields wore. Not with a rosary in one hand either but that great sinner's phallus, dripping orange stringy matter from just having been poked through some wilderness prophet's cored-out belly button. Not ready for prime time, that picture wasn't.

"Oh, I don't know. Sounds pretty profound for a well-hung bangs-anything-dead-or-alive redneck. A vision if I ever heard one."

Harry rolled his eyes. "If it is, it's a vision of the end.

Elliot shrugged, banishing the twisted William Blake scenario he'd just had in his head, of truly damned falling angels or of some savage archangel with a visage out of Hieronymous Bosch and the appetite of Baal. Making it instead into just what Harry'd said: emptiness sans existential or ethereal. Just the basic zero. "Could also be of a beginning."

And then in the madhouse, Elliot without a mirror, just sitting, swathed in the snug gauzy loops of restraints till he could hardly breathe. Concentrating on that moving, shifting, rippling scar tissue. The nightmare his face had become. Willing it to STOP, FREEZE, ENOUGH.

It made him think back to another show. Those old "Kung Fu" episodes with David Carradine he'd finally seen in reruns on a hotel television in Belfast in 1983, guest of the provisional wing of the IRA. Kwai Chang Caine, moving in slo-mo to violence he was thwarting, speaking that painfully dragged-out ENOUGH!, with all the righteous command of how God must have originally uttered LET THERE BE LIGHT! The weird sensation of shapes his facial mass of ruin took on that Elliot couldn't see, but knowing from the reaction of the doctors that these deviations could be bizarre, ferocious, sickening. It had to take a lot to make some Vietnamese doc—who must have seen some major unedited and unabridged gross-outs during the war—turn away from the panoramic psychic emetic that was Elliot's face and throw-up in the hallway.

But El worked at it, biting down hard as they wheeled him out on a cart for another shock treatment, commanding his face not to give in to the shift. And afterward doing that slow crawl back to consciousness, back to realization of self after the shockwave had been ridden down, going through his mind and taking back the pieces that made it possible to focus on stopping his face from illustrating a history of the splatter cinema in the vista of damaged muscle and tendon. Feeling the dead he'd known trying to squeeze their screams into that few square inches of flesh. Feeling dead he didn't remember at all, all very young, their childish mouths work through suffocating brick and plaster which seemed part their flesh/part not. (Why didn't he remember them?) Feeling his mother in it until he began to beat the side of his head against the floor to get her out of him again. And when blood would begin to trickle out his ear from this self-abuse, being certain that she was in that red stream, congealing on the cool floor, which he'd then spit into. Inch by inch, months consumed second by grueling second: STOP, FREEZE, NO MORE. Finally getting control. Learning to keep it. What else was a year or so in a lunatic's cell but a long spell of meditation, reflection, enlightenment?

When he'd heard that voice on the other side of the padded wall, "You the one the staff refers to as *ghostface*?", Elliot had already found the key to managing those spirits. And when he finally came face to face with that other imprisoned American and the guy said, "Ah, you don't look so bad … ", all Saab Gestetner saw were the scars: rigid, as healed as they would ever get without massive reconstruction. Fucking stone.

Nothing alive evident on that side of Elliot's face at all. Under it was a different matter. El knew that when he looked out of his eyes, all those other things looked out with him.

Chapter 11

"The crocodile's power is in the water."
—*African proverb*

The night before they left for Cambodia on the job for Mr. Tak, Elliot had a dream. It was one of those flashback things, stung with memory, maybe some of it not entirely reliable. But it was from a couple months he spent in Rwanda, a time that—even when he was awake—he had trouble defining.

Definition: often screwed as far as he was concerned.

It went like this:

He'd heard her whisper, "I love you, Elliot."

There were several predominant languages in Rwanda. The official languages were Kinyarwanda and French. Some spoke Interlacustrine Bantu. There was also a local dialect of Swahili. Elliot knew a fair amount of French and could say almost nothing in Swahili.

When he'd first arrived at this second prison, he'd asked people, *"Unasema Kiingereza? Sisemi nzuri Kiswahili ..."*

Do you speak English? I speak lousy Swahili.

Hoping he said it right and wasn't just asserting an opinion that their grandmothers took it up the ass with a basket of sweet potatoes.

It didn't take long—being one of the very few whites there—before some of the more brutish men would grope him, try to assert their dominance with a cheery buttfuck. When Elliot spoke at all it was to say "Leave me alone!"

"Usinisumbue!"

(More brutish? Most of the men—and women, too—were here because they were suspected of having been part of the Hutus that hacked and mutilated countless Tutsis the year before. Sure, some were innocent—the kids *had* to be. But many had indeed taken part in falling upon their neighbors with guns and machetes to settle old grievances or just so they could have whatever property the Tutsis owned. Brutish was simply the operative word here.)

The men who harmed him, or who at least tried to ... he snapped a few wrists, broke a couple arms, flattened some noses. Actually wishing the scar tissue on the side of his face would start to move again. That would sure command some respect, wouldn't it? Ghostface wouldn't have to put up with sodomites. Yet nothing came alive there. In ridges and keloids, no cavalry to the rescue.

Back to it: the men who harmed him, or who at least tried to ... disappeared. Guards may have taken them away as Elliot nodded off. People frequently vanished from the room. To be interrogated. To be killed in extrajudicial executions. This was the shape of revenge.

Elliot heard her murmur in a voice which floated above the manic din and crept beneath the hysteria. "Shifters, you and I," she said. "Come to the walls and let me pull you close to my heart."

"Who are you?" he wanted to know.

"Embe," was the soft reply. "Queen of my kind."

What kind?

"Are you a prisoner here, too?"

"Every shifter is a prisoner. You and I are *were,* different from most of these others. Our shapes are as mutable as the seasons."

Elliot wasn't comfortable being called "shifter." He associated this with his mother and with her abuses. He'd never carried that taint. Except in the Vietnamese mental hospital. But that had been so very different. That was less a shapeshifting than a shapehaunting.

"Please, Elliot. We can comfort one another."

She sounded so delicate, a voice of the wind through orchids. He even attempted to go to her a few times, not in his right mind, slipping back to when he'd been a P.O.W. after the fall of Saigon. But he didn't hear jazz, no saxophones, no guitars. Only jungle drums which seemed to draw their syncopation from the rhythm of his heart.

"Come to the wall, Elliot. Shifters, you and I. The same."

But he couldn't get through the press of people to reach any wall. Even when Elliot saw her shimmer on its flat surface … like a woman who has just stepped from a shower and is reflected in a misty bathroom mirror … a shape of hot frost was all she was.

Couldn't lie down. So many people. Occasion-ally—provided he was lucky at the moment—he'd catch six or seven winks while on his feet, not even able to sway as he dozed, as in a fully upright trance. Bodies in front of him, behind him, to the left and to the right of him.

Sometimes somebody would moan and then faint. He'd watch as their eyelids fluttered, maybe drool slipped down the chin from a corner of their mouth. Sometimes the drool would be speckled with blood. Their head would loll, skull grinding around on the neck vertebra. But they couldn't fall.

A real bad time came when this one Hutu had a seizure. The man might have been a grand mal epileptic (naturally he wasn't going to be given necessary medication there). Or perhaps he'd been beaten too severely and now had brain damage. His eyes rolled up to the whites and he foamed at the mouth. He shit and pissed himself. But he couldn't fall and his thrashing was limited. He grew rigid as iron. People tried to move away from him. It still wasn't uncommon in parts of the world to find folks who thought this was demonic possession.

"*Msaada!* Help!" Elliot had cried. "There's a sick man in here!"

No one came. The fellow was eventually given enough inches to spare that he slipped to the floor. Elliot thought he died there. And since the guards only came around every few days to hose the place down, the body would begin to decay. The place was so mean and primitive there weren't even any toilets. Would the extra stink be noticed?

"This looks like a nice place for an epidemic," Elliot muttered to himself.

But then that night he saw the man, managing to work his way toward the wall. Threading through the crowd, children crying as they tried fitfully to sleep. Babies wailed at the breasts of their mothers.

The shimmer, a shape of feminine curves. The man leaned toward it. The plaster might be cool so he laid his cheek against it, right where her own cheek might be. Hard to tell in that glow which happened to be all she was made of.

Then, suddenly, the man went. WENT. Cheek-first, rest of the head following. Then the body pulled behind the neck. Vanishing into that wall.

Elliot just blinked. Started then to practically climb people to reach it.

He thought about the first cell he'd been locked in. It was back in March. Right after he'd been arrested, accused by someone of having helped former interahamwe militia members reform and rearm, preparing to take Rwanda back … and this time kill all the surviving Tutsis they'd missed the first go-around. Well, he'd been pointed out as one of Saab Gestetner's mercs, this as he sat in a local tavern, drinking the foulest concoction ever to be brewed by man: banana beer. It didn't help that he'd gotten so drunk he'd started singing a rather callous rendition of some old (very old) tune from like the fucking 1920s or '30s. "Tu tu Tutsi, goodbye … " And even though he'd only been there to talk to a guy, one Jules Bucyendore, who was interested in joining the colonel's private army—a Tutsi no less—the next thing he knew he'd been clubbed and dragged to a prison in Kigali. Black and blue, rammed with a bunch of genocide suspects into the Muhima Gendarmerie Building. It was a single cell to boot, built to hold 10 people. 70 had been crammed in there.

Couldn't lie down. Couldn't sit. Couldn't move. Couldn't breathe. People fought, clawing and biting, trying to gain a purchase to climb up on others. People had rectum loads in their shorts because there was no place to squat down. The temperature and stench was like a bathroom in hell. You didn't want to be at the bottom of the pile, brother, for that was death.

Elliot had been reminded of the Black Hole of Calcutta. He didn't recall the exact year—mid 1700s. A room built to contain three or four men had been stuffed with roughly 150 British prisoners. Only 23 had come out alive. Crammed like jelly beans into a jar. Guess how many and win a free ride on the Karma Loop de Loop.

Kigali. The first prison they put him in after they practically beat and stomped the American pie out of him. Had she called to him then, too?

Sweat had run into his eyes, stinging and blinding him like cobra venom. Pooling until Elliot flashed on having heard, the year before, as Radio Milles Collines exhorted Hutus to kill

Tutsis, sparing none, broadcasting, "Get them all! The graves are only half full!"

Saab and he and the others actually had been there, gainfully employed by some higher-ups working on the sly for the Catholic Church to help defend church property and personnel. Because Hutus attacked convents and chapels and monasteries, no sacred ground or sanctuary as far as they were concerned. He witnessed thousands of chopped apart bodies clogging the rivers in 1994. He'd lost count of men's limbless trunks floating by, the floppy little penises nibbled by fish. Of women's breasts, severed yet still seeping pearls of milk. Of the decapitated, billiard ball-sized heads of infants, eyes like distant stars gone blackly nova. He remembered a backside floating by, no legs, no waistline, nothing else. Just the buttocks. And between the cheeks a length of what resembled bloody sausage casing. This victim had been raped so hard the colon had prolapsed. Maybe it had also been dragged out with a hook. And there were coils of guts swirling like rope in the current. Clouds of what must have been billions of flies hovered above. The body parts eventually jammed like logs at a narrow bend, damming the flow with unspeakable carnage.

The water had been poisoned for a long time. Not even animals wanted to drink from it. He'd see elephants come to the shore, lift their trunks, sniffing, then walk away without so much as a sip.

Elliot knew of an African belief that crocodiles housed the souls of the murdered who have returned with a hunger for revenge.

Damn, but there sure were a lot of crocs in those lakes and rivers that spring of 1995. After all the Tutsi chum ended up in the drink. Perhaps because the pickin's were so plentiful, the crocs had come from far and wide along the Nile Congo, from neighboring Zaire, Tanzania, Kenya. Even from the bamboo forests in the volcanic northwest where the peaks of Virunga reached 14,825 feet at Karisimbi. Crocs on trips to the land of (what amounted to) milk and honey.

Elliot suppressed a half-mad giggle. He had an image in his head of crocodiles carrying luggage made from human skin.

At any rate, a whole lot of reptiles, jaws snapping yard long smiles, tails capable of cracking bones, and throats guzzling the blood soaked into river stones.

He needed air! It was too hot with all this flesh everywhere. Elliot grew faint, already injured from the beatings he'd been given. Please? Help? *Tafadhali? Msaada?* Just a puff of oxygen. Two degrees of coolness. He saw purple strobe with a white diamond flash in its center, He gagged, lungs seizing. His throat closed and he couldn't even swallow. Not that he had any saliva left to swallow. He heard a wheezing—knew it was that tin whistle trapped behind his tongue. He heard creaking and realized it was the bones of his sternum and ribs.

"Elliot?" said a voice, wonderful, disembodied. A hallucination, the sort men had who were suffocating to death. Brain starved. "Let go. There are parts of you that can breathe even in here. Let them take over for you."

For an instant, he was positive he must have lost consciousness. Because he found himself on the ceiling where none of the other prisoners could reach. He languidly beat wings which were small and cellophane: open/close, open/close, open/ close. Fanning himself. Looking down where faces strained up to see him. There were dead folk underfoot of these. He heard spines crackle, arms and legs snap. He smelled blood and, as a fly, it translated into dense sugar, into warm sticky mammalian taffy.

There were also dead people on their feet, kept up by the folk pressed around them.

Someone started screaming. Others took it up.

Yet Elliot—somewhere in the center as he returned to his body—closed his eyes and opened his mouth. "Buzzzzzzzzzzzzzz."

When the guards opened the room again, there were 22 dead in that cell. Surprisingly, very few of the survivors had lost their minds. The people of Rwanda had seen and suffered too much lately to let so small an inconvenience as claustrophobia be their last straw.

Had there ever really been a time in his life when he stretched out, horizontal, supine upon a soft bed, feather pillow beneath his head? Had Elliot dreamed this?

And there had been this super bed in Singapore. A waterbed shaped like a rose. Cool against that plastic. How he wished it were there now so he could cut it open—bite it open with his teeth. Let that cool water flood the room, buoy him up until he rode a wave.

(The wall she stood within moved like a wave.)

But now he was in the second prison, Gitarama. And she had followed him there. He saw her glow upon the wall.

People had disappeared. He'd seen them go to the wall. And now she called to him to go there, too.

"We can comfort one another. We are the same," she said.

And the fellow who'd had the seizure that Elliot had thought was dead, he'd gone there just now and Elliot had watched him being pulled through the plaster. In so rapid a movement that one second he was there, the next only a memory of a shape.

So why was Elliot going there, too? Had she, *Embe,* summoned this one also? Telling him that she and he were the same and ought to comfort one another?

Maybe at this point he didn't care. If there was an out through this square of plaster, a revolving door and a dimensional slip, he wanted to take it.

Embe's voice was so seductive.

How he reached the wall, Elliot would never be sure. Maybe it was like at a rock concert when the audience picked you up and carried you like a god. But reach it he did. He touched it and found it cool, wet. It rippled beneath his fingers. He laid his palms flat against the plaster and streams trickled through his life- and heart-lines. They told his future in liquid mirages.

But when he pulled his hands away to look, his palms were bloody.

Not his.

"Elliot, come to me," she lilted.

He could see her better now. A caprice in the wall's flatness. Beautiful and weird. Her curves fluctuated, even her face one thing and then another and then a combination of both.

He saw a woman. He saw a crocodile. He was mesmerized and scared down to the on-going conga line of his elements.

"You killed him," he said.

"I've taken many," she admitted. "They butchered my family."

There was a commotion at the door on the far side of the cell. Guards were coming in.

"Elliot, don't fear me. I can make you free," she explained.

"If I get close, you'll pull me through the wall and devour me," Elliot replied, realizing as he said it that this actually sounded stupid, cartoonish.

Then he saw the bloody foot sticking out of the plaster. A piece of the epileptic she'd missed.

"I will not," she told him. "Tell me what I can do to prove it to you."

People were being herded out of the cell as quickly as thousands could be rushed through a small doorway. Embe saw them going, saw the guards taking them out. She hissed, "We'll get you all! The graves are only half full!"

Then she turned her attention back to Elliot. "You saw what they did to us? But it has nothing to do with you. We are both of a kind. We can comfort one another when the nights become dry and unbearable."

He'd been hearing and seeing Embe for a couple months now. She'd been the only sweetness he'd known. She'd saved him in the first prison when he was dying. Why would she kill him now? Wasn't as if she was waiting for him to fatten up. He'd lost at least twenty pounds in those two months.

How many had she taken, back at the Muhima Gendarmerie and here at Gitarama? Hell, children had gone missing here. People had heard them scream.

"Step out from the wall to me," he said. "Prove to me you're not an illusion and not a monster. Show me only the human shape even as I stand here, human."

(Or mostly human, he thought, touching the scar tissue on his face. But what could be more human than such damage?)

Embe nodded and emerged from the wall as if rising from a river, long black hair wet down her back, breasts streaming gemstones of water. She was a black nyad, tall and slim as Tutsis were. Her mouth was full and the color of ripe mangoes. *Embe* was the Swahili word for mango.

Someone ran through the crowd of detainees, pushing to get in as the prisoners struggled to get out.

"Tyler! I'm Jules Bucyendore. Remember me? It's been hard to find you. I heard you'd been arrested ..."

The tall, slender Tutsi saw Embe and stopped, jaw dropping.

Elliot's eyes met hers. He felt a snap of electricity, the irresistible pull of attraction. This was a queen among women.

Suddenly he didn't fear her anymore. She reached out a cool hand and stroked his forehead. Soft she was as the reeds that billow in the river. No fear. He just wanted her.

"Tyler! Here!" Jules cried out.

The man threw something. Elliot turned and caught it, seeing its flash as it spun end over end. Coming through the sickeningly fetid space of the prison cell like a crescent moon tumbling toward an eclipse.

A machete. He was lucky he caught it by the handle. But Elliot was a seasoned merc and had superb reflexes—even after two months of being beaten and starved and sleep-deprived. Maybe shifters were just better all the way around.

He spun on the ball of a foot as he came back to face her. Elliot plunged the blade through Embe's heart.

Why for chrissakes? She hadn't attacked him. And he wanted her, wanted to go with her. Actually didn't care if he would end up her meal. Actually didn't believe he would for he hadn't harmed any Tutsis, had he?

No, she'd only wanted comfort, another shifter. And maybe so did he.

Maybe.

Now he'd never know.

He'd caught the machete Jules threw him and reacted as trained. And trained to kill was what he'd always been prepared for.

There was nothing else.

Maybe he'd had a flash of his mother, Deborah Tyler. The bitch dog and goddess of his nightmares. Maybe he'd smelled the dead on Embe's breath and could see the scales faintly outlined in her complexion, like the swirling grain in rare and fine ebony.

Still he felt guilty as Embe stared at him, her eyes wide with shock and betrayal. She'd come out of the wall for him. She'd made herself vulnerable to prove her love. In that wall had been all the waters of Rwanda, maybe even all the rivers and lakes and ponds and waterfalls of Africa. She'd been safe there.

Elliot's mind chattered inside its brain. I didn't kill my own kind. I *didn't kill* my own kind. I DIDN'T KILL MY OWN KIND!

She stumbled but still glided backward into the wall, which first seemed to envelope her as a dark mass of water and then became simply plaster.

"I would have helped you, Elliot," he heard her even if he couldn't see her now. "You need healing. But it will take a greater queen than I am to do that."

Then she didn't say anything more. The wall cracked, then burst. Water gushed out. Bloody water, dark water.

Elliot rode the wave out of the cell.

Chapter 12

"When you have gone, wipe away
the footprint of death ..."
—The Rig Veda

It was slow going through such dense mountain jungle. It was late summer and heavy rains were likely without much advance warning. Mosquitoes were thick as morning mist, carrying Dengue fever as well as an especially nasty kind of cerebral malaria common in Cambodia, so they had to wear plenty of DEET. Leeches proliferated in every damp tangle. And typhus ticks made it necessary to impregnate every scrap of cloth and leather with benzyl benzoate and dibutyl phthalate. There were plenty of venomous snakes: cobras, banded kraits, vipers. Of a variety and number more than even a Texas boy used to watching out for underfoot rattlers was used to. They had to carry quinine, salt tablets, penicillin, morphine, Benzedrine, vitamins, anti-nausea pills, tourniquets, snake-bite kits, and antiseptic creams. Oh, and clean, dry socks, so that their feet wouldn't blister and then the blisters infect. Because bugs loved infection and would get in, eating their way to podiatric fame and fortune, necessitating amputation.

At dark they stopped, shook out boots, and checked one another for vermin. They rested for a night.

Elliot woke up about three in the morning. For some reason this was a time he seemed to always wake up, bladder pressing or dreams becoming too much for the mind to contain. He opened his eyes and heard a sound. A faint voice. Saab's. It was a whisper but not the kind that came from a man talking in his sleep. Was the colonel carrying on a conversation with another one of the mercs?

Elliot strained to listen but didn't hear a second voice. And yet Saab sounded querulous, as if he was doing a probe of some captured enemy, a slow but relentless interrogation.

Elliot didn't see him among the other sleeping mercs. To the right, some distance up, was the merc doing this hour's sentry. Evidently this man couldn't hear Saab. Off to his left, in the other direction, Elliot could see a thin light through the trees. He got up and softly walked toward it.

"Damn you, I know you can hear me," he heard the colonel say. "You don't fool me for a second."

Had Saab caught himself a stubborn *a khmau* renegade in one of the traps he'd set about the camp's perimeter? Or a stray from that village they were heading toward?

Elliot moved closer, toe to heel. Just to ascertain if this might be something he could help with, not really eavesdropping. Soon as he knew it was none of his business, he'd return to his spot and go back to sleep.

He got to where he could just see Gestetner. The colonel had that big pack of his on the ground, open. The light emanated from inside it. This was where Saab was directing his questions.

"How come you don't suffocate in there when the flap's down and I've got you locked tight?"

Elliot kept himself shielded by a tree, peering out from behind it. Okay, so now maybe he was spying a little. Because that was some strange conversation for a fellow apparently alone in the jungle with only his pack.

Of course, Gestenter had some weird kinks. El knew that. He tried not to judge. The man was the closest thing he had to a friend anywhere. He'd kind of taken Harry's place in Elliot's life. Not that anyone could ever really take over a brother's role, but the two men had seen a lot of hard action in their two decades together. He shrugged off Saab's excesses as he always had his brother's.

Maybe there was a blowup doll in there, and the man just felt like making small talk before sticking himself into any one of several lubed and available entrances. One way to avoid AIDS.

Once, the mercs had been on a job in the Andes, coming down on a bunch of villagers on behalf of wealthy landowners interested in entering the profitable cocaine trade. (Sort of like the job they were doing now for Tak.) The villagers apparently wanted to keep their number one cash crop. It was MAGNIFICENT SEVEN in reverse.

The colonel's group had hidden for days in caves not too far from Machu Picchu, the legendary Incan city. They'd discovered ancient mummies in there, arrayed in rows of withered flesh and bone. If these had ever worn any gold, it was plucked clean ages ago. The mouths were wide on some of the dried dead, others resolutely shut as if unwilling to give up the last vestiges of a vision they shared. Some had eyes wide; maybe they'd bulged at the moment of death—sockets scoured dry now. Others were serene in sleep.

Gestetner had spoken to these mummified bodies. Right in front of his men. Going to this one and that one, leaning close to examine the puckered features, to inhale a bit of skindust, maybe to put his tongue for a moment on an apricot rind of lip. Chatting them up with his usual smugness against objects of death. Mocking but not with the bravado of those who joked just to hide their nervousness. Not a religious man, no. But absolutely a fellow who was comfortable with grisly finality.

"Do you know I was born from a dead mother?" Saab confided to Elliot once. "My parents were arguing that night and my father shot her in the face. Immediate brain death. For some reason this kickstarted labor, and I just 'shot' right out of her other end. I've heard it said that infants born with cauls over their faces have the gift of seeing the future. But what do they get if they come out and are immediately half smothered in brains?"

Elliot had shaken his head so Saab answered his own question. "A knack perhaps for terminating the future."

Seeing the future, perceiving nothing. Nervous ticks in the eye or around the mouth which might herald the Beast of the Apocalypse. Or falling, flying, owning a cosmic abyss. Everyone around him—including Elliot himself—seemed to be at least marginally obsessed with auspicious beginnings and nebulous ends.

Now he positioned himself where he could barely make out a shape inside the pack, folded in the way some ancient societies used to tucked their dead into earthen jars. Very small and frail. Like the body of a child.

It was the body of a child. A young girl. Haloed about the head, delicate but scarred features illuminated by an inner radiance. Smiling like the molded expression on a plastic doll.

No doubt one of the afflicted Thais that everyone in Bangkok had been seeing lined up on the sidewalks for the last couple weeks. What the hell was Saab doing with one of those crammed into his pack?

And the way he leaned over it, (in a manner so intimately close to what he'd done with the Andean mummies) his features almost cartoonishly Aryan above the Asian girl's, white-blond hair making him resemble a ghost trying to haunt her, his face beautiful as Lucifer's.

Saab reached down and touched one of her hands. The fingers seemed to be crippled, distorted even as indistinctly as Elliot could make out from his position.

"Some of my best work," the colonel cooed. "Much better than what I did to Chumbhot. Well, it had been a couple years since I'd done her. You learn a lot of technique in two years. You remember Chumbhot, don't you?"

Naturally the girl didn't answer. Only smiled, not really facing him so not seeing him, more moonlight rising from her face and hair than what streamed thinly through the jungle trees.

Elliot shivered, stepped back fully behind the banyan trunk which concealed him. Took a few deep but quiet breaths. Padded back to his own tent. But couldn't get back to sleep.

The area they were in was long considered sacred by the Khmers. It was the mythical birthplace of the Kampuchean kings. The men were traveling beside a river. El looked down into it as they went past. The water was absolutely pristine, clear down to the bottom. And there in a perfect grid pattern were carved figures. Penises, all erect. What the locals called *lingas*. There had to be a thousand of them, cut directly into the sandstone riverbed.

He wondered silently, *how did they do that?*

Further on downstream, the underwater scene turned into larger blocks of stone virtually bulging with apsaras. The faces unnerved him, they were so beautiful. Living nymphs down there, mermaids, seeming to be swimming because of the ripples in the river. A man could almost rip off his clothes and jump in after them.

Ripples across their faces. Elliot touched his own scarred cheek. But it hadn't moved, no way. He'd frozen it, stopping that nonsense forever, or so he hoped. And yet there were those that looked out of the eye above that cheek. Truncated Saigon whores, burned dancers, the simperingly savage face of his mother. Even a crocodile queen. Looking down into the water, envious of those other, perfect, stone women.

"Halt!" the colonel whisper-shouted.

The men stopped. Through the trees they could make out a clearing, land which might have once been prepared for use in farming. It was a little overgrown now but not as it would be when the jungle crept back into it. There were small children walking through it, picking flowers. Each carried a double handful of buttercups.

A couple dozen of these kids, all about the same age and height. As if a school had let a class out for a field trip. But villages in these mountain backwaters wouldn't have schools like that. Most didn't have any schools at all. Not since the Khmer Rouge had systematically slaughtered everyone with any education. They'd even murdered any person who wore glasses, because that indicated they could read.

The children hadn't heard the soldiers along the river. None of them looked up. They simply bent and plucked, sweeping through the little meadow as if determined to have every flower in it.

"Narai," Gestetner told a Thai merc. "Get out and follow them. They might be from Phnom Yohp."

Narai threaded through the sopping undergrowth, pausing to pull his right foot out of the mud with a sucking sound at the boot. He moved in and around bombox trees and bamboo. When he reached the clearing, the children had already made it to the far side and were reentering the jungle, sticking blossoms in each other's hair, munching petals, giggling. He started to follow.

He was no more than three or four feet into the clearing when there was an explosion. Narai went up in the air inside a white cloud and then flopped down in a red wave. He began screaming.

"Son of a bitch!" Saab cried and went through the trees.

Elliot went with him. They stopped at the edge of the clearing. Through the waving stems of grass they could see Narai on the ground. A small man to begin with, he was even smaller now. At first glance Elliot might have guessed he'd shrunk, an easy mistake, an assumption he would have preferred to accept. But the second look showed the leg stumps spastic with shock, mangled limbs out of reach and quickly drawing veils of mosquitoes. Not that Elliot hadn't seen a lot of exploded bodies, of both comrades and enemy, but his mind always clicked at first sight, trying to turn off the gag reflex so he could go about his work.

Saab leaned down and picked up rocks, throwing one to either side of the downed soldier at a distance of about ten to twelve feet from him. The colonel pulled his arm back and threw another few as far into the clearing as he could. From these six or seven stones came three or four more explosions.

The ground shook and Narai shrieked with every concussion, the last scream finishing abruptly, without echo, blunted. The Thai merc was dead. Elliot looked at the man's face: eyes open yet full of dirt, mouth cocked so wide that he half expected something horrible to crawl from it.

Down to six men.

"Minefield." Gestetner shook his head in disbelief, staring beyond to where the children were disappearing into foliage so dense it was black. He wasn't having a problem with the minefield itself. There were an estimated four to eight million such mines throughout the country. One out of every two hundred thirty-six Cambodians was an amputee, one hundred times the ratio of amputees in America.

Elliot's jaw dropped. "How did all those kids just go through there without setting any of them off?"

And that was just what Saab was asking himself. He waved El back to the river. The other mercs stood sullenly, not even looking over to where their comrade had just died. They kept their thoughts to themselves.

Except Monivong, the former Khmer Rouge. He asked, "How many Cambodians does it take to screw in a light bulb?"

Everyone just flicked their eyes at him.

He heard no challenge so he answered, "Depends on how many it takes till you find one with arms."

Saab asked him, "Monivong, you know anything about this particular area?"

Monivong tugged at the cap on his graying head. His face was still young although Elliot guessed he was probably in his early fifties.

"Yes," he replied. "I was here in the middle of the 1970s. Don't quite recall which year exactly. The people hereabouts were very religious, and religion was not tolerated by Pol Pot, you see. We left none of the local adults alive. We had the children penned up. Aah, I remember that night."

Did he chuckle? Or was that sound he made in the back of his throat something else?

"We went to sleep, could hear children crying softly. Couldn't get them to keep quiet and we'd got tired of trying. But we figured we'd wait till morning to punish them. We were trying to show them how tough we were, so we made pillows out of the arms and legs we'd taken from them."

"Shit. How could you do that to *enfants*?" asked Vezat.

Monivong tilted his head slyly. "You know how old I was? I carried a Automat Kalashnikov and swung a machete but I was twelve."

Elliot blinked. Okay, so he's not as old as I thought.

"Go on with your story," Saab said.

"We'd gone to sleep, two guards posted. Woke up when the guards screamed. Saw snakes falling from the trees. In big slick coils. I heard so much hissing I thought a cannister of teargas had landed next to me. I jumped up and ran, saw snakes biting faces, wrapping around throats, venom squirting like juice through the air. One slid around my ankle but I went straight up, swinging out with my machete high, low, crazy, at everything that had red eyes or a tube for a body. I ran until the sun rose and I was off this damned mountain. I was the only one of my unit to get away."

A Mexican merc named Ruiz hissed, mimicking a serpent.

Monivong shuddered for a second and then suppressed it. He turned and said very softly, "Don't do that again."

Something in his voice made Ruiz raise his eyebrows and then leave off the joke.

"What happened to the kids in the pen?" asked Elliot.

Monivong simply shrugged. "Don't know; don't care. As for where that village is? It was almost a quarter of a century ago. And the jungle is constantly changing, growing over places. But I can tell you this, I think I helped put that minefield there."

Elliot turned his attention back to the path beside the river. He saw a woman appear quite suddenly in front of him. He stopped dead in his tracks with a startled grunt.

But she was already gone. Had she jumped away into the jungle? (There being no wall of relative water to fade into.)

"What?!" Saab asked, swiftly reaching for the weapon he kept closest. "What happened?"

Elliot gasped, looking right, looking left, feeling pretty damned foolish. "Didn't you see her?"

"No, I didn't see anybody," Saab replied. He glanced back to the others. Everyone just shook their heads.

But El had seen a woman, very beautiful. Enough to put the apsaras under the river to shame. Something strange about her face though. Oddly familiar although he knew he'd never seen her before. (It wasn't Embe. Nor any of his other ghosts.)

She definitely wasn't dressed like a mountain peasant.

Saab waggled his white-blond eyebrows with a smirk on his lips. "You must be having flashbacks on some of that acid we dropped in Moscow last month."

Elliot wanted to say, you know I never have flashbacks.

(Only when I dream.)

Except that, from time to time, the shock treatments they jerked him back and forth with in that Vietnamese asylum seemed to gather in the center of his forehead, spinning his thoughts into vortex dreams, then down a drain flushed to God knew where.

Elliot shook his head and just walked silently behind Saab after that. He tried not to look at Gestetner's pack. He didn't want the colonel to suspect he knew what was inside. He was sure he must have dreamed the incident anyway because it didn't make sense. Still, he wouldn't get anywhere near it. Because he didn't know what it might do to his head if he happened to hear breathing coming from within.

He stared off into the jungle instead.

And saw her again. The same woman. In gold, gemstones, and twenty different varieties of orchids. Dancing across intricate nests of vines and over veldts of moss. Hands gesturing out adorned with bells, circling round and round as if in beseeching. Or in summoning. And when she'd turn … turn … he'd finally seen she had two pairs of breasts, each mathematically, geometrically perfect. Like the celestial version of a bitch dog. Like some guru fakir's wet dream goddess. A shadow falling across the lower half of the body concealed what must be magical hips and thighs.

That face. What was it about her face?

Elliot felt the breath go out of him for a moment, as if all the air in the world has just seeped away into—nothing.

No … no it CAN'T be …

Well, of course it couldn't be. What bullshit. There wasn't a damn thing in that face that suggested anything male. Was there? It was so delicate and sweet, teasing, soft.

Yet strong. Yes, not a trace of weakness there. Self-assured, commanding. (Beseeching, summoning?)

Elliot thought toward her, what is it you want from me?

She touched one of her graceful hands along her cheek and then gestured outward again. Immediately Elliot jumped, feeling a ripple in that side of his face. The scar tissue had moved, for the first time in twenty years. He slapped his hand against it.

No! Stop! Freeze!

The movement subsided. Had it only been a muscle tick? An insect crawling across his face? (A memory of being a fly?) The web of a real jungle spider trailing across the skin?

When he looked out into the jungle for the woman again, she was gone. He realized he'd stumbled forward, hand up to his face going out to touch that pack on Saab's broad back. He quickly snatched his hand away.

Had he heard something in there? What a halo might make once the light became sound? He could feel it on his fingertips, like bells upon skin.

Chapter 13

"If one could
draw the fangs of a snake
and charm the snake to play,
it's great to have snakes.
If one can single out
the body's ways
it's great to have bodies.
The body's wrong
is like mother turning vampire."
—poem to Shiva
Mahadeviyakka

God sat amid the cobras, sleek ribbons of them encircling his wrists, winding their way through his hair, coiling into crowns around his forehead. They reminded him of the days, tangling themselves into years, then unraveling to reverse time. So that he remembered being a man.

Texas, 1951. Deborah Tyler was pregnant and due to go into labor.

She was terrified of motherhood. Her own mother had ended up in a mental institution because she ripped off her clothes regularly, going down on all fours, lifting her wet cunt in the air to any male in the vicinity. She'd been a contortionist, able to bend her remarkably supple back until she could quite literally bring her tongue into her own groin, licking herself clean or into further frenzy. Deborah had been mortified as a little girl to see her mother in this state, mouth and ass full of worms.

Deborah's husband, Lucas, had gone away to a professorial symposium on modern literature being held in Norman, Oklahoma. He'd only be gone the weekend, he promised, and left a number where he could be found at the University. She'd broken water and called in a panic. But he wasn't there, the operator assured her. The profs had trooped off to wine and dine in a private club in Oklahoma City.

Deborah screamed as her belly tossed and was squeezed from within. She doubled over with the cramps till she was down on her hands and knees, thick, brunette hair swinging in front of her face. She would never make it to the bed or even the couch. She'd dropped the phone and couldn't even pick it back up. Her fingers had curled and blunted, turning into paws right before her eyes. She did manage to slide herself into a corner, catching the cord from a lamp as she did, so that it was pulled from a table to crash on the floor. The room went dark. Her howls drifted away into the blackness. Her eyes were extremely good in the dark, always had been. But the pain she was in made her almost blind, focusing only on the torment in her womb.

If the neighbors heard, they thought nothing of it. Noises were always coming from the Tyler place. Maybe the woman there was just a screaming lover. Maybe she was a roaring drunk or suffered nightmares. They turned their television sets up or the dials on their radios.

Through the walls Deborah heard the voice of Nat King Cole, filtering from a nearby house like the disembodied voice of a ghost slipping out of a spiritualist's cabinet.

"Mona Lisa, Mona Lisa, men have named you. You're so like the lady with the mystic smile ..."

Deborah's mystic smile was a grimace, teeth glistening with saliva from some point of light which struggled to penetrate the trees in the front yard. She felt them lengthen, bruising her lips, cutting them. Then she tasted her blood, salty and sour as razor metal.

She had no choice but to lie back, to spread her legs as wide as they would go. Her hips were unhinging, weren't they, as the pelvic bone rubberized into elastic? She heard her skirt rip up each side seam, listened as her panties tore and fell away, body straining against the fabrics as the thighs stretched farther apart, and her back arched until her head almost touched her heels.

Was she suffering some kind of seizure? Would she die, her baby unable to be born, perishing inside her? Would Lucas come home Monday morning to discover her corpse on the floor, gut swollen way beyond the usual death distension because the infant within was decomposing and setting off its own gases? Would those gases have pushed it halfway out of her, until it appeared as if she'd died while trying to squeeze out a giant turd with a face?

Her spine exploded, starting in the middle and going down, vertebrae by vertebrae. Her vagina detonated. The contractions pressed hard against the lower intestine and she was certain that shit would indeed be forced out, turned to jelly, to be followed by the lining of her colon like the greasy casing to a cheap butchershop sausage. She tried to breathe as she'd heard she was supposed to. Tried to push, bearing down with vaginal muscles she knew had really just been destroyed. Why did women go through with this? Why did they allow men to put them into such an excruciating state?

She'd been born with teeth. She'd bitten through her own umbilical cord, chewing it relentlessly when she'd been born herself, the midwife pulling it from her tiny mouth like a piece of cherry licorice. This baby was biting her, had to be. Scratching at her, too, with fully formed talons, trying to get out of her meat before it suffocated in it. She reached with her hands—paws—trying to claw at whatever was cutting her in half. She felt a roundness, wet, fuzzy, warm. Instead of attempting to wrestle it out of her to fling it across the room—god kill it KILL IT it's trying to kill me!—she guided it out, gasping, her hair wringing with foul-smelling sweat. The carpet stank of her shit and urine.

She tried to see it, felt down along its rubbery torso, had it been *fuzzy*? It was a family secret that some of the women of her clan had given birth to cubs instead of babies. To hairy, four-legged freaks. And of course she'd thought about this, after she'd discovered she was pregnant, worrying about it. Especially when Lucas asked her, "Will it be *human* or … ? God, Deborah, use a coat hanger, get radiation treatments, *something*"

There was no hair. No pointed ears, no paws. She found the miniature prick.

Deborah sighed. Almost laughed, relieved it was over. "Son …"

Then doubled up again, second wave of contractions worse than the first. Blood was black in the dark but she could smell it. Before she could reach down again, before she was able to do anything past convulsing, she fainted in mid-shriek.

Waking up the next morning she could only remember bears. That they went into hibernation in the winter and woke up as mothers.

Two she had, one which had ridden down in a tide of torture. The other had gushed out after who knew how long? Both wriggled beside her, covered in red-blotched yellow-green slime which, remarkably, neither had choked on without a midwife there to scrape it. Their little mouths were open and crying, voices like Siamese cats. She studied them in the dawn light which streamed through the window. No paws, no fur, no sharp teeth in those tiny round mouths. Both were male. Both were perfect. Human.

Deborah had done it on her own and was proud. It startled her to see her legs turned backward, tweaked the wrong direction at the knees: a bitch dog's. Her hands were still paws and there was a longish brunette down on her breasts and on her flattened, sagging belly. It was the most she'd ever transformed before. She saw a drop of milk on her sore right nipple.

"Are my sons hungry?" Her voice came out throatier than she'd heard it before. A cross between a growl and a purr. She kneaded her breasts but found she was only lactating on one side. Did this mean she couldn't feed both of them?

Well, one would have to wait. Picking up a baby she began to nurse it. The other cried even harder, desperate for nourishment. The sound was needles in Deborah's ears.

"Shh, Shshsh," she cooed as the first infant slurped at the teat.

But the second wouldn't stop crying, sobs hitching into hiccups, noise making her head spin till she thought she'd pass out again.

How many times would she go through this? And what if the first son drank all the milk so there was none left for his brother? She'd never known a baby's cry could be so piercing, so deafening.

This was survival, wasn't it? The way mothers in the wild rooted out part of the litter when they couldn't sustain them all. Or maybe they simply let them starve. But she'd have to listen to that for a long time before this second child died.

"Quiet. Hush!" she shouted, and thought *oh, night's back so soon?* Because she'd seen the room go dark again.

Before she knew it she tasted blood. From her teeth cutting her lips again? No, this was not a liquid from the self. With it was a flesh tenderer than any she'd ever had. Small bones crunched between her teeth.

Strange thing was she hadn't bitten into the baby who was crying but into the one she was holding, nursing at her breast. There was a hole in its head. Nature must have done this, Deborah reasoned. This was feral motherly instinct.

No way could she turn back now. Couldn't have Lucas coming home and seeing what she'd done. And the doctor had never said she was going to have twins. She nursed the crying one till it went to sleep. Then she finished eating Harry's brother. Later she stumbled into the bathroom and vomited out a miniature hand, five pink fingers like a starfish.

Things so small flushed easily.

Some experts said that babies were remarkably keen, that they remembered things that happened before they developed proper egos and prior to being able to think in words as opposed to pure thought. They might not understand what memories were but everything was stored somewhere in the head and soul.

Harry had walked through Cambodia, seen the god dancing among the dead, recognized his own face. And he'd subconsciously accepted it. Because somehow he'd always known he had another half somewhere. He'd been searching for it in every orifice he'd ever fucked, seeking the womb it might be hiding in, waiting to be reborn or re-dead. He'd watched things crawl from everything which either was a vagina or just resembled one: crabs, maggots, blood flukes, cockroaches, even a fairly large rat once. He knew that some religions believed you could be born again into a lower form of life. Reincarnation wasn't usually further qualified as having to come from a "living" cunt. Perhaps any hole would do. Because it was dark and damp, where a soul could lurk till it was time for it.

God lifted an arm to gaze into the eyes of the cobra coiling there.

Shiva said aloud to Harry, "Yes, I'm your other half. But I am the other half of everything."

Chapter 14

"Nine hounds unleashed
on a hare,
the body's lusts
cry out:
Let go!
Let go!
Let go! Let go!
cry the lusts
of the mind.
Will my heart reach you,
O lord of the meeting rivers,
before the sensual bitches
touch and overtake?
—Poem to Shiva
Basavanna

Former Russian Communists might have currently been trying to get MacDonald's franchises, and the former Red Guard in China might have been selling bootlegged Nine Inch Nails CD's. But apparently there really were some old Khmer Rouge still running around in creaking guerilla mode in Northwest Cambodia.

There was a crack, and a bullet missed Vezat's head, instead taking out a massive orange and black striped orchid. Another shot ripped into the canteen dangling from the hip of a

Vietnamese merc named Phan. The men cursed and ducked for cover, looking up to see where the shots were coming from. Ruiz squinted, jerked up his M-16, and pumped a couple of replies into the trees. One body came down from the branches, landed with a thick *whoooff!* and heavy thud in a clutch of wild poppies.

Everybody pointed weapons up toward the branches. There were no other shots.

"Lone sniper," Ruiz said.

The man had been wounded almost too harmlessly in the arm. But he'd broken his leg in two places falling from the tree. Elliot could see the fellow had to be sixty if he was a day. Gums dark from chewing betel for too many years, no teeth, a few white hairs springing three inches from his turkey-necked chin. He was still wearing the rags from the black clothes he'd worn as *a khmau,* one of the Rouge's specialty killers.

So, not all the mass executioners retired after watching the Pol Pot trial on television, fascinated by the unfolding drama like it was a daily soap opera. Maybe he didn't know the infamous devil was dead.

Still, they approached him respectfully enough. Old bastard might have killed them all. Well, might have managed to kill one or two of them maybe.

Monivong grinned. "Former Pol Pot stooge, like me. Only he doesn't have the smarts to stop kicking a dead horse."

"Ask him if he knows where Phnom Yohp is," Elliot told the Khmer merc.

The old revolutionary just heard the name *Phnom Yohp* and began chattering, shaking his grizzled head, eyes bulging with fright. How had he possibly gotten himself into that tree to begin with?

Saab shot the man in the head. Elliot jerked around.

"Why'd you do that? He might have told us something."

Saab glanced at him blandly. "Like what? We're almost there anyway. And he killed Phan's canteen so he deserved to die. What was a man that old going to do with a broken leg and a gunshot wound in the jungle, but attract every blood-sucking insect and flesh-poison within miles. And we weren't going to carry him with us, right?"

They moved out. Elliot asked Monivong, "What did that old man say?"

"He said 'Oh, don't go there! Place is haunted!' But, shit, I could have told you that much," Monivong replied.

The Cambodian opened his pack and took out a wrapped delicacy.

"Been saving this."

Vezat wrinkled his big nose. "What's that, a dog sandwich?"

"No, Cambodians don't eat dog. That's a nasty Vietnamese habit," Monivong said, grinning lopsidedly at Phan when the man turned a glowering face at him. "This is *pong tea kon*, an egg duck baby."

Elliot's stomach turned, knowing what that was.

Monivong explained to Vezat. "Duck mama sits on eggs for eighteen days. The best eggs have great big chicks inside by then. Eat with pepper, salt, lemon, some mint. Tender meat, lots of protein. Yum! Want a bite?"

Monivong thrust it at him, showing him where he'd already crunched down. Vezat could barely see little wings and twig feet. "I got the head but still plenty of good stuff left."

"I'd think I'd rather have the dog sandwich," Vezat said, turning a bit green.

But then the near hundred percent humidity had been making him sick all morning. He'd been taking anti-nausea pills like candy. He was new to merc-work in Asia. He'd only served in the Middle East where the air was hot but dry.

Monivong chuckled. "Your people eat snails and I don't think that's much better than dining on leeches. And you favor puddings and sausages made with blood. And truffles which are just a smelly fungus like what I try to keep from growing on my feet."

Vezat stopped and put his hand over his mouth for a moment. Elliot thought the man was going to hurl.

Phan blinked at Vezat. He reached into his pack. "You really want a dog sandwich?"

Vezat let loose, proving El right.

It was late in the afternoon when they reached the village. It started to rain, practically from a clear sky. That is to say, as much of a clear sky as you could see when you were in the jungle. The drops didn't begin one at a time as rain did in other parts of the world. It descended in sudden sheets, folding branches and whole plants down in submission.

"How can we be sure this is the right place?" Elliot asked, confused, seeing nobody moving around. In such a downpour, they would have hurried into the huts, more than likely.

But there were two long rows of men sitting on the ground in front of the huts. Still and silent as the Buddhas in the Pak Ou caves back in Laos. As the afflicted Thai children on the streets of Bangkok. All of these several dozen people appeared to be in their late twenties or thirties. Every one was maimed in some way. Apparently many had once worn prosthetic limbs but they didn't now. These were left in piles in the middle of the street, like cast-off weapons by those who have suddenly taken up a peaceful path. The quickening mud rolled across the plastic flesh, and termites and wood lice had obviously been at the wooden ones. How long had they been sitting there?

Saab smiled tightly, unbuckled the pack he carried to set it gently down on the ground, unshouldered his rifle, then unholstered his favorite Smith and Wesson combat magnum, blue satin. Many preferred European makes with glottal stop names, *-umlaut* words that made the bearer feel like a real Schuzstaffel Reichsprotektor. But Saab was all-American and always had been. He casually pulled out a box of shells as well. What the hell; it wasn't as if he wouldn't have time and leisure to reload again and again. His smile uncoiled like a length of prime hangman's rope. "Oh, yeah. Dis be da place. The Chinese vampire sing, *Tao, Ta-a-a-o. Daylight come and me wanna go home!*""

He shouted to the other men through the deafening rain, "Head shots only. Fast and clean. Check the huts."

Elliot scanned the village quickly. There was no evidence of the children they'd seen earlier picking flowers in the minefield. Not seeing anyone up and about. No one able-bodied. No one full-bodied, with two arms and legs, two eyes and ears, ten fingers and ten toes. Everyone was missing *something*. And no one rose to defend themselves.

From what he'd seen of whatever this scourge out of Phnom Yohp was, no one thus affected ever did anything again but beam their smiles off into space. And these men were that way, sitting there, haloes casting prismatic arcs through the rain that cascaded onto their heads, down across their shoulders. Some inner holiness made rainbows in the storm.

Who were they fighting here? That is, who was going to be fighting back here? Which was what Elliot had always done: fight people who fought back. That was what mercs did. They went boy-scouting through private wars or in big ones if the regular army grunts weren't doing the job right. They weren't simply assassins. Nor were they terrorists: that took idealogy.

The merc only cared that the side win that was paying him. Looked better on the resume that way.

(He had an embarrassing memory of being in a helicoptor in Saigon, using the butt end of his rifle or the solid toes of his boots to crush the fingers of yellow women trying to board. And the slogging through rice paddies, being told how easy it was to kill after the first one ... Of having waited for the guilt and shame which never came because *it had gotten easy*. And how it was dehumanizing but he'd always doubted he was totally human to begin with. But this was over twenty years later, and he hadn't hurt anyone since who hadn't been shooting at him. No, because he'd had enough of those ghosts swirling in his face. And there was no more room behind the eye in the ruined half of his head for anymore.)

Hadn't hurt anyone since who hadn't been shooting at him? What about Embe? He'd thrust a machete through her heart, killing a queen who may only have wanted to love him because they were both shifters. Killed her—easy. *Easy. Second-fucking-nature.*

The colonel, Vezat, Monivong, Ruiz, and Phan began walking down the road through the village, slowly, so they wouldn't slide through the rising mud. Elliot heard guns being emptied, saw skulls coming apart like cheap movie effects, blood and brains swirling in the circles of the haloes which ringed their owners' heads like planetary atmospheres chunked with asteroids, then being scooped away in the heavy sheets of water, the red tinting the mud.

And he saw her. The beautiful woman from beside the sacred river. From the jungle. He knew it was her because of the four tits. First she appeared beside a hut, then vanished. Then behind Monivong as he reloaded, disappearing again. Then at the end of the road before her exquisite, familiar, sorrowful visage dissipated into sodden air, some haunting misty remnant of her hands gesturing, beckoning, summoning.

Elliot turned and turned, saw her one more time, back in the jungle, moving away into a jumbled stand of sugar palms. And she was dry! He glanced at the mercs. They were blasting away and not paying him any mind. But soon Saab would have to notice that Elliot wasn't following orders.

No, Elliot wasn't. He was picking up the pack Gestetner had been toting all the way from Bangkok. He was running away into the jungle, after that mysterious beauty.

He ran, hugging the pack to his chest, the buckles catching on the ropes of 7.62-millimeter ammunition which crisscrossed his jacket.

And he was thinking that the poor kid in there had to be suffocating. Even if she was in a coma or some other state of suspended animation, kids still had to breathe, right? So he stopped, gasping for his own air through the ocean the sky was dumping on him. He set the pack on the ground and undid the fasteners. Gasped again, indeed seeing the child inside as he opened it up. Not a dream, as he'd hoped it would turn out to be.

She had rainbows of her own, seeming to spark from her scalp where the rain slicked down her black hair, radiating up in pretty colors from the gruesome scars she bore.

"Can you hear me, little girl?" he cried out to her. Thinking that maybe he ought to shake her but afraid that such mistreatment of her might constitute some kind of sacrilege. Should he kiss her, lightly on the lips? No denying this was a sleeping beauty, but he'd never been anyone's idea of Prince Charming. And this was only a baby and he was no pedaphile.

He put his fingers close to her nostrils and could definitely feel her breath. The placid face just smiled up at his, eyes shut like tiny lacquered fans brushing feathered edges toward her cheek bones.

He stared at the damage on her, seeing it quite clearly now, not as he had the other night, at a distance in the dark. He stared at that hand Saab had been touching.

(Some of my best work, the colonel had said.)

Which really made Elliot shiver. In his life he'd seen some of the worst cruelty ever deliberately done to young living flesh. His own mother had abused her children. He didn't escape the sight of kids getting tortured when he fled her to go to Vietnam. In Somalia, seeing a small child that was spit-roasted for some starving freak's dinner. In Rwanda where their heads bobbed in the water like fishing lures. In Egypt where little girls had their clitorises removed to keep them pure till marriage, (often ruining their urethras so they couldn't help pissing themselves all the time afterward), sometimes the entire labia majora being scraped out so that no sign of genital 'femaleness' remained. And little boys had their testicles clipped so they would sing sweetly to Allah forever. And then up in—Iraq? Iran? One of those countries where beggars still swarmed, where the Koran's edict to give alms when asked was still honored … and children drew lots to see where they would be maimed so they would make better wage-earning gamins. Children in Bosnia raped repeatedly and buried alive in pits. Girl babies in Chinese orphanages starved or smothered and in Hindu homes 'accidentally' caught on fire in the kitchen because only males were valued. In other, supposedly enlightened, countries, conceived and born just to produce organs for an older, sickly, sibling. *There weren't any children inside that compound we sent the sarin gas into, were there? Not like Waco where eighteen kids burned alive …* And Christ what the hell had been done to those fingers to make them look like scrimshaw, like some twisted shamanistic rune-reading pick-up sticks? He'd known Saab was a kink although he'd never guessed the man was into anything this vile.

Elliot lifted her out of the pack and then resumed running, carrying her in his arms. Squinting through the rain, he'd searched, seen the dry-as-a-bone woman ahead, gesturing *this way, this way* and followed her, deeper into the jungle and more uphill. Seeing here and there in the undergrowth a carved monolith of cobras. Or stone bodies part angelic/ part puking, delirium-tremens hallucination emerging halfway through the roots of a monstrous tree. One that was either nearly convinced to releasing them, or seducing them farther into an embrace which must eventually crush or wear them away.

The girl was limp in his arms. It occurred to him he'd never held a child before. No wait, just not a living child. There'd been a little montagnard he'd pulled from a collapsed tunnel near Pleiku, skinny arms wrapped around a blowgun. He'd put his fingers to the boy's nostrils but felt no breath. He tried to do mouth to mouth but couldn't jumpstart the kid. He remembered having just sat there, shaking because the boy was still so warm, wondering why he couldn't have gotten there five minutes sooner.

(The kid looked out his eye sometimes, from the ruined half of Elliot's face. Seeing enemies everywhere, maybe looking for his blowgun.)

Up ahead Elliot spied the shape of a gateway, a gray mass of creatures beyond, gorgeous and grotesque, undulating in the rain as if bathing in it, screwing one another in it. But he didn't see the woman who'd been leading him. What did that matter now, he thought, trying to glance up at the sky to see if the storm was nearly over or if it was darker still at all the horizons. The colonel must finally be looking for him. He wanted to get this girl into shelter so she wouldn't get pneumonia. Not that he knew if she could even *get* sick.

He tried not to look at the carvings. Which was all they were. Not living ghastly hybrids in the middle of some orgy. Just a lot of weird shit cut into the temple walls. But, still, too much like ghosts in scar tissue when he'd *thought* they were jiggling, sloshing, banging each other with such a fierce finesse.

Yet they seemed to turn, didn't they? As he rushed past with the girl. Out of the corner of his eye, in almost subliminally perverse peripheral. Bestial profiles swiveled slightly, full faces pouted, pelvises tilted.

Eyes narrowed. Tongues waggled through fangs behind the lushest of lips.

What you got there? What you got there, ghostface? A present for us ... ?

Thunder bellowed from the sky, bouncing in a roar off the ancient walls, the ramshackle skew of dimensions in the courtyard producing the accoustics of ricocheting lightning bolts. It echoed like mortar right beside Elliot's head and he threw himself the opposite way out of habit, sure the colonel and the other mercs had just arrived. He slipped on a carpet of humus. He hugged the girl tighter to his chest, her face buried in his shoulder for safety. Elliot hoped she didn't strangle on the ammunition belts strung there. He wished he'd taken them off, flung them away when he'd first decided to escape this fucked-up deal. Then he scrambled back up, seeing a hole in a wall revealed in another streak of lightning, maybe actually a doorway leading inside. Elliot took it, keeping his head down, feeling the narrowness of a cool, rotten-smelling corridor, wishing he'd kept a flashlight.

Then he suffered a jolting sense of *dèjá vu*. He stumbled into a wall, forcing him to turn, and then all of a sudden the place opened up. There were lit candles everywhere. And the temple was inhabited. But not with thousands of Buddha statues.

This was where the other members of the village were. Most were women amputees, about thirty of them, looking sad but composed, as if they knew what had become of the men of Phnom Yohp but left it to the graces of destiny. And twenty-five small children sat on the floor, playing with some cobras.

In the shadows were saffron-robed … whats? Were those humans? Not much more so than the beings chiseled in stone outside. *Hissssssss*. Too-long necks and heads. No noses. Flat, wide eyes. Mouths which grinned too much and too far.

Elliot wasn't sure he should set the girl down. There were snakes in here, for chrissakes. But one of the women crabbed forward and offered a scrap of a blanket.

The women went to their knees—those that had them. They pressed their faces to the ground. As another woman began to glide across the floor from what must have been a separate entrance.

It was the beautiful one who'd led him there. Closer, and in the candlelight, he saw her four full breasts and the penis. Biggest dick he'd ever seen, save for one other. Those breasts made him hard, unable to help thinking about what it would be like to fuck those quadruplet mammaries, cock squeezed as if between four planets or four galaxies.

But there was something too familiar about that face.

"Don't you recognize me, El? I'm Harry."

Elliot felt queasy. Hell, he felt violently nauseous at the sound of that voice as it came alongside the strenuous, nearly overbearing horniness he felt. No, those things weren't meant to go together, the urge to screw an array of somic tits and the sound of his brother's voice.

The other problem was that the words weren't spoken from the hermaphrodite's mouth. They came out of the lips that had formed in the scar tissue on the side of Elliot's face.

Chapter 15

"King Soma, have mercy on us … Passion and fury are stirred up. O drop of Soma, do not hand us over to the total pleasure of the enemy."
—The Rig Veda

Monivong didn't know what was the matter. It wasn't like these men could see him. Looking down into their eyes he recognized blindness. He was pretty certain these were the adults of children he and his comrades had tortured back in the '70s. The offspring of those who had been so self-righteous that they couldn't be forced to run and heel like whipped curs. It was why they had all needed to be exterminated, every man and woman above the age of about fourteen.

Not that he had any use for the crap he'd believed then, that revolutionary diarrhea about new worlds and old worlds and dogshit dogma. His faith was in the money he kept in banks in Singapore and Zurich.

But there was a change in Monivong as he walked down the line, blasting, pop pop POP! He'd done this activity a thousand times; he could likely do it in his sleep. The rain was the only thing that kept the blood and viscera off him—except for what sloshed across his boots. He got the feeling these assholes still weren't cooperating, with or without being conscious. They were withholding something from his owning of their deaths.

Laughing at him in the cordite smoke. Possessing an essence he couldn't take no matter what he did to them.

The small bag around Monivong's neck scratched at his throat some. This was the only item he'd owned as a boy. He'd taken it from the body of a woman in a small Catholic chapel outside Phnom Penh, shortly before the Rouge marched into that city and forced everybody out. He'd stepped up behind where she sat kneeling in front of flickering candles, swinging his machete down into her back. He struck again and again, long after she was dead, just to see how much spattered blood it took to put out most of the candles. Then he'd taken her decapitated head and held it up—drip, drip—to snuff out the others. She'd been his first kill. The bag was what she'd kept her rosary in. He'd removed the rosary, crushing each bead beneath the heel of his boots, swearing that before the month was out, he'd kill that same number of people. He'd used the bag ever since to keep the essences of the deaths he'd made. The only possession he was allowed and only that because he hid it under his shirt.

He didn't have time, as a soldier, to stop with each one and manually pinch off a bit of their leaping souls. So he willed them into the bag.

It was difficult for a peasant boy, no matter how full of revolutionary zeal he was, to own absolutely nothing. To see how much others had and, hating them for it, resolve never to have anything himself. This wasn't so much. And how much could those essences be said to be worth? Nothing, except to him who'd earned them. He figured he hadn't sold out his honor.

Now he owned a great deal. He wasn't a rebel anymore. Being a merc had widened his horizons. He remained a warrior because it was thrilling. It was lucrative. And, till now, had kept him out of Cambodia. He hadn't even understood that he might be racing to other wars around the world just so he wouldn't have to come home, where who knew what karma waited to find his head ... or where whatever enemies—living or dead—waited to exact their revenge.

He tried willing these sparkling halo deaths into his bag. They wouldn't go. He couldn't get a grip on them. It wasn't the rain; he'd fought and killed in plenty of rain in the past. He'd fought on snow in the Himalayas and in dust storms in the Gobi Desert. Weather conditions never affected his capacity to command that a part of their spirits kowtow to him, since he'd driven their very lives into submission.

"Damn you all," Monivong muttered under his breath, lips sputtering raindrops.

Then he looked down at his feet ... Well, it was just mud! The storm made it swirl and then separate, congeal together with stiff skull-stuff and then spatter apart, as if he'd shot down at the ground instead of up at them.

But he shuddered, seeing it coil. Slither. Move around his boots, scooching up his legs. A piece of brainpan flaring like the back of a cobra's head, splinter of spinal cord sticking out like a venomous tongue. He grew so unnerved he aimed down at his leg—in some sort of fit, mind you, a seizure of terror so profound he couldn't control his arm—and fired at the cobra he spied which swayed, ready to strike at his balls. BLAM!

"Monivong! You trying to shoot your nuts off? Ought to let you!" Phan snatched at the smoking barrel.

Monivong stared, first at his barely-lucky crotch, where he could feel the scrotum withering in on itself in realization of how close it had just come to resembling a fully-masticated egg duck baby, then at the Vietnamese, then back at his crotch.

"Gun jerked," he told the other man, voice smooth, glancing at the tongue which lay steaming in the mud, having come apart with teeth and mouth-gum gummy bears from Phan's last head shot. Half an eyeball—bisected cleanly by a sharp piece of cheekbone, as opposed to merely having popped like a surprised dumpling—watched him from the dead man's lap. The colors from the halo were drizzling down around it, making the sort of sappy bell-like cartoon music common to old American Disney films. "I'll change weapons now."

Monivong reached into his jacket to retrieve a second pistol, glad to have something to do with his hand, a place to put it to conceal its slight tremor.

What's the matter with you? Getting old? Worse … SOFT?

"Place is haunted!" the old sniper had warned him.

Shit, could have told you that much.

Why did rain streaming through thatch roofs and hut walls, which were made of palm mats, have to hiss?

They killed them all. It was the first time Monivong had killed so many people without having an erection when he was finished. That Frenchman had one. Monivong saw him step behind a hut for a couple of minutes.

The rain stopped as abruptly as it had begun. The sun seemed to come through the treetops like a blazing mortar.

"No women or children here," the colonel said, rubbing a sizable clot of blood and tissue from his forehead, examining it for a moment, like one might snot they'd just picked from their own nose before flicking it away. "They're hiding somewhere. And we've got to find them. So we're going to start looking. Throughout every square inch of jungle in a quarter-mile radius first. Then a half-mile. So on as necessary."

Not that Saab really cared whether or not he totally wiped them out as Tak had ordered. What he really wanted now was the Soma. Tak hadn't mentioned that. Naturally! A drug lord needs drugs which bring back repeat customers, necessary for any truly profitable business. He'd no use for a substance that hooked its victims as immediately as crack did but which then afterward they had no desire for. It was self-limiting. But Gestetner had a use for it, all right.

"Where's Tyler?" he asked, looking down the ruined-doll rows of slaughtered villagers.

The man was nowhere to be seen. Had he just stepped beside a tree or a hut to piss? Vezat had but he was back.

"El?" he called out. No answer. "Son of a bitch."

At first he couldn't believe it. Not Elliot Tyler. Damn, sometimes guys just took to yellow and that was that.

Then he wondered, what if Tyler was secretly working for somebody else? What if El had also gone there specifically for the Soma? Saab couldn't let him do that.

"Okay, let's go. If anyone sees Tyler, apprehend and subdue. Bring him to me. Oh, and if you see my pack? I want that back, too."

"I have lots to spare, Colonel," Vezat offered. "Rations, first aid, even socks I'll split with you. Also a Sig-Sauer, barely broken in."

"No thanks. I need MY pack," Saab replied.

No one would dare ask why. But he shrugged, grinned, and told them anyway.

"Got to have it. My girlfriend's in there."

They didn't search for more than a few hours—slow going in the swampy areas the storm had created. Thankfully, it *was* a mountain so most of the water had continued on downhill. After it was fully dark they returned to the village to set up camp for the night. Besides, more clouds had rolled in, obscuring the lopsided moon. Just in case it stormed more, at least they could stay in the huts and have a roof over their heads. It had rained in the village again since the mercs left to nose out the drug source.

"Someone's been here," Saab stated, standing with his hands on his hips, surveying the evident change in the way they'd left Phnom Yohp.

It was an obvious remark and he knew it. The other soldiers could easily see that things weren't the same. He said it more in surprise to himself, that any of the surviving villagers would have mustered up the balls to return—however briefly.

Before they'd gone a'hunting, they'd stripped the bodies of the slaughtered village men naked, then placed them into a sloppy pile, spritzed some fuel over them and set them alight. But they hadn't exactly been carrying a bunch of gas cans; there wasn't much. It had been burning when they left, but drizzle must have put that out so that some of the victims hadn't burned at all.

"Who peeled them?" asked Ruiz of no one in particular.

Vezat rubbed his nose. "Why did they do that?"

"And what did they do with the skins?" Phan queried, adding to the number of questions.

They could see that even the bodies that were burned had been flayed first. There were fewer split places where the flesh would have burst in the heat, allowing fat and blood to run out. It resulted in far less suppuration. The end result reminded them of roasted steak and sweetbreads. Here and there a hand or a foot would show itself as unburned, its outer layer missing.

Stranger still was the veil of mosquitoes hovering in on the fresh carnage. Not that it was odd to see such winged bloodsuckers descend, but the spectrum band of colors which radiated through them was eerie. Like vampiric aurora borealis. What Dracula might take on if he bit the apostles.

Saab thought of the stupid Chinese vampire joke he'd made before they'd begun shooting. He studied the ground, but could see no footprints from people having come to do this grisly work and then leaving. The rain had washed them away.

He pondered thoughtfully on how difficult it would be for a woman to slice off the epidermis of her dead husband. Especially if she didn't have hands to hold the blade with. Perhaps she'd used her feet. Or ... was it possible ... her mouth? He knew that the women must have done it, and he also knew there wasn't a one of them without crippling of some kind. And the corpses flayed here had been deftly done.

Damn, he just wished he could have watched that. Must have been fascinating.

Was there something significant about the skins of those who'd taken the Soma? Tyler would steal his pack, thieving rectum parasite. After all he'd done for El, too. Damn, he'd gone to great lengths to acquire the teenaged Bangkok whore, barely saving her when that bitch at the gallery wanted to have her burned as a test for artistic authenticity.

Now was a different matter. Saab would have liked to see what happened if he did this skin trick to the girl inside that pack.

Chapter 16

" … whoso buys it shall have no share
in the world to come; evil then was
that they sold themselves …"
—The Koran

It was during the Gulf War that Vezat learned what he was. He wasn't but nineteen when he joined the French army, only two months before Saddam Hussein invaded Kuwait. He went over with the contingent which France supplied the U.N.

He didn't ask himself why he was there, why he'd decided to become a soldier. He knew it was from patriotic inspiration. From having helped out in a Parisian charity hospital when he was eighteen. The ward he was assigned to was filled with men, mostly old, all crippled in one way or another. And there were three who always sat together, veterans of Algierian conflict back in the '50s.

There was a specific incident: he'd been emptying bed pans and scrubbing floors where the contents of such pans had sloshed over. Vezat had also been eavesdropping a little.

The first vet, a man named Mallet who only had legs down to just above the knees, said, "Remember when we found poor Verley? Out in the desert with his eyelids sliced off?"

"Dry and white as chalk those eyeballs were, shrunken till they fairly rolled around in the wide sockets every time he tried to scream." The second vet was Donnadieu, a bit withered himself. Left leg gone up into the pelvis, left arm lost all the way through the shoulder. He'd lost some ribs on that side, too, and the metal they'd used to replace the ribs with provided no real contour to the flesh but only held in the organs. He looked to be half a man, as if he'd been bisected—vertically instead of horizontally.

Vezat knew from having to bathe him that Donnedieu had only the right testicle and half a penis, looking as if some medical student had cleanly sliced off half of it for a vivesection project.

Mallet nodded, stump tapping in his wheelchair to the rhythm of a radio belonging to one of the orderlies. "But he couldn't scream because the sun had roasted his tongue into a thin pink noodle."

The third vet was called de Givray, and he didn't say much to add to this conversation. He just narrowed his eyes, bobbing his head in assent. Which made the cup strapped under the upper teeth spill out silvery trickles of saliva. de Givray had no jawbone, no chin. The constant noises of gurgling and spewling as his phantom soft palate tried to swallow (but couldn't) kept most of the other volunteers at bay. But not Vezat. His other injuries were merely the loss of both hands and feet. The ends of these had been pared nearly as sharp as pencils points. It amazed Vezat to watch these protuberances lay still and flaccid most times, then suddenly grow rigid as erections when de Givray was excited by the talk.

"Was it any wonder we hated those filthy Algerians?" asked Donnedieu.

"So we caught that rebel bitch and were determined to make her tell us who the bastards were that did that to our pal Verley!" declared Mallet.

"Hooked her up to electrodes and poured on the juice," Donnedieu said, eyes nothing but thin slits revealing yellow schlerota.

de Givray was nodding furiously, wrists and ankles penetrating the air with savage emotion. The spittle from his cup sloshed out onto the bib arranged across his breastbone. Vezat came over to wipe it up for him and set the cup right again. Mallet pounded his fists against his abbreviated thighs. "She shrieked and struggled so hard the electrodes yanked out both nipples and half her clit. Which was funny actually, considering the Muslim girls were all *sunna*'d. So maybe she was a Christian."

Donnedieu reached his hand into his right pants pocket and pulled out a strange scrap, resembling a bit of black eelskin. "Still rub it whenever I need luck, too."

"So … " Vezat began and then shut up quickly as their eyes turned to him.

"Go on, boy. So … what?" asked Mallet mildly.

"Did the Algerians … ?"

Vezat couldn't bring himself to say it. It seemed too cruel.

Donnedieu finished for him. "Did the Algerians do this to us?"

Vezat knew he was turning very red-faced as he nodded.

"No," Donnedieu replied, grinning. "We were attending a reunion of the paratroopers from the North African group a few years back. Had too much to drink. Decided to all go jumping, and the three of us were so inebriated we forgot our parachutes! Lucky the pilot was also intoxicated and hadn't flown too high."

de Givry began laughing so hard he started choking on his drool. One of the wires for affixing his spittle cup was inhaled partway down his throat, and Vezet had to put fingers down after it.

"Don't let our stories frighten you, son," Mallet told him. "Military's a great way to see the world."

de Givry laid one of those penile wrists on Vezat's arm as Donnedieu said, "You're too strong a lad to be here, cleaning up after our shit."

Vezat joined with them in a spontaneous singing of 'La Marseillaise' in which eventually every man on the ward entered into. Even de Givry hummed and gargled the melody, what surely the famous French pride number must have sounded like if sung while being flushed down a toilet.

Vezat sent them postcards from the Middle East. Saw very little action himself. Heard the tanks booming and the rockets burning sky overhead, to finally end up so far away he never heard them strike their targets. Seldom even saw anybody wounded. Stared at the Saudi desert a great deal. Soon he grew quite hypnotized by the vast stretches of nothing. No, not nothing, he would remind himself as he gazed. Its highlights were rare but salient, points of scenery few in number, which made them all the more special for it. He could focus on one thing and it would transform into a mandala. He would stare at it until his eyes watered, until his vision turned blood red, and then after that turned white. He might be looking at something as grand as a mosque or as ordinary as a crippled beggar asking for *zakat*, the legal charity.

Six men had gone out in a jeep from the French outpost southwest of Khadhra, to make the relatively short jaunt to the U.S. G.I.s sitting northeast of Truba, there to make a switch of brandy for whiskey.

An Iraqi plane had crashed near them, shot down by the Americans. They'd seen it coming and leaped out of the jeep, managing to cross a dune for some shelter before the plane actually struck the ground. A kid by the name of Mercier was too slow and had been peppered by metal pits from the plane's near-disintegration. He lay gasping for breath, face of soft scrambled eggs, no eyes/no lips/no nose. Vezat noted that he could only hear the ragged, self-defeating inhales. There were no exhales. Very soon the inhales stopped, too.

The jeep was burning. They could hear the bottles of fine brandy exploding one by one, as the fire reached them where they'd been stowed under the seats.

"We're walking," said the highest rank among them, a lieutenant named Ouellet. He shook sand out of his red hair and then motioned in a direction for them to follow.

"*Mon Dieu*!" Proulx huffed, narrow shoulders sagging.

Vezat blinked against the sun which was practically vibrating on the sand. They hadn't exactly come prepared for a stroll. The distance between the two stations was only about ten miles or so. But, after all, this was the desert, and they'd foolishly left their canteens behind to carry all the brandy they could.

How far had they gone? Seemed like hours and felt like twice the number of miles it should have been.

"They're going to laugh at us," Maci grumbled. He tried to examine the backside of himself, where something sharp but very tiny had gotten him in the ass as he launched himself across that dune. His fingers came away with some blood on them. "We look like amateurs."

"Trust me," Gendron growled back. A small piece had simply grazed him, tearing off a piece of his sleeve, revealing a tattoo which simple said *croc*. Meathook. "They won't laugh. Not with what happened to Mercier. They'll likely courtmartial us."

"Do you hear something?" asked Proulx, adjusting wire-rimmed glasses which had skewed during his jump.

Vezat cocked an ear. He did hear a faint bell. He inhaled as a scent came to him. The merest hint of almonds.

Maci pointed. "There!"

They just came out of the desert, no jeeps, no rifles of any kind. The dust didn't rise up from the movement of their feet and the legs of the camels. Their silhouettes against the sky didn't ripple in mirage. And when a cloud passed before the sun (probably smoke from the burning plane and jeep), setting the dunes in partial shadow, there was no glint off their copious jewelry.

For a lark, Vezat slipped on his nightvision goggles. But then he couldn't find them at all.

Once they were close enough, the soldiers could see the nomads all wore heavy facepaint: butterflies, moons with stars, lions, outlandish phoenixes, simple flowers. It reminded Vezat of kids getting decorated for the price of a few francs at a provincial fair back home.

Ouellet murmured to himself, "Here among the Bedouin? Blondes? And all young women."

Two were already sliding off a camel where they'd been sitting belly to back like spoons. The one riding behind had been rubbing her ample breasts across the other's shoulder blades. Ouellet couldn't believe their resemblance to the legendary Brigitte Bardot. It was impossible that a tribe of platinum-headed knockouts like these would be living in the Arabian Desert. It was too cinematic, ridiculous. Somebody must be making a movie. But now, in the middle of a war? They undid the clasps on their bodices. Pale, huge D-cup breasts heaved out, topped with pink quartz nipples.

"Drown here," one of them offered.

The other had gone down on her knees, unzipping the lieutenant's trousers. Finding his penis only partially responding, she took him into her pouty mouth.

Maci heard him. "I see no blondes. They're women, yes. Girls actually. But they're dark, all of them. And none wearing veils."

He didn't see the two bombshells. But he wondered why the Lieutenant's face went so slack.

An exotic beauty sidled up to Maci. Her sheer skirts showed she also wasn't wearing underwear.

"I wonder if her clit's been clipped," he mused. "If maybe she has no oily insides."

"Do you want it like that?" she asked in French, as she slipped her hand under his waistband at the back, gently stroking the minor wounds he'd received on his butt, then slipping her pinkie finger into his rectum.

Maci winced, then grinned, face going red from jaws to eyebrows. "Yeah, I've never had that before."

"Then so be it," she replied, removing her hand. She went down on her back, pulling up her flimsy skirts to show him.

Maci stared at the sleek moss. There was no strip of wrinkled oyster at the cleft. She'd tilted her pelvis so he could see the dark knot of asshole, the sewn-up gouge of vaginal tunnel with the opening maintained by the insertion of splinters of ivory in the infibulated vulva. He could see the small hole she pissed through. It was as if she'd been cored out with a potato peeler, then stitched up like the tunnel into a baked goose. The thought of how much that must have hurt made his scrotum itch. But he could see she ought to be tight enough.

Proulx shook his head defiantly. "What are you two talking about? They're not even girls. They're only dressed up that way. I've heard this sort of thing went on in this part of the world."

Proulx understood it had to be some Iraqi snare. Sending a troup of handsome young men out in harem costumes. They must be enemy soldiers. They would be armed to the teeth someplace, and you could bet your bottom sou on it. His own weapon had gone up with the jeep. (Actually, to his chagrin, his own weapon was going up now.)

Several of these danced around him, shimmying their shoulders, rotating rumps and jutting pelvises in perfect sensual cadence with music that had begun richly to imbue the air. Proulx saw dark cocks beneath the gauzy fabric of their skirts. One did a series of gymnastic leaps and ended up on the sand, positioned with his head down and ass presented up to the Frenchman. Proulx gasped and quickly rubbed his glasses clean. The skirt had flown up; the cavern between the boy's buttocks was shiny—with rose oil if Proulx's nose was any judge.

But Gendron couldn't see blonde goddesses or dark teenaged girls or fey cinnamon-sticked teenaged boys. He went down on his knees, reaching into his pocket.

"Bonbon, petite fille? Chocolat, garconnet? Baiser-baiser?"

The little girl and little boy, soft clothes so perfectly embroidered with pomegranites and palms, sweet fruit and shade, stepped forward shyly for the candy. He took one under each arm and walked across the rise of a rippled dune.

Vezat shivered even as sweat ran off him, sun blinding in the sky. He saw hemp rope flop down from a camel's hump. What perched there then used whatever still existed, jaws and a hand or a foot to hold onto the rope with, getting down to the ground as best they could. Legless hips made a wide path across the sand as arm stumps dragged them over to Vezat, weaving and flat, as if the body of a fat snake had passed there. Tight knots winked as abbreviated muscles worked. Unlike the others who were dressed in gaudy, if sheer, fabrics, these were naked. He could see every nuance of lapidaried bone end and trussed fleshy stubble.

A man with no legs and no buttocks flopped onto his tiger-striped face before Vezat, presenting the crinkly scar-ridged scoop around the scrap of anus. Another who had lost most of the bottom half of his face had the remainder sewn up into a twisted hole, which was all he had for features save for a pair of sandstone eyes. He worked the stripped mouth which had been painted around like the swirling hypnotic eye some mesmerists used to employ, and he mimed some action with it that instantly made Vezat hard despite his every attempt at feigning horror and even pity. A third presented an arm, shorn at the elbow, the end of which had been whittled further to resemble nothing less than an engorged cock, similar to de Givray's. He thrust with it, pulling it back, to leave nothing to the imagination about its function. His eyes had been painted as blooming roses and his tongue waggled through the banana painted on his lips.

Vezat wanted to kiss the first man's rectal canyon, feel the pulse of red intestine barely below the remaining back flesh. He wanted to stick himself into the second man's face crater in which whirred no teeth, lay no stubble of tongue. He wanted to bend forward for the third man's arm, taking it up to the shoulder, grinding against the ramparts of scars.

He'd heard Ouellet speak of blondes, Maci pronounce dark girls, Proulx blubber about boys, and Gendron offer sweets to babes. Where Gendron had gone off across the dunes with what had looked to Vezat to be a male amputee tucked under each arm, he now heard the sounds of children crying softly, petulantly. He could see Proulx on his knees, sandwiched between two trunks with heads, buggering the one in front of him and being buggered by the one behind. Maci was groaning in a tangle of wounded flippers, and Ouellet was laughing as he frolicked with war nightmares.

And still this got Vezat so hard, his own hand grabbing at himself in desperation. But he was backing away, as sickened as he was turned on, thinking, *this is my secret desire?*

Why do we all say we see different things yet I only see devastated warriors?

The one with the dick arm reached up and touched Vezat's face with it. "Great way to see the world, boy."

He could smell betadine, minty disenfectants, the stink of bloodied sweat that ran from phantom limbs. He glanced nervously toward the camel the three had descended from and saw a single scorpion crawl from an enlarged dromedary nostril.

He turned and ran. He heard the screams of the other men begin but wouldn't look. There were the sounds of snapping, like with crocodile jaws and broken backs. There were noises too wet for the desert, of suckings and splatters and shrieks that ended in loud splops. There were growls so deep they were almost below the register of a man's hearing, as if an earthquake were rumbling up from the bowels of the world. There were twitters of so high a wavelength they were practically up in dog whistle range. Vezat's head seemed to swell with it, everything in front of his eyes blazing red and then white.

But he kept running, not daring turn to peek behind him. He had a mental impression of jackals and a string of hungry moons. The caravan's bells reverberated, gone from faint tinkling to sepulchral tolling, the knells spreading out in echo as if reaching for deep space. Sand swirled around his feet, sucking at his boots, trying to pull him down. He actually had to leap across several virtual chasms of vortices, several feet across and moving down as if the sand were in a gigantic hourglass, momentum being all that kept him from falling in.

He still had his erection, straining inside his fatigues, bumping painfully right to left. It resisted withering even as the former scent of almonds metamorphosed into a gagging reek of carrion, sulphur, and shit.

(Well, much of that—toned down, of course—was what he recalled from the hospital. The surface of his mind tried to abhor it, but the deeper part that found the damaged bodies of his fellow men to be alluring also found the stench to be a kink.)

How Vezat made it back to the base he couldn't say. He'd been overcome with the sun, with dehydration. They told him he'd been hallucinating, babbling. Where were Lieutenant Ouellet and the others? A search party never found Ouellet, Maci, Proulx, or Gendron. Although they did locate the wreckage of the Iraqi plane and, near that, Mercier's body.

"There was a caravan of ghouls," Vezat tried to tell them from his swollen, sunburned lips.

"There was a biochemical agent on board the Iraqi plane. You were exposed to that," they tried to explain.

Vezat's eyes were sun-blasted and sand-ground. Yet he could see the others in the field hospital. Mostly there for dysentery or Middle Eastern venereal complaints, there was one soldier in the bed next to his. There had been an explosion and the man had lost most of the right side of his body. He lay swaddled up like a slice of Egyptian mummy, stinking of disinfectants and of his waste products being passed into catheters.

"Please, don't leave me next to him," Vezat whined. Then his voice dropped to a rasping, dune-clogged whisper. "He looks like them."

The doctors doped Vezat up, to kill the pain of blisters the sun had given him and to quiet him. He lay upon his cot, stuporized, gazing from time to time at the burst-pruned form of the injured man, afraid to close his eyes yet at the same time glad—in a terrible, shame-ridden, self-hating way—that they hadn't moved him.

Vezat woke up with a start, in the jungle, hearing rain on the thatch roof. He'd been dreaming. He'd been out in that pile of partially burned bodies in the center of the village. The sounds had been loosely liquid sighs, hocking noises like paper being wadded up, and a *shshufffff shshufffff* of organs rearranging to accommodate other—more insistent—organs.

Voices murmured over and over, "*Sohm, sohm, sohm, sohm.*"

Vezat knew only a couple words in Khmer. This word was for *please*. Please please ... what?

And he heard, "Wia neuv ch'ngaay te? Wia neuv ch'ngaay te?"

Vezat had no idea what that meant. He only knew he was arching his back as much as he could from within the center of this collection of burned bodies. Turning his head left right, down in a reverent bow, hearing the bones in his neck creak. He was stretching his lips as wide as they would go, listening as his tongue seemed to SNAP! SNAP! like a whip. He was lifting his ass and twisting at the waist until his ribs seemed threaded like a twist-off bottle cap, and he was scissoring his legs like a swimmer in the midst of some languid midnight river crossing. His entire body thrummed in pain, ached with deep groin joy, seemed both to float and to fall in nauseous arousal. He gasped for breath, everywhere the silky suffocation of lilting mantles of flesh.

Flensed stumps had caressed Vezat, bludgeoned and poked him, ridden him relentlessly. He tasted skinless half-roasted penises and semen thick as swamp water but sweet as lychee fruit. Blisters had burst as they forced his tongue to rasp across second degree burns on torsos, flavored with ginger and soured body grease. He'd gagged on so many undefinable members, wept as more pushed up his backside, reaming him with a pitiless tenderness.

Had he managed to make it to the top of the pile? Yes …

And had seen the two poles which rose out of the center, roped together perpendicularly to form a cross. On it a crucified man was gazing down at him. Crown of thorns, halo. But no arms or legs. The nails securing him had been pounded through his shoulders and his groin. Wearing a sad smile as if to say, *these are my sufferers, my children …*

The nail through the groin was almost as long as the erection that bloomed in pain and desire there. Vezat felt a final thrusting up his backside from somewhere in the pile he was squirming upward from. It felt sharp as that nail, of rusty texture as it slowly pulled free of him, unwinding in him a burning rectal orgasm.

Now Vezat groaned, jumped up and ran out of the hut, still pursued by his dream, jerking open his trousers as he went. Ruiz, who was on sentry duty, looked over at him. Vezat nodded weakly in acknowledgement and hustled behind another hut to squat down. The pain in his lower intestine was almost unbearable. He must have picked up a bug, scorching the lining of his colon until the urge to dump was overwhelming. No wonder he'd dreamed of being sodomized. (Somehow the term "rape" hadn't applied. Vezat hadn't struggled against them—exactly. Only for moments of breath had he fought.) And he had a fever, leaving a paste in his mouth that explained the dream's other main activity. He considered if he was going to have to vomit as well, but his mouth resisted losing the memories of butterball seepings and necro-spunk.

Suppressing his grunts lest he alarm the sleeping mercs, Vezat grit his teeth till they ground, diarrhea plopping out onto the muddy earth. He supposed this might be what it would feel like to be repeatedly taken up a virgin ass. But he wasn't doing anything but theorizing on that score, for he'd never given in to his urges. He'd never had a homosexual liaison, much less with a lover of artificially-abbreviated means.

But he'd known of occurrences when prisoners had been thus run through a rectal-coring gauntlet by their captors. Vezat remembered screams and curses in other languages, the cruel laughter of his fellow soldiers, the stink of fecally-tainted blood. And he'd maintained his post, neither taking part nor intervening on the victim's behalf.

No matter, he'd not given in to the freak-lover within himself, save to masturbate away the worst of the erections when the tension became too great to bear. Usually, on a battlefield, this was simply not feasible. If you took your attention away from the danger around you to relieve a boner, you died. It was as simple as that. And Vezat was horrified that any of the others should ever suspect his soul harbored such an impurity. He was a good Catholic; he was!

Then he remembered, a time as a merc in some oil baron sheik's employ, their whole patrol going through some pissant Berber encampment, armed to the teeth to show them the righteous haughty show of what those rebels were up against. Vezat and his friend Eugene side by side. And someone under an oily burnoose heaved a grenade. It landed on the ground, the men diving in opposite directions. There was a deafening roar with crimson sand flying, sharp as peppered glass. When it cleared, Eugene was jerking spastic stumps of two legs and an arm. The fingers on the severed hand curled and pointed, then curled again into a quivering spider. Vezat rushed to him, trying to wipe the viscera from Eugene's eyes. He used his fingers to try to unblock the man's throat as he began to choke on sand and some piece of his own meat. He put his mouth to Eugene's to blow in air. Tasted the blood-flecked saliva, shivering, slipping his arm under the wounded man to cradle him.

Felt his own erection like the sneer of the devil, unable to help it. Saw in the rags of Eugene's uniform his comrade's shocking hard cock as it sputtered out an enormous wad of sperm, seasoned with blood clots. Many men died thus, it was said. So it was true. Eugene perished, rather quickly thank god, Vezat absorbing the final quivers into his own body.

Then leaning across, pretended to give his friend another last attempt at mouth-to-mouth resuscitation. But it was really a kiss. He did not wash his mouth for a long while, letting the stain of blood dry there, forcing his lips into a stiff pucker. He would not drink water for days, unwilling to let the flavor be washed away. He stood his sentry position, weeping, barely rubbing the barrel of his rifle against his crotch. This as men from the unit took their revenge on several of the Berbers who were suspected of having been the assassin. Even though no one had gotten a really good look. But it must have been one of the young ones, glistening of black hair and eyes, muscled over slender forms spiked with the eastern form of musk they favored. How high and musical their voices could go when they were finally induced to shriek.

Now. The pile of flayed corpses was still in the middle of the village of Phnom Yohp. Due to the rain, it hadn't been possible to burn them up. Nor was it likely that a suitable mass grave could be dug for them in the mud.

As he shat in excruciating tainted squirts, Vezat's eyes strayed unwillingly to this, expecting to see—what?—some truncated Messiah? There was none, not even the holy ghost of one. When the lightning flashed and lit the night up in split-second strobes, he could see that some of the bodies—even with the tops of heads blown apart and skins peeled—seemed to still be smiling.

Chapter 17

"Then Quetzalcoatl came back to life; he was grieved and he asked of his *nahualli*, 'What shall I do now?' And the *nahualli* answered, 'Since things have turned out badly, let them turn out as they may.'"
—From Aztec myth related in Spanish manuscript 1558

On guard, Ruiz watched the Frenchman go behind the hut to shit. He could hear the spurts but couldn't smell them. Nor could he smell the pile of bodies in the street.

It was probably the fault of the snot doctor. Ruiz could neither smell nor taste anything anymore. Hadn't been able to for five years.

Ruiz had beseeched him. "Doctor, *por favor*, can you help me? I can't get the carrion out. It's in my nose day and night. It fills my mouth up and plugs down my throat."

"You get nose bleeds?" asked the E.N.T. specialist in Mexico City, shining a narrow light into Ruiz's nostrils.

"Yes. All the time."

"Well, that is, of course, what you are smelling and tasting. Your own blood," the doctor concluded.

No, it isn't, Ruiz thought stubbornly. The nose bleeds were a side effect, not the cause of the morphitic drench he carried with him. It was a memory and a haunting. It was a curse from having witnessed the hideous rite in La Quebrada de Dos Medias, The Passage Of The Two Halves.

Ridiculous, this day and age. His cousins and fellow guerillas in the insurgent group Los Manos (an indigenous peasant movement in sympathy with the Zapatistas who'd formed further south in Chiapas) from the tiny village of Trueno might have believed in these improbabilities, but Ruiz was not a country peon. He'd grown up in the city; he'd been to university. Once, when they had been out hunting, he'd pointed out what looked like a likely place to go looking for quail. His friends had shaken their heads and told him in whispers, "No, we don't go there, *primo*. It's a bad place. *Los bestios de la crepusculo … la sangre pavana …*"

Right, beasts of the twilight did a blood dance up in this secret mountain grotto.

(But since it turned out to be real, who then was the educated one?)

(Before God, I'd give anything and everything to still be ignorant of this horror.)

In those days, he hadn't needed to go to the snot doctor. Ruiz's mother had died and he'd taken her body home from Mexico City, back to Trueno where she'd been born.

He'd never been outside that giant metropolis and he was amazed—once the pollution was lifted from his sinuses—how sweet air could be. The corn flowers and pampas grasses, agave cacti and mango trees. And in the mountains surrounding the valley Trueno was situated in, timber was harvested. Sometimes when the winds were right, he could stand in the street and smell the cedar the lumbermen had cut miles away.

Ruiz had stayed, long after his mother's funeral. He'd grown close to his cousins. He'd joined their cause, against the caste system the wealthy few exploited. He'd put aside his books and donned the black bandanna over his face, learning how to use weapons. And—okay, let's admit to facts. He'd met the most beautiful of women. Ah, the crux of any true given situation. He was introduced to a distant cousin, seventeen, black hair down to her waist, eyes of deepest smoky topaz. She walked in beauty like the night … "Maria, I just met a girl named …"

Love could bring out the romantic revolutionary in anyone.

They'd been together for a year, and she was going to have their first child any day now.

Trueno was a very small place. There were eighty-six people living there. Seventeen were children too young to fight. Twenty-three were old people and also unable to take up arms. Another nine were crippled due to recent skirmish-related injuries. One was the church's non-combatant priest. Twenty-five were women (including Maria), busy with caring for their children, elderly parents, and/or ruined husbands. This only left eleven able-bodied rebels to go about the business of struggle.

These eleven had gone off into the bush, piled (stuffed was more like it) into an old jeep to join the militias of several other villages. They were going to stop a company called TorquemadaCorp—known for the thorough polluting of any countryside surrounding its plants—from building in their state. NAFTA hadn't put any money in their pockets and they didn't want to see the land suffer the slow, poisonous death which awaited it if the factory went in.

"Come home to me," Maria pleaded, touching Ruiz's face, bringing his hands down to lay across her swollen belly where he could feel their child kick. "I'll be standing right here, in the street, till I see you returning."

They'd been sure the company would resist. But Los Manos hadn't expected Mexico's president to send in the army—although troops had been sent into Chiapas on New Year's Day. They'd fought well into the night, mostly automatic weapons hammering the darkness.

Ruiz had smelled cordite, fire, blood: nothing unusual or of an amount too great to be borne. He rubbed his nose on his sleeve and continued firing, ducking, rolling for cover, shouting slogans.

The soldiers were better equipped. Pinned down, the villagers were basically shot to pieces. When they finally managed to scatter, there were only four from Trueno alive. Ruiz and his cousins: Julio, Diego, and Emilio.

Emilio had come upon the others on the road. He was driving what was left of the jeep, and they were glad it was at least still moving on all four wheels. Ruiz had a minor head wound, looking worse than it really was. A bullet has creased right on the top of his skull; it poured blood front and back till it seemed at first glance the injury had begun to bisect him. Julio's hands were bleeding. Diego had a shallow shoulder wound. Emilio had a bullet in his leg but didn't complain as he floored the accelerator with it.

No one greeted them as they entered the village street. The sun was coming up so most people should have already risen.

Ruiz frowned, not seeing Maria. She always waited in the street for him, even if it took days. Perhaps she'd gone into labor. In which case she'd be in the tender care of the midwives—and not waiting in the street. Maybe news had preceded them about the TorquemadaCorp debacle, and she'd been told he was among the dead. In which case, no, she wouldn't be waiting in the street for him now. It was just as well. If she saw the blood which had run down his face she might be shocked into some danger with the baby.

He lifted his head and sniffed. He should have smelled coffee, bread. But nobody was cooking.

Julio pointed. "*Oiga*."

They listened. A door was banging, softly. They could see it ajar, moving back in the wind to slip forward again, not able to close. It struck with a thud, muffled against something that kept it from completing the arc that should have ended with striking where it would latch.

Ruiz got out of the jeep and went over, ignoring the throb in his head. It was Paulo Granada's place. The crippled Mano was lying on the floor, body in the doorway. He'd been shot one time in the face.

A check of the street revealed ten dead. The nine wounded rebels and the priest had headshots, massive damage. Ruiz imagined someone walking up in the pre-dawn and swinging a shotgun from the hip like some movie desperado, blasting, again, again. Everyone else was gone.

Of course, they must have been abducted by the forces of TorquemadaCorp. People had often disappeared from villages sympathetic to either the Zapatista National Liberation Army or Los Manos. This was revolution.

"It wasn't that long ago," Ruiz said. "The bodies are barely cold."

Inside, he was freaking out. God, where was his wife? At least she wasn't among the corpses here. Maybe she was still alive. But he felt the blood on his face and was determined it not be tears.

"I'm an excellent tracker," Julio declared. "The trail is an easy one. Moving almost sixty of our people, how could it not be? It goes up into the mountains."

"*Esta lejos?*? Is it far?" Emilio asked, glancing at the petrol gauge.

Ruiz saw it was low and shrugged. "There's some gas in old Rodriquez's store."

Diego ran to get it, since Emilio couldn't because of his leg, Ruiz was having a bit of trouble with dizziness, and Julio couldn't actually carry a gas can because of his hands. Ruiz smelled the fuel as Diego poured it in, smelled the exhaust as Emilio gunned the engine and they took off.

An hour later the way grew too rocky, and they had to get out. Ruiz could see his cousins chewing their lips as they came to the entrance of The Passage of the Two Halves. All he could think of was Maria so he was hurrying, pushing himself beyond his head wound, beyond the exhaustion of having been up for two days, having fought ridiculous odds and barely escaped with his life (if not his entire scalp).

Everyone but Ruiz crossed himself, murmuring a prayer. The gap in the mountains was narrow, traversable on foot or by burro. There were ugly vacant patches where the once-lush array of trees had been stripped.

There was a roar of grating thunder. Anyone who lived anywhere near the timberlands knew the sound of the lumber saw. It meshed with screams and weeping. Underneath it, Ruiz could make out words, being spoken by numerous chanting voices. It came in the native language of Nahuatl, still spoken by many Indians in this part of Mexico."

"iuhqui tiyez in …"

(you shall be like this …)

He could see an old endless chain conveyor, moving through a stand of cedars.

"noquichtiuhm nohueltiuhe …"

(dear brother, dear sister …)

There were people running the belt, standing at its beginning, end, and at stations in-between. They were mostly naked, except for thick, steel-toed work boots which looked so out of place with the rest of their physical adornments. They were draped with cheap loops of garish paper snakes, the kind that popped out of joke cans. There were headdresses of bright feathers, apparently handed down from some time immemorial since parts had gone bald, the feathers clearly missing. And here and there were some fabulous pieces of gold jewelry, fantastically wrought, valuable, old. The nude bodies were painted with a single, carefully straight black line that ran up from the crotch, through the cipher of the navel, between and equidistant of the breasts and shoulders, centered through the lip, between nostrils and eyes, through the hair to go down the back again, straight upon the spine, vanishing cleanly through the butt cheeks. Some were men, others women. On the men, the left testicle had been removed and a large circle was drawn around the left nipple, apparently to simulate a feminine breast. On the women, the right breast had been severed, weights attached to the clitoris to make it long enough to imitate a penis.

"*Madre de Dios!*" Ruiz muttered under his breath. "What freaks!"

"Ometeotl, Ometecuhtli, Omecihuatl … " they chanted.

Aztec wannabees. The god was the one the ancients had called LordLady, the He and She of Flesh, All-begetting Father, Universal Mother. A hermaphroditic being who in some secret cosmic coition began everything in existence.

Sort of a fuck yourself, therefore you are and so are we.

The cousins were close enough they could see the log saw and what was being run down to it. Appropriated from some lumber mill or perhaps discarded by the company as outdated machinery, it was capable of handling six- to ten-foot hardwood tree trunks, splitting them vertically.

Chanting continued, "tlatlauhqui totonqui yayahuic coacihuiztli … "

(the red heat, the dark pain …)

Ruiz just froze. Not even sure if Julio, Diego and Emilio did the same. A shudder passed through him, down in a thunderbolt from the bullet crease at the summit of his scalp, electrifying his skin and veins until it felt as if he'd been descended upon by a cloud of locusts.

The villagers from Trueno were in a knot, bound hand and foot, watched over by more of the strange cultists armed with shotguns, machetes, fat head-pounding cudgel *things*. People were lifted onto the moving belt one at a time, "priests?" down the line making sure there were no "log jams." It was like a sick update of some old U.S. PERILS OF PAULINE movie, without the hero arriving in time to prevent the serrated teeth from chomping into tender flesh. Muscle. Bone.

(Jesus, aren't we the heroes, Ruiz thought. But he couldn't move. Was it the head wound, worse than he'd suspected, finally affecting his brain so that he was little better than stone? Where was Maria? In the group waiting to be tossed onto the conveyor? Or—at the end?)

The air filled with the grinding and ghastly shrieks and fine scarlet spray that rose up to tinge the mountain air pink. The only word he could think to describe it was from his college days. Hypnopompic, referring to hallucinations which a terrified dreamer might perceive, right after waking up and persisting until they were fully awake.

He could feel his own scream rising but it was stuck in his throat. Forced back down by this unbelievable stink that was suffocating him, rolling up his nose and between his lips. It was slaughterhouse musk, as the saw not only severed what it met but digested what it touched, letting it fly up like woodchipper spew. Legs were held apart to expose crotches, a nightmare of bone skree and arterial spurt infinities, separating layers of human as easily as a fingernail went through cobwebs. The blade whirred and sliced up, the parting intestines like the Red Sea itself, if that sea were full to bursting with boiling cherry eels.

And it was worse, godawful worse, because it was full daylight. No grisly nuances left to the shadows or to the imagination. Truly, blow by blow.

Down at the end, where the halves were pulled from the belt, a team of these creatures was praying, chanting, sewing. Dark jam mushed between raw, hasty sutures of some greasy sinew. Catgut maybe. Some kind of gut.

"auh in axcan ticzazalozque, Teteo Inta, Teteo Innan …"

(but now we shall glue it back together, Father of the Gods, Mother of the Gods …)

There were sudden, sodden queasy plops which Ruiz realized were the noises of people shitting themselves, waiting to be thrown onto the belt or as they were laid upon it, brown smears flowing down the conveyor to churn with the thick blood, spraying onto the cultists who lifted them hand and foot and who paid no attention to being doused in excreta. Ruiz had shat himself, as had the three men next to him, watching all with a mesmerized, vicious paralysis. A stench must accompany that, but it either blended with or was lost entirely in the reek from the bodies put to the saw.

(There's a boundary to horror then, Ruiz thought distractedly. Distractedly? Hell, no, he couldn't have been more focused. Yet he considered almost outside himself: there's a limit where the terror and its smell can't get worse. Because a man's capacity for it has finite borders in the senses.)

Why couldn't he move? He was enveloped in some rose-colored porcelain vertigo, like a chick trapped within an egg it was fated never to break through. His own blood in his eyes probably. Emilio limped forward, bringing up his rifle. He'd used it as a crutch to help get him through the pass. His finger spasmed on the trigger over and over but the weapon was empty. No one had any ammo left after the battle of yesterday and last night.

A guard glanced over and saw Emilio approaching. It (Ruiz couldn't grant the person a sex since they had obviously chosen not to possess a single gender identification) jogged the thirty or so feet to him and swung a sparkling machete. Emilio's head flew, body going forward two more steps before it pitched.

Julio was also running forward, crying, "Papa! Mama!" Seeing his parents there, thrown onto the belt like logs of primavera, the white mahogany. His damaged hands were up, barely able to clutch his rifle but he held it like a club.

The priests looked vaguely annoyed. Julio was stopped with a couple bullets. He crumpled, feet from the belt.

Diego was going toward the end of the conveyor, seeing the halves of his fifteen-year-old sister, the right discarded, the left attached to the right half of a wizened old man. The two didn't fit well but it was better than the left half of Ruiz's aunt Rosa, sewn to the right half of a little boy, he emerging out her side like a shriveled twin, the edges of organs flopping out through the sloppy, ill-fitting, sutured edges.

One of the priests spun around as Diego got right up to him. The thing thrust the long sharp needle through the cousin's eye and deep into the brain.

Ruiz saw Maria, one of the last, heard her begging for the life of her unborn baby. He started to run forward, his legs tingling and numb. He'd thought all the blood on his face was from the head wound—and much of it was—but a great deal was because his nose was bleeding. Profusely, as if to exorcise the dreadful meat stench from itself, the flow bubbling over his lips, pounding out in scarlet waves that made his whole face seem to have a carnal rhythm all its own.

The guards watched him, strangely not lifting weapons to kill him. Staring at the line of blood drawn straight down his face and chest from the bullet crease on his skull and the blood gushing from his nostrils.

And he couldn't help but think of the name of the place. Quebrada de Dos Medias. The Passage of the Two Halves. He knew he looked somewhat rendered in his own blood the way they had painted themselves, the way they were severing the villagers and then putting them together. To be two halves. Like the god Ometeotl.

In Nahuatl he heard them. "Xolotl, tlamacazqui, Xoxotl, ce-tecpatl, tezzohuaz titlapallohuaz ..."

(Double, Spirit In Flesh, Double, blood-stained knife ...)

Two priests strolled down, taking Ruiz gently enough—all things considered. Restraining him, forcing him to his knees. So he couldn't go to her. And Maria with eyes popping watching her own descent, priests holding her thighs apart, the blade hitting with a relentless gout and geyser, up through the pregnant abdomen, through their child, milk actually spurting from her nipples as the saw split the ribs and breastbone between them.

Down at the end of the conveyor, idiot-fiends in paper serpents stitching her to some teenaged boy. The other half of her discarded, half a fetus hanging out of half a belly.

Ruiz was woozy from loss of blood, only upright to still watch because he was being held up on his knees. But he must have been hallucinating by then, gagged on the odor of carnage the like of which no one could have smelled since the Aztec altars in Teotihuacan slaughtered sometimes thousands of people a day. The hot sun already fermenting the riven viscera and buckets of waste until the drone of approaching flies could be discerned beneath the shrieks and reverberating racket of the giant buzz saw. He must have been mad by then because it wasn't possible that the sewn-together halves moved, struggled to rise, flopped getting up, maybe only one leg long enough to stand on so that they hopped a few steps then fell over again. It wasn't conceivable that, as they wheeled like spliced gyroscopes, the look in their mismatched eyes was jubilation. That the half-head of his Maria, long black hair stringy with blood and brains, had a crinkle at the corner of the mouth, tweaking upward in an insane grin.

They had toppled over, alive for only seconds maybe, or hideous minutes. But the Aztec freaks were wild with it, cheering, chanting, singing.

Ruiz thought he was splitting in two, from the bullet crease downward, pulled apart by grief and corpse-reek. He lost consciousness. When he woke up again, he'd been moved, dumped outside some nameless little village. No one believed him when he babbled out his story.

He wasn't surprised.

He went to a neurosurgeon but was told the head injury was well-enough healed and the nose bleeds were not a result of it. The death stench remained, overpowering, monstrous.

"Can you help me?" he asked the snot doctor.

"Oh, yes. It's quite simple."

The E.N.T. performed a minor office surgery, cauterizing the weakened veins in Ruiz's nostrils. The nose bleeds stopped. But he could no longer smell anything—nor could he taste so much as a spoonful of menudo.

Somewhere in-between noble struggle and failure, love and grief, ideology could lose its hold. What might wait beyond death had no respect for righteousness. He hardened, senses dimmed, switched allegiances, determined to earn something for his troubles if he was going to fight. He didn't know if this contained a deathwish or not. He didn't think so. He fought very hard as a soldier. Who wanted to die when death turned out to have different rules than first suspected?

Just look at those drugged locos on the streets of Bangkok, grinning up in vapid rapture, not needing to eat or breathe. Beyond catatonia and on into something no one could say was really alive. And these old freaks here in Phnom Yohp he'd helped splatter, the same. Who called that living? And that pile of skinned corpses—also very Aztec! It had made him do a double take, coming back from looking for that gringo Elliot, reminded of the cult of Xipe Totec that had skinned its sacrifices and then worn the skins. Flayed, burned ... yet he had an uneasy sense that they weren't quite what he'd call dead. He expected them to get up—or try to. Teetertotter around, jubilation in what eyes the mercs' bullets hadn't blown apart, mouth corners spasming up in demon grins.

The Cambodian jungle steamed around Ruiz. Vezat came back around the hut he'd gone behind to shit. He looked nauseous.

"You okay?" Ruiz asked him.

The Frenchman nodded weakly. He looked down the street at the heap of corpses. He trembled, pinched his nose between his fingers at the reek, and smiled, shaking his head. He then went back into the hut where the others slept.

Ruiz shrugged and stared on into the darkness. For a moment he tensed, finger on his weapon's trigger.

What was that? A figure moving around the corpse pile. Dancing, dressed in a human torso-skin and mask. Part man, part woman. LordLady. It leapt high upon the mound of bodies, gesturing up to the heavens with hands that carved a metaphor for creativity out of an air full of despoilment. Then it jumped back down, destruction clinging to its back in purple shadows.

Ruiz didn't fire on it. What? Was he a fool?

It was only a *fantasma*. Of a god of his ancestors, *Padre y Madre*. Father and Mother. *Noche y viento*. The night and wind.

Chapter 18

"Now have we conquered and obtained,
and from our trespasses are free.
Shine thou away the evil dream, O Dawn ..."
—The Rig Veda

Night and a nameless village. Boy four years-old watching the sky streak white and yellow. Ripe fire bursting on the ground. People running without sure direction, screaming, changing into something else when the bombs hit them. He didn't understand coming apart, saw it as a transformation very mystical. Into the mist that totally sundered meat can become.

No one to take his hand or lift him up, to race for somewhere safer. He just stood there, on almost the only spot where nothing came down. The dragon roar overhead winged away, even as the thunder fallen on the ground reached a certain steady din before it began to sputter/flicker off.

There were littered bits of flesh everywhere, reminding him of the charred scraps of firecracker paper which he'd once seen strewing the ground after a festival. Bones had turned into bamboo splinters and sawdust. He saw the foggy shapes of the villagers rise from the raw mounds they had manifested into. The place was mountain-remote so he'd never before seen anything of the war. As they floated out of the ruined streaks, he heard them whispering, weeping, cursing.

Where am I?

Is that you, Bao?

Fuck you, Christian god, Buddha, Quan Yin, allgod!

Alone now, the child began to follow them as they wandered the burning debris, before heading for the path that took everyone down into the caves below their mountain, where they'd always agreed to go should planes come. Had they not been caught sleeping after even the moon had set, they would've heard the engines coming and fled into these caverns. There was suppose to be a sentry, staying awake and listening to the sky. But he must have dozed off—or run away.

The little boy toddled behind the misty villagers, crying to be picked up and carried. No one paid any attention to him. He caught up with the one that looked like his mother except she was all-white now. He reached up to grasp her hand but couldn't catch hold, his fingers closing on smoke.

There was one moving through them he didn't know from the village. It was a man/woman combination, ashes heavy on its feet, a garland of skulls about its neck. It danced through them as if leading them. Or as if simply reveling in their presences. It grinned forcefully with silvery sparkling teeth and wept tears tinged with a pink blood. The night seemed to tumble down to hang as a mantle across its shoulders.

It was the only one that took any notice of the child, winking at him through the moist banners of the villagers.

A voice filled the boy's head, repeating over and over, *This is my gift to thee. Oh, joyous! joyous!*

The cloudy specters here resembled those he'd often seen, traveling along the old road, fog people on fog elephants, in armor such as some of the ancient cave statues wore, swinging swords of the sort of graying light that crept through summit stones at dusk. Making a torturous journey back from a battle waged centuries ago. These, too, had never paid any attention to him when he called out to them, asking where they were going, where they'd been.

The child had asked his grandfather once, "Who are the white people on the road?"

"How many are there?" his grandfather had sternly inquired, instead of answering him.

"Many times more than there are people in our village," the boy replied, not knowing how to count so he couldn't say there were hundreds or thousands.

The old man had been startled, hands shaking, hurrying to make sure there were no Americans there. He'd been angry coming back, finding nothing, no one, not even the footprints of an army.

"There's no one. You must never lie like that ..." grandfather began harshly.

"Not even the one who dances them along?" the boy asked.

"Which one is that?" asked his grandfather, leaning down to him to hear better.

"It's both a man and a woman. It has a necklace of heads stripped to bone. It seems so happy—and so sad."

The old man's toothless jaw dropped as he exhaled, "Shiva!"

But now the boy couldn't find his grandfather. He ran after the people he'd known all his life, themselves a white folk now. He stumbled over stones on the mountain path, falling, skinning knees and hands, nobody pausing to get him upright again. His own mother, ignoring his cries, blind to his tears, her hair and fingers trailing behind her like torn rice paper. So he managed to get to his feet by himself, hurrying to catch up as the cavern mouth opened, darker then even the surrounding night. During the day, the cavern's entrance didn't seem like anything to be afraid of. But now it terrified him to have to go in there, like the jaws of some enormous animal.

"Wait!" the little boy called out. "Don't leave me behind! Mama!"

Down in the caves they shrieked, finding no sanctuary. Their voices were so high-pitched, the boy covered his ears while tasting copper in his mouth. He didn't try to keep up with anyone anymore as they began running, misty pale streaks skewing every direction, caroming through the interconnected maze of caverns. They vanished into the black, slimy walls, re-emerged rising in coils from the spined horns of stalagmites, dripped down from the points of stalactites, and passed through each other to co-mingle cloudy limbs and then separate. It was dark down there and he couldn't see, only able to detect where they were by the shimmer of white skins and hair.

It was the dancer who led him back out again. Or so he thought, for the boy had followed the sound of bells, the footprints dusty with ashes. He later saw the being again, dervish-whirling among the same color refugees on the road, soldiers both Vietnamese and round-eyed American stumbling while bearing incense-stick rifles, valleys full of them.

He ended up in an orphanage someplace, not able to remember how he came to be there. He'd sit in the window and watch as a stream of pale people wailed while going past, or silently trudged, accompanied by fog dogs, fog tigers, fog birds. The stream grew steady till there was no break in the line save for the skull-bedecked dancer weaving a spiral through their ranks, as the noise of artillery boomed both distant and near. Fire painted the horizon or flamed so close by that the orphans could hear large numbers of trees crackling like some peculiar percussion instrument.

When the boy was seven, his throat grew very sore and a fever shot through his blood. He was put to bed where he burned for days, the pallet growing sodden as all the water boiled out of him. After that he could no longer see any white people, nor hear them as they asked one another where they were and what had happened, or as they cursed the forces which had killed them. He did not see the one who accompanied them, mourning and cheering them on.

Phan woke up, sweating, clothes damp as if he were still sick with fever. He blinked, trying to shake a rain of perspiration from his eyes. He remembered he was sleeping in one of Phnom Yohp's huts. Someone was moving around him. Probably one of the other mercs, getting up to drain a full bladder.

As his eyes adjusted to the dark, he could tell it was no one in fatigues. But Phan still couldn't quite make them out. Their shape had somehow caught the moonlight from outside, painting it an eerie white.

A couple more drifted past the entrance to the hut. Phan reached for his gun with one hand, trying to nudge the merc sleeping nearest him awake. He wanted to whisper, "Hey … hey … we're not alone. Some of those crazy Khmer's have come back …"

Vezat rolled over, spit sloshing around his gums as he reluctantly opened his eyes. Phan poked him, letting a hissing exhale be the only attempt at communicating their danger.

The Frenchman glanced around. "What?"

Phan's jaw dropped. He pointed to the shapes in the street, to the one pacing the hut's interior. Then that one drifted outside to join the others.

"We've got company … " Phan said, voice soft.

He hoisted himself onto his haunches, duckwalking to the doorway.

Vezat saw no reason not to take his comrade at his word. He grabbed his own weapon and then placed a hand on the colonel's shoulder. Gestetner's eyes popped open, immediately conscious.

"Phan says he saw people in the street," Vezat related in a hush.

Monivong was making little back-of-the-throat noises, limbs jiggling, squirming, as if dreaming of unpleasant things inside his clothes. Saab put a hand over his mouth, not eager to have the man wake up with a scream. The Cambodian shuddered awake, eyes goggling, then made out his commander's voice in the darkness.

"Street," was all Saab told him. It was all that was necessary to relate the message that there were unfriendlies outside, and where.

The four slipped toward the doorway, weapon barrels picking up stray flecks of light. It was no longer raining. The sky had obviously cleared and stars were out, the moon ogling the village like the slick ophite of a cataract eye.

Phan fired. Once, twice, three times. He emptied his gun as he jumped out of the hut into the street. Then he snapped out the spent clip and reloaded another.

The colonel, Vezat and Monivong stared at him, then looked back at the street. They couldn't see anyone. Then they saw the line of bullets dance toward Ruiz as he leapt to his feet. The Mexican cried out, *"Alto! Alto!"*, diving for the ground, his own gun shot out of his hands.

Phan watched his blasts zip through fog bodies milling about the square. Dozens of crippled men limped, crawled, slid from hut to hut and around the pile of skinless, semi-burned corpses. Beyond that, flitting between the trees where the jungle began, others moved, most of them Asian and many in a variety of strange garb from other times, some of them American soldiers of the myriad peoples that the U.S. held, every skin white no matter what race the features indicated. He could see the confusion in their eyes, the helpless terror contorting phosphor faces.

Phan cocked an ear. What was that he heard? Just a burbling at the edge of sound. The way one might detect the cry of a frightened child so far away that the wavelengths don't quite reach a conscious manifestation of noise.

It was nothing he could entirely separate. It was a winged rustle of languages, sonances flapping at some window to his brain. He couldn't distinguish the separate meanings but somehow he recognized *where am I?, is that you … ?, fuck you gods of spirit spite and hereafter cruelties …*

And there—who was THAT one? Wiggling hips and shaking shoulders around the site of the cremation, eyes rolled up in rapture, feet soiled in ashes despite the rain. Not with mud—only ashes.

Suddenly Phan began to shake, violently, buttons and zippers on his clothes clacking, teeth banging, heartbeat in his ears roaring like the engines of bomb-dropping planes. He jumped as the colonel carefully relieved him of his gun—even though it was empty. Ruiz was slowly getting to his feet, patting himself, determining he hadn't been shot.

"You nuts?" he shouted at Phan.

"You don't see them?" Phan asked Gestetner, voice a warble of uncontrolled fear.

"No," Saab replied quietly, scrutinizing his man to see if he'd have to put him down.

The Vietnamese looked surprised, then just sat down in the mud and hung his head.

Chapter 19

"And, being so much kinsman to the dead, I walk
contented to the peopled grave."
—"Sonnet 29"
Rudyard Kipling

Ivan Gestetner took his own life in prison. The son born from the wife he shot had been given over to Ivan's brother Micah. Uncle Micah worked as a driver for the head of the Varanasi branch of the American spice company Thousand Seas, garnering exotics in northern India.

Varanasi was considered by the Hindus to be the holiest city in the world. It was the spot where Shiva chose to make his earthly home after his marriage to Parvati. It was on the banks of the sacred River Ganga, a body of water which, it was said, had once flowed through heaven.

The building Uncle Micah kept behind the company boss's house was used partly as a home and partly to warehouse the spices. The walls, furnishings, everything there smelled of cardamom, figs, nutmeg and ginger, cassia. Cashew nuts and pistachios were stuffed into large burlap bags which heaped across the floors. There were stores of balsam from the Himalayas, pepper from the Malabar coast, and tea from Assam.

Scents of fenugreek, cloves and mango helped Uncle Micah to sleep at night—along with a more secret herb among the stash of those often-illegal mysteries he himself collected when he wasn't busy chauffeuring his employer. These sweetly covered the stench of cremation fires. Varanasi was where pilgrims traveled—sometimes thousands of miles entirely on foot. It was a place where, if they died while in that city, their sins were expunged and their souls were freed from the cycle of rebirth, ascending immediately to heaven. Those who didn't go there with the precise intention of dying, went to bathe in the sacred river Ganga, to be washed of their transgressions.

The smell of death didn't bother little Saab, who had lived for about ten years in Varanasi, since he was only a few months old. He was comfortable with it, believing it to be as natural a part of the air he breathed as the blood from the goat sacrifices made at the Durga Temple—south of Benares University, the heady roses and jasmine which poured forth from local gardens, and the wet scent of the monsoon wind coming up from the southwest in June.

They lived next door to a widow and her three sons. Captain Roopali had died a couple years before in a skirmish with Muslim Indians farther north. They'd had three sons: Siddhi, Shrinivasa, and Bhaskar: a year older, the same age, and a year younger than Saab who was a decade old in the last year he knew them. They had been brought up in the strict Hindu sense, honoring the caste system which separated people who were from different stratas of society. Captain Roopali had been a warrior and thus of the second highest varna, Kshatriyas. Micah's boss—even though an American and presumably not to even be considered in matters of caste—was a merchant, which was the third varna in India called Vaishyas and the strata below their father's. Mrs. Roopali only barely deigned to nod her head when the American spice merchant greeted her on the street, but was not too proud to silently accept the gifts of spices he sent over to help out the widow and orphans. But

Micah was only a servant, thus of the Shudras, *two* castes below. (That is, had they been Hindus from Varanasi, instead of foreigners. Could this have actually made them even lower?)

The kids weren't allowed to associate with Saab, which annoyed him to no end. He would see them playing soccer in their yard, stopping, seeing him out of the corners of their eyes. He sometimes got the impression that they badly wanted to include him. He was husky for his age, tall as most other American boys were, and it would have evened the numbers out so they could each team with two members apiece. The brothers would confer, then bite their lips as they remembered their mother's stern admonishments, and turn away from him.

He hated them for it. Anyone would have thought their departed and sainted daddy had been a general or something. Instead of just a captain who tried to interfere when the Muslims at the garrison where he was stationed decided to butcher a sacred cow for a feast. To be shot to death over a steak seemed the height of idiocy to Saab.

"Hey! *Shubh prabhat,* guys. Good morning!" he called to them one day, a book in his hands. "Hey! Soooooo, there are four varnas, right?"

They glanced across the yards at him, showing only their profiles. They didn't nod but just observed, blinking. Looking just like those stupid sacred cows as far as he was concerned.

"The Brahmins, then the Kshatriyas—that's you guys, the Vaishyas, and then the Shudras—me. We won't mention the niravasitas since they're untouchables, okay?"

Siddhi, Shrinivasa and Bhaskar were still looking at him, wondering what he was getting at.

"Anyway, only the first three varnas are allowed to hear, learn or recite the Vedas, correct?" Saab asked, not really expecting a response. Then he grinned, opened the book, and began to read. They were close enough—separated only by a row of hyacinth bushes—to see the title was The Rig Veda. "'He conquers godless and malign enchantments, and sharpens both his horns to gore the Rakshasas.'"

They gasped. Sacrilege, eh? Ass reaming the big cosmic Moo.

He continued, "'Loud in the heaven above be Agni's roarings with keen-edged weapons to destroy the demons.'"

The boys cried out and covered their ears.

"'Forth burst his splendors in the Soma's rapture. The godless bands press round but cannot stay him …'"

Saab had to stop, he was laughing so hard. He threw the book down, shouting, "Don't let them Rakshasas get you now!" Then he tra-la-la'd off. When he looked behind him, he could see they were still shaking, not in the least sure what to do.

He flung back one last bit. "Sikh, maryjain, Sikh. Brahma's just a figure of speech!"

He went down to the river, as he often did for want of any other activity. He loved the bustle and Ganga hurdy-gurdy, the temples, the sheer oldness of the city. Varanasi could be traced back at least three thousand years. He would sometimes go to a high point where he could watch part of the Panchakroshi Road which ran for 36 miles around the city. On it was a constant parade of those on pilgrimage, the very old hobbling along like sacks of wrinkles and despair, the sick in jostling carts, the crippled dragging themselves until their bodies were only whispers of dust. They awed and amused him at turns, amazing the boy that anyone would put themselves through such torment to bathe in the nasty Ganga. The river was full of waste and the ashes of the dead, slicked across with sacred cow shit and black, crunchy cremains.

He'd occasionally seen a figure, hazy but gorgeously grim, dancing up and down the steps of ghats where cremations were done. He'd seen statues closely resembling this person and knew he was seeing Shiva. And what a wonderful god this must be, superb, apparently liking the smell just as Saab did, attracted to the death because he was the deity of death. And Saab found death so interesting, a passage to another realm where caste systems mightn't matter, because the strong ruled in such places, didn't they? Not the entitled.

But in this world one's ultimate responsibility was dharma, he heard preached as surely as a Bible thumper in the Baptist belt back home redundantly harangued about the evils of strong drink. One did as one was born to do. The filigree merchant sold his silver. The stone mason carved giant penises for Shiva and cow figures for the Gai Ghat. Untouchables put their hands into unclean filth to remove the carcasses of fly-bedecked cows from the marketplace and of those pilgrims who collapsed dead on the road upon entering Varanasi, their bodies riddled with cancers and plagues.

And what was Saab born to do? The god of death danced in the darkness as cremation fires lit the city, up and down the ghat steps, to the summits where the pyres burned and blood bubbled with body fats, down to the riverbank where the ashes were then strewn upon the face and arms of Ganga, mother goddess of the river. Saab would see the god seem to glance his way, knowing the boy could perceive him.

And Shiva would wink, as if to say, "Yes, the dark accepts you; death accepts you. You were born to this."

Other times Saab would walk the intricate maze of alleys and winding streets, inhaling deeply, filling his lungs with the sharp/sweet air. The sun would spike in hot bolts off the golden domes of minarets. It would wink between the pinnacles of towers in abandoned 18th century palaces. He would hear chanting and the gongs from hundreds of temples, some of them richly adorned edifices which were sliding slowly in the

Ganga, where their carvings—like fabulous tattoos and scars in stone—would be lost forever. Such a waste!

There were the colorful bazaars where silks and filigree trinkets could be bought, where *tali chawal* fried rice balls and *gulab jamun* sweet dumplings could be bought from vendors to snack on. These last always reminded Saab of donut holes in Karo syrup, hardly competition for chocolate cake and ice cream, but curiously satisfying considering their rank simplicity. Here were road-side barbers, moneychangers, urchins begging from the European tourists. There were *sadhus*—priests—smoking *ganja,* the holy weed, smoke creating vortices around their thickly bearded chins and enigmatic eyes.

There were the endless ghats, flights of stone steps which led down to the river. On these he would see hireling priests performing rituals under tacky umbrellas. Washermen knelt on the bank, rhythmically flogging clothes clean. Astrologers cast horoscopes. Yogis twisted into all manner of astounding contortions. Children splashed in the river, playing in the swirls of ancestor ashes, as nearby pilgrims piously immersed themselves, men naked and women fully clothed. He would watch as the women would emerge, soaked to the skin, peeling these sodden garments off in front of everybody to put on dry saris. Their bare tits and buttocks reminded him of the pictures in magazines Uncle Micah kept in his room, except only seldom as attractive as the ones posing in the skintrades.

There was constant noise, flamboyant with omni-present funeral processions, the ringing of bells, pounding of drums, trilling of flutes. Smoldering cremation pyres which made the entire of Varanasi seem to be filled with the strange incense of human taper. There were streets lined with lingas, stone erections pushing up toward the sky. Every so often some tourist would be turned out of one of the main burning ghats—

Jalsain or Manikarnika—for trying to sneak in a camera with which to take pictures.

Saab would hang out near the Dasashivamedh Ghat, dedicated to Sitala. Because she was goddess of smallpox, he hoped to see infected pilgrims visiting, sores dripping until their skin might have been pocked wax. He was usually disappointed. What a misnomer.

He liked to visit the Trilochan Ghat. This had two turrets between which most of the local vultures sat, leaning anxiously forward with their black wings rustling from time to time. They watched the water of the Ganga expectantly, waiting for lunch to float by. He would stare as they caught a glimpse of something, their wings beating and beaks opening to emit a guttural SCRAW! as they swooped down after it. He would try to make it out. Offal, more than likely, squeezed out of some splashing child's grungy backside. Or maybe part of a body which hadn't quite burned completely before the ashes were spread upon the surface of the river. And once he even spied half the head of a goat, sacrificed at the Durga Temple. It had floated down, one sideways pupil of an eye and one curling horn directed at the sky. Its brains had spread out around it, curdled, reminding him of clumps of cheap bathing soap which had been used to rub some poor slob raw until he'd bled.

June came and the monsoon wind was late. The temperature had been in the triple digits for weeks unending. People were desperate to see the rains arrive. The river's level had grown so low that it moved sluggishly through the city, little more than mud. People dragged themselves about their duties. The *chandal* outcasts, who were employed to burn the bodies at the ghats, were passing out from the heat of the fires.

Saab liked it. He'd always liked it hot. The way it could make others dizzy yet sharpened his mental faculties to crystal clear made him feel superior. Well, that was superior, wasn't it?

The way he could walk through the color-rippling hell of it, high on mirage images, smelling burning flesh, watching everything wilt and wither ... And those three spazzes who lived next door barely able to bear it, standing in the yard, turned to the southwest, watching for the storm clouds to begin gathering on the horizon.

"Not yet, mother," they would chime to the woman in the shadowy doorway to their house.

They would be helping each other to stay on their feet, none of the houses in Varanasi airconditioned in the 1950s, except for a few of those belonging to Americans and Europeans with more money than a raj. But the building the chauffeur lived in with his nephew wasn't. The heat and dryness was considered good for the spices.

Saab gyrated, a hoola hoop slung around his hips, showing off.

"Doesn't affect me and I'm not even a native!" he called to them, jeering. "If you're so special, how come it's bothering you and not me? Strengths are suppose to belong to the higher castes, aren't they? Passed down from the fathers?"

Siddhi, the oldest brother, turned, fully facing the American boy for the first time, and glared. He snapped, "Your father was a murderer. He killed your mother, didn't he? You only survive this heat because he burns in hell."

Saab heard Mrs. Roopali gasp in the doorway, whispering some reprovement. Saab didn't know whether it was because her son had uttered such a terrible thing or because the boy had spoken to the American Shudra at all. Siddhi blinked and hung his head, mumbling something which might have been an apology. Shrinivasa and Bhaskar grabbed him as he slumped, either from the oppressive heat or shame, and helped him back into the house.

Saab was livid. How dare they mention his parents. He stormed about the yard, tearing up rose bushes, letting the thorns rake his hands, ripping branches from frangipani trees, murdering entire families of gardenias. He moved into the building he and Uncle Micah shared, kicking over barrels of fragrant spices, clouds of red billowing as he stomped a load of cinnamon sticks. He found a small shesham wood box, containing a tiny package of a faintly yellow-green powder which could only have belonged exclusively to Micah. If he was caught with it, he'd get the ever-lovin' whaled out of him. But he didn't need much. A pinch or two would suffice.

At the bazaar Saab purchased a few coconut cakes, called *narial ka halwa*. He sprinkled the powder on them. It looked like dyed crystals of sugar. When the Roopali boys came outside again he approached them, coming to the hyacinth bushes which bordered the two yards.

"I bring these as a peace offering," he told them slyly. "Not to make us friends, for I guess we can't be that. But I know you spoke only out of anger, because I taunted you into it. This is my way of saying I'm sorry. *Meherbani se*. Please."

He knew that food prepared or served by a person of lower caste could be consumed by someone of higher caste if it had been fried in ghee. Ghee was clarified butter. It was considered to have a quality of sacrament to it because the butter was derived from the milk of the sacred cow. This rendered it acceptable, just as a Christian might accept something from an infidel if it was washed in holy water. Took away the contamination. And what child could turn down sweets if given half the chance?

"*Dhanyavad*. Thank you," the boys said, bowing slightly, then quickly grabbing the cakes.

Not long after, Saab heard the murmurings of monsoon wind begin. It was an aeolian sound, humming through the minarets and towers, tones like *sadhus* vibrating holy names. This interwove with the weeping of Mrs. Roopali next door, now very much alone with no more husband, no more children.

Saab saw the black clouds gathering on the horizon, forks of lightning dancing like the god of death.

He darkened his skin with makeup and drew white horizontal lines across his forehead, like the followers of Shiva did. He dressed in a simple, seamless white robe, traditional for funerals. He went to the ghat where the boys were to be cremated and was unchallenged, believed by the attendants to be a cousin. What did they know? What did they care? The mother wasn't present. She'd collapsed and been put in hospital. No one else was there to say anything.

Apparently the Roopalis actually did have money. The pyre erected for the brothers was of expensive sandalwood, the perfumed smoke helping to disguise the smell of combusting meat.

The taper of burning straw lit the wood. The bodies began to cook. Saab smiled to himself, laughing inwardly. The powder hadn't killed them. It only put them into a deep sleep which looked like death. So, his father was a murderer, and sons inherited their fathers' castes? Are you watching, daddy? Are you proud? I have recognized my dharma early and taken the first step in the beginning of a long and bloody karma.

The clouds rumbled in, thunder drowning out the usual clamor of Varanasi. Lightning tongued the ground, shattered stones in ghat steps, making the attendants scatter. Saab backed up against a wall, underneath a short open pavilion, watching the pyre, cursing under his breath as the clouds opened and rain came down in sheets.

"Oh, not yet …"

The funeral pyre for the Roopali brothers smoked thickly, hissed, spat, and went out. There was a shifting upon the sandalwood logs. The brothers woke up and climbed out. One of them was blackened all over, hair burned away, fingers melted into flippered hands, genitals vanished into a smear of pimpled grease. The second had burned enough he no longer had arms and his mouth was a charred hole, the teeth within black as jet prayer beads. The third had only burned until he was etched by the fire, seemingly covered in a Sanskrit of split skin, his body swollen like a tattooed dumpling.

They stumbled to the pavilion, some flesh sloughing off in the rampage of the rain, bobbing away in the torrent like oysters in wine. Saab cringed, seeing they were headed his way, horrified and repelled. They curled up next to him, hugging his body for warmth as the cool rainwater seemed freezing to them.

What? Couldn't they see who he was? Didn't they know what he'd done to them?

Perhaps they didn't see him, eyes damaged by smoke and flame. Perhaps "death" had altered their perceptions of caste and revenge.

Or maybe they saw only the disguise he wore, skin darkened, white sideways lines on his brow.

Their ruined skin crinkled against him, rubbing off on his own flesh. But it didn't make it crawl. Instead he discovered he was strangely aroused, a new kind of heat permeating his groin. He slipped his arms around the two at his sides, as the one in the middle lay its head in his lap and sighed a puff of blue-gray smoke. When he hesitantly caressed the left one's head, his finger brushed against an ear which crumbled at his touch. It was at that moment Saab experienced his first orgasm.

Leaning over, he put his tongue into the right one's mouth, tasting the stewed gums and charcoal teeth. He ran his tongue along, feeling as if he'd stuck it in burned butter. He fingered the shoulder stumps, then played with the braised tip of the little penis, crumbly as fried bacon. Saab broke off a tiny piece and put it in his mouth, savoring its heat, its salty sweetness. The boy—Shrinivasa, or was it Bhaskar?—arched his back, emitting a brittle wail, grinding his skull against the stone of the pavilion wall. In pain? In ecstasy? Both?

Saab traced the bleeding patterns in the third one, curled into his lap and twitching. They were so deep and sure, they might have been made with the sharp tip of nearly molten metal. They bewitched Saab, making him think of the erotic bas-relief he'd seen at some temples, ripples of carnal panorama which was exquisite in so much devastation.

They died in his arms, in his hands as the storm pulsed, the Ganga quickly rising to overflow the lowest of the ghat steps. A nearby temple which had been slowly sliding into the waters for years now went the rest of the way with a colossal groan, its pillars folding like the weak legs of a palsied pilgrim. Saab felt the tremor beneath him as the ground shuddered and took it as a sign that the earth itself had just experienced something sensual, blissful.

Saab saw Shiva, not dancing now, only sort of floating through the rain.

"For you!" the boy cried exultantly.

He expected the god of death to smile and bless him. But Shiva frowned sternly and shook his magnificent head.

Surprised and depressed, Saab disengaged himself from the bodies he'd been fondling. He ran into the next temple, and the next. Every statue he saw glared at him, angry, disapproving, rain gushing around their stone faces like tears, gouting around the hard mouths as if they were spitting at him. All the gods, hundreds of them in depictions of Shiva, scowled at him with revilement for his crime. Even Kali with her violent gaze and Hannuman the merry monkey god hated him.

Why, was this not his dharma? Had Shiva lied to him?

Or was there a secret he'd discovered that no boy—indeed no man—should ever uncover? A pleasure the gods hoarded, jealously keeping it only for themselves? That which it was only their dark duty to accomplish and enjoy: the love of total wreckage, the feasting upon mortality. (No wonder Shiva danced where bodies were burned, and Kali swirled lasciviously with skulls about her throat.)

Well, he knew it now. And no matter what they felt about this upstart, he must have been destined to. He could feel the fate of it hard between his legs and pounding to distraction in his ears. He would never let go of it.

In Phnom Yohp, in the rain again, he saw Shiva near the pile of partially-incinerated corpses. This was different from the image of the god he'd first seen in Varanasi. This was the androgynous version he'd seen many times since in statues and paintings.

It danced slowly, in elusive illusionary leaps and shutterspaced twirls, intricate braids flying. It turned its face toward him, away from him, toward him again.

And it clearly despised him.

PART THREE

The Cosmic Man

The Cipher's Prelude

Sometimes his wasting art depressed him. Realizing he could only do so much damage to any single individual.

If only victims came in chains, like paperdolls. The imagination could be employed to run riot so much further. He could do series, making each atrocity a sort of microcosmic incarnation. They would be produced in volumes, portfolios, each with its own irrevocable destiny and dharma.

But that was not to be, alas.

The best he could do was the best he could do. What infracted maya he could create was limited to his human state. Surely only the gods were capable of grangerizations on a cosmic scale, the subtle or grotesque alterations which might evolve a species to a higher level of wickedness ... or bring it to the brink of extinction, a poetical act in and of itself.

Sometimes he could hear them, the little ones who'd died under construction, as he remade them in his own inimical style of tigering artifice. For he had—as all the wasting masters like him—created a place of illusion where models/victims were compelled to go, bearing the salacious and allegorical scars with which he'd decorated them. They cried out in Spanish and Portuguese, Egyptian, dozens of Hindi, African and Oriental dialects. Making a babble so poignant, so inundating of puericide child-choir tintinnabulation, that he strained to hear them better, smiling secretly like a homicidal Buddha wherever he was. And, as soon as was convenient, taking opium or whatever it took to phase himself back into that place where they must wait for him, all the flesh-chiseled sculptures and pith-engraved lithographs who were his slaves.

Chapter 20

"I was alone
inside.
Shedding
the visible dark ..."
—poem to Shiva
Allama Prabhu

Elliot felt his state of shock bleeding away. Could this really be Harry? No ...

But it could be his brother. Transformed how?

How? echoed the beautiful face, answering from Elliot's own scar tissue.

Remember ...

They were back in Texas, playing in the yard among all the trees. They were about eleven and twelve, with little brother Arcan maybe six. There were two neighborhood kids with them, a school friend of Elliot's named Steve who was eleven and a girl named Tina who was thirteen.

"Fuh-fuh-fffling us hu-hard," Tina cried gleefully, perpetual stutter nothing that made her self-conscious.

Harry had been nominated to be the first 'it' for Swing The Statue. He could fling a kid around like one of those G-force machines they used to train astronauts. Till your face screwed sideways and your mouth threatened to end up as a permament fixture on the other side of your head. He shook the brains loose and put the bottom of your stomach somewhere up on Mars.

He was as big and strong as a high school fullback. Tina gasped every time she saw him, staring always at his crotch because of its omnipresent bulge. She'd brushed up against him at school in the hall, asking coyly, "Thu-that a sock fuh-fuh-filled with quarters in there, Harry?"

Harry swung baby brother Arcan first because he whined to be the first. He grabbed the little boy by both hands and lifted him clear off his feet, arms strong as carnival cables.

Elliot recalled watching the spin as it blurred, seeing Arcan's body seem to change, slimming into a lithe bullet, feral as a cat on a trajectory popped from a cannon toward the moon. The face altered, too. Not cartoon sideways G-force but something eager with fangs. Blood spewed, making rings about the two boys as they went round and round, as if all the rings of the planet Saturn were bright crimson.

"Ohmygodddstoppp!" Elliot had yelled. "He's hurt ... puthimback down!"

Something must have cut loose from the little boy, some kind of seizure. A brain vein exploded, gushing out in a game gone horribly wrong.

Harry didn't seem to hear but whirled twice or thrice more before letting go. Elliot screamed, breaking immature boy's voice rising in a ripple of birdy pitches. He didn't wait for the little brother's body to splat against an oak tree but sprang forward.

Arcan landed, skidding on his sneakers through the grass, trying not to windmill his arms but to remain as he was cast. Unhurt except for a foolish grin of dizziness. His resulting pose was one of a beast coming up from a crouch, or cringing into one in some vicious defensive maneuver, the way a wolf coiled up before springing on a deer. It was so weird, Elliot had to laugh, seeing no blood. But it was a decidedly nervous cackle which came out of him, high pitched in that voice boys have before the deepening that comes with manhood.

Harry snatched at Steve and spun him, shoulders looking as if they buckled under his tee-shirt, the way they would on an older boy. Harry wore a trough in the ground where his feet dug in, heels tearing sod in an ever-widening arc.

Elliot saw Steve's head separate, a flower whose petals have burst in a sudden spring storm. The blood made not so much circles as a mist of scarlet pollen which hung about the two boys. Then—faster—the head flattened. Fasterfaster, the head vanished.

Elliot didn't try to stop it this time but stared, fascinated. If it had seemed terrible on Arcan but obviously hadn't been anything more hurtful than a silly mirage, Elliot wouldn't make a fool of himself. He watched Harry let go and Steve soar, falling, legs subtly flailing to gain a standing purchase as he came down. His shoes tore through a patch of Deborah Tyler's rose bushes. Thorns clearly embedded in the frayed jean's legs. But Steve—to his credit—didn't cry out or try to extricate himself from the mess he'd landed in. He wobbled only a bit, hands and arms rising and lowering to get a balance like a surfer riding a wave. Yet he fell anyway, rose bushes snarling his ankles. He came down with a thud on his face, arms out wide in some kind of embrace to the earth.

He didn't try to get up. This was how he fell and so he must remain.

Elliot whispered, "You okay?"

From a mouth of dirt came a positive, muffled, "Mmuhhuhmph."

Now it was Tina's turn.

"Suh-wing me hard, Harry," she begged through wet lips.

She was big-breasted for her age. Her nipples were erect against the fabric of her cotton shirt, which clung to her with the late summer sweat of a Texas September. Harry couldn't help looking, the boner in his pants threatening to burst the zipper. It had actually popped his belt into the next higher notch.

"Spuh-spuh-spin me and thuh-thuh-throw me like you want me!" she demanded.

He grabbed her hands and turned, leaves rustling down around them so perhaps he'd set up some sort of vibration, his feet doing a tantara that loosed a tremor into the ground. The damp shirt almost whipped off Tina, riding up her chest to expose her slim ivory waist, the round white curves of the bottoms of her breasts.

"Huh-harder! Fuh-fuh-farther!" Tina cried.

Elliot was aroused, waiting for the blouse to fly off completely. Lucky there were so many trees in his parents' yard, nobody could see this from the street.

But then with the mixture of red leaves raining from the trees, her flesh seemed to have holes in it, gouges, ragged and wealed.

Harry flung her. She landed on her ass, up on her elbows with grass stains, legs splayed apart, seam at her crotch splitting a little, shirt miraculously just above her jutting nipples. Her face was flushed, hair tousled, lips parted like some centerfold in a dirty magazine of their father's, expression begging for it.

"El … " Harry held out his hands, strength already cording through the tanned but soft fingers. (No, not soft. There'd never been anything soft about Harry.)

Elliot grabbed hold and they ran in place a bit, as if doing some stupid square dance do-si-do but with a demolition derby determination. Then Elliot felt himself go up, bound in a centrifuge, feet leaving the ground and stomach hurtling for his throat. His heart skipped beats and his colon clenched, the way it did on the tilt-a-whirl at the circus when the guy running the ride could be taunted into really cranking it up.

Harry's face became a blur, became weird, softer (no … there'd never been anything soft …), lips more succulently petulant and appealing than even slutty Tina's. And suddenly his brother was stark naked as he whirled him, breasts (not two of them but FOUR!) appearing to pop with a golden firmness and hips like some sultry movie star. Rachel Welch or Ursula Andress maybe, one of the muscular types that always made El's heart race in the theater—not like those scraggly twiggies that were showing up on the new underfed fashion scene. If Elliot had been attracted to "them", flat and bony, he'd be afraid he was destined to be a faggot—a fate worse than death in any part of Texas. But damn it DAMN IT he was seeing his own brother as a woman for SHIT'S SAKE so *was* he a queer boy then? Because looking down he could see Harry hadn't become all She but still had that prodigious erection that had always marked him as—well—HARRY.

Well, with four such prodigious breasts, why not Raquel AND Ursula, twice the woman, two times the majesty?

Elliot then seemed to see himself through Harry's eyes. His head was on fire, half his face melting, bubbling, flesh full of monsters the like of which not even a Hammer Film Saturday Extravaganza could dish up. He whimpered, tasting bile, afraid he was going to spew.

The brothers, shocked, let go of each other simultaneously. Harry stumbled back, arms feeling half-yanked from shoulder sockets, eyes bulging. Elliot flew, landing miraculously upright, but with one arm up as if reaching for some giant's grasp and the other arm down, making him appear to be outstretching to help someone to stand. There was a throb in half his face. He must surely have struck a tree with it, skidding past, scraping bark and skin down to wood pulp and bone. But he'd hit nothing and the agony of that pulse ebbed away. Like the echo of a scream made in a nightmare, dreamed while camped in the woods, is carried away in the wind before fully waking.

Tina had gotten up and sidled over to Harry, standing oh so close, not even bothering to pull her blouse back down. She whispered to him and he raised his eyebrows. She took his hand and led him behind the house.

"Where they goin'?" piped Arcan as he saw the game was over and relaxed his statue stance.

"To play a different game," Elliot replied drily.

Arcan gazed up at him. "Can't we play it?"

"Maybe someday," El answered, smirking. "But not now."

Steve pulled his face from the ground, spitting clods and grass blades and the seeds from late season dandelions.

"Hey, I think Harry killed me, ya know?" he grinned. "I mean, I bit the dirt, right?"

And then the memory shifted, and Elliot could see what had happened when Tina lured Harry behind the house. She'd slipped off her torn jeans and plunked her rosy butt down in the grass, legs spread the way she'd fallen in the game.

"You fuh-fuh-flung me good. This must be the wuh-way you wuh-anted me, right? So fuh-fuh-fuck me already."

Harry had knelt between her thighs and put himself inside her like he knew just what he was doing. As if it was him, Elliot could now feel the friction of heat and scratch, building moisture. Could taste vanilla wafers fuzzy on Tina's teeth and strawberry grease from gloss on her lips. Could smell her as a mix of cheap Evening In Paris perfume which came in a big blue bottle at the drug store (reeking like violets up a rectum), and a salty milky kind of musk that rose up from her sex. Could sense the intolerable pressure about to explode from his balls and then *it did* but he still kept going, never growing soft, the burn and the build beginning again.

He felt hands in his hair, his head snapped back. He was pulled off Tina and dragged backward. There was Deborah, fingers curled into claws, spittle flecking red lipsticked lips curved downward. A deep throaty snarl growled out, "Little bitch!"

Tina started to scream but Deborah quickly punched the girl hard in the throat, silencing that cry into a pulp-splintery gurgle. Then Harry's mother was on her, biting and clawing, mouth making disgusting sucking noises that Harry/Elliot understood were the swallows of Tina's blood. Deborah stood, chest heaving, and, picking up Tina's feet, began to hawl her through the back door into the kitchen.

Tina was no longer trying to scream or plead but was busy enough just trying to breathe. The trachea had been crushed, cutting off her air supply. The larynx, likewise, was damaged and filling with blood. She was drowning in it. Sputtering in a wheezy choke that sounded like *fuh-fuh-fuh-fuckckckck!*

"Get in here," Deborah Tyler barked at her eldest son, face contorting in a closed loop of the expressions for fury, lust, hunger.

Harry crawled in on all fours, looking whipped, erection bobbing between his legs. She locked the door, blood thick and bubbly over the threshold.

"Get me the big butcher knife off the counter," his mother ordered as she leaned over the twitching girl. She said to Tina, "So you think you're woman enough to steal my little boy? You're what? Fourteen, fifteen? You haven't yet earned the right to be called a woman! You think you're going to eat up my boy?"

She just shook her head at the girl, slowly and with a fierce grin. The girl was strangling but staring up at her, transfixed by something moving in Deborah's face.

Harry reached a trembling hand toward that knife. Elliot could feel that he wanted to stab it right into Deborah's catlike eyes. He could do it, too, while she was hovering over Tina, not looking at him, not *commanding* him. Then his mother swung her gaze from the girl and back to her boy. Suddenly he didn't dare even consider putting the knife into Deborah. He could see pieces of Tina's flesh in his mother's mouth, hanging like peach peel from her teeth. He closed his fist on the knife handle and handed it to her.

She hacked a piece of meat from the still-breathing Tina's breast and thrust it at him.

He just stared.

"Go on … " she said, not to be denied.

She cut off another and stuffed it in her own mouth, chewing defiantly. When he didn't do the same, she cuffed him up against the side of his head with a fist which was looking more like a paw every millisecond.

Harry ate the piece of Tina, aware that the girl could see him doing this. It struggled across his teeth and gums, marinated in frothy blood. He had to close his eyes so he couldn't see Tina watching as he swallowed.

Deborah crouched. "She's dirtied you."

She began to lick him clean. He could feel her tongue slick with Tina's blood erasing the traces of the girl's lubrications and his own cum. He could hear Tina's gargly sputters as they slowed, then ceased. He could have sworn the linoleum cooled noticeably by several degrees beneath his bare feet.

He said nothing as she fed the girl to the rest of the family over the next week, in roasts and thick stews, in sausages and blood puddings. He went into the bathroom after each meal, sticking fingers down his throat, trying to throw up but unable to, the flavor of both stomach acid and strings of lamblike meat making his hard penis seem to be granite, grinding himself against the sink as he leaned over it.

The word went out that Tina had run away, probably with a gang of bikers that had roared through town about the same time. Well, with the reputation she had, it was easy for folks to accept.

Elliot shivered in the caverns, the faces of female demons in stone not as horrible as what he remembered of Deborah's. He didn't judge Harry. He could—without even trying—recall the texture of her spit on his own balls. There wasn't a beast among the bas relief of crumbling rock more animal than she'd been.

He heard Harry's new voice, of bells and silk inside a mouth on the side of his face, purring from scars. Here, see in this tangle of carvings only the Insurrection of the Lotus. It is a shuffling indigo between the statues of rutting danavas that exalt the act of love even as they wantonly seem to debase it. It is the intentions of a lust which was born not so much of evil as the kind of all-encompassing hunger that denizens born to abandon must own … or be owned by. It comes with a cosmic finesse of abominating which practitioners of a more aesthetic path can never fathom or imitate.

"What's that supposed to mean?" Elliot inquired, feeling his own lips working to form a question posed to a being speaking through a hole in the side of his face.

It was Harry who actually spoke this time. "Our mother was nothing like them, yet everything like them. A mother of beasts cannot help being what she is. Even Kali devours infants she is striving to protect. What is the fortress that shields if not icy stone reared from boiling magma? It was her path."

Did this mean Harry didn't hate their mother anymore?

Remember …

Time might not have gone anywhere. Everything which had happened after a certain moment can be a dream. Saigon's fall, the helicopter, the madhouse, then being recruited by Saab Gestetner as a mercenary warpig, then opening the stolen pack to see the face of an angel inside.

He and Harry were on R & R and it was 1972. Yes, they were in Bangkok. Or Singapore. Or Shanghai. Someplace exotic with such things going on in the shadows that lay in velvet beneath lilies. They were at a very unusual theater, where white-gowned midgets were stuffed into the uterus of a dead elephant and then emerged naked with sapphires and pearls between their teeth. There was no Banyon beer or plum wine, but only a strange brandy pink as a virgin's pierced cherry, laced with opium, served with red poppies floating in it.

A dancer had stepped onto the stage. Her dress consisted of very un-Thai wide bell sleeves and full skirt of golden scarfs that fell to her knees. As she began to dance, these veils were caught in some contrived draft blown gently from someplace backstage. She seemed to billow as she swayed and pirouetted in a style more common to Russian Bolshoi than to the wrenching movements of classic Thai dance. She came up on tiny toes and lifted a thigh high, turning around in a spin that fully revealed the waxy bud of her clitoris as those skirts came up, and the slick armpits beneath the sleeves.

It also showed with sickening finesse the puckured raw flesh that had healed beneath where her skin had been stripped away. This skin had been stretched, and stretched, over years, pared with amazing but cruel skill away from the layers beneath, rubbed with oils, tanned, made tissue thin, silk veil thin. It had been artfully woven with gold threads, sewn with little rhinestones smaller than tears. It rustled from her shoulders and down the tops of her arms with no underpinnings beneath. It had been sheathed from her waist and down the buttocks, pulled up painstakingly and gently, the exposed meat beneath treated constantly with ancient medicines that smelled both sharp and sweet from the stage. There was the glaze of drugs in her eyes but she must have long since become inured to the agony.

"How did they keep it from rotting?" Elliot murmured out loud.

"It has rotted a little," Harry commented, inhaling a sugary sourness. "But these guys over here in the east invented doctoring."

Some of the patches were iridescent green or blue, others almost black. But somehow the dying process of the cells had been suspended.

She held her arms out to the audience. And it was Harry who stood up. He climbed to the stage and she put her arms around him. Elliot could hear the rustle of her skin as it draped around his brother. Then they were moving in a slow waltz, the tiny stones sewn into her veils moving across Harry with the soft tinkle of miniature bead curtains.

"I was made for this," she told him … and somehow Elliot could hear it. Whether he could when the two brothers were actually there together or not seemed unimportant. He could hear it now. "Fuck me to pieces."

Harry opened his trousers and lifted her skin skirt. She bounced upon her toes to spring, legs wrapping about his waist with a sound like rice paper and very ripe melon. The audience gasped, then cheered as the rhythm of the couple was accompanied by the sounds of drums and gongs. The delicate material of her body gown tore like paper tinsel, floated off in wisps in that wind from offstage, went down in gossamer skimmers into the crowd. Some tore it like a saffron lice from their hair in shudders. Others dropped it into their goblets to lie among the poppies in their drinks. Harry could clasp her nowhere that didn't come loose to stick in his fingers like cheap ostrich plume. Up close he could see the bloodshot veins in her eyes, smell the deathmusk about her like a combination of myrrh and half-fermented peaches.

And then Elliot clenched his eyes shut in a wince, becoming Harry up on stage, moving with this dancer of mortified cellophane, hands and fingers holding her against him informed of the weatherworn weight of butterfly wings. What it felt seemed to him that he was clasped with some giant mothlike creature whose wings everywhere crackled and frayed with contact.

Nevertheless he rode in and out of her to the drunken applause of the audience, plunging into an organ vessel limp with its own partial decay. He could feel the dying within the cold, cobalt womb, tell that it was detonating up and upward with his orgasm in a corrupting spiraling plastique-like jizzum through her innards, the ripples of rupture which must turn the deep blue flesh to purple, then to a black-sheened scarlet, finally to the white of fire on bone.

He looked out at the crowd and could see himself sitting out there, El of the passive face, not cheering with the others, only dragged along as usual, a witness without agenda who never formed judgements. He saw that Elliot face and caught himself trying to think out across to it (get me out of this, won't you? come up on stage and separate me from this degradation. you're the only one who can ...)

The dancer did fall to pieces in his arms, the thin clinquant veils of stretched skin caving, crumbling to flakes and powder, to motes of particle human. She slipped to the floor, a torso with stick limbs of dried yellow jerky, all grace lost in the desiccated rumple of herself. He (Harry/Elliot/combination) swallowed, stepped back, tried to shake the dust of her ruined silk-screen flay-scarfs off his clothes, tried to wipe the shreds of her wilted lettuce uterine lining where they stubbornly clung in his own emissions on his ever-rigid cock. Not showing his disgust because Harry Tyler could and would fuck anything, and maybe remain unable to show it and maybe not, because that was a part of Elliot inside him at the moment, grossed out, able to observe abomination without comment but not to be close up against it/touching it without some godawful shudder … But he Harry/Elliot/ *somebody* was thinking that she reminded him of an insect which has left some stage of itself behind—larval perhaps, chrysalid—but then which can't proceed to the next. Only floundering there, half of anything and half of nothing, born to shrivel and die without completion.

The god/goddess mouth, the mauve-frosted lips with copper-clapper tongue in the side of his face murmured. And Elliot couldn't lift himself out of the sequences he was thrown into. Similar to drug revelries, similar to fever dreams. Yet more real than memory, for memory was such a liar …

Harry and Elliot had said goodbye to Steve, and watched him go walking off down the tracks. Their friend was moping about a girl. Lately Steve was always depressed about something.

"Man, you need to go home and get some sleep," Harry'd said, noting the other teenager's dark-circled eyes and stoop. "You can dream about her. Can always get what you want in your sleep, can't you?"

Steve had just stared at him, through him, past him, too, perhaps. And replied, "No. Dreams are worse."

Elliot had been alarmed by the boy's voice when saying that. Because it was such a concrete affirmation. Because Elliot's dreams were often worse than reality, which considering the Tylers' home life was saying a great deal indeed. Even though Harry was always glad to sleep, escaping into some other world obviously better suited to him than the one Deborah crept through during waking hours. And obviously better than the one Elliot (or Steve) fell into at night. It was another thing of Harry's for Elliot to be a bit jealous of. Clear-skin envy, penis envy, dream envy.

Harry chuckled, slapping Steve on the back. "Come on, man! You're going to college in two years. You got that slipped disc in your back so there won't be no rice paddies for you. Us handsome types'll be in Vietnam. You'll have all those coeds for yourself. Don't let this little high school suzie creamcheese wilt your pecker!"

Steve shrugged and said, "Love's boat, crashed against the daily grind."

Oddly enough, Elliot recognized that. Because Steve and he were both in advanced English classes together—the only subject Elliot excelled in being that one. Recently they'd been studying poets of the Russian Revolution. That was a quote from Vladimir Mayakovsky. At least Elliot thought it might be. It was from one or other of those cheerful Bolsheviks.

Steve went his way down the tracks, and Harry and Elliot turned back toward the road to head home for supper. The sun had gone down and the moon was rising like the light from a spectral locomotive. It was late September, as it had been when they'd all played Swing The Statue together, the time when Tina ran away a few years ago. The trees were turning early, as they had been then. Sometimes, in this part of Texas, autumn didn't arrive till early December, summer lingering like the sweats and nausea off a bad fever. Red leaves were already falling by twos and threes. Out of the corner of Elliot's eye, they could have been drops of blood.

Elliot thought it odd Steve would recite this particular piece, considering that Mayakovsky—providing, of course, that it *was* from Mayakovsky—had committed suicide over some woman. El was a bit confused about this, remembering another Russian Revolutionary poet who'd killed himself, too. One of those two boys put a gun to his head and blew his brains out. But the other—was it Mayakovsky?—laid down beside the train tracks, putting his head on the rail …

Elliot grabbed Harry's arm.

"Jesus, Steve's gonna kill himself," he replied in a gagged voice.

"What makes you think so?" Harry asked, jumping.

But they ran back, just in case. Just in case it had been Mayakovsky who wrote "Love's Boat, crashed against the daily grind", and just in case it was him that waited for a train to come along.

And it churned inside Elliot's guts hearing a goddamn train coming as he opened his mouth wide until the corners of his lips split, shouting, "Steve!"

Remembering the game, with Harry flinging him and all of them in and out of some sort of oblivion. Seeing Steve's head separate like some ghastly cemetery-arboretum marigold, become a cloud of wine nimbus, then flatten, then vanish in the whirl.

It wasn't quite simple to say that this was how they found him. The body had spasmed when the train struck Steve, either because a train was naturally a lot of massive weight speeding to hell on rumbling metal so that it jerked the body as it connected with and crushed the head, or because at the last split second Steve cringed convulsively in mortal anticipation of being struck. The arms had flailed up and caught in the gigantic wheels—either before or after the head popped, the legs following as the spine arched and snapped. He'd been spread like a fly through the blades of a fan. More, considerably, than love's boat simply crashed.

And Elliot hated that he hadn't been able to save Steve. He was sure he'd had a premonition. He was sure Steve had been hinting (save me ... get me out of this, won't you?) when he quoted that bit from (yeah, *whoever*). He couldn't understand why he'd been able to see it coming, only to have that information be useless. He would have wanted to save Steve, so why couldn't he?

And then, weeping, clawing at that haunted scarred side of his face, trying to drag himself out of these images, Elliot found himself in the bathroom, twelve-years-old, standing before the mirror, popping zits. Searching for signs of *the shift* without even being obvious to himself about it. Making a few secretive hand passes that only a repressed suburban American freakmother would think out of the corner of her eye—*if* the bathroom door happened to be wide open—might be her boy masturbating but which were really just invocational gestures to some god of beasts, his lips murmuring START, MOVE, CHANGE.

Harry walked in, hung like Grendel, Leviathan, Satan, Michelangelo's David. In fatigues, so they weren't really just kids in Texas but had to be staying in a hotel. Maybe it was the night after Harry'd danced with the leather butterfly.

Elliot asked him, "Do you believe people can see into the future?"

And Harry had his pants open, was holding his Ever-Ready, Ever-Hard dick in his hand. Only it was a bayonet. Only it was a gobbety bloody drumstick from some poorly-cooked, inedible buffet they were serving down in the dining room. Only it was a wand of incense.

He answered, "You're seeing into the future now, little bro."

Elliot stared into the mirror as suddenly it was Harry standing in his place, squeezing pimples he'd never had, semen bursting out of them, raw liquid gold pouring out, stars being forced to pop from the craters and trickle down his face like glitter. Suddenly it was Deborah standing there, pawing her blemishes, tiny wolves and cat things crawling from the weals to bay up at the moon of the mirror. Then it was just Elliot again, only he wasn't in a bathroom but in a helicopter, and he was stepping on a woman's fingers to keep her from boarding as Saigon side-flipped into insanity. He was watching Sarin gas drones being sent into an occupied building where there might be children. He was walking behind a man carrying a pack he knew for a fact contained the cramped little body of a living (well, sort of) girl.

And Elliot hated that he'd done those things. He hated that he hadn't been willing to die for some principle which nagged him in its purity. He detested in himself the weakness that kept him from pulling back from shit to announce that he'd be going a different direction now.

Of course, that bathroom mirror was still there and now he fell through it. Looking down at some weird slant-eyed hermaphrodite that two grunts from his unit were holding down, telling him, "We know you like some strange knotholes but we bet you a month's pay you won't fuck this moi!"

With Rosh, Jansen, Crowell, Graham and Katzeff circling around this odious event, it was Elliot between its legs, bashing it in the face as it struggled and cursed him. Elliot grabbing hold of its gleaming breasts and feeling its cock and balls rub above his own as he rammed into its dark cunt. Elliot, dead in his mind, feeling the thing come in his face, waking up finding the other soldiers had skinned it and hung the skin in a tree. Elliot seeing that skin crawl down again in the moonlight because the soldiers were too close to discovering the village. And Americans were known for leveling innocent villages even if they so much as *suspected* they might be harboring VC. It went to each man, a mouth opening with nothing at all behind that raw taffeta mask still bit holes into them and spat out peculiar jungle *non-realia* which swarmed all over them or which turned, capering, hole in the skin where the ass had been—nothing in there either—but which still shat a curdling darkness that blacked them out.

It was Elliot having it turn to him afterward, just turn, a pirouette on an empty skinbag of a foot, eyeholes full of green swamp gas. Trudging back in the morning, only man who survived.

Had he survived? Had he begun a transformation of incarnation without death having to intercede first? Or had the thing pressed against him, as he had earlier forced himself against it? Had the flapping scraps of its genitals been like a fist of darkness up his ass where he lay on his back like a woman? Had this twirly, jerky strip of dick then pissed out a scalding light that sprayed down his throat like the golden showers of a fiend who has drunk sulfuric acid? Had the mouth vomited out more of this light in curds that sang of Bodhisatvas, burning, and birth?

Had it used this mouth of incinerating light to chew into Elliot's head where he'd been dead already? And had those brains that chugged from crunched-open skull started out gray but taken on rainbow colors?

He'd screamed, there among the tropical trees, soul throttled out, soaring up, dizzy into a sky blistering with light, stars everywhere, some kind of seed bursting out of some eternally-engorged spectral dick of him which created more stars. He felt the terror pass, a euphoria overtaking it. It seemed he was coming apart to make the universe stretch farther, worlds boiling out of it like sapphires and emeralds. Comets were spewing from the ends of his fingers as he splayed them in front of his face. Space and time intersected through a chakra point in his forehead until, with a stab of fabulous pain, he could feel every inch and second simultaneously.

He'd screamed, there in the jungle, spirit raped and disemboweled, finding himself running down a mountain. Demons were running with him, laughing, shrieking, tearing up the rocks and soil with their taloned feet. He was grinning like a loon, going so fast he knew he couldn't stop even if he wanted to. But he also knew there was no way to end this wild slide downward. Beyond the sound of the insane jubilation he could hear the jangle of a universe coming unhinged, rattling like the jabber of teeth in skulls.

He'd screamed, and found himself in the cavern, Harry's warm/cool hands to either side of his face, weirdly beautiful features close to kiss him softly. Whispering, this time not from Elliot's scars but from Harry's own mouth, "It's all right. This is my gift to thee. Oh, joyous! Joyous! This is the lesson of *mokhsha,* salvation. Not for crimes you have committed, though we must always accept responsibility for what we've done. But for having allowed yourself to be thrust from your path, from your dharma. By our mother, by the government, by this man you call the colonel. We atone when we allow destiny to enter our lives again, for peace or destruction or both, and when we take up whatever road this incarnation was intended to walk."

And, as a matter of fact or course, it *was September*. Elliot closed his eyes, sensing himself floating to the cavern floor. He felt four moonbreasts press against his chest. Shiva entered him, not in any way violating or painful. The delicate tissue of the anus did not tear or even seem to stretch. And the god member that took him felt nothing like flesh. Elliot shuddered, feeling arms and legs wrapped around him securely, then more arms as an extra pair slid from beneath the first, as if a key had been turned in a secret lock to cause these to appear from hidden recesses in the god's ribs, and a tail was squeezed from the last vertibra in the spine, squeezed out like a long turd only it was flesh and it wrapped itself to lock Elliot's and Harry's legs together. In one moment he was going upward in a space-bending rush with his brother, seeing nebulas and novas spark, flame, generate all manner of alien life, and also racing down the mountain, seeing demons, hearing time crack like a billion eggs.

Elliot would have reeled with shock had he been able to move. Briefly he heard Embe's voice, *You need healing. But it will take a greater queen than I am to do that.*

The god pulled out, caressed Elliot's face where ghosts shrieked and ranted, their eyes and mouths open like infected pimples, bullet holes, stab wounds. As his fingers touched, each one closed, melting back into that which was only a ripple of plain scar tissue. No longer haunting. And voiceless.

Chapter 21

"Sometimes I am man,
sometimes I am woman.
O lord of the meeting rivers
I'll make wars for you
but I'll be your devotees' bride."
—poem to Shiva
Basavanna

Elliot had been quiet a long while. He might have even slept for a few hours, exhausted.

After he'd arrived at the cavern with his brother, the women and children had disappeared for a while. But now they were returned. Most of the women were collected together, praying softly—he assumed—for their men who had been slaughtered in the village. The children were gathered around the Thai girl he'd rescued from Saab Gestetner's backpack. They were gently washing her skin with what appeared to be milk, especially careful around the bizarrely sculpted fingers of the left hand. They were singing very lightly to her as one of them combed her hair, arranging a many-hued orchid into it. The brilliant flower paled beside the glittering aura around her head.

They had stripped her to perform these ablutions, and Elliot could now see clearly the abuse which the rest of her frail little body had suffered. He considered the kind of beast that he knew Saab to be and wondered how he could ever have thought of the man as his friend, turning a blind eye to excesses he'd seen the colonel perform.

Harry said that Saab (among others) had taken Elliot off the path he'd been meant to walk, whatever that was. That Elliot had let himself be strayed by the stronger will of others. Harry thought that was the worst sin a person could commit. It seriously fucked with fate, which ultimately could screw with the balance of the entire universe. Of course, Harry was Shiva now; Harry was God. So his ideas were likely to have taken a decidedly metaphysical turn than when Harry'd only been Harry, and mostly concerned with where he was next going to stick his cock.

Elliot trembled, wishing he had cigarettes ... a pack or three would suffice. Even though he didn't smoke. Because he knew so many guys who smoked when they were unnerved, giving the twitch in their fingers something constructive to do. It was better than just letting them convulse, like a nest of spiders each chained by a single leg. It was better than being tempted to stick his hand up his ass just to keep them still. He was wishing he had a drink, some potable the color of burnt almonds and aged at least thirty years, to dull the beating of his heart. He was wishing he had a few Valium, or some Halcion, or Quaaludes. Barbituate clouds to calm him.

Of course, maybe what he really needed were some antipsychotics, because this had to be an episode. Soon he'd discover he'd been on the shock table again, strapped down, rubber stopper in-between his lips, volts caroming him into this place of mutilated dolls and godbrothers.

He observed the girl's scartattoos, every bit as evocative as Elliot's scarhaunts had been—before Harry quieted them. He half-expected to see them START, MOVE, CHANGE. He wouldn't have been surprised to see the headless corpse on her belly begin an obscene dance. Carvings of sewage-breathed vampire vetanas and bestial rakshasas with blood-and-shit-matted fur might have marched off the blister-burn moonscapes of her flesh, a parade of the damned even more frightening because they adorned the body of some sort of Thai Mary Magdalene.

"Her name is Sirikit," he heard Harry say.

Yet when he glanced that way, the god was sitting in full lotus, every nuance of the dual genitalia as visible as the individual facets of a precious gemstone. The eyes were closed, lips pressed together, nostrils flaring first on the right side, then on the left, as if Harry was only inhaling through one and only exhaling through the other. A pose of deep meditation.

Elliot wondered if he'd taken that first step toward what Harry'd called *atonement* when he stole this Bangkok child—this Sirikit—away from his old friend and commander. (After refusing to take part in the slaughter of helpless villagers, a definite switch from his usual go-along, pick up your gun, it gets easier with every one you pop.)

Still, that didn't ensure that Elliot was fated to be some sort of hero. Maybe he'd been meant to be nothing, or had been intended to invent some evil weapon which would ultimately destroy the world. Harry'd said that destruction could just as easily be someone's path as creation. And that it was just as valid: cosmically. The only importance was that the destruction in question serve some higher purpose.

What Elliot had already accomplished had been a lot of destruction. But apparently it was done only because of pressure on him by outside forces. So … what? That meant it was bad. (No shit, Sherlock.) But was it necessarily bad if it was what he'd been meant to do?

El sighed, feeling weary, mind taxed to understand. He stared at Sirikit's warped fingers, horrific totem figures he thought would surely commence to performing some grotesque puppet theater. Had that been a part of Saab's path—and was it okay if it had been what he was fated to do?

There was no way in anyone's belief system to accept what Gestetner—and others—had done to this child.

She glowed: indigos, malachite greens, jonquil golds suffusing an otherwise rose light. He felt humbled in the sheer serenity that blossomed from her. He was certain he ought to crawl over and kneel before her, kissing the bottom of each foot once. He believed if he could, he would give her his own left-handed fingers, so she wouldn't be crippled this way.

The children had finished adoring and adorning her. They began dancing around her quietly, feet making only soft shuffing noises on the cavern floor. A cobra slithered between them and coiled into her lap, going to sleep.

Elliot looked away, to where a mound of flower petals lay in one corner of the cavern. Buttercups, orchids, lotuses. He saw them shift, begin to slide. He watched the head of a young woman rise up through them, petals falling from her face like scented water droplets from a bath.

He gasped, suddenly breathless by how beautiful she was. He hadn't seen her when he'd come in with Harry. And he'd have noticed her. She was no older than nineteen or twenty, face perfectly molded, high forehead and cheek bones, almond eyes with long lashes like black lacquered fans, a full mouth. Her long straight black hair cascading down her sleek back seemed to sparkle with the various blooms. She was possibly the most exquisite woman he'd ever seen anywhere, coming up through the flowers as if invented by them. The burnished shoulders and round, topaz-nippled breasts (even if only a single pair of them), arms rising over her head as she stretched, blossoms falling away to reveal a small waist and the flare of her hips.

Elliot held his breath, waiting for her stand and finally shake off the last of the petals. The children must have covered her up as she'd slept.

But then he understood she was standing. On the stumps that went no farther than a couple inches below her hips.

Yes, all the villagers of Phnom Yohp were crippled. All except the children. And their god.

She looked at Harry and smiled shyly. She put her hands together and bowed in obeisance. Then she walked over to Elliot, using her delicate hands as feet to propel her along.

"I am Cheanneary Ry," she told him. "Have the others told you that tonight is almost the full of the moon?"

El shook his head.

She gestured toward Harry in his tranquil repose.

"Shiva sent me a dream just now," she whispered, and Elliot marveled at how her breath smelled of anise. "Tonight we will be confronted by the men you came with. They come to kill us all and to take the Soma."

Elliot was startled. Although why should he be surprised? He'd suspected that the colonel wouldn't give up until he'd found the drug. And that he wouldn't be satisfied until every person from Phnom Yohp was dead.

She bit her lip and then lightly touched Elliot's arm. The brush of her fingers sent electricity through his veins.

"The question is, brother-of-god, what will you do then?" she asked.

He took a breath and replied, "Atone."

Chapter 22

"When the void forms of one's own thoughts are shining here, May the Buddhas, exerting the force of their grace, Cause not to come the fear, awe, and terror ..."
—Tibetan Book Of The Dead

The god, the Thai girl Sirikit, the twenty-five children, and the snake-faced priests remained in the cavern. The women went into the jungle, fully aware that the mercs were looking for them.

"We can't let them find the temple," Cheanneary Ry explained to Elliot. "We must protect the Soma."

Elliot remembered one of the dreams which had been shown to him. Of how the U.S. G.I. carrion-knothole-fucker Harry Tyler had come to be transformed into a god. The soldiers had come *then* to the temple, finding the hermaphrodite. The thing had returned after its murder specifically to *protect* the *village,* to prohibit them from harming it.

So why was the scenario now reversed, the villagers (the women anyway, since all the men had been killed) putting themselves in danger's way to shield the temple?

Well, there were the children to consider. Logic said that without them there would be no village in the future.

And the Soma hadn't been there the last time. No, the Soma was something that this incarnation—the Harry incarnation—

of Shiva had brought back into reality. (Or whatever was passing for reality.) Elliot got the distinct impression that this particular Shiva was different from previous ones to be personified in Nagas Wat. He was stronger; he had a farther-reaching purpose.

What could such a purpose be?

Elliot went with the women. There was no way he could allow them to go unprotected. He felt deep inside that this was part of his path, a section of the destiny he was supposed to fulfill. It seemed odd, doing this on gut sense, without anyone ordering him to, without a payment being made for his services. As a matter of fact, he didn't really expect to survive this, being outgunned five to one. If he had the element of surprise, he might fare better but …

And Saab must be determined to kill him. Not being a man to give a shit why you betrayed him, he wouldn't wait to ask for Elliot's reasons after all their years together. He'd just have him held down while he drew out that Smith and Wesson, and with one hammerfall at a time blow gaping holes into each of El's knees and elbows, laying a bullet into the groin, the intestines, and finally the heart.

Elliot didn't look forward to the meeting. He'd come to really hate Gestetner in just the last few hours. He suspected he'd always hated the colonel, but had suppressed the force of will necessary to let himself realize it. It had been easier just to go along with the notion that the man was his comrade, likened even to his own brother. It was simpler to play along with the devil, told where he would go, when he would shit, and whom he would shoot.

Elliot might have chosen to remain behind with Shiva, to make sure that Gestetner didn't show at the temple and threaten the kids. But he had a queer foreknowledge that the people in the temple would be all right if the others left.

Actually, it was Cheanneary Ry's foreknowledge, from the dream that Shiva'd given her.

(Growing up with him, who'd have ever guessed ol' Harry could give anyone dreams of prophecy?)

It was a bit slow going through the jungle, many women being without one or both legs. Only Elliot carried any weapons, his Glock pistol and trusty AKM.

They went down into a bowl between one mountain knee and the next, a field of rapeseed in full yellow flower, the plants so tall that the heads of the crippled women disappeared beneath the blooms. The wind shooshed through softly and El felt strangely alone, being the only one tall enough to be standing higher than the plants. There were petaled ripples around him and he had to suppress a shiver, because it was as if *anything* could be moving through those flowers.

They crossed a little bridge at the river, looking down, seeing many golden carp, fins flashing a red orange in the late sun. Just down from this the water was carpeted with pond lotuses, so many that it seemed the group ought to be able to walk across them and remain afloat. On the other side was a stand of bamboo, emerald plumes bowing in the breeze like courtiers lowering their heads before an emperor.

Coming night turned the trunks of trees silver. It altered the color of Cheanneary Ry's face to that of shining moonstone. Elliot had to constantly swipe at vines and brambles that snagged him as he went through the undergrowth. He marveled at how the women never seemed to get anything snared in their long black hair.

He smelled mango trees and glanced up. What was that up there? Loose and dangling? He imagined a sky full of kites, bamboo whistles tied to the strings, a sudden downdraft swooping them in a fall to be caught in the branches.

What a curious paper or cloth they were made from. Brown and black, wet from last night's rain.

And the way many of the corners were long, too long.

Then Elliot could see that some had faces. And some only had the parts of faces.

He paused and stared, mouth hanging open, as he understood these were human skins.

Cheanneary Ry saw he'd stopped and made her way back to him.

"They are from our men," she explained. "When the soldiers left the village the first time we went back. They had tried to burn them but we took the skins anyway."

Elliot was disbelieving. How could these women—many of whom didn't even have hands—have accomplished such a terrible task? Not only to deftly separate the hides from the bodies, but to climb the trees to get them up there? He attempted to picture in his mind armless or legless women shinnying up mango trees. With a mixture of revulsion and amusement he was greeted with an image of breasts and buttocks like round mango fruit, getting a disturbing, yet arousing, mental scent of fruity sweetness and female musk working together.

As if knowing what he was thinking—about the dexterity necessary, that is—she replied, "The children did the work."

Somehow that vision was worse. Twenty-five very young children—who would only be in kindergarten back in the states—having to flay the corpses of their fathers and then arrange them up in the high branches of trees they might also have many times eaten the fruit from.

There came a sound of bodies moving methodically through the undergrowth up ahead. Low chatter, men's voices. There was a slap—probably at mosquitoes. Somebody cursed in French. The mercs.

Elliot frantically waved to the women. "Get down!" he whispered hoarsely. He glanced about but really didn't see a lot of decent cover from which to mount his solitary defense.

But they wouldn't obey. They stopped and stood, as if waiting to be observed. El gasped. What? Did they *want* to die?

Cheanneary Ry was looking out toward the eastern sky, her eyes narrowing into darkly feathered slits, mouth clearly set in resigned determination. Over the mountains, the lopsided moon was rising, white as bone, spilling rays that descended the sky thick as pale mist.

The mercs came through the trees and Elliot could see the colonel. Saab saw El, too, standing with the women around him. The man smiled in a hard, thin line that exposed no teeth. He drew his Smith and Wesson and shot the woman nearest him right in the head. The stumps of her arms came up to cover her face as if in some late expression of self-defense. Then she rocked backward into a bed of braided vines. Mosquitoes immediately swarmed the blood.

Phan had been staring, eyes wide, looking this way, that way, as if at things no one else could discern. When he shot, it was in a strange random pattern, certainly not at his own men but not at the women either. The fact that he actually hit a couple women was by sheer accident, as if he'd tracked spirits who then passed in front of these unfortunate targets.

Monivong raised his weapon and fired in rapid succession. Three more women fell, bright red-and-gray orchids blooming through their hair.

Elliot had snapped up his AKM and began shooting over the women's heads (which wasn't too difficult) and at his old comrades-in-arms. He'd seen the Mexican bring down a woman with one leg and a crutch. Ruiz was now taking aim on a woman with no arms and only one shoulder, giving her the appearance of always being in mid-shrug. Elliot squeezed off and saw a round split the top of Ruiz's head. The man spun, twice in a widdershins circle, before coming down to sit upright on his ass in the undergrowth. The Mexican looked stunned, blood running straight down the center of his face as if the bullet had been the first chop of a machete intending to split him directly down the middle. The man then touched this, running a forefinger in the line between his eyes, down the bridge of his nose, the center of his chin. He began to shriek, "Maria, Maria! Dos medias, noche y viento!"

Vezat brought his weapon up almost in startled afterthought, firing, striking a woman not ten feet from him. She fell to the ground and writhed, just a torso and head, bullets having not-too-cleanly blown apart her lower jaw. His eyes widened and he crossed himself, fingers brushing his crucifix as he did so. He shrank his touch back, glancing down at the cross and seeing the image of his Savior rendered upon it, sans arms and legs. Elliot's weapon spat metal which caught him in the shoulder, arm, and side. He fell back, then rolled to distance himself from further spray.

Gestetner gave Elliot an annoyed frown as he went down on his knees, grabbing a woman to thrust in front of him as a shield.

Still, he chuckled as he called out, "Have to do you later so I can do you slow, El!"

Then he fired a single, deliberately errant bullet that skimmed the side of Elliot's skull, knocking him to the ground. Afterward he pressed the pistol'smuzzle against the back of his whimpering shield's head and pulled the trigger. He knew the spray he saw on the other side of her was the blowout of the front part of her brain and most of her face.

Elliot twitched, what felt like a mallet slamming the side of his head. His AKM drifted from his fingers and he lay on the earth, unable to get up.

He could see the skins in the trees. They were crawling down from the branches, moonlight turning the partially burned skins into reams of ghastly Halloween-colored crepe paper streamers. He knew he must be hallucinating. They couldn't really animate that way, puffing with invisible innards which somehow lent a colorful glow to the outside—as if a spinning rainbow disco globe whirled within each. They lighted on the ground and began to move toward the mercs. One stepped across him, skin of the feet dragging across his chest like a lukewarm snailtrail. And ... was that a smile as it glanced down at him? Through the crinkle of the mouth that was what a crack in midnight must resemble?

Monivong saw something dangle from a tree directly to his right. It coiled and snapped at him. He tried to ignore it, knowing it was only the vision of a cobra, like he'd had before. He wouldn't make a fool of himself again in front of the others. But when it sprang and latched around him, squeezing about his arms, forcing him to drop his gun, he managed to cry out before it also began to choke him.

Monivong could see them, in the trees, and this one brought its face near his, mouth split and hissing.

Only there was nothing inside the mouth, just as there was nothing within the eyes. And he could see it wasn't a serpent at all but the skin of a man, mottled from burning until its surface resembled the dappled scales of a cobra. But from the underbrush, cobras *were* coming, slithering out of the vines and out of the rotted fruit of fallen mangos. They snaked up his shaking legs, working their way under pants cuffs which had been tucked into his boots and now somehow weren't anymore.

(Was he also seeing them drop from the trees, the sky? Like rain! Just as they had before, years ago, when those damned brats got away. Like soot-dappled, neck-swelling snow. Air-full-of-cobras! Landing on everyone, the hissing from all combined so loud that it sounded as if the atmosphere of the world was suddenly leaking away into space.)

The cobras crept up Monivong's thighs and burrowed their swollen-necked heads into his ass, working upward through the rectum until his spine snapped from the enlightenment of this deadly kundalini. Others found the spasming sacs of his testicles and the frightened leach of his dick. As they bit down, the skin that was still squeezing him brought its own mouth up to Monivong's and fastened this over his lips.

And if he'd believed it to be empty inside, he discovered it was not. Sizzling cobra venom began to spurt from it, shooting like a thick acid sperm across his tongue and down his throat. He twisted and gagged, jerked at every balljoint and connective juncture to attempt to loosen the thing's grip on him.

The little bag he'd always kept around his neck was rubbed at the cord, rubbed until it came off, opening as it struck the earth, the captured souls inside taking flight like a flock of startled nightingales. His own spirit was sucked into the skin of the thing clutching him.

Ruiz sat on the ground as two skins came at him from opposite sides. They didn't have heads, as he knew they must have been blown apart when these hides had graced living men. Neither did they have more than stumps for legs. But they were as strong as if they owned the arms of wrestlers, taking hold of his head, one to each side of the further crease Elliot had made of his skull.

They also had these ridiculous, scrappy, twizzle stick-made-of-fried-tripe dicks, empty as balloons not yet blown up for a kid's birthday party. But they erected, looking for all the world like circumcisions-in-reverse, where the cock meat has been removed but the foreskins remain. These were jammed without ceremony into his ears where he could have sworn he *heard* blues, greens and yellows pierce his eardrums. The creatures thrust corrugated, rainbow air-bloated hips, screwing into his brainpan with needle thrusts as they began to pull apart the two hemispheres of his head.

But he was already insane, certain he'd ridden the slide of the great buzz saw. And that these were gods ... not of the Lord/Lady Ometeotl but of Xipe Totec, the Flayed Deity. Ometeotl mustn't have been able to get a visa to travel out of Mexico, so Xipe Totec had come to finish the job of making Ruiz into the holy divided one's image.

Even with his ears plugged (and his eardrums speared?), he could hear the noise his skull made as it cracked. He could see with each eye the change in perspective, as the right half went down one way and the left half went the opposite. He briefly tasted coppery blood mixed with semi-petrified nuggets of snot that dumped from his split sinuses into the shucked reservoir of his mouth. He heard several of his teeth as they sprang from his gums like kernels of shocked popcorn. And then, mercifully, he knew nothing else.

Vezat managed to get to his feet. He saw the abbreviated *truncated* shapes dancing the cripples' own graceful saraband toward him. He tried to bring his weapon up to shoot them but was paralyzed save for the single-minded part of his anatomy which was growing very hard. (Naturally, it could have been because Elliot shot him, getting him in that shoulder and arm, knicking a nerve.)

The sight of the maimed women hadn't done anything for him—except for seconds only, as the armless, legless one he'd shot convulsed, seeming to be a man. Aroused Vezat was, but also terrified. Even as his erection dribbled lubricant when by all the rights and rites of freaking out it should have been pissing a font, his ass squirting shit into the seat of his trousers, flowing in greasy lumps down the backs of both legs.

"Ne plus," *he murmured.* "Ne Plus, ne plus."

No more, no more, he pleaded over and over as they began to touch him with their strange taffeta limbs, illuminated with the same ophite halo the village men had worn—only inside now. As they came at him across the ground, more fell from the nearest trees onto Vezat until he was born to the earth by a sea of mangled skin. They pulled down his fatigues and he couldn't help it … he arched his spine, ass thrust up. His dysentery-bruised sphincter muscles clenched, fluttered spastically as their flotsam gummy flap-cocks rammed into him, turning his bowels to more mush with each thrust, tearing with wet sheet splits and gargled farts as the Frenchman pig-squealed.

It was like his dream in the village, of rut in the pile of corpses, as he swam through them to find some bit of air to gulp down. He tried now, even as he ground backward into their rectal-assaults, to find a way up through the carrion mound, even as his own hard granite erection passed through various mouths, the hollows at the backs of their throats taking on an aspect of tarnished silver and mephitic fire opal.

And then their wide mouths fastened onto him in all places, biting down sharply (how? without *teeth*, he wondered), fangs like what shrapnel must feel like when it came up in tissue-rending, bone shattering arcs from a fool's tread upon a landmine. He floundered in the orgy of skin-sans-flesh, his breath cut off abruptly, back-of-the-deep-throat exquisitely. He felt the gouges they chewed into him fill with acid and honey, as agony and orgasm cast him out into a viciously happy oblivion.

Phan was still squeezing his trigger, even though he'd long since run out of bullets. The fact that he carried plenty more, that all he needed to do was to stop long enough to reload, meant nothing to him. He saw the ghosts everywhere, the dead of wars recent and distant past.

He saw the god of battlefields (and of cremation grounds) dancing through the throng and tried to shoot him. But the being only glided away, laughing, spirit eyes mad with a sorrowful euphoria and spirit nostrils flaring with the stench of eternal carrion. He could see the skin creatures crawling down from the trees, blood flowing down the bark behind them like mango juice. Or perhaps it *was* juice, the mangos bursting like ripe heads in a village square. He could see the little women, mutilated as if they *ought* to be among the ghosts. He could see the colonel seeming to be very surprised as skin things began to rush him, an odd but not ungainly movement like the rustling of bolts of kaleidoscopic silk, moonlight visible through them making ghastly inner auras even more compellingly gorgeous.

Phan watched Gestetner take off, running through the trees, his expression not the one of horror and fear that the situation would have required, but of puzzlement and a raw determination to survive. One of them was too close behind him. Gestetner turned and shot it, the bullet ripping through the skin and making a ripe, puncture noise, as a jab at a tire innertube might make. It halted, seemed to shrivel, leaking prisms. Then it shook itself, an unsettling action of a wound attempting to gather its edges back. It plumped up again. But by that time Colonel Gestetner was far ahead. Still, the skins pursued, visible as full-spectrum spectral lanterns being carried through the trees, not the least bit hampered in their movements the way that living amputees are by their afflictions. But then their feet (or whatever they had as the lowest parts of their bodies) didn't really seem to touch the ground. They glided; they spun. They *flew*. And, at that, they would surely overtake Saab Gestetner eventually. There would simply be too much night and too much jungle in-between for Phan to get to watch.

Phan realized the colonel's gun had made a booming sound, something his own weapon wasn't doing.

"Oh," Phan muttered to himself and finally paused to reload. He then brought the gun up and fired. Again. Two more women fell, having the bad luck to be where there were ghosts he was trying to stop.

Then another woman reached up and grabbed his gun.

"Don't be afraid," Cheanneary Ry told him. "Once you join the parade, you'll no longer be able to see any of the others. Do you recall, long ago when you were a child and the Americans bombed your village, how the ghosts couldn't find one another? You have but to be one among them to no longer see them."

Phan trembled, sobbed, and let her take the weapon. He closed his eyes as several of the skin things descended on him. When the pain was gone and he opened his eyes again, he discovered he truly was alone. But he was hardly comforted by this.

Elliot had seen as Cheanneary Ry went boldly up to the Vietnamese—as he was shooting, mind you—and calmly grabbed the barrel of the gun. How fine and courageous she was! She took it away from him and then set it on the earth, where a cobra began to slither along the length of it, twining, forked tongue flickering along the muzzle like a lover. She walked on her hands back to where Elliot lay, side of his head thrumming like some industrial-sized tuning fork. She cradled him in her arms.

Elliot felt her soft hair on his face. It trailed in the blood on the side of his head like a painter's delicate brush, the kind an artist only used to draw tears and the subtlest of shadows with. He gazed up at her and murmured, "Ry?"

"Don't speak, *lowk,*" she said in the voice of the mangrove's dove.

"Ry?" he persisted, a bit loopy with pain. "You're the most beautiful woman I've ever seen."

A blush rose from her jaws to her cheeks. She stroked the side of his face tenderly but didn't seem to believe his words. After all, no woman without legs could be all that.

"I mean it," he assured her.

She whispered, breath issuing out almost harshly, "No, I am a *freak.*"

Then she called to the other women, those who had survived. A dozen or more had been killed. The colonel's people had been responsible for the murders of over three quarters of the adult population of Phnom Yohp in a little over twenty-four hours. They came up, limping or dragging themselves, weeping, fingers or knees or hair stained with their sisters' blood.

"Don't ever say that," Elliot told her, trying to reach his own hands up to touch her face but finding he was unable for the moment to move a muscle. "You're the goddess of—(here he wondered, what was Shiva/Kali not lord/lady of? And he didn't know so he just made something up)—the goddess of roses on moons and of bells struck through birdsong."

He gathered from the kindness in her eyes that she was really in love with somebody else. He just didn't know who it was.

She traced his cheek with her cool fingers and wiped blood from the side of his head with her long hair. Then several of the women, herself included, lifted Elliot up and started back to the temple.

Chapter 23

"Drink of this mead, rejoice in it;
Delighted go by paths on which the gods go."
—The Vajapeya

Elliot was woozy. He hadn't lost consciousness, either while being carried back to the temple or as he was treated afterward for Saab's pure-stroke-of-marksmanship Smith and Wesson swipe to the side of his head. He'd been given something warm to drink. It looked like milk and tasted of strange flowers.

His brother came to sit beside him.

"Have I just drunk Soma?" Elliot asked, eyes flickering to sight of the girl Sirikit.

She who was smiling without a mind. He didn't know if he relished such a chance or was scared shitless of it. Of course, it was possible to really want something badly simply because it did frighten you so much.

Harry shook his head. "It's only something for the pain."

Elliot squinted, seeing the form of his already much-altered sibling as it misted, shifting. The feminine aspect faded and Harry was reconfigured as Krishna, as he was depicted in the battle on the Kuruksetra plain in the beginning of "The Bhagavad Gita." Pronouncing to Arjuna, *I have become Death, the Destroyer of Worlds.* He was the iconoclast in the center of the avatar and—simultaneously reversed—the creator at the heart of the vandal.

Elliot squeezed his eyes shut tightly, till his lids ached and lashes ground off, skull throb rising and falling in a crescendo of cymbals and out-of-tune flugelhorns. When he looked again, it was the Shiva persona he'd come to recognize as his brother's new self, part male/part female, a little bit country and a little bit rock and roll.

"Did I do good?" he asked his godbrother. "Was this atonement?"

"You've begun. To be shriven, you must return to the source, the incarnate imperative. Begin again where it first started to go wrong for you. It might be a place; it might be a state of mind. You can't change what you've done but you can alter what you might eventually do."

Elliot tried to smile, but he knew he only looked confused. Did this being sound like a god … or a psychoanalyst? And the method such doctors used in their psychoboogie treatment that brought out every nuance of the 'anal' in psychoanalyst. He'd really asked because he wanted a pat on the head, a nudge and a wink, something to imply he had the chance to turn things around. What he'd gotten were further complications.

"What happens if I fail?"

Shiva closed one gorgeous eye, lashes like black jungle ferns. "Failure is an illusion. All the emotions we struggle with—the things we seek and what we run away from—all illusion. And that is *maya,* which is what binds us to the painful wheel of birth."

Elliot thought back to when he'd compared trying to get control over the shift in his face with the character off KUNG FU. Slo-mo commands and mystical tonal manipulations. Now Harry reminded him of that priest David Carradine had played. Harry was Kwai Chang Caine, moving in so many separate parts per second, but he was also a god who—because he *was* time—could disrupt it. Bringing up his hand and making a profound utterance. Not *Enough!*, but *Atone!* Now, in addition to those nifty tattoos of tiger and dragon on the forearms, he had mouths in his palms.

(Which made Elliot giggle, despite himself, thinking about an adolescent boy jerking off, and a mouth in that location being able to give the kid a blowjob at the same moment. Very con-fucking-venient, even though by all intents and purposes the kid's dick ought to be emerging from the back of his hand. Except it didn't because there was a dimensional screw and skew there someplace.

And even when he came, and the palm mouth swallowed it, it stayed inside the flesh, because milk did a body good, helped build it twelve different ways toward the path to enlightenment, integrating him into the ultimate, transcendentally-experienced cosmic man.

The lips smacked afterward and said, *we know what you've been up to!*

It made him blush, red flushing his face in a horrible wash of nausea and Christian guilt. Was it damnable for him to think such thoughts about a god? Especially while that god was—what?—delivering commandments unto him? Thou shalt not consider masturbation and God in the same heartbeat … And staring at those breasts must be as vile a sin as undressing the statue of Mother Mary with your eyes at communion. Thou shalt not think *Mother Mary full of grace* … and *Hey, babeeeee!*

Back to Kwai Chang, in and out of flashbacks to temples and serene bald guys and dancing violence, this plot-interwoven spiel about Tao and *chi* and STUFF that could leave any normally level-headed redneck folding himself into a tight fetal ball for protection. What the fucking hell did it mean? If failure was an illusion, and accomplishment a chimera, did that suggest that defeat laid a fifty-pound egg that ruptured the out-hole and that nothing sucked like success?

"Then why does it matter?" El dared asked, expecting lightning to strike him.

No white-hot bolts came; Shiva didn't even frown. So perhaps it was okay to actually ask questions here.

Shiva did cock his lovely head. "Matter?"

Elliot blinked, pain drug swirling through his veins—probably some locally-produced opiate—numbing his lips, making them feel thick and frozen as with novacaine (Kwai Chang Caine) at the dentist's.

He plunged on. "Yes, then why try at all? If it's so much nothing."

Shiva smiled and Elliot could see Harry very much present in it. "Oh, it isn't nothing, bro. It's the difference between the dream and the nightmare."

Elliot considered then that ol' Harry had finally lost it, blathering a load of pseudo-righteous psychotic-rap Hindubabble which would earn him CC's of Tra-la-la Trilafon, Mellow-Out-Man Mellaril, and regular trips to the ECT room under more 'civilized' conditions.

He pictured the great god of destruction with electrodes at the temples (double-entendre?), biting down on a rubber bit painted like the round egg of the world. The juice was turned on, and as he arched his back and blue steam spurted from his nostrils and ears, every single patient in the asylum berserked, then smiled and went catatonic with rainbow haloes, as the demons came out of the padding in the walls to have orgies with the heads of orderlies.

One of Shiva's one thousand and eight names included one which translated out to "mad."

Ramakrishna said, "The true saint behaves as though he were mad."

But then the sheer sight of this being, the *presence* he could feel next to him that made him shudder with memory of soaring up into stars and racing down the mountainside in the arms of … Elliot couldn't doubt.

There'd been sex between them, hadn't there? Shiva had actually entered him, like a heat-seeking salve up his rectum. The god had ridden him up into those stars and down the side of that mountain, screwing tightly and unwinding eternity all in the same orgasm.

And if that had really been just Harry that he'd been fucked by, Elliot would've been utterly grossed out and shitting little bricks of moral outrage all over the place.

(As if Elliot had ever really reacted to anything with what approached a sense of moral outrage. Surely the fact that this would even occur to him—now—meant he'd been touched by a god.)

Elliot, his head bandaged, explained to them that Mr. Tak would probably send another team. A man like Tak didn't appreciate things done in half-measures. He considered the village of Phnom Yohp to be a serious threat to his drug trade, and this rivalry was something he simply couldn't abide.

And even if the kingpin realized that a drug like Soma could not be a source of repeat business and, thus, had severe limitations, he would still feel obligated to wipe out the village because he'd sworn to do so. To fail in that would cause him to lose face.

(Failure is an illusion? Not to a maya-challenged dirtbag like Tak.)

"What can we do?" asked Cheanneary Ry.

Elliot glanced at his brother, who stood in the shadows under an archway in the courtyard. The dawn's light canted in sideways across the walls of Nagas Wat, illuminating him in dapples, making El recall the skins which had climbed down from the trees.

What had happened to those things after the mercs were dead and no longer posed a threat to the temple? The gibbous moon had set; they'd shriveled and fallen to the ground, the colorful lights in them winking out like the spent half-lives of fissionable materials. The women had taken Elliot back to the cavern but then returned to dutifully and with reverence collect these flayed countenances, putting them with the rest of the remains back in Phnom Yohp. Then all were given an honorable cremation, complete with sweet incenses burned in offering and songs being sung.

Elliot turned back to the women and said, "I can take you away from here. Back to my country, to where I was born. In Texas."

Returning to the source, was it?

Cobras slithering across the ground hissed what sounded like *yesssssss*.

The priests with the too-wide mouths seemed to smile approval.

Shiva nodded in the recesses of sun-played shadow.

The women trembled. None had ever been more than two or three hours from the village.

Several voices piped at once, *"Wia neuv ch'ngaay te?"*

"Is it far?" they asked anxiously, every one of the almost twenty female survivors eventually taking up the question, anxious about it. Their voices high in bird chatter, trying to imagine a journey that might take them a whole day or two to complete. That was a very long walk. None of them had been on Pol Pot's forced march from Phnom Penh. Their killing fields had been right here, in about five square miles of jungle.

"Is it far?" Cheanneary Ry asked Elliot, wondering how long she would have to walk upon her hands. Would she need to use her appliance legs?

Shiva whispered under the archway, "How far is far? The universe being created is far in the past. Destruction is always nearer than you think. Put the two together and they make a distance of a single step, good with blood."

Elliot saw out of the corner of his eye as the monstrous carvings rippled, flagrant with carnal cruelty. A demoness rode the face of a compliant Brahman with the scissors of her sex, his severed penis grasped in her webbed fingers. She seemed to turn her face toward El and gave him a sidelong wink.

Giving his attention back to the god under the arch, he perceived a tiny cyanic quasar nictitation from one of Shiva's eyes. Elliot sighed, trying not to have to hazard a guess as to how much blood would come from the distance.

Chapter 24

"Now let your Soma juice be poured; be not afraid, O Kali's sons. This darkening sorrow goes away…"
—The Rig Veda

She felt him lean across her. Had he turned the lights out? Had she gone hysterically blind?

No, his shadow cast over her was just that thick. It eclipsed everything else she might have seen: the knife, the bobbing of his erection, the face moving-changing-what would it become next?

She could feel the stinking blackness of that penumbra as it nullified her personality, as if covering her in smears of shit scooped from the worst sewer imaginable. She couldn't scream through it, couldn't breathe through it. Her breath had been suspended, cut off until she choked, chest aching, lungs deflated and quivering like bats hanging upside down in a poisoned cave.

When the tip of his knife dug into her left breast, she had air again, enough to try to shriek with. He backhanded her and stuck something into her mouth. It tasted of blood and silk, part of the nightgown he'd sliced off of her. Having thus muted her, he began to cut wedges into the breast, the way a cook would slice a pie. Then he peeled each strip of skin back from the flesh beneath. He cored out the nipple. He worked to insert the end of his cock into the wound, his voice a curious mixture of moans and growls.

If she'd ever believed this thing was a man, she didn't anymore.

Leah Limerick woke up, found she'd overslept again. Light was streaming in through lace curtains at the windows. The scars on her body hurt, but not as vividly as in the nightmare. They were as the dull cry of a patient on the burn ward, so drugged that all they could emit was a warbled sigh, like a distant ambulance siren winding down.

She climbed slowly from bed and crept to the closet. There, she closed herself in to dress in the dark, so she wouldn't have to see what the monster had left her with. Even if that covering darkness made her smell shit, caused her to taste blood.

Flashbacks were the tools of despotic memory, trying to get you to accept—through event repetition and cruel rote—that the trauma you endured was integral to foreordination. It was always meant to have happened. There was nothing you could have done at any time to prevent it. It began as fate and wound up as history. You were left to recall it, to ponder and weep for the power of destiny.

Leah stripped the bed, replacing the night's used sheets with fresh ones. Then she left the house to take her walk. Every day she strolled the empty streets where people had moved away after the base was closed down.

She'd moved to Machenville, Texas two years ago, four years after the government decided that Whitman Air Base no longer had much strategic value since the end of the cold war. The missile silos had been padlocked, the bombs dismantled. Anyone to do with the service was cashiered or transferred out.

Many civilians had moved, believing the place to be toxic. There were only three or four thousand people left, out of a previously thriving community of about seventy-five thousand.

She'd heard the rumors, of course. About the leak at a so-called secret lab at Whitman. About biological weapons and a failure that wasn't practical in terms of warfare because it took years to fully manifest in the host.

"But you'll be okay 'cause you had to be exposed to it in the first few hours after it oozed out of that tube the lab tech dropped," the paranoid conspiracy-theory nut named Joe told her. Possibly lent some credence because he was scratching at this plethora of pimples he bore on his arms. "You didn't live here then so you don't have to worry. The government don't care 'bout the rest of us. Except to monitor how we're doin'. They know it's not contagious. That's how they get away with claimin' there wasn't no lab and no disease and therefore no leak. It's how they don't have to compensate us for anythin'. Naturally, it's why they really closed the base. Everybody else who left'll die off eventually, the soldiers who were here and their families, gettin' cancers and such, the townfolk spread across the country havin' tumors or failing organs. And thems that makes too big a noise'll just disappear prob'ly."

Leah only talked to him—or had been talked at by him—the one time, when she moved there. He ran the Ryder place where she turned in her rented moving truck after she'd arrived and unpacked.

No one else seemed to discuss it. At least she never heard anything, eavesdropping when buying groceries or at the bookstore or the pharmacy. She tried to avoid the company of others as much as possible. No matter if they coughed, splattering gray mucous, or if they were losing their hair and what grew back in was a color different from what had grown there before, or if they had pimples and blisters. They still didn't look as bad as Leah did.

Besides, it wasn't as if Leah had transplanted herself to make friends who didn't know what had happened to her. Not as if she'd gone there to build a new life. She didn't think a new life would be possible, not with the scars she bore, outside and within. She'd merely found a spot to wait for death. However long that might take. It had already been two years and it could be twenty more, or thirty. What better place than a desert, where every tall shape in the blowing dust looked like the specter of Death?

No, she didn't want friends, needed no one to commiserate with. It wasn't true that misery always wanted company. Often misery simply wanted to be left alone.

Whatever people there were hanging on to the town lived on the south side of Machenville. The rest was a ghost town. Since the area was desert, it was practically a caricature out of an old western. Tumbleweeds floated down the streets; doors and gates banged forlornly in the wind; dust covered everything. It put Leah at peace to walk there, matching the vistas of her mind where she felt safest. In scenes abandoned, no one to stare at her scars, no one to threaten her.

It had been years since she'd been attacked by the rapist who became animals. She'd been released by the hospital, torn body and mind pronounced healed—as well as could be expected, what with the kind of memories she bore.

She'd moved away from her old house, the one which had become a museum and mausoleum to pain. She'd drifted out of east Texas, west to Machenville. Not a bit like the place she'd lived in all her life before the man who became a cat, then a wolf, finally a ghoul had slashed his way through her serenity.

The canyons would turn colors. Sometimes the strata seemed to run with the hues one might expect to view in purgatory. The way of knife cuts down from the nippled pinnacles of the breasts, blood sluicing like lava out of ruptured volcanos. Canyons would go blue and black in that moment, just after the final rays of the sunset bloodied them. The way of a vulva in which various blunt instruments had been thrust, bruised, night descending for a long stay.

Leah would sit on her porch and stare, contemplating Death, turning Him into a lover in her mind. She'd slowly run her hands across her dress where the scars corrugated the skin beneath, fingers plucking at where the cerise quartz gems of her nipples had once been. Her touch deepening down the belly to find her crotch.

Would there be feeling in this spot tonight? Or was it numb as ever, the nerves damaged beyond repair? Would she caress herself and remember that there was only ice between her thighs?

Leah took her walk in the mornings, through the ghost town, surely as likely a spot as could be to search for Death. She'd catch her reflection in the windows of the empty stores, think she saw ruined people staring out at her, realizing it was only herself, quickly turning away. She'd relocate her gaze at the vacant houses, silent schools, lonely parks.

But one of the parks wasn't empty today. Tents had been set up during the night. She thought she saw an Oriental woman walking by on stilts but realized they were only long prosthetic limbs. Other Asian women were serving bowls of simple food to a group of children sitting on the grass. All the women were injured in some way, in profound ways actually. It caused Leah to cringe, shutting her eyes to try to wish them gone.

Leah felt her fists ball up at her sides. She considered this to be part of her place, uninhabited, exalted because it was hollow. It needed to remain blank for her to feel safe. So who were these people? These trespassers in her soothing nowhere?

"Can I help you?"

A man—a white American—approached her from an artificially-grassy slope dotted with transplanted and spindly live oaks. Leah blinked, observing that one side of his face was heavily scarred. She didn't like to see hideous people. She always got the impression they wanted you to feel sorry for them. (Maybe another reason she didn't seek friends among Machenville's sick population. Commiseration, never!) She could spare no sympathy apart from herself. And she didn't feel kindred with them just because she and they shared an obvious defect. She preferred her solitude, inside a forsaken location. Waiting for Death.

"There's not supposed to be anybody here," Leah said bruskly, as if challenging his privilege to be in a place the rightful residents had deserted.

"There's no rule against being here. People have moved out. It doesn't mean new ones can't move in." His response didn't sound like he was rising to her challenge. He said it nicely enough, with a smile that twisted up from the ruined half of his face. It made Leah wince, wondering if her own scars did that to her smiles.

Did she smile anymore?

"Do you have permission?" she asked, intending to turn this motley-looking crew of squatters in to—well, in to whoever would be the appropriate authorities. Then they would be evicted and the place would be hers again. Hers, and hers alone.

"Yeah, we do," he replied. "With what we're paying your city fathers, we'd better have. It's temporary. A few months. We're an advance team of the Cambodian Circus. We'll be wintering here. Most U.S. carnivals go to Florida for the season but since I'm from Texas originally …"

"Yeah?" asked Leah suspiciously. Was it really the devastated side of his face which bothered her, or was it something about the other half? Something reminiscent of … ? A resemblance to … "Where-abouts?"

The man gestured around them. "I was born right here in Machenville. My folks were passing through, on their way back to east Texas—that's where I grew up, not far from Dallas. Their car had blown a rod, so they had to stay in a motel while a garage made repairs. My mother heard the coyotes howling."

Leah nodded. "Lots of them around here."

"Sent her right into labor," he added, looking wistfully off toward a stretch of unmown grass where a coyote was nosing, across the street from the park, snuffing up the scents of the earth.

It had once been carefully tended St. Augustine, but without being kept up by city crews the local flora was quickly creeping back in. There was evidence of Texas bluestem, sideoats grama, and even some creosote tarbush. No wonder the coyote felt at home.

And do I detect a little of the wolf in you? Leah bowed her head. Did she really believe that her private ghost town would remain hers forever?

A few months, he'd said. Wintering. Would they, then, be gone by spring?

Could she stand it that long?

"I'm Elliot Thomas," the man said to introduce himself, extending his hand. "I'm—er—the agent for the circus here."

She didn't take the proffered hand, but stared as a sheet of rice paper blew out of a tent. It bore the imprint of a rubbing off stone, the sort she'd seen in museums and estate sales, taken from temples and palaces in Southeast Asia. But those usually had the figures of dancing girls or some such exotically bucolic nonsense on them.

This was much larger anyway, at least eight feet wide, as if it was a section taken from part of a high wall of bas-relief. It unrolled, practically at her feet. She gasped at the bestial acts displayed within, graphically committed by creatures both hideous and gorgeous, seeming to be actually doing these things at that moment as the paper rippled in the breeze coming in from the desert.

Leah's face flushed, the deep knife-gouges along her stomach and where the flaps of her breasts had been stitched up grew hot, as if newly pared, as if boiling with blood.

He bent and quickly rolled up the sheet. A woman came hurrying from the tent the paper had blown out of. She ran on her hands, not wearing prosthetic legs like the woman on the stilts. Leah couldn't help but notice how beautiful she was. It painfully reminded her of her own shortcomings. It shamed her, thinking she could be jealous of someone with no legs.

"*Som dtoh!*" the legless woman said to the man. "I'm sorry, Elliot. That was on a stack near the opening and a little twirl of wind just swept it up before I could catch it."

"It's okay, Ry," he told her.

The Cambodian woman felt Leah's stare and smiled, doing the most graceful bow imaginable, especially considering she had so little below the hips. How did anyone with such a disability manage to move like a dancer?

"The war left many of us like this," she explained, voice calming as a dove's. "The circus everywhere in the world has been the refuge of those who were unwanted by the rest of society: the cripples, the freaks, the displaced. Here we've found where we are accepted, where we can belong."

Displaced. Wasn't that what Leah was? Yet where did she belong? Certainly not in a carnival. Perhaps not anywhere.

Yet when she accidentally caught sight of her reflection … what did she see but a freak show?

Who was she to judge anyone? Who was Leah to stare?

"I didn't mean to offend you," she said, and hoped she'd managed to convey her sincerity.

The Cambodian woman smiled radiantly and bowed again.

Then Leah thought of the pornography in the rubbing. What kind of circus had things like that in it? Maybe some act in a tent closed to anyone under eighteen. Like the old hootchie kootchie shows. SHE SHIVERS, SHE SHAKES; SHE QUIVERS AND QUAKES! COME SEE LITTLE SHEBA, LADIES AND GENTLEMEN. SHE WILL SHOW YOU THE FLESHY MYSTERIES OF THE ORIENT! ALL FOR ONE THIN DIME!

"The mayor's invited us to display some of our entertainment at the upcoming two-day Festival of Fears. I believe it's a combination of Halloween and the Day of the Dead?" Mr. Thomas remarked.

Leah nodded. It used to be a big deal before the base closed, the fiesta bringing the usually-separated factions of gringos and Mexicans together. People who normally didn't associate much came out to mingle in the two days-and-nights party. Somehow it was an even larger affair now, virtually every person who still lived in Machenville emerging from their deserted desert shell-shock to pretend the town was its old self.

"I hope you'll visit us then," Elliot said.

Except that Leah didn't go to fiestas, hadn't attended this one in the two years she'd lived in Machenville. She wouldn't be able to stand it if someone—anyone—accidentally mistook her for the type who flaunted their unnatural looks for money.

Leah mumbled that she'd think about it and then turned away, anxious to be back on one of the empty streets. She caught sight of a tumbleweed, ball of intricate desiccated branches, floating like a spirit across the cracked asphalt in an empty Wal-Mart parking lot, the shadow it cast long as a tall man, spectral. She made toward it, desperately, as if the key to her salvation lay within its barbed wire-like tangle.

Not that Leah really expected to catch it. Loving Death could never be as easy as embracing a dead, dried-up bush.

She'd dreamed again.

He'd come in her mouth.

Then he'd straightened up, still straddling her, and put a cigarette in his own mouth. He lit it, sucking, the end glowing red hot, puffing, inhaling fire, exhaling smoke much paler than his shadow cast upon her.

Then he took that burning end and made patterns in her skin. She jerked with each time the scorching tip touched, spasming as if it were the frayed end of a live wire. She smelled herself scorch, flesh and hair shriveling.

She'd thrashed, spine arching as tormented nerve endings sent messages of pure unadulterated seizure through her entire body, the sperm he'd made her swallow coming up and projecting out from between her lips in white-hot bile. She bucked.

And somehow knocked him off.

She usually awakened to dawn like a peeping tom through the curtains. She would glare at it viciously, resenting its spying when she was so vulnerable. But it was still night out and the only light leering in at her was that of the half moon.

She slipped from between the sweat-soaked sheets, gaze elevated to the ceiling so she couldn't even accidentally look down and get a glimpse of pie-wedged breasts, daisy chains of cipher-round burns, livid in that roentgen moonlight. She reached out blindly for her robe on the chair and put it on, covering herself up.

It never occurred to her that it might be odd that a rape victim would choose to sleep naked. It was a most vulnerable *dishabille.* Did others wear heavy pajamas which virtually rendered the parts of their violated bodies hermetically sealed? Or flannel granny gowns with high snug collars and sleeves that cuffed tightly at the wrists, long long hems which snarled their legs so much as they thrashed in nightmare flashback that it would be almost impossible for an intruder to unravel the twist of fabric and limbs to expose the tender crotch?

Leah always slept in the nude. Although she never had before she was attacked. She felt the slick sheets on her, the plushly textured night …

Leah went outside, sitting on the front porch. Where she lived was just beyond Machenville proper, although it was technically within the city limits. It had a fantastic view of the desert and canyons. The sort of grand panorama that photographs were taken of for the cover of TEXAS HIGHWAYS.

Yet Leah had gotten the place cheap.

Because of the history of the ground that began a few feet from the porch, extending out to where a stand of alligator junipers—punctuated with spiny sotol plants—decorated the side of the road which lead to the base.

Sacred ground, for some. It had been used as an Indian burial spot since long before the white man came west. During the Civil War there'd been a skirmish between forces of the Confederate Army and Union troops. The dead had been buried there. After that war, a local rancher was ordered to free his slaves. He refused, shooting them and defiantly burning their bodies on that spot. During World War 1 there was a camp for German P.O.W.s near Machenville. The influenza outbreak that caused some 25 million people worldwide to perish, half a million of them in America, killed off many of the prisoners. This was where they were laid to rest.

Battlefield. Cremation ground. Graveyard. Most folks just weren't comfortable living there. The wind could produce a high keening when it gusted over twenty miles an hour, bringing up a strange black dust which resembled ashes. The rare rainstorms wept, causing the red sap from the scraggled limber bushes to streak the ground with gory crimson. The Mexicans called this bush the *sangre de drago*, or dragon's blood. The few rainbows to arch from such storms, if springing from or ending there, ran red and black as the back of a whipped slave. A tornado ripped through Machenville once, a few years before. It swept through the new cemetery on the other side of town, churning up graves, hawling out corpses, to deposit them right there on the ancient site of death.

Leah had gotten the place very cheap indeed.

It didn't disturb her. She'd never seen any ghosts. Perhaps she would have liked to see ghosts.

Maybe it was why she slept in the nude even though she'd once been raped and mutilated. Because ghosts might be substitutes for Death, Death-as-a-lover by proxy.

She shivered in her robe now, even though it remained warm out. Late October it was, but sultry anyway. How had she thought of such a thing? That she would strip herself each evening and wait for the spirits of the dead to slide across her? Not repulsed by her scars, only full of need, hungry for the warmth she generated. Because—despite everything which had befallen her—blood still coursed through her veins, the heart pumped its lonely desire through the chambers, the brain flickered and synapsed with Leah's wanting to be held and caressed even if she never consciously expressed this. After all, the Death-as-a-lover she sought wasn't a carnal wish; it was intended as a bearer of tender surcease.

(Death as a lover?)

"I want no lovers!" she whispered to herself, hissing through her broken teeth.

It was only a metaphor for lying down and passing on, pressed between clean sheets.

She changed the bed every single day.

It was a thing about eradicating the filth at scenes of a crime.

Just as a rape victim desperately wanted to bathe, to wash away the defilement.

(Death as a lover …)

And she slept naked. And thought now about the spirits.

Perhaps the ghosts would need her so much, they could end up hurting her. In an effort to feel where there was no more flesh to feel with, they might grip too hard. Their bones would bruise her. Their mouths would press dust against her face which they might expect her to swallow, as if it were the only seed they could offer. They would overwhelm and bear her down, till all their relative revenant weight pushed the bed through the floor, the wood cracking, creaking, splintering as the bed further descended into the ground, driven by passion in the spectral tons until it was deep in the impotent desert. There they would be able to claim her, again and again, in every strata and among all the other dead things of the ages. The desert would shake so much from this taking that there would be an earthquake. The sides of canyons would cave; the mountains would granulate and avalanche onto the town; the fossil reefs would shatter.

It wasn't as if these ghosts would be deliberately brutal. They wouldn't use knives or wield the glowing tips of cigarettes. They were just ash people, dust folk.

Displaced.

(Prisoners of Death?)

(Love slaves?)

Leah shut her eyes tightly, saliva flooding her mouth, a roar in her ears. She crossed her legs and pressed the thighs together as an ache heated there, sliding up into the womb which usually was beyond feeling. Her hands traveled down, fingers probing, squeezing, tracing bull's-eye circles that got smaller and smaller, more precise, assigned mentally to parched finger-bones and the sharp edges of pelvic husks. She shuddered violently, to the point where euphoria and nausea were a single unit in transcendence. And then she hated herself, the tingling rapture fading, the sickened feeling persistent. She despised herself for indulging in such bizarre, wanton rape-fantasy.

How unfeminist, how politically incorrect to allow her anxieties and loneliness to drag her into such debased imaginings. That women had rape fantasies at all was supposed to be a male-generated myth. But especially that a rape victim would permit herself such a vulgar, self-degrading reverie was even more appalling.

But didn't Leah have needs? Didn't she hunger past the forced limitations of a ruined body? Wanting to be caressed, adored, swept away? And since she'd shut herself off so stringently, freezing up at even the approach of another person, wouldn't she have to be carried off into the night to be loved at all?

Leah heard chimes, muffled as if thrumming through the burrograss. There was the soft shuffing of gourds, surely only strings of dark brown beans which suspended from the mesquite trees. And there was a bell, as of one of those weeping raindrops shattering on the spines of a prickly-pear cactus.

She opened her eyes.

A figure was dancing across the ground, near the road, its back to her. The hands gestured out, snaking, palms coming up seeming to be filled with sleeping juncoes and chickadees, then making fists to reopen filled with night-blooming cactus flowers.

Leah held her breath, not sure if she was imagining this. Was she finally seeing one of those love-obsessed ghosts, or should she run since there was obviously an intruder?

The figure turned and, in profile, Leah could see by the shape of heavy breasts that this wasn't a man. The arms came up, hands invoking with semaphore, with the language of the deafmute, and blindly reading the Braille of air as if the wind was patterned with intelligent bumps, reaching for stars. The arms bent at elbows, swung quickly side to side, and then folded together in front, movements progressively faster until Leah almost believed this person had four arms instead of two.

The dancer turned again and was facing her. The moonlight fairly rolled across the bronze flesh, turning it the shades one sees when a soft light is shone through a yellow diamond. Leah could now see the prominent phallus, bobbing beneath the flat belly, itself beneath those magnificent breasts, not as large as she'd first suspected. They only seemed that way because there were two pairs of them.

The dancer grinned lasciviously, each tooth a fire opal fang arrayed in a semicircle about a sharp-ended, red velvet tongue. It stomped its feet, these turned in at the ankles where bracelets of golden bells jangled, softly muffled by tufts of hairy erioneuron that sprouted upon the old burial place, the ancient sacred ground. The being made little jumps, crossing its feet sometimes in front, sometimes behind.

It sprinted, pirouetting across the arid soil, head tilted back in joy.

Leah noticed that the dust plumed, eddied, swirled around this being's feet. Tiny inch-high whirlwinds, finger-length tornados, dusty vortices peppered with the seeds from broom snakeweed. The ground itself trembled, shuddered, as Leah had with her orgasm of a few minutes before. Out of the earth came the chanting of native voices, of sabers clashing against steel and cannons booming. Out of the air rushed the stench of bodies being consumed by flames, and of flesh simply, slowly, inexorably rotting after disease has wasted it.

And the dancer moved faster. The skin took on the appearance of strata, or the stripes of a tiger. A necklace of skulls chattered about its slender neck, whirling round and round the opposite direction of the dancer's turns. The long black hair, previously bound up with gold pins and jewels, came unbound and went electric. Zapping out as if static with serpents. The being reeled until Leah thought it drunk, its luscious red mouth opening to rave what Leah couldn't understand but which she guessed to be fragments of insane poetry and song. This, even as shrieks and sighs rose from the gyrating ground like geysers. The undulating hips thrust into the wind which had risen to a point where it skreed up from the canyons and howled down through ravines. The erect cock impaled the wind, as the creature bent at the waist, scooping up handfuls of churning soil, wisps of ghostly mist expiring from it in thaumaturgic/turgid motes. The dancer rubbed this into the godly dick to fuck air and earth together, an act undeniably both lovemaking and ravage.

Leah was terrified. And completely aroused. She'd never witnessed anything so totally deranged and powerful, sensually fanatic and of obviously supernatural generation. She was shocked to discover that, while absorbed in watching this—debacle, she'd stood up from the chair and walked somehow down the porch steps, bare feet stopping just at the beginning of the graveyard.

Had she actually come down here on her own? No! She must have been levitated, spirited down against her will. And yet there was the flush of heat in her face even though she was certain all the color had drained from it, the blood running down to irrigate the senses beneath her old scars, phantom limb-nipples erecting, itching to be pinched beneath her robe.

Take it off and be naked here. Join the dance, the dance that shakes the loins and spirit …

The gorgeous being faced her but didn't seem to see her, topaz eyes rolling up to pearl whites. The skulls on the necklace about its throat were bleeding at bleached eye sockets. The hissing of the snakes in its hair aspirated a sibilance of sitars.

Dance with us … open your mouth and legs … open your third eye …

Leah's gaze was riveted on the dancer's erection as it twitched, pulsed, and suddenly burst out a thick jizzum …

… of black butterflies, blood-red fireflies, and green bottleflies.

Everything fell silent.

Leah fainted. Was somehow back in her bed, dreaming the ghosts had come out of the earth. They had streamed en masse into the house but didn't have sex with her. Instead they lifted her up, hundreds of dust hands, and carried her out into the night where her real lover, Death or a god or both, awaited.

Chapter 25

"We come but to sleep.
we come but to dream:
It is not true, it is not true,
that we come to live upon the earth."
—Ayocuan, from CANTARES MEXICANOS

Elliot sighed, massaging his temples with his fingertips. When he'd rented the park—expecting it to be temporary until he could buy some land—he hadn't considered he'd have to do a lot of explaining. But he couldn't have too many questions asked. Yes, he'd made up the notion of the refugees from Phnom Yohp being part of a circus. It had been a quick lie.

A merc of Elliot's stature made a lot of contacts in twenty years, many of them introduced to him by Saab Gestetner. Enough to manage to sneak some people into the country. He'd made very good money, seldom spending much, investing wisely. And Harry had shown him jaw-dropping treasures hidden in the temple which further facilitated the economics of such a move.

Part of a circus. It might have been a philosophical metaphor, unconscious but telling. He hadn't actually thought they would be asked to perform.

"Well, they're just the advance group. Looking into a proper location. You know, it takes time to look at real estate … " He'd hemmed and hawed to the mayor.

Wishing he had a gun so he could just blow the guy's head off. Those ways had been much simpler, the solutions of a professional soldier. See, how easy it got after the first one? After the hundredth? The thousandth kill?

But Elliot wasn't that person anymore. He wasn't even going by the same last name. Well, Elliot Tyler was supposed to have died in Saigon a long time ago.

"Oh, I'm sure you can come up with a little something," the man persisted, grinning broadly. Elliot noticed he had bleeding gums. "Help liven up the fiesta. It's been basically the same thing for years, rides and games and such. We could use an exotic shot in the arm."

Harry had been at his brother's elbow at city hall, elegantly dressed as a veiled woman, fairly swaddled in silk wrappings. It made him resemble some mysterious dragon lady out of an old film noir movie. The mayor stared, inhaling deeply to constantly have the scent of jasmine perfume render him dizzy. It masked the smell of his own skin, which looked feverish and sallow.

"I think we can indeed," Harry purred, effecting an accent used to diphthongs and bird-cooed softenings on the hard consonants. "But it will be different from what you are accustomed to. Some will be for public consumption, but there will be a tent reserved for a more private showing. Not everything of the Orient and the jungle—how do you say it quaintly—has a 'G' rating?"

The mayor chuckled phlegmatically, then choked slightly on whatever loosened in his throat. He clucked. He winked. "Oh, yes ma'am. I quite understand. I served in Nam."

"We would never wish to shock anyone," Harry added, lowering his gaze coquettishly, long lashes shading the shy eyes. "No one will be admitted without—*thaa mait? niak yuhl te/niak s'dap baan te?*—Eye Dee?"

Elliot bit his tongue, watching this display. Thinking of the brother who would have knocked out the teeth of any man who might look at him like this guy was looking at Harry now. Not that the mayor understood that this wasn't really the most exquisite 'woman' he'd ever seen. And it wasn't as if Harry was just done up in drag or anything. He'd changed; he had ALL the working parts. What the man saw was the heaven Harry—no, *Shiva*—intended him to see. And heaven was apparently not out of Harry's jurisdiction anymore.

Elliot just felt that things would have been safer if they could have remained as anonymous as possible. Why didn't he just say they were refugees from the minefields and Pol Pot? Because that involved more red tape than could be imagined. Medical visas and questions of political asylum. The boys who sneaked the women and children in hadn't wanted any messes. That was that.

Keep a low profile.

Right. We're just wintering here. In other words, this is our off-season and we don't want to be bothered. Elliot wasn't an entertainer. How could he know that everybody expects them to be at the audience's beck and call three hundred sixty-five days a year?

Guess it was sort of the same as being a merc, at that. On stage or in the theater of war, what was the difference? You jumped when summoned.

Harry rose to bow graciously, indicating they would now depart the mayor's office. The mayor took the god's gloved hand and kissed it. Elliot couldn't help but wonder if the mouth that lay at the center of that palm was smirking.

The children were hurting one another, methodically wrenching limbs out of joint—without even as much as a wince or tiny peep out of them as the muscle popped. They bent each other's fingers back till the joints audibly cracked, while El cringed.

He ran forward, horrified. "Stop that! What are you doing?"

Cheanneary Ry, who was also watching their progress as she sewed, laughed. "Don't worry. They're not torturing each other. It's an exercise. For them to be dancers. It widens their young bone sockets and expands their ligaments."

Little arms moved back, shoved backward still, like branches in a relentless wind. Elliot made a face, seeing them pressed more until the elbows were back as much as 40%. It looked excruciating but the little faces were all solemn, concentrating intensely as if in the study of some reasonable martial art.

"It's distortion training," Ry explained. "The Cambodian dance is a wrench dance, performed with arms and legs bent at angles, shoulder blades pushed together, the belly contracted practically to the backbone. They have been learning this for more than a year now."

Elliot saw how they wriggled themselves into this bit and brace position, and it made him ache. Yet he'd seen films of this kind of technique, the dancers in spired and curled costumes of filigree and shiny sequin mosaics which had to be sewn onto them, piece by piece, before the performance began. The films had been made before Pol Pot included the royal ballet in his list of enemies, and the art form almost disappeared from the earth.

"My mother was a dancer," Cheanneary Ry said, gazing off into the sky. "I would have been, too."

Elliot had heard how she'd come to be born and how the man Sarun Chhuon had rescued her from her dead mother's womb. The same man who had brought the Soma to Bangkok's abused children. El wished he could have met him, the one who'd gathered together all the wounded kids of Phnom Yohp and cared for them until their god returned. He wished he could thank him for having brought Ry into the world. But Elliot knew how Sarun Chhuon died and it made him sick, to know he'd ever been with the people who could do that to such a man.

Mokhsha.

Salvation.

Atonement …

(That's what I'm doing, aren't I? It's why I'm here, trying to put together a decent refuge for these women and children.)

Elliot wanted to touch Ry's shoulder, to tell her how beautiful and how perfect he believed she already was. That if she hadn't become a dancer, like her mother, it must have been destiny. But surely she already knew this.

(It's human nature to pine for what we don't have, to wish to remake ourselves. We don't have to atone for that, do we? It's not a real attempt to thwart fate.)

Elliot knelt beside her in the long grass, felt it rustle against his legs. Now could be the moment to tell her he loved her. A statement he'd never made to anyone, anywhere.

But the god appeared at the opening to the large tent which had been set up as his temporary temple. Cheanneary Ry immediately turned her attention there. She gazed and sighed, the longing so apparent in her eyes that Elliot felt a stab of jealousy. Then of guilt. Then only of grief, beguiled by adoration for both of them.

Chapter 26

"Santa Maria, madre de Dios, ruega por nosotros
pecadores, ahora y en la hora
de nuestra muerte, amen."
"Saint Mary, mother of God, pray for us sinners now and
at the hour of our death."
—Catholic prayer

October 31 arrived: Halloween, the first day of the Fiesta of Fears.

There were tables of carved pumpkins, orange and black cotton candy, caramel apples. Alongside were Mexican delights already put out for the Day of the Dead which would be tomorrow, November 1: sugar skulls with maraschino cherry eyes, little chocolate corpses, ghastly cookies, and *los panes de muertos*—the bread of the dead. There were cheeseburgers and tamales, french fries and mole, beer, lemonade, and pulque.

A booth sold turn-of-the-last-century photographs of dead children (*angelitos*) dressed in their best clothes, as they used to be posed with grieving parents or siblings or maybe the family dog. Other booths sold traditional U.S. costumes—the best sellers usually being the monster or slasher out of whatever the last big horror movie was. There were places selling cheap clay skulls with movable lower jaws, cardboard skeleton puppets dancing at the string's pull, expensive skulls in monoliths of lava, crystal and jade. There were little scenario shadowboxes with skeleton dolls done up as soccer players, firemen, angels, souls in purgatory, brides and grooms being wed by a skeleton preacher with the logo beneath describing their vows as *Hasta que la muerte los separe* or 'Till Death do them part'.

Everyone in Machenville was there, except for those who were so sick as to be bedridden. People coughed, spat into handkerchiefs or into the dust, scratched at lesions or at their heads as hair fell. And cheerfully rode the rides.

There was a merry-go-round of death figures. Riders got to sit in the arms of the grotesquerie of their choice. They could swoon and be turned round in the arms of pasty-faced vampires of either sex or reapers with scythes. There was a werewolf, a vulture, a Frankenstein's monster, a man with crazed eyes and bloody hands and a knife.

This last one was where Leah rode as she came to the fiesta after all. She shivered, staring up at the killer's face, waiting for it to … what … transform? Her scars seemed to bloom afresh.

Why had she come? Because she wanted to go to the Cambodian circus. The dancer she'd seen, moving across the graveyard so provocatively, had looked vaguely Oriental. It must have been someone from their group. And she knew she needed to see this person again. She'd been able to think of nothing else since. She'd actually gone there first but they weren't set up yet.

"We're sorry," the woman called Cheanneary Ry had told her. "The children need a little more time. Please come back in a couple hours. Okay?"

And, reluctantly, Leah had moved away, trying to get a peek into the biggest tent. Where she sensed—by the moisture gathering between her legs—that the one she sought waited.

When she saw the sign advertising the hermaphrodite—FOR ADULTS ONLY—she knew that was who it was. She hadn't dreamed it. Hadn't imagined it in her lonely mind.

Somebody who wouldn't laugh at her. They were both different, clearly outcasts of this world.

Displaced, yes ...

Leah had thought constantly about this special being, dreaming about it as she slept naked between her clean sheets. The need she felt—the love, what it had to be—was sweeping her away. But not into the night as Leah had once believed that Death as a lover would have to carry her. Her passion was just as aroused in the daytime, and she was discovering it to be something she couldn't repress, couldn't deny. And this wasn't Death! This was a genuine person, unusual, perhaps a little insane. You had to be, to dance so wildly over a graveyard.

Leah trembled at that last attribute: madness. She ran her fingers over her dress as if to smooth the fabric. But really she was touching the scars of knife gouges and cigarette burns. Nervous as a bride?

Surely such a creature as this man/woman dancer wouldn't turn her away. Might accept the gift of her love. Could be—must be—lonely, too.

There was a Ferris wheel spinning like incarnation. The seats were carved into skulls. People sat in the opened jaws, a tinged red steam being shot from a vent at the bottom—presumably for hell. A tall coiling pipe shot out a golden mist at the top of the ride, for heaven. Round and round we go. And where we end up we might not want to know.

There was a tilt-a-whirl. Usually somebody always threw up on this ride. But in the city limits of Machenville—so near the closed base—there was a retching noise like engines grinding on a stalled highway. Everyone aboard vomited. Watching from the sidelines, it must have seemed almost comical, a gross skit off Saturday Night Live that made you laugh so hard you gagged. Faces going greenish-white blurred as the machine whipped them about, faster, trapped within dozens of gyres-per-minute. Bile mixed with burritos and hot dogs rained outward in a centrifugal chili-spray. There was so much that the gears clogged and the ride cranked down to a halt. People lurched off, burning eyes full of water, not willing to look at each other, to have to accept that there was something wrong with all of them. Each found a place to sit down until the nausea passed, or crowded into port-a-potties lined up at various places within the carnival. Eventually they returned to the fiesta, ghastly grins forced across their faces.

Maybe the next thing they'd do was something a mite gentler. Like going through the house of mirrors. Only to have to see how they appeared, fallen and regrown hair rendering their heads like the bodies of 1957 two-toned Chevies. Noticing how they stooped, hands a bit palsied, feet shuffling like the walking dead. The pimples, blotches, blisters and lesions. Laughter slowed down, sped up, congealing until it had to ratchet to a stop like the puked-into gears of the tilt-a-whirl. Many of the women wept, tears making trails through the make-up they'd lately taken to wearing thicker than ever before. Some of the men swore softly. Children bent double and vomited up entire miniature skulls, gleaming their sugar-bone whiteness in a pink-flecked pool of stomach acid. Or the limbs from candy corpses came up and out, partially dissolved, as if the kids were throwing up pieces of their own deteriorating little systems.

Out of the house of mirrors.

BUY, BUY! the vendors exhorted/extorted while being dressed up in long black cloaks or as killer clowns, faces streaked until unrecognizable with stage blood, rubber worms affixed to wriggle from their cheeks as they shouted. They offered wares of pain-shrieking noisemakers and cheap boxes filled with sound-chip maniacal laughter, stuffed teddy bears-of-darkness, kewpie doll succubuses, psychotic raggedy ann's and night-stalker raggedy andy's, rubbered-beanie-baby-buggerers. Spend like there's no tomorrow. BYE BYE!

Leah saw Asian women finally wending through the crowd, one using the stumps of her elbows and knees to successfully juggle glass globes filled with smoke, a second throwing and flawlessly catching an array of wickedly curved or wavy-bladed or serrated knives with just her feet and teeth. There was a woman swallowing fire, exhaling it in the shapes of cobras and tigers. There was a troup of them performing unusual acrobatic routines designed for amputees.

One operated a booth, giving away free cups of some Cambodian milkshake.

She'd smile and offer these to people going past. "Different! You try ..."

Leah reached out for one but the young woman pulled back. "Oh, not for you," she murmured softly, very politely.

Leah frowned. "And why not?"

"The big tent is open now," the woman replied, tilting her head as if passing on a secret.

Leah gasped, feeling giddy. She turned back and headed where they'd earlier been setting it up. How close would she be able to get? Would the hermaphrodite recognize her from the other night? Had it even noticed her?

She passed the one called Ry. She was doing some kind of fortune telling gig. As Leah walked past, she heard her telling someone, "I predict you will smile soon and be filled with happiness. All your troubles will be conquered."

A few paces later, a woman told her husband what the psychic had said. "She promised I'd be smiling soon and happy. There won't be any more trouble."

He chuckled and scoffed. "Yeah, well, that seems to be what she's telling everybody."

Elliot shook his head, trying not to laugh out loud as he listened to the hired barker calling an audience to the big tent. It was clearly posted as being only for those over eighteen years of age. Driver's licenses and other picture I.D. were being checked to prove folks were as old as they claimed. El was a bit shocked that some of the kids trying to sneak in looked practically ancient.

It's because they're sick, he reasoned.

The barker clamored, "She shivers; he shakes; it quivers and quakes. Come see Little Shiva, Ladies and Gentlemen. You will be shown the fleshy mysteries of the Orient! Only a dollar!"

Outside, the twenty-five children in their precious little costumes performed traditional dances, to the delight of the crowd.

Just outside the tent's opening was a bowl full of money, where those entering had placed their admission fees. The only person seated there was Sirikit. She beamed the colors of her heavenly halo in all directions. Anyone who'd even faintly considered not paying—or who'd even thought of snatching at the money and taking off—found they couldn't. Their eyes riveted to the young girl's face, then to the bony totems of the ruined left hand which was laid gently to a side of the bowl.

"Isn't that one of them ... ?" a woman began, mouth flopping open and closed like a startled fish.

"Saw 'em on CNN. Bangkok, wasn't it?" her husband agreed, a tremor in both shoulders as he nodded with a bobble.

"You goin' to tell me what's inside's weirder than this?" asked the wife. She brought her own fingers up, open sores on them running, and gingerly touched the corona that shone about Sirikit's head. Rose and azure rippled across the woman's hand. Gasping, she pulled back. "Oh, it's hot!"

It wasn't until she'd gone inside that she noticed the blisters on those fingers had closed and were no longer oozing. It wasn't as if they'd healed outright, just been soothed.

El stood inside the tent, not completely convinced when he looked around that he'd left Asia at all. The wide charcoal rubbings made from some of the main bas-relief had been put up. With the potted rubber trees and sugar palms set about, misting hoses secreted about the perimeter, and with the veil of smoke of sandalwood being burned, he might have well been back in the temple of Nagas Wat. With the god dancing, naked skin burnished even bronzer with a glittering paint until he created perfectly the illusion of a living statue, and with women playing flutes, drums, gongs, and the strange eastern version of the xylophone…

Shiva danced the night before, yes, before the carnival opened.

Elliot had seen the women pressing the mushrooms brought over from the jungle, curious quartzlike fungi, clear as the moisture in a kiss. Crushing the pulp further to squeeze out an ultimate juice. This they strained through silk and mixed with milk. Then Shiva drank. It was afterward that Shiva danced, in ecstasy.

Elliot had heard his brother Harry's voice inside his head, its original Texas twang eradicated and the brutish threat it had often employed strangely stilted. *I dance creation into existence … or I dance the end of the world.*

Elliot had been unable to breathe, aware his heart seemed to have stopped beating. His chest hurt. Time stretched out on an impossibly long red tongue.

Next thing he knew, his brother, the god, was pissing into a big bowl.

"It will be greatly diluted," Cheanneary Ry whispered. "It will take much longer to take effect. Hours. A day, perhaps."

The dance Shiva did now was not frenzied. It was graceful, yet active enough that audiences could tell the combination of genitals was real: nothing obviously faked fell off. Women gasped and blushed. Men either chuckled or were slack-jawed silent. Some tried to look away in embarrassment. But wherever they turned, they saw the cavorting abominations in the rice paper perimeter, vague though they appeared through the manufactured clouds of mist and incense. People often had to look twice, gawking, unbelieving that such positions were even possible. Lutherans, Methodists, Catholics, and a herd of dyed-in-the-wool Southern Baptists ought to have been outraged. But it had become a mightily jaded world, at that, hadn't it? They might have seen almost this much on the cable.

Hell, we know we're dying. It could be mass hallucination. It might be the moment when the damned begin to see visions of heaven and hell. These are the last days ... for us anyway. "Shall thy wonders be known in the dark?" Psalms 88:12, hallelujah.

Elliot saw the woman who'd challenged their presence in the park. She was entranced, at the front of the crowd, eyes unblinking so as not to miss any divine gesture or sublime expressions. She leaned forward, kept back only by the velvet theater rope which separated the audience from the entertainers. She reminded him of love-struck teenagers at a rock concert, capable of throwing themselves at the feet of their idols just to be noticed, impressionable eyes bespeaking volumes of a willingness to die, *just die,* for a chance to go backstage.

No, this was more serious than that. She swayed on the balls of feet, hypnotized—no—concentrating, focused, determined to be the tallest tree when lightning might strike.

Then Elliot heard, "Come on, we ought to be getting back. It's a long drive yet."

"Aw, Lucas," replied a wheedling female voice. "Can't we stay for the rest of the carnival? We can always go back tomorrow—or the day after."

"No." The man's voice was firm. "I have to get back to the college."

"But, I'm hungry. And really thirsty. Can't we get something to eat. At least to drink? There was a booth giving milkshakes away."

"Absolutely not. You get something in a place like this, no telling how sick you might be on the road."

Elliot saw the old man, now indeed an old man. His father had only been in his forties when Harry and Elliot had run off to go to war. Now he was a creaker. But he still had some pretty young thang on his arm.

The man glanced back at the hermaphrodite.

"How do you think they faked it?" the girl asked him. "Because it can't be real, right?"

"Honey," Lucas Tyler said drily to his date, "you wouldn't believe what can be real."

The man barely glanced at Elliot, present for—what?—this brief cameo in El's life. He hadn't recognized either of his sons.

Chapter 27

"Shall the hood of the cobra appall me—
The loneliness of its eye, the eye of the mountains
Through which the sky eternally threads itself?
The world is blood-hot and personal
Dawn says, with its blood-flush."
—"Totem"
Sylvia Plath

Leah dawdled through the hours at the carnival, waiting for the late of night when the other fiesta-goers would leave. She knew she couldn't simply remain in the hermaphrodite's tent. It would seem too strange. So she'd forced herself to go, dragging her feet as she exiled herself from the tent.

She didn't ride any of the rides. Leah couldn't actually go near them, so bad was the stench of vomit there. She'd lingered briefly outside the house of mirrors, shuddering, the contour and crater's depth of each of her scars nattering at her, trying to make some connection with the repulsive idea of reflections. She didn't even consider going inside.

Leah made herself drink a soda. And she ate a barbecue sandwich because she could see the meat was rare in places, seeping blood which she curiously savored. The juice rolled across her tongue in the molecular configuration for RED, defining some need in her, representing the passive predator.

She tried again to get a sample of the drink the Cambodians were giving. She was aware she did it just to be refused again, albeit with excruciating politeness. Just so this would reinforce Leah's belief that she was expected by the dancer who called himself (herself?) Shiva. And that everyone in the Cambodian camp must know about it.

How? Why? Had he spoken of Leah to them? She found what this even suggested to be very compelling. Mutual attraction. Destiny.

Until that rendezvous with her incipient lover (Death? Dancer? Freak?), she had to suffer the urgent crowds. Trying hard to convince themselves and everyone else that they were enjoying this deathfest. She found herself studying this person or that one, scrutinizing couples and children. She was struck with an unsettling *déjà vu* that all of them were dying. And not only because of omnipresent manifestations of the so-called bio-bug the air base was supposed to have accidentally unleashed upon them.

It was something more: a sense that these folks were going to perish, together. And it was an imminent thing, so close she could feel the rotting breath brush her face as it stalked past, marking them as a plague's possessions. They weren't going to die of the sickness, especially not the way of polemics, some tomorrow, some next month, next year if they were lucky (or unlucky) to endure so long.

Was a plane going to fall onto the fiesta? Was a tornado going to come tearing out of clear southwestern skies? Would there be a wildfire, sparked from the lady fire-eater or a sterno can heating tamales or some fool's cigarette? A crazed gunman at the top of the skull-seated Ferris wheel, where the gold mist simulated heaven and from where he could send down judgement like God Himself? The wheel would be stopped, yes, symbolic of the end of incarnation.

"I don't know," Leah whispered. "I don't know what's going to happen."

She saw Cheanneary Ry, overheard her giving out the rote prophecy to a man with bleeding eyes.

"I predict you will smile soon and be filled with happiness. All your troubles will be conquered."

The man hobbled away, blinking red clots of mucous in the corners of his eyes.

"Why did you tell him that?" Leah asked her.

"Because it's true," the woman with no legs replied simply.

"No, it isn't," Leah argued. "They're all dying."

"Most of us die," Ry explained.

Leah sneered, letting out an uncomprehending laugh. "*Most* of us?"

The Cambodian smiled and nodded, long black hair shimmering as it slid across her shoulders and down her breasts.

"Yes, but here, *here* is an unusual town. Where almost everyone is going to reach a living nirvana. We usually toil and struggle through each incarnation, our tears and pain intended to teach us what we need to know before we can stop having to be born. For some it takes a hundred lifetimes, for others a thousand, still others a million times enduring the shame and hardship of birth. But in this place almost all will find it, tonight."

Leah scoffed, turned away, shaking her head with the bemused wonder of the condescending unbeliever. Then she glimpsed the woman who was giving away the little cups of milkshake. With a light to her eyes and the righteous expression of the priest who doles out sacred wine and wafers at communion.

"Oh, dear JesusGod," Leah said between the gusts of twin sharp exhales. "You're poisoning them ..."

Leah spun in place, seeing people with colorful little Dixie cups of milkshake, eager to have some since it didn't cost anything. Old sick men, coughing mothers and their small pimpled children, rednecks and Mexicans with brown or black hairfall and blond or red growing back into the balding patches. Sipping, slurping, draining in a single greedy gulp to crush the cup and toss it.

"Stop!" Leah attempted to cry out, the word strangling in her throat.

Cheanneary Ry made no attempt to prevent her. The woman ladling milkshake didn't pause. Leah stared, trying to run through the crowd, to slap cups out of hands. She tried to scream.

But she couldn't. She only watched in sick fascination as the cups were poured, changed hands, were tipped back to trickle between unsuspecting lips.

When would it hit them? People had been drinking it all day. It was after dark by a couple hours already. No one had fallen ill.

(How could you be so sure? They were already sick, throwing up, staggering. Would a couple more symptoms be noticed … or ignored?)

At one time soon, would—ashes, ashes—they all fall down?

Leah sobbed, fists clenched, trying to overcome this sensation of being beguiled by an unfolding tragedy which presented itself as unstoppable. She wouldn't, couldn't just remain a damned observer, not interceding to warn them. She must try to save at least someone.

Her teeth chattered as she squeezed out a desperate, whiny, "Pleeeeeaaaaasssseee!"

A couple glanced her way, cups in their hands.

"Don't drink it!"

Images of Jonestown, Guyana flickered across her mind. Nine hundred insect-ridden corpses, men-women-children, poisoned with fruit juice laced with cyanide. The gruesome vista of what had been called the People's Temple. Temple. Holy Place. Refuge for Worship, axiomatic of the Reverence of Higher Glories and Benedictions. Flies buzzing about bloated bellies and contorted faces, jungle heat percolating deathwish and deathpresence with a sullen synchronicity.

"Poison!" Leah finally managed to shriek.

She started to run through the crowd, yelling at the tops of her lungs, "They're poisoning you!"

Folks arched eyebrows, frowned, or laughed outright. Yeah, this was the crazy lady who lived out by the old Indian burial ground. The one who spent a lot of her time walking through Machenville's ghost town. The woman who wouldn't talk to anybody but always cringed away as if you were about to bite her on the ass.

"Don't drink it," she cried, catching her shoe in a dropped caramel apple, stumbling, skidding on a patch of melted ice cream.

She saw several children munching candy skulls, washing it down with milkshake, and ranted at them, "You won't live to see the Day of the Dead. *This will be the Dead's Day if you don't listen to me!"*

In the old Aztec religion the skull was a symbol of resurrection. They had believed that life was a fleeting moment, a dream from which death awakened them.

And indeed she pictured Death bending across these children, prepared to kiss them into Its special brand of consciousness.

A man with a guitar who'd been playing softly now swung around and glared hard at her. "Hey, gringa, don't talk to my kids like that!"

"But they're going to die … " Leah started to say, about to finish it with *if they drink that stuff.* But the look on his face throttled the words in her throat. It wasn't a look like he was going to hit her if she didn't shut up. It was sadder than that; it was a look of helpless resignation. A man who couldn't save his children or himself.

The kids were crying.

Then Leah saw the tent, thirty feet behind the guitar man. Where the hermaphrodite had danced for fiesta. He was standing in the entrance, beckoning to her with those graceful hands. He was there quite naked but nobody else seemed to notice. Maybe they couldn't see him at all now.

"Is he only for my eyes?" she murmured out loud. She had no problem anymore with thinking of the dancer as 'he'.

Feeling the stares of the crowd burning silently on her, then feeling it even stronger as they turned away, Leah walked to the tent and went in.

The tent was empty except for Leah and the god.

This was what he was, wasn't it?

Inside, the mist and incense smoke played across his body, obscuring the erection, then revealing it slowly along its length like a sword being drawn from a sheath. In Leah's peripheral vision the wide rice paper temple rubbings rippled, seemed to hiss, garbled phrases she couldn't quite make out but which she was certain were either words of love or obscenities meant to incite her. One in the same.

Join the dance, the dance that shakes the loins and spirit.

"Be revealed," he said.

And she knew that meant he wanted her to disrobe. This was hard for her but it showed how much she wanted him that she complied. What was she revealing but her scars? The shattered fault lines of her flesh? But as she took off her clothes, the sandalwood fog wreathed these manmade imperfections into a frosted origami. If it was possible for such physical devastation to be rendered beautiful, hers was.

Dance with us …

She trembled, hands up over her missing nipples and carved breasts, like any shy maid. He opened his arms and she felt the knotted cords of his hair snake around her when she stepped into his embrace. She couldn't believe how erotic just the sensation of his hair against her skin was.

It didn't bother her a bit, the unusual combination of breasts pressing into her own chest and engorged cock hard against her stomach. It was a physicality completely uninformed of treachery, that of a being invented entirely by sex sent to rescue her with this sensual conglomerate of mysteries.

Leah pulled herself onto tiptoes, lifted one leg so that the erection slipped between her thighs. He, in turn, moved his hips back and forth to rub across her clit.

"Be revealed," he said again.

Confusing her. She'd stripped. What more could he mean?

And then everything slipped: the years, space, distance and memory, the dissolving of time in matter's absence. She was in East Texas again, in bed, waking up to a bolt of lightning turning bright her windows, outlined abruptly in the dark. Thunder shook the glass but no rain followed. There was only a scream bisecting the night.

Leah hurried out from between the sheets. She grabbed for the phone to call 911 as she heard another scream. It was coming from her neighbor's house. She knew Rob Gaines had been working the late shift at the plant. Carmel and the little boy were home.

Leah punched the buttons. Tried again. Heard a thin line of static, interspersed with nothing. The line was dead. Lightning must have struck the wires.

She'd seen the news. There was a serial rapist stalking the city. Finding women unprotected. Leaving a trail of razed lives.

Leah ran to the kitchen and grabbed a knife from the block on the counter. She went out the back door and across the two yards, unseparated by a fence. She began looking through the windows. Through one that bared the master bedroom, she saw him cutting the gown from her friend's body, light from a single lamp turned on next to the bed. His profile was too feline, teeth mincing together, ears seeming to be laid flat against the skull.

Leah really had intended to do the right thing, to save Carmel, to stop this—well, there really was no better choice of word in this instance—*beast*.

But a liquid heat rolled through her, making Leah limp, the kitchen knife in her hands slipping from her fingers to fall into the grass. She was unable to do anything but watch.

The rape, the mutilation with blade and teeth and cigarette, her own body sizzling, spasming with each violation. She urinated, or was she just that wet with lubrication that it trickled down her thighs? She chewed her tongue and the insides of her mouth, grinding her teeth. She gasped, came, wept, failing to run to any of the other houses in the neighborhood for help. Observed the outrages with a shivering, perspiring voyeurism she couldn't thrust from herself. All she'd managed to do was creep closer to the window, fingertips clinging to the ledge, nose pressed to the glass, breath fogging it until the scene within became a vile ballet of destruction committed through a misty filter.

She hadn't cried out, "Stop!"

To the rapist or to herself.

She wasn't able to keep from touching herself, eyes focused and unblinking, pupils going achingly dry as those tears she'd shed vanished. She pinched her own nipples viciously as Carmel's were gouged out, raking her nails through the fabric of her gown and robe, over her breasts and down her stomach to match the geysering route of the attacker's knife.

Leah's entire body thrummed as Carmel's spine arched and she somehow bucked the beast off. The woman was bleeding and screaming out of her mind. She jumped from the bed with scraps of flesh trailing. She stumbled to a dresser, jerked open a drawer, yanked out a gun. The rapist foamed at the lips, spitting a string of invective so vile—so horrible—that Leah knew she'd treasure every word of it, despising herself for this.

(Where's my compassion for my friend? My empathy for this other woman? If I were actually in the room with them, would I obey if he told me to hold her down for him? Would I snatch the gun away from her to save him? And what part of him would I want to save most? The cat, the wolf, or the ghoul I've seen him be?)

He leapt across the room at Carmel. She stuck the barrel of the gun into her mouth, her finger working the trigger.

The force of the sound made by an exploding 38 jarred Leah from the window ledge. Blood, brains, and skull fragments splatted the glass in pebbly clots, a molar striking one pane, starring it with cracks spreading out like a rock thrown from a semi into somebody's windshield. Where the back of Carmel's head had been a gory gray/scarlet mist swirled for a split second, then condensed to spatter back and down in smithereen rain.

The sound of Carmel's child came crying from somewhere else in the house. That was when Leah faded out. The police had found her there in the back yard, cowering beneath the window, rocking back and forth in imagined agony.

Then had come the hospital.

The doctor commanded the orderlies to strip her in front of the mirrors. He would repeat, "See, Leah? There are no scars.

You weren't wounded; you weren't cut or burned. Your body is unmarked."

In much the same way that he had the patients suffering from severe anorexia stand naked before the mirror, using his mantra of, "See? You're not fat. You're not overweight at all."

But she'd known he was lying. There weren't enough drugs in the world they could force into her to fool her into believing the scars weren't there. Of course they were! They hurt her all the time, twinging in the least of the pain, burning nerves all the way to the bones during the worst.

Every morning the nurse would come with the meds. Leah would be taken from her room for a session with the mirror. The crew would come to strip the bed. They changed the sheets every day. Because patients in madhouses tended to piss and shit themselves as the nightmares bombarded them. They sometimes even tore and chewed the sheets to shreds.

The guilt had transformed her. She'd become the victim she'd spied upon. Leah was just able to believe by half that the only stain upon the soul was that of indifference. The other half must be the sin of appetite.

Illusion ... a voice hissed in her head.

If life was an illusion, it was a fractured one, legion with ruptures and breaches which rendered any fantasy incoherent.

Leah had not been a victim. She had not been harmed.

But the scars hurt her, now! She felt them as their edges seemed to sink further through her flesh to scrape bone!

She opened her eyes, knowing she was being clasped in embrace. Temple, TEMPLE, ***TEMPLE***. Worship, refuge, within some colossal subterranean *chaitya*, antipodal to anything even remotely connected with divinity as she'd always been taught it to be. Devotion, propitiation, sacrament ... mouth and dicks in oral benediction. She was bent forward and penetrated from behind by a cock surely comprised of a barbed harpoon, which entered, then pulled back a little, snaring a corner of tender rectal tissue, almost pulling this out before the instrument rammed deeper in. Her spine was creaking, threatening to snap as she was bent backward, the cleft between her legs gutted and guttered up to her navel by jaws full of fish hooks. Her head lay in the lap of a rat-faced creature that thrust its multi-needled phallus into a raw hole in the back of her neck, sending shock waves into her brain and down each vertebrae. An unkempt female that was little more than a wasp with breasts and almost-human countenance straddled Leah's chest, reaching behind itself to hold up and out of the way the striped stinger that rose from the corrugated crotch, then sat across Leah's face. She gagged, smelling/tasting sharp ammonia, burning forests, and the kind of cheese which might be made from blood.

Dance with us ... open your mouth and legs ... open your third eye. We will fill and overfill everything.

She could somehow see the god off by himself. He was dancing, head tilted back in rapture, eyes closed, feet stepping lightly, surely across the bare ground of the tent. He feinted left, then somersaulted toward the fray of used and using flesh. Yet without ever connecting. He'd whirl away again, in three-dimensional dervish.

Leah realized she was scarcely of a single dimension. But rippling. Cascading and undulating in a chaotic misalignment of up/down/left/right. And the creatures that debauched her—cruciating her with such venereal lust—were the ones she'd seen ... in the rice paper mural!

But they didn't feel like paper now. And even with the tissuey rustle and the bannerlike wavelike motion, she knew they were stone come to life. Neither did Leah seem to be paper as they used every orifice and invented new ones, loving her as they dismantled her, strung her back together, fucking savagely each neural nuance.

And the god, who'd summoned her to him, was symbolic of her fantasy of the man with the knife, loving her and then handing her over to the forces of the night.

The all ... the full ... the horror that brings us joy.

The never-solemn rites of jubilant demolition.

She'd been put into the paper, had become one with the stones, martyred by dark love, granted the center of her pain. The atonement she required to give her wretchedness meaning.

And how did she appear to him, as his gaze swept the wall of rubbings (as they rubbed and ground against)? One of her eyes rounded to its maximum, veins within shattered in terror and torment's extremity. The other eye rolled up to pupil-less white in rapture. Her own heart in her left hand, a lotus flower in the right.

She sagged, a sandstone rag doll, each bone silted down after having been dislocated, then broken by the rarest and most physically impossible (or at least inhuman) positions of coitus.

But she didn't fight. She welcomed it, not quite Death. Nothing so single a unit or limited a condition. But a lover by her own twisted definition. Lovers, *plural*, the darkest modes of which insisted upon reconfiguring a body utterly. Otherwise it couldn't exist within the sheer boundaries of this orient and disorient.

She shrieked and smothered, bit and clenched and gripped with teeth and ribs and thighs. Was ravished, devoured with desire, murdered under the carnal barrage, then brought back again and again because they so cherished her they couldn't forsake her. She was forced to join the dance, bending, opening, blossoming in the ultimate display of her fantasy.

Carried off into the night.

PART FOUR

Festivals

Preface To Zero

Was he the only one who saw the scarring of the world? That its time of cosmic commencements and turbulent Ages—Archeozoic, Cambrian, Cretaceous, Jurassic, Paleozoic—comets and searing sun bursts, the swivel upon a fragile axis, ice age, starstorm age, axe age, sword age, brother against brother, had left it exquisitely etched in suffering?

No, he knew there were others out there, like him. He'd felt them, in proximity of severe ether, reaching out through the mute spheres of pain-bringing on other planes. Tempests of souls, vital with compulsion, constantly and relentlessly adding to those sworls of defacement, that history of disfigured adornment.

They were the heroes of the most rugged, impious individualism, defying the gods, stealing divine thunder and pleasure. Putting themselves at the center of the universe where darkness bloomed in kaleidoscopic bruise. They spat in the eyes of all immortals and kept the human race from completely becoming slaves to heaven.

I am monster and freethinker, builder upon the blaspheme, rewriter of the narrative of man through the use of scriptures of misery.

And it's the souls of the children I send out, remade, afflicted but wise, who will cry out to the universe to beware, to not trust the vulgates who preach that there are things which belong to the gods and things which belong to men, and that men should never covet what the gods adore.

Dharma? Duty?

My only duty is to myself.

Like the beast Aleister Crowley once said, Let This Be The Whole Of The Law.

Chapter 28

"Notions and tickets, short circuits and folding mirrors.
I am mad, calls the spider, waving its many arms.
And in truth it is terrible,
Multiplied in the eyes of flies."
—"Totem"
Sylvia Plath

The rides were still going when the screaming started.

How long could one night go on?

As long as a scream could ride a single exhale.

And if it were thousands of screams—or rather, the screams of thousands? Spirits thrown into another place, no one saw the simple monsters of the merry-go-round that continued to turn their bodies, circumnavigating the dark. The Ferris wheel of incarnation went from life to death to life, like an emperor at the Colosseum games who couldn't make up his mind: thumbs up or down to the gladiators. The tilt-a-whirl had been hosed down repeatedly, but no one threw up anymore. The rictal grimaces plastered on their faces looked like the sideways slides of astronaut trainees, blurring in G-force tests.

The hall of mirrors was empty.

The carnival train—mostly for kids—chugged without much smoke, miniature cars filled with faces pale as those on candy skulls, as many teeth showing with jaws snapped open wide as possible to wail. The tracks continued to trundle the insensate bodies through the cardboard cut-out ghost town, with old west gunslingers and lawmen popping out to slaughter one another, no audience conscious to enjoy the spectacle.

A trio of teenagers in the extra-large handicapped stall in the men's bathroom fired up a spoonful of Mexican black tar. They shared the needle, thought they knew in the resulting rush what it was like to skim dimensions. Then the Soma caromed them in another direction entirely, where only gods enjoyed the buzz of hunger. On basalt slabs in the giant place, they saw what leered down, poised to pick apart the moist meat of souls.

Elliot watched the paper rubbings, the women having smeared Soma on them as his brother danced. The figures in them surged, flatly alive, the strips of rice paper running a motion picture more repulsive than any porno snuff-fest he'd ever seen Saab rent. He was surprised the milky liquid didn't ruin the charcoal, didn't pock the paper. The screams outside the tent began shortly after, matching and going beyond any human din he'd ever heard in war.

The refugees from Phnom Yohp went through the fiesta, shutting off the rides, getting people safely down, turning off the fat fryers in the booths, putting out cigarettes burning between paralyzed fingers. The twenty-five children, no longer dressed in bejeweled costumes, gathered wildflowers—bluebonnets, painted daisies, marigolds—and put at least one somewhere on the person of each screamer. That took the rest of the night.

Shiva danced through the streets.

Those who hadn't gone to the fiesta because they were too sick wondered what was happening. A few managed to sit up in bed, straining to listen to the commotion through the walls. Those with families couldn't help but notice when none of their loved ones came home. But they couldn't go out looking for them.

A man took out his cell phone and dialed a number.

"You were right, Colonel Gestetner," he spoke into it when he'd reached his party. "They're here. And it's getting weirder by the minute."

Sirikit smiled. Focused on light of moon silver and pale prism rose. She floated in it, weightless, careless, buoyant. Not to be chained again within the womb, learning the claustrophobics of physical existence. Not to be expelled again in a flood of uterine water and blood, to then forever fear being overwhelmed. If incarnation was a word made flesh, then this freedom from sorrows was a hush of profound torpor.

Shiva danced, followed at a discrete distance by Cheanneary Ry. Her love for him poured out through her eyes. The screams she heard everywhere were nothing, she knew, but the sounds made by those enduring labor pains. Giving birth to themselves anew, released from the redemption of *samsara*—the seemingly interminable cycle of reincarnation. This wasn't by the usual offices of fleshy conception into a womb receptacle, but through a spiritual journey provided by this god.

Was he not the fairest living incarnation of Shiva that Nagas Wat—and now the world—had ever seen? She'd viewed the others, all eventually become part of the epic carvings about the temple grounds. It was an iconographic index of variety. Bearing anywhere of from one to nine pairs of arms, from a single pair of breasts to as many as a dozen teats, some Shivas with tails and others without. Some were highly muscled while others were softer-lined, curves more voluptuous, sensuous as opposed to warriorlike. When their times came, they took their places among the monsters in the primordial *mudras* of the beings who have always existed at the edge of the mind of homo religiosus.

With kisses and teeth, tenderness and violence, fascination and repulsing revelation.

In her hands, Ry had one of the little ballet costumes she'd made for the children. She tore small pieces and scattered these across where Shiva put his feet, as if leaving in his wake shreds of her own bridal gown.

She hadn't been jealous when the woman who walked the ghost town came to be with him, summoned, to be loved by him. She hadn't been frightened when he gave this woman to the beasts in the rubbings. She knew Shiva was wise, granting Leah Limerick what her soul cried out for.

Cheanneary Ry didn't ask, "What about me? My soul cries out to be in your arms."

She didn't dare ask it. She'd already had the image flicker across her mind, just as the other prophecies the god allowed her, tickling along the synapses. She'd been there—or would be—in Shiva's embrace. She'd seen herself lying down with him, his body black in shadow, visible only in misty jewels of ruby, diamond, opal and pearl, skin smelling sweet, limbs twined about her languidly, his eyes closed in rapture.

Shiva danced, past the merry-go-round where people reclined in the arms of abominations. Not unlike in the rubbings she'd helped to make in Nagas Wat, before Elliot brought them all to Texas. (But these didn't move, didn't reveal epithymetic genitalia which could eat as well as fuck victims.)

Ry knew she would be granted her most profound desire. She just didn't know quite when it would happen. It filled her with joy, with a sense that she would soon know completion. She would have continued to follow him without this, accepting that she was but an undesirable and insignificant woman. But to know that she would someday be flesh to flesh with him, cheek to cheek …

She knew that Elliot loved her although she couldn't imagine how. She had seen a glimpse of what he perceived when he looked at her and couldn't understand why that vision he had of her was of a perfect being—which she knew she wasn't.

(No, the only perfect one she was aware existed anyplace was dancing a few feet in front of her.)

It made her feel sad that she didn't return his feelings. But in her intuition she knew El was never meant to have a wife—only children.

Harry's head tilted right to left, viewing contorted faces he passed. The mouths splitting back into the most wrenched of grimaces, eyes bulging and etched with the bloodshot outlines of the mountain ranges of hell, muscles pulsing/twitching as they tried to describe in their own sinew the countenances of demons they could see on the other side. As if those in the suffering stage of Soma were beginning to shift, taking on the semblance of anything but the haplessly human.

And as such it touched whatever remained of the human inside him. He felt a shudder rumble through, uncharacteristic of the god he'd become (or of the god who'd become *him*). He saw a woman lying on the ground, squirming in spiritual agony, having rucked up her dress to reveal the tiny pink rosebuds on her underwear.

He was aware that his former self would once have had no qualms about taking advantage of this comatose female. He would have gone to her and torn the panties off, kneeling between her legs, hoping her convulsions would make those inner muscles grip him real hard as he slammed himself inside her. He'd have ground bone to bone until the orgasm leapt him out, into a place he'd always considered to be oblivion and which he'd always been convinced must be attained by force.

But he didn't go to her. Rape was another animal, a jackal of a different night.

He passed a booth which had earlier sold candy skulls. It had been knocked over, the grinning confections rolled to blanket a corner of the fairground. He walked across these, feeling them crunch beneath his feet and being happy as the lord of death, just as the lord of love would be joyous walking barefoot across a carpet of rose petals.

He danced up the steps of the huge trailer that contained the house of mirrors. He could hear the rumbling of an air conditioning unit beneath, hidden from view by the plywood skirting which surrounded the area between the trailer's floor and ground.

He went in, the cold air making the mirrors seem faintly smoky. He felt the golden bells on bracelets about his ankles shiver up his legs, the femurs inside his thighs vibrating like tuning forks. The Nagas tail slid from the base of his spine, a sensation not unlike that of the kundalini serpent awakened in the first chakra to travel upward into the center of the brain.

He wasn't really sure why he'd felt compelled to enter this place. *Could* god be compelled? Perhaps it was only a way to find some silence from the din of screams. But why would Shiva do that, shrinking from a destiny he was responsible for weaving? It wasn't anything which ought to have bothered the god who cherished both hideous and beautiful.

And yet it was awful. To Harry at least—even if such suffering had never disturbed him before. The squeals and shrieks rattled his skull bone practically down into skull dust. The sight of the woman, helpless, her features turned horrible in the truest sense of the word ran a liquid current so cold through his blood that the veins fogged, his arteries chugging like the air conditioning unit.

He was responsible for this. Part of a plan he'd formulated—or which had been devised for the vessel of his body and soul to implement, no matter how Harry born-as-a-man might have felt about it. Back when he had some sort of human autonomy. Back when he wouldn't have seen any part of that woman in the dust there as anything but a vagina and maybe a pussy-mouth.

The god had danced him inside this place, the smells of sandalwood and vomit pervasive. The sight of a dancing prodigy was multiplied many times until the reflecting maze resembled nothing less than the wrap-around gestalt of the death-orgy that spanned the temple walls back in Nagas Wat. And which now hung reproduced in rice paper and charcoal in the main tent.

There, surrounded by the mirrors, views of himself with breasts, a tail, hands up in sudden visual shock with mouths in the palms open to gasp in holy terror.

No longer dancing, the bells jangling down into silence, infinities of a freak-who-was-prince-of-time everywhere he turned.

There was almost nothing present in the physical reality confronting him which reminded him of the Harry Tyler he'd been. The man, the lean tough not-to-be-fucked-with cowboy who'd survived death in a hundred southeast Asian shitholes, had screwed death in a thousand demented and damning ways. (A shortchange, considering there were one thousand two hundred fifty aphorisms of sex as divine merging in the Kama Sutra.)

In the Tantric system, sex was employed through its many positions and with the proper meditations as a tool to attain self-mastery and redemption. Both the Kama Sutra and Tantrism were an elaborate codex of dance in sex as the ultimate and most illuminating creative force. As opposed to the negative and nihilistic postures Harry had favored, wandering blighted landscapes seeking the most putrescent of ventages, sick with the need to defile. Dance to him had been a naked girl in a peep show booth, gyrating as the tokens were inserted in the machine.

"I'm a man; only men debauch; only men are this perverse."

I dance creation into existence ... or I dance the end of the world.

What Harry saw now, reflected back at him and backward like some mutated joke on the process of incarnation, wasn't a god. Wasn't a vastly supernatural being who was at the very hub of the next cycle of the world. It was a pathetic mutant, a nightmarish sex-doll tricked out at some illegal, underground porno-plastic surgery crankerie. As if he'd entered that dancing booth years ago to be with all the others who hadn't quite achieved the intended godhood.

Yeah, old Harry had fucked some strange knotholes.

Until his karma came down on him in a serious cosmic crunch and he'd *become* one.

Atonement.

(Return to the source.)

He'd done that all right. He was his mother's son. He'd changed, metamorphosed, ah hell SHIFTED more than Deborah ever had, or any of her breed and brood.

He'd sought empowerment through abusing every hole he saw as the womb of both Madonna and Terrible Mother, the saint who bore her pain nobly to give birth but then devoured her babies. Now he was that archetype, complete with a pussy scented with new lotus blossoms and stinking of carrion. He was the hole he'd always strived to first rule and then destroy.

Had he really made it to godhood? And if so, so fuckin' what? How was he any better than the wreckage that had called to him from behind the window at the peep show?

Harry stared at the mirrors and then screamed, sound shattering each one like lightning through the ego. Then he hung his head and wept like a drag queen.

Not a man anymore. Not a woman. Only a broken emblem.

Chapter 29

"They don't know the day
is the dark's face,
and the dark the day's."
—Poem For Shiva
Allama Prabhu

They each had a photo of the man with the half-scarred face. He was to be found and taken, alive. There were twenty-five little Cambodian kids to be rounded up as well.

Everyone else was to be shot. Every single person in Machenville.

Other methods had been considered. The release of a gas or toxin. It could have been released after Elliot and the children had been safely spirited away. It might have looked as if the slow illness leaked by the base years before had finally killed them. Except the government had put a lot into repudiating there'd ever been such a bug. And how to explain the other seventy-odd thousand people scattered across the country? They had lived in Machenville when that leak occurred. And although they were sick, they didn't also die?

Video had been taken. People screaming. *Everyone* screaming. A bit of computer Hollywood and it would be obvious they had gone berserk, killing each other. As if they'd all been slipped PCPs in their nachos and been hooked up to Marilyn Manson music.

But the contamination had been by that weird new substance Soma, and who knew what a drug like that was capable of? Look at what it did to those kids in Bangkok. Even though none of them had become violent. Hey, the hallucinogens from the 1960's used to make some people horny and happy, and it caused others to jump out of windows, right? Beer could make you relaxed and farty or you might just get ornery enough to kick the shit out of folks at a soccer game.

Saab was fully prepared to blame it on some fucked-in-the-head Vietnam vet named Elliot Tyler—listed as killed during the war but having been in hiding all these years. He'd worked for infamous Thai drug lord Tak in a heinous plot to introduce this vile and godless new buzz to the planet. Had used it on the Bangkok tyke guinea pigs—and on a Cambodian village where the occupants had also gone insane and killed each other. Locational testing was all the rage. Saddam Hussein used a town of Kurds within his own borders to try out a biological weapon and shrugged off the casualties. Even the U.S. had a history of using its people when testing the effects of things like LSD and atom bombs.

And where was this Tyler freak? He'd been tracked back to this country, to Texas where he'd set himself up under an assumed name in Machenville. Mostly ghost town, small population, isolated in the desert.

Not to worry. Saab wanted him alive but he didn't intend for him to live too long. He had plans. He didn't like being betrayed.

The cleaners arrived in trucks from Whitman Air Base, where Colonel Gestetner waited with Outfit techs who were going to test the Soma and examine the children. The colonel said they'd tramped carefree through a heavily mined meadow, picking buttercups, not setting off any of the bombs laid out in a tight grid. He was theorizing that some property of the Soma must have rendered them able to do that, although he couldn't imagine how.

"Find that drug, boys," he told them sternly, "or don't bother coming back."

The cleaners had seen the tapes of the streets of Bangkok, lined with smiling catatonics. There would be a few thousand of these, no fuss, some muss. If it was necessary, then they could do it, American citizens or not. That's how they came to be hired by an organization like the Outfit in the first place, because silly notions like moral imperatives never got in the way of their doing the job. The pay was good, the benefits fantastic: medical and dental insurance, 401 K, license to kill.

They came in about 11 P.M., saw the carnival lights blazing in the darkness. The moon was up high, centered in the sky and lopsided. They could hear screaming so loud they thought at first that there'd been a disaster on one of the rides. But nothing was running but the lights. There was no activity, no crowds running to or from some catastrophe. People sat propped up against buildings or were lying on the grounds, unmoving except for the wide extending of their jaws.

There wasn't supposed to be screaming. These folks were supposed to be sitting like Southern California guru-wannabees, lotus-style pretzel legs, grinning silent mantras, with psychedelic haloes of the surrealistically witless. No fuss …

This reminded the guys more of serious bummers, what Woodstock might have resembled if everyone had taken bad acid and gone into some shocked paralyzed psychosis. (Or had gone off on a mass deep end and begun slaughtering each other, like the story for this was going to go. Would have made a much better movie, huh? Instead of those boring hours of one peace-righteous band after another playing before 400,000 longhairs screwing in the mud. A few semi-automatic weapons sneaked in under long-fringed jackets—hey, no metal detectors there, right? Others using nails and teeth, eyeballs spurting, jugular veins being chewed through, storming the stage, jamming drumsticks through Country Joe's eardrums and planting the stringed necks of Gibson guitars up the draftcard-burning asses of the likes of Crosby, Stills, Nash and Young. Knocking Baez's teeth down her Commie throat. Taking Joe Cocker and … well, that was obvious.)

They spread out, fanning through the carnival grounds. Pop, pop, pop, gunfire erupting like festival firecrackers. Shrieking heads falling silent, arcing out in marshmallowy bone bits and sodden red corn flakes. Some muss …

"Have you noticed they all have flowers on them?" one cleaner asked his buddy, zeroing in on the bluebonnet tucked into the breast pocket of a guy's shirt.

"Hippies," the bud chuckled. "Love children. Takes me back to when I was just a pimpled kid in the national guard."

"I came all prepared to blow the heads off—ya know—like those damned krishnas at the airport," another said.

That conjured up an image and the three men burst out laughing, singing together, "Hare Krishna, Hare Krishna! Krishna Krishna, Hare Hare!"

They investigated the trailers, able to tell by the screaming before they went through the doors if there was anybody inside. There were no noises coming from the house of mirrors except for a particularly loud air conditioning unit the compressor must have been going out of. They went inside anyway, found no one, just piles of shattered silver glass and air so cold their testicles shrunk. They did see what appeared to be stained ice spilled from some kid's cherry-flavored drink, and spatters from it all melted down the steps outside. Of course, maybe it wasn't ice inside at all, but the drink had merely wetted the glass shards until it resembled ice.

There were Asian women amputees in a couple of tents, huddled together, not screaming until the cleaners opened up on them. Then they yelled plenty for about twenty-thirty seconds.

A couple truckloads of men drove off to check the rest of town. Went through houses, shooting people in their beds. These hadn't been doing the drugged wail either, but gazed up at their assassins with milky eyes, barely able to move under the covers. Started to go through the ghost town but realized about a mile into it in all directions that there was nobody there. No one lived in that part of town anymore and all those who were ambulatory had gone to the fiesta.

Elliot earlier dosed himself up with shit to help him sleep, trying to block out the screams. He wasn't needed anyway, not that he really fully understood what Harry believed he was accomplishing. Dharma, right. But wasn't giving all these people Soma a direct interference with *their* dharma?

Or did gods have directives which didn't follow the same "mortal" paths?

The Bangkok children had been freed from their lives of sexual enslavement. Some, like Sirikit, from mutilation as well.

The men of Phnom Yohp were needed to protect the village's children later because the coming of the mercs had been foreseen. Or were they freed from their amputated conditions? Or were they rewarded for their dedication to Shiva, the women kept alive to care for the kids?

The folks of Machenville had been freed from the illness they shared, which would eventually have degraded them even more physically and emotionally, until they must die in agony. Or was there yet another reason? Something Elliot couldn't guess. Something he wasn't sure he wanted to ever know.

He recognized the sound of gunfire in his dreams and—soldier that he was—forced himself awake. He ran out of his tent, smelling carnage, the bitter liquified rust of gallons of free-running blood, the sweet/rot feculence of spilled guts, the oily vapor of cordite. The air had already been vinegary with the stench of fear, as all those who were caught in the first stage of Soma were seeing distant horrors but relaying them in terror pheromones here.

El looked around, trying to find his brother and Ry but not seeing them. Had they already been killed?

Men were carrying baskets of crystal mushrooms out of the main tent. He could see the children of Phnom Yohp gathered together in a knot. They were about to be herded onto the back of a truck. The kids were startlingly calm, beautiful faces gazing up at their captors with unafraid eyes.

Elliot saw Sirikit, sitting on the grass, scars bathed in moonlight, rainbow of her halo turning frosty in the lunar silver rays.

"No!" Elliot shouted, rushing forward as a man turned to Sirikit, weapon raised with its barrel inches from the twelve-year-old's serene face. Damn, if they were taking the other children alive, why not her?

All the colors in her halo disappeared save for red.

He prepared to leap on the man, to wrench the gun away and use the barrel of it to smash in the guy's skull. But there was a sudden, sharp pain in the back of his head. A harsh white light extended out of his vision, then bent like the Bifrost Bridge. And then there wasn't anything at all.

Chapter 30

"If you say
you and I are one,
you were me
but I was not you."
—Allama Prabhu to Goraksa Shunyasampadane

Saab Gestetner was sent into Vietnam in 1976, to infiltrate a mental hospital with the intention of investigating rumors of an American G.I. being incarcerated there. Information had it that the doctors called him 'ghostface' because he possessed unusual powers to alter his features. Such a person could be useful in covert work if he really had the ability to radically change his appearance by will alone. Old episodes of *Mission Impossible* aside, cosmetic disguises weren't that good. And they took time and convenience to apply.

But it wasn't going to be easy. The war with the U.S. had only just ended with Saigon's fall to the VC the year before. Americans weren't exactly popular. He would come out of the jungle, raving like, well, a loon. And they might see he was crazy, not hurting him because *you just didn't do anything to guys like that*; it was a universal shyness of the holy protection of the lunatic. Or they might beat him, sodomize him with the rigor mortis-sized dick of a dead water buffalo, and drag him off to a snug little bamboo cage in a P.O.W. camp. Or they might figure oh, what-the-fuck? and just shoot him. Saab was aware the latter was the most likely scenario.

But, then again, they'd whup-assed the mighty United States and might be feeling moderately generous toward those stray soldiers who'd ended up lost and insane and half-eaten by foot and penis fungi.

Yeah, right.

Saab figured he'd been sent on this mission because a higher-up had heard a rumor about his extracurricular art projects and predilection for particularly young models. Not that he knew who'd found out and ratted on him. But the Outfit was as full of sharks ready to eat their way to the top as anyplace else. He wasn't intended to return, of that he was certain. But he'd surprise them.

He emerged from the trees stark naked, orchids in a garland around his neck, sticking out his ears, one out his ass, offering the trio of soldiers from the handful of white grubs he was eating.

He said to them in flawless Vietnamese, "Good morning, I am Ho Chi Minh!"

Their guns had come up at first sight of him but no one pulled the triggers. They stared at him, faces unreadable, obviously waiting to see what he'd do next. It was apparent he wasn't armed, unless there was a grenade hidden behind that purple orchid up his rectum.

Then he announced, smiling and bowing, "Good afternoon, I am Mao Tse Tung!"

Pronounced *mousey dung*.

The three soldiers glanced sideways at one another.

He mushed-munched through a couple more squirty grubs and then nibbled one of the flowers on his garland. He said, "Good night, I am Jane Fonda!"

"Jane Fonda?" one of the soldiers repeated.

Then they broke up, laughing their butts off.

That day's miracle was on his side. He ended up at the rice cracker bin, Vietnamese doctors seeing him safely locked into a room. He had his hands cuffed behind him and his feet manacled but they gave him some lovely drugs.

Which even under the potent influence of—hell, he'd taken stronger buzzes than that on R & R—he wouldn't reveal his true mission. Because, certainly the Vietnamese wanted to interrogate him.

"Why are you here, G.I.?"

"Bar-ba-rel-la. Bar-bar-ba-rel-la!" he sang, shaking his long white-blond hair. His equally platinum whiskers were kept well manicured around the mouth, resembling a woman's groin. He was prepared to suck some cock if he had to. It really was less annoying than taking it up the ass. Unless, of course, they first did it up your ass and then expected you to suck.

"Why are you still in Vietnam?" he was asked.

Saab smiled, batting his lashes. "I came to Hanoi to help, don't you know that? During all that criminal bombing! It was on TV."

"The war is over. What do you expect to accomplish? To fight another war?"

"Goodness, no! Why you certainly beat the pants off us, 'scuse the expression." Saab managed a girlish blush.

"Are you CIA? Where is the helicopter that dropped you off?"

"Are you the Black Queen? And I was brought here by Pygar, the blind angel."

He was wheeled into the shock room. They hooked him up to the ECT machine, rubber bit between his teeth tasting of the fifty humid mouths that had chewed down on it before. He didn't resist the voltage but jumped with it into the darkness. It was a place he'd visited often on his own so why should he fear it now? So many people saw their worst nightmares in the realm the electric convulsive treatment took them to. Saab saw his best ones, stalking across the gash of horizon, karma-stained in his vocation's demanded duty.

He ran down a street paved rather unevenly with squirming little bodies, leaning as he went, swinging a long kris, severing fingers and noses that poked up. He pissed in a gutter lined with tiny backsides. He wandered between alley walls composed of sad cherubic faces, gouging his initials everywhere, harvesting tears as he created a mural which was the transcript of black dharma. Hedgerows of spinal splinters and scrimshawed scraped-pate anomalies advertised in windows at a gallery of his desires, where inside all the art were works-in-progress he could slash his way up to and reform on whim.

He came to a jungle temple, the statues and bas-relief in stone done all in children. And as each rock wept, he whittled at the petrified smiles, at miniature genitals, while somewhere nearby an incense burned that reeked of the shit that comes from being breastfed.

When he regained consciousness, he whispered to a man who was either a doctor or a captain, "Do you have any children? I'd like to tell them a story. About a boy who kept a magical cricket as a pet. Every night he took it out of its matchbox and set to work on it with tweezers and a sewing needle. And finally he turned it into a spider. The spider got away, growing huge because it had once been a magical cricket and knew how to use the maya. It wove a gigantic web, which shimmered in the moonlight. The boy walked into it in the dark, thinking it was only a patch of harmless fog. And when the spider rushed down to him and he stared it in the face, the boy cried, 'What are you? Are you going to hurt me?' And the spider replied, 'I used to be harmless; I used to be a cricket. My dharma was to chirp. But I've been remade and my dharma has changed. Now I'm hungry all the time.'"

This man who was either doctor or captain looked askance at another who was either an orderly or a soldier. "Doesn't he sound like what you'd expect ghostface to, if he bothered to speak to us?"

"But if it was ghostface, you couldn't be sure which mouth was talking. The one where usual mouths are located, or any of the horrible others which open in the side of his face," the second one replied.

Saab was taken back to his room. Leaning against the padded wall, he thought he heard somebody on the other side whistling. Nothing he recognized, a nameless piece of jazz. He'd tried to get into jazz himself once. He'd suspected that because it sounded like jizz that he'd like it. But the jizz the jazz poured abundantly came only out of pain and emotion, and not from the violence he preferred his orgasms be derived from.

He didn't know if Vietnamese listened to jazz or not. He took a chance and asked, "You the one the staff refers to as ghostface?"

"Yes," he heard softly replied. "Are you American?"

"Does Andy Warhol like Campbell's soup?"

"Is the war still going?"

"No, ended 'bout a year ago. That's when Saigon fell."

"Yeah? I was there then. But our chopper crashed and I woke up here. Did we win?"

Saab was silent a moment.

"No," he answered. "Weird, isn't it? To think that America actually lost, beaten by this bunch of little gooks in a little gook country."

The man on the other side of the padded wall chuckled. "Righteous," he said.

Saab was mildly surprised. "Why's it righteous?"

"Because America's become a nation of werewolves."

Saab thought about that. He nodded to himself. Not only because he thought it might just be true, but because he rather liked the idea.

Two weeks later. Or so. Time here was hard to gauge. It wasn't like he had a window to see the sun going up and down.

He heard the orderly speaking to the guard in the hall. The one that stood between the doors to his room and ghostface's, sentry-present because they were Americans and therefore highly suspect.

The orderly had brought Saab's injection. Saab had been getting used to it, less and less affected as each day passed. Not that he'd been as helpless off it as most patients would be. He did too many drugs on his own to be that susceptible. He had one of those systems that eventually acclimated to chemicals.

Always putting him in search of the next neural overthrower.

"I can let myself in," the orderly said.

The guard mumbled something. There was the jangle of keys.

Saab remained limp, slumped upon the soiled padding, waiting for him to close the door. Then he jumped to his feet so fast he caught the orderly completely unaware, head-butting him before the man could cry out. The orderly fell back, stunned, half-conscious, a purple and red streaked goose egg rising on his forehead. His fall had been muffled by the padded floor.

Saab rocked onto his back, wrapping the chain between the leg irons around the man's throat, squeezing it like a linked garrote, hearing the wet splop as tubes and cartilage squelched, then mushed. He released the pressure and swung himself around to look over the body. The Vietnamese had the key to the door but not to the cuffs.

Saab was a slender man. Lying on his back again, he squirmed his narrow hips through his arms until he had his hands in front of him instead of behind. He grasped the orderly's forearm and wrenched it savagely, bones snapping, flesh parting as the separated ulna jabbed through. He bent carefully but quickly and extracted a splinter of bone. He sucked the gore from it to clean the point, tasting blood and marrow. He started to spit this out, then thought better of it. Hadn't been getting much protein lately. So he swallowed, finding it gritty but satisfying. He filed the bone shard's point finer, grinding it against his teeth. He used this to pick the lock of the handcuffs. Then he sprang himself from the leg irons.

Medieval mechanics. Some Vietnamese had fought with pitchforks during the war. He loved backward countries.

Saab stepped behind the door and called to the guard, raising his voice a couple octaves to imitate the orderly he'd heard only moments before. When the guard stepped in, Saab plunged the hypo needle into the base of his neck and hit the plunger.

Now he was free *and* he had a gun. He unlocked the other American's door. The man looked up from where he was sitting on the floor.

Saab grinned. "Ah, you don't look so bad. I've seen worse. Hell, I've done worse to people."

Around the corner another corridor branched off. A second guard had his back to them, lighting himself a cigarette that smelled like it was at least half Mekong marijane. Saab started to raise the weapon's butt end in preparation for creeping up behind him but ghostface was already stalking up so fast, so silently. He took the man's head in both hands and twisted it.

There was a crack to do any psychotic chiropractor proud. Now ghostface had a weapon, too.

They passed the shock room. A doctor and an orderly were tying down a female patient. The doctor spoke to her in low, reassuring tones but she was clearly terrified.

"No, please don't send me to that place. I can't go there again," she pleaded.

Ghostface put a round through each of the staff member's skulls.

"You don't have to go there again," he told her in Vietnamese. "If I let you go, will you just run away? Beyond the hospital and into the trees? Any other jungle's got to better than this one."

She nodded, crying a little. Ghostface undid the straps. She got up and skittered down the hall. Saab raised his weapon to shoot her in the back but the other man put a hand on the gun to lower it.

"What are you doing?" Saab asked him, appalled. "She'll sound the alarm."

"I doubt it. She's more interested in getting the hell out of here. Anybody wired up to that machine wants out. And if they see her loose, they'll start chasing her and she'll be trying to get away from them too much to remember us. She probably thinks she hallucinated me anyway." Ghostface arched the scarred, hairless eyebrow on the ruined side of his face.

But Saab knew right then that this man would never make a covert operative. He had scruples. And he made excuses for them.

But Gestetner did find out that Elliot Tyler was one hell of a soldier as he effortlessly killed six more people as they made their way out of the hospital and off the grounds. Saab let him do it, just to see what he was capable of. After all, this wasn't a military installation, just a madhouse. And there hadn't been more than the two guards and the captain who'd interrogated Saab as far as army presence went.

Out in the wilderness, Elliot survived like a wolf.

(Werewolf American.)

Saab was a little disappointed, especially when the face didn't move at all. There were no alter-egos, no disguises, no hauntings. A shame, since it was quite the piece of wreckage art. But he figured he could use this guy anyway. The man's dharma was clearly that of the quintessential soldier. Okay, he could still do that, working right alongside Saab. Without ever having to know what Gestetner really did.

As for the higher up who'd sent Saab in after ghostface. Jimmy Carter was elected, there were some political changes in the organization, the man was no longer there.

When you were properly fulfilling your dharma, destiny had a way of taking care of you.

The cleaners returned to Whitman. Pronounced everyone tidied up. Saab had previously considered having them burn the bodies. This was desert area so it wasn't like a torrential downpour would make them hard to incinerate. But, shit, three thousand of them? That wasn't a simple bonfire but a major conflagration, the image it brought to his mind one of stinking acres of burning tires.

Besides, burning the corpses wouldn't have gone with the disinformation of the townspeople going berserk on Soma and killing each other. (The cleaners had used weapons that it was possible to obtain at a gun shop—like the one conveniently near the carnival grounds which had been broken into and looted. They threw spent weapons on the ground when they were through with them.)

Saab remembered those skins coming after his mercs. He'd escaped them, yes, but had lingered—hidden—watching when they lost their power as the moon set. What the hell they were he hadn't a clue. But he knew that somebody had skinned those dead villagers. And his troupe hadn't gotten any hits in Phnom Yohp but the men; the women and children had been in successful hiding. Now those women were dead also and the children were here. So there was nobody left to do the stripping.

Elliot was brought in, unconscious, laid on a stainless steel gurney, strapped down.

The colonel made sure he was standing over him when El finally opened his eyes.

Chapter 31

"That which through sleep or darkness hath deceived thee and lies down with thee, And will destroy thy progeny,—even this will we exterminate."

—The Rig Veda

Cheanneary Ry had gone to him when he screamed and the mirrors shattered. She'd cut her palms walking across the broken glass, to kneel beside him and rest his head in her lap. His eyes stared up without comprehension. Shiva couldn't move nor could he speak.

Then she heard the gunfire begin outside.

They were early! The people who'd been given the Soma hadn't yet passed from the maya of hell into living nirvana.

She knew she must hurry to hide Shiva and herself. There was no time to get him anywhere other than beneath the trailer. It was hard to drag him across the sparkling shards but there was no choice. He weighed more than twice what she did, and she needed her hands to walk on. She had to use them to pull him along, sliding on legless hips, the glass shredding her flesh. Tears leapt from her eyes as she arduously dragged him to the door, muscles stretching to their limits in shoulders and arms as she pulled him down each of the few steps.

The body of the god also bled, leaving between the two of them quite a trail across the glass-littered floor and down the small staircase. Ry pried apart a section of the plywood that skirted the bottom of the trailer, not able to hear the nails pop because of the noises from guns.

She didn't like that trail, smearing and clotting in the soil as she heaved Shiva beneath the floor of the trailer with her and patted the plywood board back up as best she could. But there was nothing she could do about it. If they were destined to be caught there and killed, then so be it. But this didn't fit with what she'd foreseen. There were too many things which hadn't happened yet. And this wasn't how she saw herself lying down with He whom she loved.

So she cradled Shiva down there, under the house of broken mirrors. Which was a metaphor for maya, wasn't it? She heard boots mounting the steps, going inside, crunching on the glass, leaving, thunder and more thunder, getting more distant as a storm receding to the horizon. The man in whose body the god lived remained in his catatonic state. It must be the man, for how could a deity become so paralyzed with whatever epiphany he'd suffered in there?

She stroked his forehead, murmuring, "Shshshsh. Shshshsh."

She quelled her own terror by closing her eyes in the dark and imagining she had legs. That she was a moving mantra of limbs and torso, immaculately perfect in Cambodian ballet costume, golden and bejeweled. She undulated like a lotus in the wind, bare feet touching the tiled floor of the palace lightly as soft rainfall, the illusion she created with gesture and step a synchronicity of flesh and infinity. In the physical act which was second in holiness only to sex: dancing.

And after what seemed like forever the guns stopped, the killing had to be over. She opened her eyes. God was in her arms and she had no legs.

But still Ry didn't leave the space beneath the trailer of the house of mirrors. She was afraid the men with the weapons were still out there. That if she took Shiva back outside, they would be seen and murdered, and everything she'd witnessed of the future would never happen.

Dawn came. She could hear the birds, singing as if no atrocities had happened during the night, in that manner which birds have of going beyond all horror to react only with pure joy at each day's beginning.

She noticed Shiva was looking at her, his beautiful eyes sad. He smiled as anyone does who has felt the passage of thousands through the sieve of mortality. Then he was turning to push open the plywood. He was wriggling out into the beginning light.

"We have much to do," he said to her.

She followed him, glimpsing the bodies of the other Phnom Yohp women, shot to pieces. She stayed behind him as he went directly to their main tent, where he'd danced the day before.

"In this fiesta the people of Machenville were celebrating," he began. "Yesterday was Halloween. Now it is the Day of the Dead."

Cheanneary Ry knew that it was impossible to think that Shiva and she could flay all the bodies by nightfall. The moon was going to be gibbous, too. But what about the children? What about the Soma?

And even if it could be done, what kind of risen would these make, having been terminated before they could leave their terror behind?

The god marched up to the rice paper where the charcoaled images of demons cavorted.

Yes, she'd seen them actually move, when smeared with Soma. But there was no Soma now. The killers had taken the mushrooms.

He began to intone, voice guttering deeply until it vibrated like the metal blade of a scalpel. Using his own nails, he tore into the veins of his arms. He bathed the paper images in his blood, crooning to them, smearing swathes of red across the figures copied from those at Nagas Wat. He stepped back, four nipples hard, erect penis moving up and down like the baton of a symphony's conductor, arms open wide the way of one who summons another to come, be embraced. He ran his fingernails across the breasts and in sharp circumnavigation of the head of his cock till the nipples and dick squirted more blood.

Ry trembled, watching as the shapes did more than just move this time. They began to coalesce, to step from the renderings, in flesh not of rice paper but of meat. There were beasts whose live, quivering breasts were fanged bats which hung upside down from their chests. There were monsters whose erections were the curved beaks of giant ravens; the testicles were their empty eye sockets filled with flies. There were all the other incarnations of the living Shiva who had existed at Nagas Wat. There was even Leah Limerick, vortices in place of nipples spinning like black water going down drains, the split of her tail one long uninterrupted gash filled with wounds which opened, suppurated, then healed, opened, suppurated, then healed. Her smile was full of teeth which were nothing but the glowing tips of cigarettes.

They shambled across the tent floor, curdled breastmilk, glacier-sour cuntjuice, gelatinous and viral semen dribbling across the ground. They went outside and began to flay those who'd taken the Soma and then been killed. They worked as fast as whirlwinds, even spinning, talons and teeth deftly removing flesh as single units. Or they passed into the corpses themselves through some kind of carrion osmosis to then lift off the skins from the inside, as anybody would take a gown off their own bodies. Then they picked these up and carried them to the canyons and arroyos beyond the limits of the city. There were no mango trees so they used the branches of thorny mesquite and alligator juniper to lift the skins toward the sky.

And afterward, blessed and released by Shiva, they raced into the wall of one of the canyons, resuming their positions of lust and despoiling, grinning profiles and silhouettes of fucking death, part of some ancient rock face once again.

Shiva led his army of skins to Whitman Air Base. The ICBM silos rose like ithyphallic ziggurats, housing the missiles that were supposed to have been dismantled. Still pointed at other countries, most of whom hadn't taken theirs apart either. They loomed in the dark, like giant rakshasas waiting to spring on the unwary traveler.

There was only one skin which housed the rainbow light. It belonged to Sirikit, bouncing along like an elegant balloon. The others lurched and staggered, black as the center of subdermal gangrene inside, the skins of the hands clenching and unclenching fists. And what faces there were contorted from the horrors the Soma had caused them to suffer in that vast cavern of basalt slabs and unholy diners.

The sentries at the gate looked up and saw them coming down the road.

"What the hell … ?" one of them asked the other.

"Look like people in costume," the second man said, lifting his weapon. "Halloween was last night, wasn't it?"

The first man stepped out of the guard cubicle and stood in the middle of the road, hand up to halt them.

"No trick or treating here, folks. You can just turn around and go back to wherever you came from."

Because, hell, he knew they couldn't have come from Machenville. There was nobody alive there anymore.

They came closer, and it was apparent the heads on many just weren't shaped right. Not the way of people with whole heads. And they were naked, weren't they? Actually he figured they must be wearing nude suits, like the genital-simulated chicken suits you used to see on people who wanted to streak but who didn't have the courage to skinny down to nothing.

Except for the tall woman at the front. No, some guy who couldn't decide if he wanted to be a female impersonator or a bitch dog, considering the extra tits and the tail.

"This is a military facility, sweetheart," the first sentry said to this he/she thang. Except neither sentry was a soldier. They were Outfit boys, and everyone presently on the base worked for the CIA. "So you'd best take your playmates back to whatever faggot party you dropped your Cinderella shoes in."

But the group kept coming. Man, there had to easily be a couple thousand of them. The second sentry picked up the cubicle phone to alert Gestetner.

It rang and he heard a scream. He looked up to see the first sentry being forced down, the butt of the weapon he'd held being rammed into his mouth until it emerged out the back of his head. The phone rang again and he dropped it, trying to get out of the hut before they could grab hold of him, too. Up close he could see there was absolutely nothing inside the stretched open mouths or in the ragged eyeholes, nothing but swirling black smoke.

He could hear a voice in the phone, saying, "Gestetner here. Hello?"

He couldn't help but think of Romero's *Dead* movies, from *Night of the Living Dead* to *Dawn of the Dead* and whatever had sought the dinner of flesh beyond that. But these weren't cannibal zombies with fish white eyes and cankerous tongues, loosening teeth chomping down as their sheer ravenous numbers overwhelmed the living.

nothing, nothing inside but black smoke …

You had to shoot 'em in the head, make sure you get a head shot, blow out their brains, stoppin' 'em dead in their cemetery-slime tracks. That's what it took to stop a Romero dead, chittered the terrified yokel at the back of the sentry's mind.

Except he could see there weren't any brains in the heads—those that even had enough of a head to house a brain. He was looking through smoky glass in vague human contour, dark air puffing in disquieting shapes, conjuring up the half-memories of what very young children perceive in shadows.

Hands that didn't look as if they ought to have any strength in them grabbed him and pulled him down. And began pulling him apart. Joints popped and then dislocated, skin and ligament making a sound not a bit unlike that of wet towels as they tore.

Chapter 32

"A hundred autumns stand before us, O ye
Gods, within whose space ye bring our
bodies to decay ..."
—The Rig Veda

"Where are the kids?" Elliot asked.

"Being examined," Saab replied.

"And my brother?"

Gestetner's brow furrowed. Who? Arcan Tyler was a dead suspected serial rapist. And Harrold Tyler had vanished years before, after retiring from the army, no one having seen him since.

Unless ...

No matter. From what he'd read of El's brother Harry, the man was an animal with no artistic finesse.

He shrugged. "If he was in Machenville with you, he's dead now. If he had a hand in bringing the Soma to this country, well then, I thank you both."

Elliot thought of Ry, of the other helpless women. Of watching Sirikit being killed with no more consideration than the assassin would give while swatting a mosquito. His teeth ground audibly. "Soma?"

"Yes," Gestetner said, smiling. "From what I've seen it possesses a certain potential for manipulation. We won't know exactly how until we've fully tested it. You get to be the first. To test it for us, that is."

Saab produced one of the crystal mushrooms, sitting in his hand like a knarled peyote button some shaman had transformed into a desert diamond. "Almost beautiful, isn't it?"

He snapped his fingers and a man came forward to force Elliot's jaws apart. The colonel dropped it into El's mouth and then signaled the jaws be forced shut again, where they were held, the upper and lower sets of teeth painfully crunched together until El could taste the silt as enamel flaked off. Saab stroked Elliot's throat as one would a puppy you'd just given a distasteful pill to.

"Swallow it, swallow. If you spit it out, I'll have to pick it up and drop it back in again. Then it'll be dirty because it's been on the floor! And we'll keep doing it until you do get one down," Saab cooed sarcastically.

His throat underwent a spasm, involuntarily choking down the mushroom. He grimaced, wondering what it would do to him. After all, it was totally unprocessed. It had been neither crushed nor strained nor drunk by a god to be transformed into Soma. In such a virgin state, was it hallucinogenic? Would it be poisonous? *What will it do to me?*

Que sera, sera. What ever will be will be.

The phone rang. Saab had sentries out to watch for anything weird—like bodiless skins skipping up the yellow brick road. Not that he expected it but you never knew. It rang a second time and he picked it up.

"Gestetner," he said brusquely.

No one said anything back.

"Hello?"

He heard screams being relayed from the other end of the line.

He hung up and punched another line. When they picked up, he said, "Let's do it. Close the building down."

This was where the germ that sickened the people in Machenville had been made. The place was fully equipped to be sealed off in the case of a biohazard emergency. Most of the men who'd done the cleanup were not in this building—just Saab, a couple guards, and the doctors who'd been brought to examine the kids. Too bad.

He hung up and punched another code, accessing him with those people beyond the walls. It was picked up. He said, "Just wanted to let you know you guys are probably going to have some company."

He heard gunshots and shrieks in the background. Duh, guess they knew this already. No one had said anything on the other end. They seemed to be holding the phone, not speaking, not breathing. If the colonel had been inclined to that sort of thing, this might have made his skin crawl and his balls cinch up. Saab hung up, assuming that what now held the opposite receiver likely *didn't* speak and *didn't breathe*.

He turned to Elliot and saw the man was having convulsions. He strained against the straps binding him to the gurney, spine arching, head banging back on the table until metal rang, eyes rolled up to whites. And his face moved on that ruined side. The scar tissue was swirling like soapy streaks in dishwater.

One of the doctors came in, glancing down with surprise at the prisoner's contorted expressions. But his reaction was brief; he knew who he was working for. And he'd known the colonel was going to be giving this man the drug. He just told Gestetner in the voice of flatline, "We've examined the children. Thought you'd want to know right away."

"And?"

"Extremely unusual. Every one's a hermaphrodite. Twenty-five of them. All from a single remote village. You know what the odds are? And with as much as they are similar in appearance in every other way, I'd almost have suspected they were clones. Of course, we can do a DNA test but that'll take some time ..."

Saab stared at the doctor for a moment.

Serials, strings, paperdolls. Limitless—nearly—options. Sequential canvases and quarry marble for consecutive outrages. A tingle ran up each of his vertebrae and he felt himself growing hard.

They had come to him, too. Ended up in his hands. His artistic, wasting hands. And some people said there was no god. And that there was no such thing as destiny.

Or dharma.

In his case, black dharma.

He heard air hissing through El's clenched teeth. The scar tissue was riding up like billows in beginning tidal high, whitecapped. And was that—could that—have been a little eye he'd just seen, opening in the hollow beneath the cheekbone? Like a shark coming up under that tide to look out of the water for the moon. It closed and nearby was a miniature rosebud mouth, gasping, lined inside with pearly baby teeth. Ghostface, yeah! After all these fucking years, it was about time.

Damn. Saab really wanted to watch this. But he needed even more to go see those twenty-five possibilities. It was the kind of opportunity to come along once in a millennium. To just the right iconoclastic *figuriste*. Inscribed tiny clits and cartouche little dongs, glyphic rumps, graven limbs, lost-wax process on nipples, acid-etched eyes, dye punched tongues. And finally he could experiment with his idea of intaglio on the deep insides of the rectum. If the Chinese could paint the interiors of snuff bottles, why not?

What is it the wasting man seeks?

Twenty-five identical freaks.

"Watch him," he instructed the doctor. "If he goes into cardiac-arrest, give him adrenalin, CPR, whatever, but hang onto him. If he goes completely nuts, try a tranquillizer. Keep him alive because if anything happens to him, I'll fuck you through both ears."

Shiva and Ry slipped inside the building thirty seconds before it was sealed off, dodging the slamming of a metal door. Outside the skins were swarming over everything. *Dia de muertos. Santa Maria, madre de Dios, ruega por nuestros pecadores, ahora y en la hora de nuestra muerte, amen.*

Shiva knew the children were here. He felt them in his testicles and in his womb. He recalled getting huge, boulder big, four breasts bursting with milk, needing to lie down in a spot where the moon shone into the temple.

The cobras had hissed like midwives, but it was the snake-faced priests who'd delivered the twenty-five babies. Yes, hermaphrodites were supposed to be sterile and certainly couldn't impregnate themselves, but this wasn't an ordinary androgyne. This was a god.

This was god. And the twenty-five little ones would become gods. Living incarnations of Shiva, all existing at the same time in the world of illusion. The cobras flicked their tongues, licking up the seas of blood and afterbirth. They coiled into cradle shapes the infants could sleep in. The priests sang their strange susurrating music as their heads undulated on the long necks. And Shiva rode the pain, stomach like a sail vibrating in the wind, hips crackling.

Now his children were prisoners here.

"They're in this place," Ry stated, seeing this fact in his eyes.

He didn't even need to nod. He tried to send them a mental message, not to fear because he'd come for them. But he knew they weren't afraid. Even though they were only children, barely five-years-old, they wouldn't be frightened, would they?

He realized that if he could be frightened for them that they, too, could know terror.

"I think I feel where Elliot is," Cheanneary Ry told him. "He needs help. He's been given the mushroom without your blessing of it. If I don't go to him …"

Her voice trailed as her expression took on a faraway look. But, then, it was Shiva who'd given her the ability to see. He nodded and she hurried away on her hands, palms silently pattering across the concrete floor.

From a few doors down on a long corridor came the eerie sound of a voice forced past a mouth full of foaming saliva. It gargled in a suffocated basso profundo. Shiva recognized it as belonging to Elliot, even though El was more baritone than base. There was pain in it, horror in it, and the part of him that was Harry wanted badly to go to him.

But his children were—oh … this way, and hurry … He saw in his mind an altar covered in flowers and bread, then in milk and blood. And then an altar which was only covered with tiny cracks, as if no one had come near it in centuries. In the first image were the striped shadings of both darkness and light, but in the second there was neither, only a colorless emptiness. As if the universe had ceased, not in any logical way which might have included explosion, for there was no dust upon that altar.

A part of a poem came to him, something Harry the man was remembering. Something he'd heard in school or recited by his shifter-bitch mother who'd been heavily into verse.

This is the way the world ends, the world ends, the world ends. This is the way the world ends, not with a bang …

But the last words weren't right. They were in no part T. S. Eliot, and all Harry Tyler.

... but with a who-gives-a-shit?

He came to a door. No, it wasn't the right door. This wasn't where his children were. But ... what? Someone inside drew him to open it, ever so quietly. He sensed a nada-being, separated utterly from light and darkness, nasty, *other*. Daring to believe itself demonic with a purpose. But it wasn't the higher purpose Shiva recognized. Black dharma? Was this a concept he'd heard before someplace?

Well, all through the epic varnas of men there had been those who tried to put their fates above the touch of gods. Those who could not only manipulate the great illusion but create corners of that maya for themselves. Places even the lords of destruction couldn't reach and utterly outside the possibilities of earthly *mokhsha*. Where only a mortal man who had learned the road into it while wearing the beast's insignia could travel.

"Who are you?" Shiva whispered. He thought in a panic of all the faces Harry had worn, realizing none of them had been the beast. Harry had not been a shifter like his mother.

He could only get flashes of this location, beyond his dominion. Ruled over by a man worse than any vampire, rakshasa, or ghoul that fucked and feasted on the young simply by virtue of the fact that he had made such a place—out there—for himself.

And in this thing's mind were Shiva's children!

"Colonel Gestetner, I feel these children were placed in my care. No, I'll not just hand them over to you," a young man in a white doctor's coat was saying.

"Your colleague didn't seem to possess your sensibilities," a tall, very blond man replied coolly. "And I'm in charge here. You will retire for the evening."

"I just can't do that," the doctor argued.

"How long have you worked for the Outfit?"

"About six months. After I finished my residency."

The blond man sneered and prepared to leave. He hadn't quite turned around so he didn't see Shiva glide silently into the room. Amazing how not even the doctor—who was more or less facing that direction—saw him. But Christians often believed God was everywhere without ever being able to see Him. "Good night, doctor."

"I'll report this," the doctor said indignantly.

The blond man arched a platinum set of eyebrows, picked up a AKM which lay upon a table. Sloppy of some guard, leaving that there, wasn't it? He whispered, "Have it your own way. You will retire forever, then."

He fired, a spray of bullets that splatted the man against a wall which was a good six feet behind him, turning his white smock into that more suited to the red garb of the Buddhist monk. Skullbone flew, revealing the rippling bubblegum-colored silk of the brain. Both eyes had vanished beneath a bloody lava. A burst into the chest and neck had forced the tubes of the throat up into the mouth, and the doctor thrashed briefly, choking on this, even if in truth he was already dead.

Saab turned now, seeing the beautiful hermaphrodite, long black hair in jeweled braids falling across the breasts, the erection like a cudgel of gold. It was not the way he'd seen this being every time. Some showed it as a warrior, others clasped in coital bliss with a consort, others still as having a blue throat. But he'd often enough seen the depictions of androgyny as he'd grown up in the east, as well as present from time to time in his dreams. How surprising it was to see such a creature in the flesh, outside the landscapes and landmines of the brain. Yet the colonel accepted this, as fey epiphany, warily, and not with a little awe.

Well, he'd seen him before, hadn't he? When he'd been a child of ten in Varanasi. And had been despised for his choice of sacrifice.

"Shiva," he said, more to himself than to the unusual prodigy before him.

The being graced him with a slight bow of the head. But thought 'who are you?'

There had been the time in Phnom Yohp. Some of the mercs had seen him dancing where the village men's corpses had been piled high. The Shiva who'd been Harry didn't know him personally beyond that. But there were so many parts to the prism ... One refraction of that might have seen him. Yes, and tasted the bitter outlaw maya this criminal would make.

Shiva felt it. Rippling down the hall, coming through the walls at him. It was a presentation of the place this white-haired man had built, scar by scar, childish tear by tier. A location the human monster liked to walk, lord of it, master of its abominations. Not unlike so many such dens of darkness in which god and demon cavorted and careened. Only there was no chance of release from this place, no possible mouth of pain's end which led into the fiendish stomach where rebirth was begun. No balance existed here, only constant eating, raping, maiming. There must always be that shred of hope that the nightmare would fade back into only a dream, and that those who seemed so remorseless could—between the falling drops of blood—turn into saviors.

The sensations of this place washed over Shiva like a particularly icy tide. It was horror without meaning behind it, torment without purpose. Yet all he'd been able to get were flashes from it. Where precisely was the rest of the vision coming from?

All he knew was that this evil man planned to take the twenty-five little gods there, through the vehicle of the most hideous of desecrations.

"You will not do that to my children," he told Saab.

"Do what?" Gestetner asked mildly.

Shiva threw the images he'd received back at the man. The colonel briefly swayed on his feet, taking the vision in, letting it flow through him to settle finally in his groin. Shit-eaters still shit, and you couldn't throw shit into a shit-eater's face and have it do anything but increase his appetite. He thought, *cool.*

Saab grinned. "Oh, that. Why not?"

"They will be god, living incarnate," answered the musical voice.

Saab thought it was like the amalgamation of all the most dick-yanking phone sex voices he'd ever heard, making him almost as hard as he'd been just considering what he could do with all those mutants.

Heeze and sheeze and heesheeze. Like the difference between flesh and spirit, perfection and crapulence, the white light of love pure-and-chaste-from-afar and the blackening spunk of sadistic usery. Papamama, brosis, outee-innee. World a giant blue green testicle, moon a gold-silver breast and vice versa. Can't tell the sex of the players without a pogrom.

The quintessentializing prospect: the dick of reality in the cunt of oblivion. Birth with footnotes, death with foreplay.

But what he saw in the god's eyes infuriated him, being the sum total of all who'd ever loathed or humiliated him for his predilections. All those statues in Varanasi staring down at him without pity, in the rain judging him, hypocritical on the subject of dharma. They who ought to have understood and comforted him but who wanted the sum of human suffering to remain on their plate, at their discretion.

In other words, no difference at all. But in the eyes of this intrinsically wigged-out being Saab saw everything he'd ever come to hate.

"You mean like Jesus, the living incarnation of the son of God? Or the Dalai Lama, the living incarnation of Buddha? Giving us poor and lowly even more things to be looking over our shoulders for: seeing what books we're checking out of the library, tapping our phones, investigating the contents of our stomachs looking for that stray item which only the gods may eat?"

(Shit-eater. Waster. Black feculent coprolithic ejectamenta dharma.)

As Saab feinted toward the door, Shiva leaped. Saab brought the weapon up and smashed him in the face with the stock end. Shiva reeled, blood gushing from a broken nose, and collapsed in a stunned backward flop to the floor.

Saab exited with a peccant grin, closed the door behind him, punched a code on a panel to lock it. And then walked on down the hall, boots echoing like satisfaction.

God saw sparks, very similar to the motes of burning dust during creation, flashing on and off before his eyes. He put his hand out to pass through them. Felt them whisper the jumpstart heat of universal ignition against his fingers. Then watched as they winked out, leaving him with the searing nova of the crushed cartilage in his nose.

He got up, reconsidering the benefits of being in a living body. He lunged for the door and found it locked. Yes, he could force it open; he had the strength.

But his senses cleared further. He realized he could hear the rattle-firing of a rapid-output weapon and the screaming of children.

Rage swelled in him, urged on by pain, and he let loose with every ounce of power in him. He didn't need codes or passwords or keys to bypass the failsafes of what resided in the silos at the base. He was god; he had attitude and wherewithal. The ICBM's rose and were loosed, the land-based missiles and long-range bombers preprogrammed to their targets. He didn't need to understand anything concerning the propulsion systems and propellants, the internal guidance systems, warheads, or reentry vehicles.

He simply sent them.

And the missiles in those other countries—who'd agreed to disarm but who hadn't really—responded.

And while it was Krishna who'd said, "I am become Death, the Destroyer of worlds," Shiva repeated it now because it was the right thing to say. As his third eye opened, the pupil reflecting an image of mushroom clouds, and white fire filled his mouth.

Up went down, down went up. The earth's crust bit into itself and a great wet red wind gibbered.

Devouring it all. Burning it all, as he rode in restless ascent and descent an apocalypse in which all the species and races heaved the startled sigh of sudden extinction.

Past this was a void, absolute and empty.

He fell through it, up's-and-down's new skewed permutations.

A vision of the end.

And he owned it.

Like running down a mountain with demons, soaring starward, and the jangle of a universe coming unhinged.

He paused … Because Shiva was the god of death and destruction, but also of creation.

And of time.

He relented, heart breaking, swallowing back the provoked spark. It swept in reverse, up becoming up again and down becoming down. The missiles were recalled, the silos went silent.

Nothing had happened.

Nothing was that easy.

The act of it still resided within him. He'd sucked it back into himself and he alone was burned. He'd fallen and didn't realize it. He looked down at himself and could see he was covered in radiation sores, iridescent along the darkly immolated flesh, like the jewels of stars across a night sky.

Chapter 33

"He who also realizes the truth of the body
can then come to know the truth of the universe."
—Ratnasara

Ry ran down the hall, hips swinging, remarkably fast considering she ran upon the palms of her hands. One of the two guards still inside the building saw her from the back on a monitor out of the corner of his eye and thought because of the blur of hair, the gait, and the running on the hands that Ry was a monkey escaped from a lab. The doctors with the Outfit had brought primates on which to do some testing of the Soma. He chuckled, thinking the beast was likely leading the scientists on a merry chase. He had no intention of helping them unless they called. He stretched, casually smoothed out a wrinkle on his suit, and waited to see if they would, indeed, buzz for him to come pursue the monkey.

Ry stopped at the door where she could hear Elliot. He'd stopped screaming and there was in the place of that noise a droning, like the sound of grief underwater. The urgency she felt compelled her to further haste. She set herself down, hips flat to the floor, and reached up to put her hand upon the door handle. It wasn't locked and turned easily.

Was that Elliot?

The body strapped to the gurney was a mass of writhing flesh, no longer merely confined to one side of the head. The skin throbbed and boiled, a roiling magma of sustained, terrible vitality. It slapped and lashed together, forming faces and small hands clenched into fists and claws, raking empty air in an effort to escape, revenants trapped within scarred orbits.

Elliot had become a very choppy sea, scarcely resembling anything close to a body anymore. He had changed from ghostface, metamorphosing into ghostflesh, physical self transforming into a chamber of horrors.

Not quite entirely submerged beneath this, a germ of consciousness remained. Wondering: have I been here before? In the madhouse, riding the shock wave?

The faces foaming out of him had been marked by savage ritual, some with eyelids carved and the eyes themselves removed, some with an attempt made to stab a design upon the pupils as a Chinese artisan would etch a bead of amethyst. Some had noses cut off and tiny scenes engraved within the sinuses in grisly shadowbox until they were reminiscent of opened Faberge eggs. Some had all their teeth pulled and the gums burned with acid into patterns, tongues forked or filigreed or stripped into three sections and braided. Some had scalps shaved, peeled back to reveal raw skullbone and this scrimshawed like Bering Strait walrus tusk ivory.

They flinched upon Elliot's swarming body, heirlooms of a mad fucker's legacy. Ry felt overwhelmed with pity, both for Elliot and for the children haunting through him.

A doctor in a white lab jacket frowned as he studied Elliot's changes, having become more alarmed and intrigued as it migrated from being confined to the man's face into rapidly consuming the entire being, reminding him of nothing less than a voracious flesh-eating bacteria. It was when the little mouths everywhere began to gape and sputter, trying so hard to scream their pain and outrage that the doctor shook himself out of the trance the sight had put him into, reaching into his pocket for a hypo.

"No!" Ry cried out, not knowing what the needle contained but sure that it might react dangerously with the Soma mushroom, possibly even killing Elliot. She flung a chair at the man as he turned, seeing her there for the first time.

The hypo clattered to the floor, the doctor falling against the gurney. He lunged for a nearby table and slapped an intercom.

"We've got an intruder. *Hurry!*" he barked into it.

He brought up his foot to kick her and she grabbed it in her hand, twisting till it was at a right angle from the ankle. A woman who'd always needed to walk upon her hands developed a lot of strength in the fingers, wrists and arms. The doctor cried out, losing his balance entirely as she then shoved him with his foot. As he hit the floor, she leaned in to snatch up the fallen needle and plunged it into his leg.

There was the sound of steps and a man in a dark suit jumped into the room. The guard's weapon was up and he fired at the woman he saw, mind taking in the odd circumstance of her being only about half a person. There was a silencer on the gun. A softly exhaled explosion zipped past her head as Ry threw herself down and rolled. The guard began to fire again when he saw what lay upon the gurney. He'd helped wheel that thing in there, only then there had been a man upon it. But there was no man there now.

His jaw dropped as his trigger finger paralyzed.

A mass of kindergarten from hell was effervescing through the straps, a gory festering seltzer, achingly mute, choked into a strangled derangement where insanity must have already been present. It was as if someone had taken a huge ladle, filled with the souls of tormented children, out of some demon's cannibal cauldron and dumped it on the stainless-steel table.

Except it didn't slosh apart, retaining its cohesiveness as if bound together inside some invisible bubble.

A nervous giggle spewed through the guard's lip as he thought, absurdly, *is it soup yet?*

But it was rising, en masse, osmosis through the restraints. Getting off the table and flowing at him. Lashing out in an undulating ripple, like a windy banner that looked like silk but was really made up of fine razor threads. There was sharp pain, agony, as suddenly his hands holding the weapon were slashed off, falling to the floor, blood gushing from the trauma at both wrists to spatter directly into some of those infantile mouths.

How did it hold its shape, seeming so wet? It was a slippery column of open wounds fuming upright, staggering—on what? there were no legs—across the floor, motivated by separate minds to go this way, then that way.

"Elliot!" Ry whispered urgently. "We have to go help the children."

But this thing was composed of children, a lacerated convulsing jello of them. Tiny palms pushing out, stained with stigmata, some with flayed fingers wiggling like cherry licorice sticks, others with bones skillfully removed so that the fingers were only fleshy tubes flopping about like flaccid penises. They jammed against the elastic fiber of the substance encasing them, stretching it out a bit, twitching as it bounced back to keep them imprisoned. The faces strained, shaped like the ruined visages of botched late-term abortions pressed against a plastic surgical garbage bag.

The doctor moaned on the floor, groggy, then from a yet prone position on his back reached out for the guard's fallen weapon, picking the man's severed hands from around it, ready to fire at the horrible thing and hang what Colonel Gestetner had said.

Ry scrambled over, skidding on her palms, throwing herself onto her stomach to grab his genitals with both fists. She squeezed as hard as she could, feeling the testicles squelch like lychee fruit, the dick pop like steamed pig's knuckles, the total purchase pulping like a fish head used to season a rice dish. The man didn't even scream, the air lodging in his throat, trapped within a trachea which was trying to collapse in on itself from shock. He let go of the weapon, hands tremoring toward his crotch, trousers blooming with blood and a yeasty squirt of electrified semen, the last ejaculation he'd ever have.

"El! You have to hear me," Ry babbled, desperate to reach what consciousness Harry's brother might still retain. Was there a shred of him sane enough inside this phantom stew to even try to help Shiva's offspring? "We have to go down the hall, to save the other children. Before … " she paused, hardly able to even articulate such a possibility, " … they are made to join these you carry."

She tried not to be unnerved as she reached out to touch the throbbing mass of faces and hands, jerking her fingers back as a tiny gigged rump appeared, cored-out asshole opening and closing like the mouth of a suffocating fish.

"Elliot!" Ry called again, plaintive, persistent. "Elliot, come on …"

For a moment she could see El's eyes, opened near the top, buzzing with a bloodshot gaze of static. The blob of contused wraiths swung about and followed her into the hall.

The second guard had just come up, more quietly than the first. He saw the blob and froze, but not before he fired. Another silencer. She barely heard the two bullets which struck her as she fell the short distance to her ass. Blood pumped out of a gaping hole in her shoulder and she was unable to see through anything save one eye now. Had the bullet grazed her forehead, or pulped clean through it? She brought up a trembling, spastic hand, (from the arm at the uninjured shoulder, the other not responding to her brain's call for action). She patted the wound, stared at her fingers, scalp/pulverized bone like chalk dust/a wiggle of pinkish gray curd. She knew she ought to be dead. Perhaps she was and it hadn't registered yet.

Ghostflesh bent and lifted her in what felt more or less like substantive arms. Passing the guard who'd wet and shit himself and was gibbering, "*I've* never hurt a child; I've *never* hurt a child; *I've never hurt a child* ..."

A wet tentacle of pastel ectoplasm snaked out and wrapped about the guard's neck, snapping it, as if not caring or not believing his protestations of innocence.

Down the hall. Ry gestured to a door. "In there."

Saab had only entered the room himself a few minutes before. The two guards had silencers on their guns so he hadn't heard anything. He'd been standing there, looking at the twenty-five children, stripped naked for their physical examinations. He could see the twin genders on a few closest to him, sitting lotus on silver gurneys and on the floor. Tiny penises but all erect, making his head swim. Their faces were more beautiful than anything he'd ever seen: flawless, golden as the first sigh of the dawn's sun, long black hair in silk across their shoulders.

He let his imagination run. How to use a scalpel and a very fine set of chisels to raise and sculpt bone and flesh to resemble the reliquary towers, spangled chedis, and ornate facades of both Southeast Asia and India, where he'd learned and enjoyed himself so much. How to insert miniature tapers to burn at strategic locations—the jutting tips of shoulders, for example—recalling the occasional torch of an oil refinery which stained lapis skies to sooty gray. How to flail expertly with chain and leather to create canyons, similar to those here outside the air base, staining the wounds so they were striated in the colors appropriate for that terrain. How to parch and wither certain patches of skin so that it resembled the mummies he'd seen in the South American caves. If one could remove the eyes, perhaps salting the sockets, and retracting the lips to expose the teeth in perpetual rictus, it might be possible to even make the face appear mummified without causing the death of the model too precipitously.

Saab casually sniffed his fingers, imagining the scent of blood and shit. He rubbed the stock of his gun against his erection, mashing it against the zipper, thinking of how it would ache rubbing against bone and cartilage. He smiled, because they were all looking at him, eyes narrowed as if studying him. As children might, peering into true darkness for the first time, curious as to what the meaning of evil could really be.

How many would eventually be in that gallery devoted to his work which existed on that other plane he'd manufactured? The place he liked to journey to whenever he took the right opiate or received the correct number of volts or the sound wavelengths and pitch which were perfect in a child's screams.

"All of you," he answered his own question. "You'll all be my narcotic. You will each be a masterpiece."

Art and karma: consequences of a deadly ecstasy.

The fruits of dark dharma: waste and exaltation.

But the door opened. The twenty-five would-be gods shifted their studious gazes to what was behind him. Saab turned, weapon ready. And saw … a part of that other-realm of his. Cherub-cobbled streets and angel-baby walls, the ragamuffin handiworks immortalized in its dismal yet genius alleys.

In a jumble of meat and slimy blood *walking?* toward him. It had a legless Asian woman in its hold but set her down. Some of the blood on it was hers, but not all.

But how could they be here? They ought to be in the other place, where he sent them. A set of eyes, a man's, older, near the top, regarded him furiously.

Was this Elliot? Had the Soma done this to him? Swarmed him over with spectral swirls of Saab's kids, springing from every part of him: bulging from his torso, bumping his arms and legs, squeezing like bubos out of his armpits and in boils from his genitals. Little eyes focused on Gestetner from this wasteland of unsteady flesh, small hands spasmed while reaching, snapdragon mouths parted.

And screamed at last, fully, shrilly.

Released as they shot out at him, scoops of disembodied veal landing on him, in splopping hamburger heads full of rivet teeth and gooey goober hands with nails of broken brick.

Saab fell onto his back as his finger jerked spasmodically on the trigger, AKM splattering the ceiling with bullets. They dug in, hooking under his skin, infesting, shaking him like hundreds of small but starving dogs. All the obscene patterns he'd used on them blossomed on Saab's flesh, sizzled down through the muscles, hissed into bones and turning the marrow into searing jelly. Something of sulfuric aspic slithered down his throat, detonating his tongue, popping the teeth like fleas between fingernails, eating away the trachea like it was a short fuse on dynamite. Excruciating pain hallucinogenic as the theophanies of saints torched by Romans and electric as a thousand bare wires. Should have fucking crossed him over to his favorite vacation spot. But somehow they kept him right there, in three crucified dimensions, love slave, hate slave, canvas of retribution.

Their shrieks and the gun being jerked off till it emptied, plaster and shattered light fixtures cascading down in slicing dust.

And for a moment it seemed as if the whole world ignited. Careened sideways through a fire of monumental proportion. What nerve endings might feel like invaded by so many vengeful jaws and claws. What it felt like when the heat was so intense it even ripped the soul apart with the massive radiation that had to be Eternity stalking.

But then that winked away, like visions of cataclysm and rapture did. Where was he?

Not in the room with the little freaks at the base …

He'd crossed over. He'd made it! To his home away from home …

Opened his eyes that he was sure had burned away, melting down his face as his skin became shredding wings of flame.

The street he knew so well rippled as if a fault line beneath was quivering. Children congealed from paving and climbed out. The walls smoked in musky mirage, and their little prisoners here, too, found cohesion, crawling down to the ground. At the end of the street, his gallery, the maimed poured out through the double doors in a crippled but angry quadrille.

Not all of the street came apart. Where Saab stood was still entirely solid. Looking down he could see a host of small but steel hands, felt them grasping him firmly, holding him there as surely as if he'd been set into a bucket of concrete.

The urchins came toward him across a ribbon now of blood-red fog, holding in their hands and swinging every device he'd ever used on them.

"Waste," he heard them whisper. "We have the victims' dharma to do."

Had something happened?

Apart from a sudden rush, not unlike the most intense from a really large dose of LSD. Flashbacks on Vietnam?

Elliot stood in the room with the children from Phnom Yohp. He'd dreamed his scars had swelled over his whole body. He'd imagined he'd shifted into this face and that one, shapes full of a history of agony.

Then he'd dreamed the world ended.

Saab had forced the Soma on him. He'd gone nuts. He'd had some pretty wild notions.

But he patted himself. Nothing. He touched his face.

And found no scars at all.

Ry groaned behind him and he swung around.

(Had there been someone else there, in the room, with him and the kids and Cheanneary Ry?)

Maybe. There was an AKM on the floor, expended shell casings every-bloody-where. Part of the ceiling was shot to pieces although the kids were okay.

Ry was not. She'd been shot, bad wound in the shoulder and worse one in the head. He bent to her, his heart going weak. There was gore in her silky hair, one eye burst like a grape.

"We have to go to Shiva," she said.

Elliot picked her up, exited the room, feeling the twenty-five kids following. Let her gesture where down the hall.

He tried the door. It was locked. There was a keypad but he didn't know what code it needed.

"I can't touch it," she told him. "You must."

She had the sight. The god's gift. But she was dying.

How could he do this?

Because El had sight, too. This was his personal shift, above and beyond what his heredity had worked through him. It was a changing—not of skin—but through years and events. Never as clear in images as what Ry had, but then she'd been given her visions by a god.

(Oh, and hadn't he? Didn't all such gifts come from the gods?)

He extended one hand gingerly, tremulously, so as not to drop her or move her uncomfortably. His fingers paused while he concentrated, thinking *please, please, don't let me screw this up.*

He couldn't think out to it, hoping his scars would whisper the code. So what did he do?

He cleared his mind, of all the horror, the jungles and deserts, the minutiae of his life.

The sequence came, in numbers that seemed like the letters in a prayer. His fingers tapped them out.

They went in.

"Harry?"

Elliot could barely murmur the name. Was that his brother, burned upon the floor? Yet there were no traces of fire around the room. Only a slight scorching on the tile where Harry was, the way El had seen in photographs taken of people who'd spontaneously combusted.

But this hadn't been just a burning. The man's body was covered in sores, leaking lesions.

Ry smiled.

"He's in shadow, rubies, diamonds, opals and pearls across his skin," she said softly. "So beautiful. Put me down with him."

The burned arms came around her. How sweet he smelled. Of sacrificial godflesh and blood boiled into wine. Shiva turned his head slightly and put his cheek against hers.

"El?" And it was Harry's voice. "You have to take care of my children. Until their time comes to dance across the earth."

Elliot nodded.

Cessation

Sirikit's color blazed.

The skin wrapped around her light moved slowly past the corpses strewn about the base. The moon would set soon. Which would free her. She would shift beyond the living nirvana into true nirvana, bodiless, non-physical, free.

But the others, the people of Machenville, had no such colors and no light. Their skins puffed with darkness. For the Soma they had drunk hadn't been allowed to help them beyond the pain. The moon would set all right, but they would yet be trapped within their flayed hides, within hell.

Only she could lead them.

"Gather!" she called, voice a hummingbird's exhale out of the rosy tissue of her hollow mouth.

They came from around the corners of buildings, Outfit blood dripping from the tubes of fingerflesh. They came out of doorways to buildings other than the one where they couldn't enter, where the metal barriers had sealed Shiva inside. They struggled, mouth- and eye-holes full of blackness. On those without enough of the heads intact to own these, the orifices of the urethras, assholes, cunts leaked this sloe terror.

They made a semicircle around her, waves of cold shivering off them.

The cosmos spun, overturning. Sirikit was the butterfly again. She hovered high, high above the feasting hall, basalt slabs below covered with the wriggling forms of sufferers awaiting the debauchery of gods. The necropolis turned inside out, subterranean for an orgy of every torture conceivable. She flew, not far from where the parasites spat out threads to climb down to the carrion on. They eyed her, rubbing their filthy legs together, eyes rolling in greasy hundreds, vertical mouth slits full of human paste. She remembered they'd had human faces before.

But this wasn't entirely her hell. There would be nuances. For her the worst she'd seen had always had a human face.

Now her beating wings sent little breezes which caused them to scuttle away, afraid to become trapped within an arc of her rainbow.

Down below, a demon buried its multi-pronged face between thighs gruesome with an emptied gut, necklaces of entrails still twitching with the peristalsis of fear. Another had scooped a woman's belly open and was squeezing the exposed ovaries. Eggs plopped out far too large for human ova. These then cracked with tiny females—each bearing the unfortunate woman's face—streaming out in sticky yolk, snatched up by the monster to be crammed into a smacking red mouth. Another creature squatted, expelling a foul greenish shit, swarming with flea maggots, dribbling in noxious steam. It then grinned as the foul rectum expanded, telescoping out. A partner beast shoved a man's head into it, as he gurgled and gagged, as his skull cracked and his shrieks echoed into the scurfy tunnel.

More. Rapes by geared, ratchet-dicks. Sodomies with gig-hook cocks. Forced fellatio with members tipped with chittering sharkheads which ate their own way down the throat eating them. Commanded cunnilingus into muffs bristling with needles and into cunts which twitched behind a clit of scorpion tails.

"Let go!" Sirikit shouted down to them. "It isn't real."

The carnage and perversion continued, punishing, terrorizing, rendering hopeless.

"It's maya," she whispered, realizing she didn't really have to yell. "It's a magic you could blink away if you truly had eyes. But you don't have eyes anymore. So stop trying to close them."

Up from countless black altars strewn with those debased again and again, faces upturned, as if distracted from what tore them apart by the tolling of a single soft bell.

Were they listening?

She glanced up to the ceiling of the cavern, seeing a tiny pinprick hole. Through it was a speck of brilliance.

"It's just a deception, collected from every life reborn again and again into pain, layered with billions of nightmares."

She smiled inwardly, understanding this for the first time herself. She'd created the place as much as any of them, as everyone had who'd ever slipped, bloody, from a womb. She hadn't really had to be eaten by Shiva and then birthed out through his exotic justice in order to find peace. But she'd needed to be shown the direction by him. So she could then show these people.

The hole above was blooming, like the velvety rose of a birth canal.

"It's maya," Sirikit murmured. "A fantasy. This place is the last dream of the world."

The sufferers shrugged, skin sloughing off, blood raining against the basalt, bones clattering away. And then they ascended, right through the grasps of their abusers, cutting through the webs of the mites on strings.

Sirikit flew higher and they trailed in the dust of her wings.

Giving up the last illusion.

Meet the Author

Nell Anne 'Charlee' Jacob was an American author specializing in horror fiction, dark fantasy, and poetry. Her writing career began in 1981 with the publication of several poems under the name Charlee Carter Broach. She began writing as Charlee Jacob in 1986.

This native Texan is best known for her graphic explorations of the themes of human degradation, sexual extremism, and supernatural evil. Her first novel *This Symbiotic Fascination* was nominated for the International Horror Guild Award and the Bram Stoker Award. Her novel Dread in the Beast tied David Morrell's Creepers for first place for the Bram Stoker Award for Best Novel of 2005, and her poetry collection *Sineater* won the Bram Stoker Award for Best Poetry Collection in 2005 as well.

Bibliography

Novels and Novellas

Containment: The Death of Earth
Dark Moods
Dread in the Beast
Haunter
Season of the Witch
Soma
Still
This Symbiotic Fascination
Vestal
Wormwood Nights (novella)

Collections

Dread in the Beast and Other Atrocities

Flowers from a Dark Star (poems)
Geek Poems
Guises
Heresy (poems)
Sineater (poems)
Skin (narrative poem)
Taunting The Minotaur
The Desert (poems)
The Indigo People: A Vampire Collection
The Myth of Falling
Up, Out of Cities That Blow Hot and Cold
Vectors: A Week in the Death of a Planet (with Marge Simon)

Collaborations
Chim+Her
Four Elements (with Marge Simon, Rain Graves, and Linda Addison)
Skins of Youth (with Mehitobel Wilson)
The Best of Him+Chim+Her

Curious about other Crossroad Press books? Stop by our website: http://crossroadpress.com
We offer quality writing
in digital, audio, and print formats.

Subscribe to our newsletter on the website homepage and receive a free eBook.